Elizabeth Ann Hill comes from a long line of Cornish people, although she herself was born in Barnet in North London. She grew up in Cornwall and Wales and spent some years working in the hotel trade, where she acquired a keen insight into human character. After a series of secretarial jobs, she now works part-time for a Cornish antique dealer. She has been writing since early childhood, and at the age of 26 won a prize in a short story competition run by *Woman's Own*.

By the same author

The Hidden Spring

ELIZABETH ANN HILL

Pebbles in the Tide

PARRAGON

First published in Great Britain by
Souvenir Press Ltd 1989

Published by Grafton Books 1991

This edition published 1993 by
Diamond Books
77-85 Fulham Palace Road
Hammersmith, London, W6 8JB

Printed and bound in Great Britain by
BPCC Hazells Ltd
Member of BPCC Ltd

1

On a lonely road across a wilderness of heath and granite carns, a pony and trap was travelling. It carried a young couple on their way to Penzance, for this was the first week in June and the last day of Corpus Christi fair. Except for the jingle and beat of the pony's harness and hooves, their passing scarcely disturbed the silence of the moor, for they spoke very little as they rode along. The girl sat contentedly beside the young man, her arm linked with his, and sometimes they exchanged a few words or a smile. They had been together since childhood and knew each other too well to feel any need for constant chatter. The year was 1857 and their engagement was already nearing its first anniversary. Less than a twelvemonth now remained before their wedding day.

Jenny and Richard had been inseparable friends from the very first. The understanding had existed between them for so long that the ring and the promises were given almost as an afterthought. It was what everyone expected, what their parents had always wanted, as natural and predictable as the turning of the seasons.

Beneath her shallow-crowned straw hat with cherries on the brim, the girl's face was round and sweet, her skin, hair and eyes three different shades of brown. The polished dark waves reached halfway down her back and the pink cotton frock was her very best, kept especially for outings with Richard. About her neck hung a small circular charm – a latticework of gold and silver wire, the threads twisting and coiling in an endless knot.

'There,' he had said, placing the chain round her neck

5

and fastening the clasp, 'that's your life and mine, woven together from beginning to end.'

She had always adored him. There was no one to compare with Richard, and Jenny knew that he was meant for her, made for her by God and by kindly Fate.

Happily she glanced up at the young man beside her, watching the breeze ruffle the curls of his dark hair, his eyes, with their thick brows and lashes, intent on the road ahead. Despite his betrothal, Richard Rescorla could seldom walk so much as a hundred yards through the streets of his home town without encountering some young woman eager to wish him good day and delay him for a while in conversation. The daughters of the fishermen and shopkeepers, the pert and hardy bal-maidens, even the occasional young widow, were all inclined to cast inviting glances at the tall, slim lad with the humorous black eyes. But there had never been any real question as to whom he would marry. Everyone agreed that it was bound to be Jenny Varcoe, the sailmaker's daughter, and no one was at all surprised when the engagement was made official on her sixteenth birthday.

Jenny had no doubt that Richard was aware of his appeal, and she accepted as natural the touch of vanity she sometimes sensed in him. Perhaps he was a little pleased with himself, but never had she heard him mock or disparage anyone else. Oh yes, he was apt to be impulsive – but never ill-tempered. He could, it was true, be thoughtless, but she would not have dreamed him capable of cruelty. Furthermore, he was John Rescorla's only son and certain to inherit his father's boat-building business. Richard, at eighteen, had less than two years of his apprenticeship left to complete and would then be earning a full shipwright's wage of seventeen shillings a week.

Why, indeed, should he not be pleased with himself?

thought Jenny fondly, for she was as proud as could be to know that he belonged to her. Sure of his love, she had long been collecting items of linen and other household ware for the home they would share. And since their marriage was a foregone conclusion, she had already shown the depth of that faith, for neither of them had the patience or the self-control to wait for the parson's blessing and a distant wedding night. Why, in any case, should she play the coy maiden with one to whom she was already so close?

Richard was in buoyant mood that day as the trap rolled on down the road. Like Jenny, he was greatly looking forward to the fair. He had lately been feeling restless and troubled by a vague sense of confinement, so a little novelty and excitement would be very welcome.

They arrived in Penzance just before mid-day. The sloping main street of the town and all the little sidestreets leading to the harbour were packed with crowds and the sideshows, stalls and exhibitions they had come to see. Bathed in a din of hurdy-gurdies, tambourines and fiddles, people pressed and elbowed their way along in the quest for a good view of the marionettes or the waxworks, the best spot from which to stare at the dwarf, the fat woman or some similar unfortunate. Pulsing with energy and vulgarity, the fair had lured its usual quota of pickpockets, some from as far afield as Bristol or London. A smart frock coat and air of distinction were often accompanied by swift, felonious fingers, and a purse might be deftly removed while its owner haggled with a stallholder or listened to the nonsense of a quack doctor. Miners came dressed in fine black coats, their women in silk frocks – clothing purchased with money which could have been more wisely spent on food or repayment of debt. There were fishermen from every port and cove for thirty miles or more, farming folk from the bleak, windy countryside of Penwith, quarrymen from Lamorna and St Keverne. Many were credulous, most were uneducated, easily duped by the charmers and fortune-tellers or exploited by the prostitutes. But none of this ever discouraged anyone. The victims might return chastened to their homes this year, but they would still be back for the next fair, just as silly and every bit as likely to be robbed again.

Jenny wanted most of all to visit Wombwell's menagerie, so the couple spent an hour marvelling at the wild beasts, and the exhibition of deadly spiders and snakes from Australia. Afterwards, Richard took her to one of the refreshment booths for a plate of hot beef and potatoes.

'We must take home a present for everyone,' she said, washing down her meal with a mug of raw cider. 'I want to buy a new tobacco pouch for Father, and you must choose something for your sisters.'

'We'll go and see the fire-eater first. There's plenty of time, maid, and I've seven shillings still to spend.'

'Seven shillings? Richard, that's more than a week's wages!'

Her accent, like his, was a soft burr, warm and drawling.

'No matter,' he said grandly. 'Father's given me an extra fourpence a week, so I'm not short of money.'

Taking her by the hand, he began to push his way through the crowd towards the caravan with tongues of flame and the name 'Incendio' painted on the side. There was clearly a performance in progress, for puffs of fire could be seen blooming and disappearing into the air above the spectators' heads.

When it was over, Richard bought a pound of sugared almonds and peppermints for his younger sister. From a sly little gypsy woman with a tray of beads and fancy buttons, he purchased a tortoiseshell comb and some coloured ribbons for the elder one. Hawkers and established tradesmen alike had set up straggling lines of stalls to offer their goods. Fairings, cakes and ginger beer were sold alongside dishes of cockles and winkles. Bags of marbles, wooden hoops and penny whistles lay jumbled together on makeshift stands in company with baskets, ornaments and crockery.

Determined to miss none of the amusements, the couple worked their way through the congested town from end to end. By late afternoon they had watched the travelling theatre's unseasonal performance of 'The Orphan's Christmas'. The brass band was now slightly out of tune, having taken a lengthy break at a public house nearby. Continual shrieks of ribald laughter, together with the bickering and jostling of the crowd, were beginning to tire them both, and Jenny was upset when approached by a pathetic creature who begged twopence to show her his crippled legs. Richard quickly hustled her away, reaching back to pass the man a threepenny bit as he went. For all the merriment, the costumes and the music, there was also a sad and ugly face to the fair.

Among its least attractive features were the brawls, which grew more fierce and frequent as the day wore on, for every public house was filled to overflowing. When morning came, many landlords would be reckoning up the damage to their premises, while some of their customers still lay drunk in the street.

Fights of an organized kind were also taking place and, since Jenny would welcome the chance to sit down, Richard suggested they might go to the boxing match, where the combat was better ordered and money prizes were at stake.

It was while they sat watching an uneven contest, which drew nothing but jeers from the onlookers, that Richard's attention was diverted by the sight of a young woman walking down the high terrace to his right. She looked familiar and he soon recalled that he had noticed her in his home town of Porthgullow on one or two occasions in the past. Unlike most of the other girls, this one had never spoken to him. Indeed, she was seldom seen at all in that part of the town which huddled round the harbour, for this was a young lady from one of the smart houses built up on the hill behind. She was fair-haired and fashionably dressed, her demeanour one of delicate superiority.

Perhaps it was this faintly disdainful air that served to provoke the two drunken quarrymen who stumbled out of a tavern just as she passed by. What appeared to Richard a graceful manner and lovely refinement had clearly struck the men as haughty.

Barring her way and thwarting all her efforts to sidestep them, they first taunted and then propositioned her in no uncertain terms. Outrage and mounting alarm began to cloud the young lady's face. She made a move to turn and go back the way she had come, but one of her tormentors snatched her parasol, mincing to and fro with it and slurring his mockery of the girl's protests. The second man then clamped an arm round her waist, delivering a wet, noisome kiss to the base of her throat as she squirmed and squeaked in distress. He reeked of beer, sweat and gunpowder, and his victim began to scream for rescue.

Richard leaped to his feet, followed by two other men. They bounded up the steps onto the terrace, whereupon the first quarryman flung the parasol to the ground and took to his heels. His companion, busy clawing at the girl's bodice, did not hear the approaching footsteps until it was nearly too late for escape. However, when he saw that retribution was almost upon him, he released the

10

young woman and shoved her backwards out of his way. With a squawk she tumbled over, to land in an uproar of flying skirts and petticoats. Her attacker, meanwhile, trying to evade capture, staggered off the edge of the terrace and fell into the street, a drop of nearly five feet, which quite stunned him. Drawn by the commotion, a number of onlookers came to snigger. Three wild-haired prostitutes had emerged from the tavern and were screeching with mirth as they pointed and sneered at the young lady.

There were many among the bystanders who found the matter comical, but Richard saw nothing funny in the girl's humiliation. It seemed to him a shocking thing that such beauty and dignity should be abused. While the other two men removed the dazed quarryman to the police station, he hastened to help her up, supporting her as she fussed with the folds of her dress. His worried face was the first thing she saw when at last she raised tearful, china-blue eyes to thank her rescuer.

Richard picked up the parasol and handed it back to her.

'Are you hurt?'

'Merely shaken, sir, I think.' She took swift note of his features and his good Sunday suit. Her eyelashes fanned coyly and she gave a demure little smile. 'I am deeply grateful for your assistance.'

Her gaze wavered briefly as Jenny came running up to see what was going on.

'Richard, what was all that about?'

The fair girl made rapid appraisal of Jenny Varcoe and a slight crease appeared between her finely arched eyebrows, which were almost as pale as the skin itself.

Richard had not heard Jenny's question. He was mesmerized by the new face before him, the closeness of this

11

fragile, pastel-coloured creature who seemed composed of marble and primroses instead of common flesh.

The young lady did not acknowledge Jenny's presence, but turned again to Richard. 'I dare not imagine what might have occurred, had you not come to my aid. You are truly a gentleman, sir, and a most courageous one.'

Richard made light of his deed – as well he might, since he had done no more than lift her to her feet. Privately, however, he was thrilled to receive praise and admiration from such a lovely woman.

She wore a dress of sky-blue grenadine with a small lace collar, five rows of flounces to the skirt, and white puffed undersleeves beneath the fabric which flared from shoulder to elbow. Under a little hat adorned with forget-me-nots, cornflowers and a dark blue feather, the shimmering hair was smoothly dressed in coils. A dainty beaded reticule hung from her wrist, and Richard noticed that her hands were very small, encased in white gloves.

'It was nothing, Miss . . .?'

'Tregear.' She hesitated for a second, then added confidingly: 'Susanna Tregear.'

'I'm Richard Rescorla. Oh – and this is Miss Varcoe, my intended,' he said, having finally realized that Jenny stood beside him.

Jenny smiled at Susanna in genuine friendliness. 'You must have been very frightened, Miss Tregear. I hope your lovely frock isn't soiled?'

'I thank you for your concern, Miss Varcoe. I confess I am somewhat upset, but I shall no doubt recover. As for the dress, I shall never wear it again, for I fear it would always remind me of what has happened here today. It's of no consequence, in any case. My father is a draper, you see. He has an establishment here in Penzance, and others in Truro and Porthgullow.'

'Oh,' muttered Jenny. She felt somehow slighted by

Susanna's dismissal of the frock and its importance. 'I've plenty of others,' the tone implied. 'A lady has more than one good dress.'

'Porthgullow? Oh – then yours is the shop on the corner of Covenant Street?' Richard said.

'So you know of it? Of course, the Porthgullow branch is the smallest of Papa's establishments, but the town is so charming that we chose to make our home there. I live in Morven Terrace.'

He nodded. 'I've seen you once or twice before, though 'tis clear you've never noticed me. I'm often in Porthgullow and I live just a few miles west of the town. My father's a shipwright and has his premises in one of the small coves along that coast.'

Susanna's eyes widened. 'It's strange, then, and most regrettable, that we've never met before.'

Jenny, still smarting from Susanna's slight, put in sharply, 'Don't you think 'tis rash to be out alone today? There's always trouble at a big fair.'

'I came here with my papa,' explained Susanna. 'However, because he was obliged to visit some person on a matter of business, I took the opportunity to make a few purchases, thinking that no harm could possibly befall me in so short a time.' She turned soulful eyes upon Richard, then sighed deeply. 'I suppose it was silly of me. No woman of good character can afford to venture forth, however briefly, without a man's protection.'

She opened her parasol and twirled it gently above her head, so that the ruffles and blue rosettes fluttered busily in the breeze.

'I think we'd best try and find him,' Richard said, 'to be sure you're not molested a second time.'

At that moment, however, a florid little man in a fawn-coloured suit came hurrying down the steps from one of the sidestreets and called out as he spotted Susanna.

13

'Oh, there's no need – here he is. Papa,' she said, when he arrived at her side, 'may I introduce Mr Rescorla and Miss Varcoe.'

The man extended his hand to Richard and raised his hat to Jenny.

'Mr Rescorla has just delivered me from a dreadful ordeal, Papa. I was accosted by two ruffians and my honour gravely threatened, but this gentleman saved it most gallantly.'

'Good Lord! Well, please accept my gratitude, sir. Susanna's my only daughter and very precious to me.'

Richard bashfully shuffled his feet.

'Are you certain you're all right, Susanna?'

'Yes, Papa, truly I am. And do you know that by happy coincidence Mr Rescorla lives near Porthgullow?'

'Is that a fact? Then I'm sure we'll meet again, young man. Indeed, we'd be glad to have your company for what remains of the day. Susanna and I are going to look at the menagerie. Perhaps you and Miss Varcoe would care to come along?'

Jenny's mouth tightened and she looked a little troubled.

'I don't want to stay any longer, Richard. We've seen the menagerie and everything else, too. I have a headache and I'd like to go home now.'

His brow knitted in puzzlement and slight annoyance as she tugged at his arm.

'That's a shame,' said the little man, 'but we understand, my dear.'

'When is your wedding to be?' enquired Susanna.

'Next May,' supplied Richard.

'Well, well. Allow me to wish you both the greatest happiness.'

'Thank you, Miss Tregear, and good day to you.' Jenny

began to steer Richard away. 'And to you, sir,' she added more amiably, as Mr Tregear once more raised his hat.

Susanna murmured a farewell and turned with a flick of her skirts, laying a hand lightly on her father's arm as they went on their way.

Richard lingered for a moment, staring after her. Jenny noticed the look on his face and was filled with a sense of resentment she had never known before. She had summed up Miss Tregear as patronizing, disliking the high, imperious voice, the prim little smile and the lofty tilt of her head. Here was an idle young woman with the benefit of money and a genteel education. Like the quarrymen, Jenny felt antagonized by her and was vexed that Richard could admire such a person.

Mr Tregear's visit to Penzance that day had little to do with the fair. He had been to see his accountant and the interview had not been a happy one. Susanna, prattling about her fright at the hands of the quarrymen, failed to notice how preoccupied he was, how his shoulders drooped and his forehead was furrowed with anxiety. Driven to anger by the sound of her voice, he finally snapped at her.

'Why couldn't you wait for me, Susanna? I've troubles enough without having to worry about your whereabouts and your safety. If I'd known you'd do something so foolish, I wouldn't have brought you with me.'

Father and daughter were walking among the cages in the menagerie and had paused beside one containing a pair of brown bears.

'I did wait, Papa, for nearly an hour.'

'Had your patience only lasted another ten minutes or so until I concluded my business, that incident in the street would not have happened.'

'I simply wanted to buy a thing or two,' sniffed the girl.

15

'And you're very unkind to chide me when I've just suffered such a dreadful experience.'

Her father gave a snort of irritation. 'Eager, as ever, to waste my money, and nothing must delay you. Sometimes I marvel at the way you run through your allowance each month; never a penny left over and none of it spent sensibly. You've no care for anything but finery and fashion.'

Susanna regarded him blankly. 'But our fortune is founded on those very things, and all my frocks are made from our own fabrics by our own seamstresses. Naturally, I must purchase my hats, shoes and jewellery elsewhere. What is wrong with that? How else should I use my allowance?'

The brown bears grunted and bawled, and Mr Tregear's ruddy face grew redder still as his daughter turned her head, presenting a haughty profile.

'By heaven, I wish you were married, my girl! Believe me, I count it no privilege that I still carry responsibility for you. Susanna, you are twenty-seven years old and the burden of providing your upkeep should have passed long ago to a husband.'

The pinkness of outrage washed across her cheeks.

'How can you say such a thing! As if it were my fault I've twice been let down!'

'You know my opinions on that, Susanna. We won't argue the matter again.'

'No, Papa,' came the pettish retort, 'there's little point, is there? In the end, the blame is always mine.'

For a long moment he was silent, then he said quietly: 'You must accept a large share of it, my dear. But . . .' He hesitated and now surveyed her with a strange look of sorrow and helplessness. '. . . so must I and so must your mama, for it was we who spoiled you and made you what you are. If only we'd taught you to be strong and resourceful, instead of vain and selfish.'

Insulted, she opened her mouth to protest, but the weariness and woe upon his face caused her to swallow her words. Papa was not his usual self today. There was something badly wrong, but she could not imagine what it might be.

Laying a hand on her cheek, he shook his head. 'Dear Lord,' he sighed, 'what will we do with you now?'

Susanna was nonplussed. 'Do with me?' she repeated. 'What do you mean, Papa? You seem afraid of something and you're making me frightened too.'

He sighed again, took her arm and walked on. 'Daughter, there's something I have to explain to you and I suppose this is as good a time as any. It's bad news and there's no way in which I can soften it, but I'll make it as simple as I can.'

He waited until they had passed the cages filled with monkeys and shrieking parrots, and led her down beside the row of heavily barred boxes where the great cats were kept. In the last one, a single black panther lay silently watching the passers-by with baleful yellow eyes. Mr Tregear paused here and turned to his daughter.

'Some years ago, Susanna, I was tempted into making certain investments. At the time they seemed extremely promising, so I borrowed quite heavily in order to raise the capital. Naturally, the bank required security and I gave them a claim over much of our business property.'

Susanna understood little of commerce or finance. Even so, she did not like the sound of this arrangement. The blue eyes were fixed intently upon her father and he shifted his gaze uncomfortably as he went on:

'To my great distress, the ventures failed and the money was lost. Nevertheless, I was hopeful that we could still repay the bank from the proceeds of our drapery shops.

17

The legacy from your grandmother also helped to reduce the debt, and indeed, for some time it seemed to be under control and no great threat to us. I asked no sacrifices of you or your mama; I wanted my family to live well, but . . .' Nervously, he cleared his throat. '. . . I'm afraid I was too complacent.'

She felt a rising surge of panic and disbelief. Their wealth, soft as a cushion and solid as a fortress, had pampered and protected her all through her life. How could their money, always relied upon and taken for granted, have been in jeopardy all this time? He might as well have told her that the ground beneath her feet could dissolve and disappear.

'You see, my dear, there's been much competition in the fabric trade of late. My shops are no longer the biggest or the best, and the takings have fallen steadily in the last two years. The bank has, on several occasions, granted me more time to pay. But yesterday morning I received a letter, an ultimatum.'

'No,' whispered Susanna. 'Oh, Papa!'

'We have just twelve months more and then they will call in the loan. That's why I went to see my accountant today. I'm sorry, daughter, there's nothing to be done. I know of no way to obtain the sum in time, and I see no point in turning to other moneylenders. We won't lose everything, but we will find ourselves in severely reduced circumstances. There's no fear of starvation and we'll still have a roof over our heads, but you'll have to do without most of the luxuries and pleasures you've enjoyed in the past.'

'I don't believe you!' The words were uttered low and fiercely, but there was a tremor in them and a shadow of fear on the delicate face. 'It's preposterous! A wicked, wicked lie! I won't listen to any more of this.'

In his cage, the black panther stirred, slinking forward

on his belly towards the bars. Like all his kind, he could smell terror. The movement caught Susanna's attention. She glanced around, met those malignant eyes and pictured poverty, like the panther, a dark, terrible thing creeping up on her.

Her father regarded her sadly, for she had turned a ghastly waxen colour.

'What is more, you must be prepared in future to earn your keep. It seems certain that we'll lose our establishment here in Penzance, and also the small one in Porthgullow. I have hopes that we can keep the branch in Truro, but in order to do that we must give up our home in Morven Terrace. There are living quarters above the shop in Truro and they'll have to suffice for us. Of course, I'll be forced to dispense with most of my staff and my plan is that you should serve behind the counter.'

Her mouth had dropped open as he spoke and she shook her head in furious refusal. 'I will not! I cannot!' Her voice was shrill with desperation. She stamped her foot and tears spilled down her cheeks. 'I was never raised to do such a thing and you cannot ask it of me now!'

'I must ask it, since you have no husband. That's why it grieves me so much that you've lost two chances of marriage. I cannot continue to support a spinster daughter in comfort and idleness, and that's all there is to it.'

Susanna thought she would faint. The noise and bustle of the fair had receded to a dull hum and flicker of movement, and seemed a long way off.

'Come along now, and stop crying.' His manner had grown gruff again, for he knew that sympathy would only make her weep the more. 'You had to be told and I'm glad it's over and done with. Lord help me, I have to face your mother with it next, and I don't relish the prospect of watching the pair of you sniffling over dinner.'

19

2

Jenny sat with her hands clenched in her lap, sorely out of temper as the pony and trap rattled homewards. It was only when Richard mentioned Susanna's name that she pricked up her hears and paid full attention to what he was saying.

'What did you think of Miss Tregear?'

'I didn't like her.'

'Oh? That's a pity.' The road took an uphill turn and he shook the reins as the pony began to dawdle. 'What do you find wrong with her?'

'She's high and mighty.'

'Jenny! She said nothing unkind.'

'She didn't have to. Men only hear the words that are spoken. A woman hears a lot more besides.'

'Rubbish.' Richard frowned. 'You didn't have a headache at all, did you?'

'Yes.' Her tone was unconvincing.

'Come to think of it, you were rude to her.'

'She was looking down her nose at me! 'Twas just as though she was cut crystal and I was an old tin mug. And how you fussed around her, too!'

'Dear Lord, I believe you're jealous.' He stared at her, half amused, but exasperated at the same time.

'Of that? Hmph! She's just a featherhead,' sniffed Jenny. 'Conceited thing, bragging about her father's shops.'

'I'm sure she didn't mean it that way.'

'I suppose she thought I was shabby,' muttered Jenny. 'I know her sort – no use to anybody. Too much money

20

and nothing to do but spend it. I suppose she's got a houseful of servants running round after her, and I'll wager it took one of them more than an hour just to pin up her hair like that.'

Richard began to grow impatient. 'It's not often I hear nasty talk from you and I can't say I care for it. Jenny, my love, we've had a good day, haven't we? Why spoil it now? There's nothing to sulk over.'

She chewed at her lip and stared down at the whitened knuckles of her hands. 'I'm sorry, but I don't like it when people are scornful of me.'

Richard slipped an arm about her. 'Look, you're taking it all the wrong way. I was no more than civil to the lady, and she made no jibe at you, so let's forget the matter, eh?'

The girl smiled weakly and wished she had managed to hide her feelings. But Richard's words had done nothing to change her opinion of Miss Tregear, and what he called 'civility' still looked too much like worship.

I've eyes to see and I'm not stupid, she thought irritably. He stood there gazing at her like a great besotted fool, and spoke as he would to the Queen herself.

Richard's thoughts had indeed dwelt long and keenly upon Susanna's fairylike hair and magnolia skin. He suffered a small twinge of guilt over this, but stronger still was the sense of annoyance that Jenny could read him so easily. He loved her dearly, of course, but there were no mysteries between them and therefore little excitement.

The seven o'clock sun hung halfway down the sky as they travelled the last few miles of furzy common. Ruddy-brown and wiry, splashed with the livid yellow of gorse, the moor looked scorched and crisp that evening, with all its colours glowing. At length, their route began to lead upwards to the summit of a hill, where tumbled stacks of boulders emerged from the covering of bracken on the lower slopes. On the other side ran the north coast road, and beyond it the harsh Atlantic cliffs stretched away to left and right, tapering into a haze of distance.

At the foot of the hill, Richard turned eastwards along the broader main road that would take them the last three miles to Porthgullow.

The town, with its population of five thousand, occupied a deep indentation in the coastline of Cornwall. There was only one road into Porthgullow and the first building they passed on the way down the hill was the parish church, with its square tower and slightly tousled grave-yard. A few small but genteel houses were built nearby and the track then continued for half a mile without a sign of human dwelling before the town suddenly came into view.

A branching road to the right led to the smart area reserved for the well-to-do, a little colony of the affluent, the heart of which was Morven Terrace. Richard glanced curiously at this turning as they went by. He had never visited that section of Porthgullow, though he knew every ope and alley of the lower part.

Although the surrounding moors were dotted with tin mines, Porthgullow was first and foremost a fishing port. Between the east and west quays lay three hundred yards of waterfront, facing a shelving beach. To the east of the town, a curving arm of land sprawled far out to sea. A scattering of rocky pinnacles, half submerged, stretched for a quarter of a mile beyond the tip of it. On the largest of them stood a lighthouse, with lamp and bell to warn of this menace, which had claimed lives by the score in centuries past. On this same side of Porthgullow lay the five-acre shipyard of K. B. Annear, where brigs, barques and clippers were built.

Almost without exception, the people who occupied

the warren of granite cottages made their living from the sea by one means or another. Most were drift fishermen, long-liners, crabbers, and those who catered to their needs. In the mornings, when the catches were landed, the jetties would bustle with jousters, fish merchants and horse-drawn carts. With the contours of a heavy ocean swell turned suddenly to cobblestone, the tangle of narrow streets rose and fell in surges of slopes and hollows. A disorderly maze, built without regard for bewildered strangers, the paths and alleys were punctuated by flights of steps and tiny shortcuts.

Apart from Covenant Street, which boasted an ironmonger's, a bakery and a pharmacy, together with Tregear's drapery, there was no particular concentration of shops. Instead, they were scattered all over the town, tucked away in opes and corners. Those enterprises closest to the harbour were chiefly concerned with the fishermen and their boats. Here were the chandlers and ropemakers, the shipsmith, the barkhouse, the suppliers of blocks, spars and pumps, nets and baskets.

Here, too, was Varcoe's sail loft. It occupied the upper floors of three adjoining cottages. The sailmaker's home was the third from the end, and he shared the loft with the riggers who dwelt in the last two houses of the row. A flight of outside steps allowed access to this workroom without the need to pass through the living quarters underneath.

Bob Varcoe was a widower, a bluff, heavily built man whose hair and beard were always unkempt. He was setting out his supper when they went in, and Richard was asked to stay for the meal. There could, in Varcoe's opinion, be no better husband for his daughter. Richard was the son of his oldest friend. The lad was strong, capable and hard-working. Jenny would be loved and well provided for, and she would take a respected name when

23

she married into the Rescorla family. There were wealthier men, to be sure, but none Bob liked so well.

'You've had a fine time, I take it?' he said, as they sat down to eat.

Cutting himself a lump of cheese, Richard glanced across the table at Jenny and raised enquiring eyebrows. 'Well?' he asked, teasing. ''Tis for you to say.'

For a second or two the girl eyed him dubiously, and then a sheepish grin crept across her face. 'Yes,' she said, spearing a pickled onion from the jar and dropping it onto his plate, 'we did, we had a lovely day.'

And how silly, she thought, to make a fuss about that woman.

3

Richard's home lay three and a half miles from Porthgullow, and it was dusk by the time he reached the turning to the cove, signposted by nothing more than a wooden board tacked to a tree. Shaded on both sides by hedges, in which bramble and honeysuckle vied for space, the stony track was wide enough for just a single vehicle. Richard made his way cautiously, for should he meet another cart face to face, much backing and manoeuvring would be required before either could make any progress. Halfway down, the path branched to the left along a short spur of carriage track, ending at a five-barred field gate with the name 'Boskenna' painted on it.

The square granite house beyond was built on a ridge, a position that gave fine views of the sea from some of the bedrooms but allowed only a quarter of an acre of land. There was just space enough for a kitchen garden, chicken run, furze rick and decently distant privy, together with a few outbuildings, the largest of which was reserved for the pony and trap. A small, rectangular portion of ground remained at the front of the house for grass and flowers.

Climbing down from the trap, Richard opened the gate and led the pony through. Then he fastened the latch and hitched the reins to the gatepost, before collecting up the things he had brought from the fair. He started up the path to the front door with its small porch.

Inside was a square vestibule with flagstone floor and a row of coatpegs on the wall. An inner door faced him, and opening it, he walked along a passage to the parlour on the left, from which came the sound of voices. Among them were the piping tones of a child – and they rose to a squeal of excitement as Richard put his head round the door.

The parlour at Boskenna was not large and contained just two easy chairs, the best of which was occupied by the compact and muscular man who was Richard's father. His nine-year-old sister, Esme, dressed in her nightshirt, was perched on her father's knee, while Judith, the elder girl, was sitting quietly in the window seat. A square table and big glass-fronted corner cupboard, together with a hearth stool and the late Mrs Rescorla's upright piano, took up the rest of the room.

The display cupboard was filled with glassware and china figurines. An engraved punchbowl on the top shelf was surrounded by inverted tumblers, rummers, and goblets in green and red with long, twisted stems. On the table was a cranberry glass epergne, and a pair of prints adorned the wall opposite the fireplace. One depicted Vesuvius by day with a column of smoke winding sullenly skywards; the other was a lurid impression of the mountain in full eruption by night.

As Richard came into the room, Esme scrambled down and ran to her brother, stretching up for the bag of sweets he held above her head.

'What have you brought me? Oh, Richard, please let me see!'

She jumped and snatched as he dangled it just beyond her reach.

'Don't torment her, for pity's sake,' said John Rescorla, grinning. 'She won't go to bed till she has her present.'

Richard handed Esme the sweets, together with a few small novelties for good measure. There were gasps of gratitude and delight, and she scampered across to show Judith her treasures.

'How was it, then?' his father asked him. 'Did Jenny enjoy the fair?'

'Oh yes, we saw all there was to see. Here . . .' Richard fished in his pocket. '. . . I've brought you a tin of cheroots.'

The shipwright took them with a murmur of pleasure, a smile transforming his broad, brown-skinned face with its darkly intent eyes. Looking down at him, Richard was suddenly aware that his father's hair, once as black as his own, was now partially grey.

John Rescorla was a skilful, industrious man, content with his moderate prosperity. He cleaved to the Church of England and was generous to a sensible degree, preserving a balance of shrewdness and good will in his business dealings. His only real fault was a tendency to stubbornness – a trait of which Richard also showed signs – and he seldom lost his temper. He had, on rare occasions, been moved to rage, but always with grave cause. At the age of forty-three he was, like Varcoe, a widower, having lost his dearest Ellen some three years past. Only Sundays, funerals or special events moved him to put on a suit. Most of the time he dressed, as now, in the same type of flannel trousers, linen shirts and woollens worn by the men he employed. Only his manner of quiet assurance set him apart from them, betraying the fact that he had received a little more schooling, that he was the owner and master.

Esme, blissfully crunching a sugared almond, returned to clamber once more on her father's knee and feed him a peppermint. The wavy hair that fell to her waist was the colour of autumn bracken. Her upturned face, laughing up at him, was freckled, the features sharp and questing, with eyes and brows of a light toffee-brown. Esme's gaze was always on the move, dancing here and there, examining everything, dismissing, admiring, wanting. There

27

was no peace in it, but evidence of a great and urgent appetite for life.

Richard turned to his other sister, holding out the comb and ribbons.

'Judith, these are for you.'

The girl took them with a gentle smile and murmur of thanks.

'I hope you'll wear them?' There was a coaxing note to the question.

Judith nodded shyly. 'Of course I will,' she promised.

Richard, however, had his doubts about that. At fourteen, Judith was very plain and quiet, not given to primping of any sort, despite all persuasion. Her oval face was framed by straight, heavy hair that was very nearly black. The set of her mouth expressed a certainty that all was as it should be, and the grey eyes were calmly thoughtful. Capable, sensible Judith, the reliable, the willing, the one who would always shoulder burdens and forgo a treat in favour of someone else. With dignity, tranquillity and all the patience of an adult, she was quite unlike Esme in every respect.

The little one clasped her arms fondly round her father's neck. 'I'm going to have a new yellow frock when I'm Jenny's bridesmaid, aren't I?'

'You might, if you behave yourself in the meantime.' The child began to giggle and he slapped her lightly on the backside. 'You like Jenny, don't you, maid?'

Esme nodded happily.

'So do we all.' He turned to his elder daughter. 'Put her to bed now, Judith – and don't let her take those sweets with her or she'll eat the lot before morning.'

'I'd best see to the pony and trap,' Richard said, accepting a goodnight peck from each of his sisters.

He went outside and lingered for some time over the task, recalling the events of the day. The outing had done nothing to cure the discontent that troubled him. In truth, he felt more restive than before.

'Anything new at the fair?' asked John, when his son came in again and flopped down in the other armchair.

Richard's gaze flitted away from his father. He pursed his mouth and shook his head. 'No, 'twas same as always, just like every other year.'

The Rescorla family had lived and worked at the cove for more than a century. John's father and grandfather had both been builders of fishing boats, and he had therefore inherited a well-established business, together with Boskenna.

It was a plain but substantial house, built round a passage which stretched to the kitchen at the rear, with a staircase to the five bedrooms leading from the right of it. The kitchen was large and square, dominated by an open hearth with a six-foot granite lintel across the top and a recess so deep that three men could sit within it side by side. A fire of peat and furze burned here summer and winter alike, for all the boiling and baking and the scalding of cream depended on it.

Boskenna's only domestic employee was a corpulent middle-aged woman named Hannah. She declined to live in, returning each evening to the cottage she shared with her father down in the cove. During the day, however, Hannah did most of the family's laundry and performed wondrous feats of simple but tasty cookery with only the aid of a trivet, two large boiling pots and a cloam oven.

The house boasted a small dining room – regularly used when Mrs Rescorla was alive. The daughter of an Anglican minister, she had always insisted on certain standards of behaviour. Since her death, however, the family had adopted the comfortable habit of eating in the kitchen.

It was for his late wife that John had bought the pony and trap. He would not see his beloved Ellen, a woman gently raised and nicely educated, walking back and forth to Porthgullow to fetch supplies. It was also useful to carry the children about and had lately been a great convenience for Richard and Jenny.

From some of the upstairs windows, the roofs of the building sheds could be seen on the beach below. John and Richard had only to walk a hundred yards farther down the lane each morning to reach their place of work.

Beyond the final bend of the track lay a sheltered blue-green inlet. The cliffs were clothed down to the last fifty feet in rough grass, where pads of sea-pinks flowered in summer. The bare rocks below were the colour of dark tobacco and the water at their base lay deep, calm and unclouded. White sand, combined with ground-up shell, gave the beach a texture like that of coarse sugar. It was an easy landing place for a boat, and an equally good spot from which to launch one.

Rescorla's workshops stood some forty feet above the tideline. The yard was surrounded on three sides by an eight-foot stone wall, with double gates at the front and a wooden ramp leading down to the water. On the left hand side the cliff itself completed the square enclosure, and a great natural recess in the rock provided an extra building bay, for use when the workshops were full or the family received an order for a craft too large to be built inside. Of the two building sheds, the lesser one served only for gigs or seine boats. The larger one, however, could comfortably take two luggers and a small crab boat at one time. A lean-to timber store stood against the wall on the right hand side of the yard and was normally piled high with various kinds of elm, oak, pitchpine and larch. The steam-box and boiler, together with a small storehouse for tar, oakum and other materials, adjoined the main workshop. Although Rescorla's enterprise was a modest one, it was usually busy. John could not recall a time when his building bays had stood entirely empty, for fishing was the livelihood of many local men. His reputation brought him much respect, together with a steady flow of repairs and new orders.

He had always found the peace of this little cove more agreeable than the bustle of Porthgullow and he was, after all, not without neighbours. A number of cottages clustered there, some within a few feet of the sand, others perched on any patch of level ground to be found among the slopes behind. Most of the occupants were fishermen, but a few were his own employees. These were company enough for John Rescorla. Although quite affable with his family and a handful of carefully chosen friends, he was not what most would have called a sociable man and he liked his privacy.

During the week that followed the fair, Richard and John worked late each evening. Their day in the summer months would normally start at six in the morning and last for twelve hours; this Tuesday evening, however, found them still busy at half past nine, as dusky-blue clouds began to roll up from the skyline. Rescorla's oldest employee, a dour individual named Rufus Adams, had also stayed on, and he was working alongside John on the forty-foot lugger under construction in the main shed.

Pausing for a second, Rescorla glanced across to the other end of the workshop, where his son was ramming hemp between the planking of the new crab boat. John grinned and turned to the man beside him, knowing that Richard could not hear them above the clang of the caulking mallet.

'The boy's been full of yearning and soulful sighs since he came home on Saturday night. 'Tis a long engagement, I suppose, and he's growing impatient now. He didn't say much about the fair, but he keeps smiling to himself and

31

staring off into the distance as if he'd just met Jenny for the first time.'

Rufus put down his hammer and sat back on his haunches for a moment. 'Ess,' he said thoughtfully, 'I nawticed he didn' seem quite hisself.'

'Well, they'll have a long life together, God willing.'

'Hmm, thass a fact. He've made his pledge good 'n early, specially fer a boy wi' s'many maids givin'n the glad eye. Lads like Richard d'more offen go courtin' this one 'n courtin' that one fer lots o' years 'fore they decide to wed.'

'Richard has more sense. He could find no better than Jenny and he knows it. I married young and I've always been glad of it.'

Rufus nodded. 'Aw, ess, ess, she'll make a fine wife for'n, I knaw.'

A tough little man with iron-grey hair, a scooped nose and jutting chin, Rufus always exuded an air of caution. He was fifty-three years old and had been employed by John Rescorla for thirteen of them.

John hammered in a final nail and rose stiffly to his feet.

'That's enough for tonight.'

He slipped out between the frames of the boat and dropped to the floor, which was littered with wood shavings and piles of sawdust.

'Leave it, Rufus, and come up to the house for an hour. We've elder wine and sloe gin. Richard, come on!'

His son glanced round and John jerked his head towards the door.

'You needn't wait for me,' the boy said. 'You go on, I'll lock up.'

John picked up a lantern and extinguished two others, leaving the last one for Richard. It was dark when he and Rufus stepped outside. They walked up the lane in the

32

circle of lantern light, with Rescorla still talking breezily of his son's forthcoming marriage.

He's right, I knaw, thought Adams, as John sang Jenny's praises. There's none better'n the li'l Varcoe maid. Still, I fancy the boy've bin pushed a bit. Betterfit he'd had a chance to sow a few wild oats 'fore tyin' hisself down.

4

With its leafy surroundings and lofty position, Morven Terrace hardly seemed part of Porthgullow. Perched high on the hill above the cottage rooftops, it spoke of genteel detachment, of prosperity and comfort not to be shared by those down below. The terrace consisted of a dozen three-storeyed houses, each with bay windows to the ground floor and a small lawn in front. There were larger gardens to the rear, enclosed by high stone walls and stocked with rhododendrons, camellia bushes and various flowering trees.

Number three was the home of Mr and Mrs James Tregear, and one warm afternoon in July found their daughter Susanna sitting morosely upon the garden swing, fretting about her future.

Four weeks had passed since Corpus Christi fair, and Papa's evil tidings had filled her mind for every waking moment. She could not resign herself to what lay in store, nor could she think of any agreeable way to avoid it. Her mama had made a few suggestions, all of them horrid in Susanna's view.

She gnawed at her thumbnail, rocking gently back and forth on the swing. How could such a calamity befall her? How could everything have gone so terribly wrong? Mama and Papa had raised her to expect so much from life. An only child, she had always been petted and pampered. To want a thing was to have it, and every little whim had been indulged. There had always been money – plenty of money. She could not imagine life without it. But then, there had also been a time when she would have laughed at the notion of finding herself still unmarried at the age of twenty-seven.

It had happened, all the same. Miss Susanna Tregear, with her pretty face and lovely hair and all her splendid clothes, had twice been jilted.

'It's no surprise to me, my girl.' Papa's words, spoken after her first disappointment, sounded again in her mind. 'A beautiful woman is forgiven many things, daughter, but you go too far with your temper and your cruel tongue. Oh yes, you're sweet enough as long as you have everything your own way. You're quite charming until you're thwarted – but then it's tears and tantrums and spite. God forgive us, your mother and I always pandered to you, but you won't easily find a husband to tolerate such behaviour. He was a man of good family, Susanna, and you've lost him. Well, you're only twenty, so I daresay there will be others. I just hope you've learnt something from this. Try to control your petulance next time, and don't be so capricious.'

His voice faded away, replaced by the creak of the swing and the piping of a chaffinch high in the magnolia tree. Susanna raised her head and sighed wretchedly, her gaze roving about the garden.

Yes, there had indeed been others – numerous suitors and eventually another proposal of marriage. And she had tried to be less difficult. Yes, truly she had. Perhaps, on one or two occasions, she had forgotten herself and allowed some unattractive traits to show, but she did not think this the real reason for the second fiancé's defection. It was significant, she told herself, that he left her for a young French lady whose papa was wealthier than her own. Mama had thought so, too, but Mr Tregear had yet again blamed Susanna – and he was not the only one. When she found herself alone once more at the advanced age of twenty-five, there were fewer men eager to court

35

her. Some had already married, but others, hearing rumours of her temperament, chose not to seek her company. To be jilted once was merely a misfortune; to have it happen twice seemed to be a stigma.

And now, on top of everything else, had come this financial disaster. Sometimes she pictured herself behind the counter of Papa's Truro shop and her pride shrank from this awful vision. Susanna had already suffered pinpricks enough from 'friends' who flaunted their wedding rings and their pity for her single state. Many of them made regular shopping expeditions to Truro and word of her situation would soon spread. She could not stand the thought of one day serving them, and women like them, of running back and forth at their beck and call, thanking them for their patronage. Dear heaven, she could never do that.

It was wrong, so wrong, that she should find herself in this predicament, she fumed bitterly. Hard work and spinsterhood were for others – for plain women, common women – not for Susanna Tregear, who was meant to have everything.

A wellspring of rage suddenly bubbled up inside her and found for its target the chaffinch, trilling its one monotonous note over and over at the top of the magnolia tree. Furiously, she seized a stone and hurled it at the bird, which simply flew off to another tree and went on chirping in the same irritating way.

Exasperated, she stood up and stalked off into the house. She had sat for too long, in any case, and her back was beginning to hurt. A fall from that same swing when she was eight years old had left her with a spinal weakness which forbade her to lift or carry anything heavy or to stand for long periods. The small of her back would grow stiff and sore if she slumped when sitting or had no support against which to rest. Sometimes it helped to walk for a while, and at others she had to lie down. On this particular day, she decided to go into the town and spend what remained of her month's allowance.

She changed into a plum-coloured redingote and put on a hat of plaited straw. Beneath it, a black velvet ribbon was skilfully interwoven with the gleaming blonde hair.

The walk down the hill took a quarter of an hour and she went first to the shoemaker's to see if her new kid boots were ready. They were and she paid for them with her last guinea piece. After that she spent a pleasant ten minutes in the pharmacy, where she sampled a new cologne and bought some *pot-pourri*. Finally, she paid her usual call at Papa's shop, and there collected a favourite frock which the seamstress had taken in at the waist. Shock and anxiety had recently caused Susanna to lose a great deal of weight.

It was as she emerged from the drapery that she heard a voice offer the greeting: 'Good day, Miss Tregear. You're well, I hope?'

She looked up and saw before her a person in working clothes, with open waistcoat, shirtsleeves rolled to elbows and a red neckerchief tied at his throat. For a moment she was at a loss – and then she remembered him. Of course, the young man she had met at the fair.

'Ah – Mr . . .' She groped for the name and recalled it just as he was about to prompt her. 'Mr Rescorla.' Her eyes flickered uncertainly over his shabby garb. 'How nice to see you.'

An errand to the sawyers had taken Richard into Porthgullow that day, and his plan had been to call and see Jenny for an hour before going home. At the sight of Susanna, however, this intention slipped his mind. He smiled and nodded towards the packages she carried.

'They look heavy. Could I help you with them?'

She hesitated. The parcels were not at all heavy. On

37

the other hand, it was a tiring uphill walk to Morven Terrace and she was flattered by his offer. Susanna loved the attention of men and this one was very attractive indeed. Not of her own level, of course, but pleasing all the same.

'Well, I hardly like to trouble you. I'm on my way home, you see, and it seems an imposition . . .'

She let her words trail away, leaving him the opportunity to dismiss them.

''Tis all right, I've plenty of time.'

'You're very kind. I fear I'm a great nuisance to you.' Susanna sighed prettily and handed him her packages.

They strolled slowly up the hill and it was nearly a quarter past four when they reached the gate of Susanna's house. As she took the parcels from him, she supposed she ought to make some gesture other than a mere word of thanks.

'Will you come in for some tea? It would please me greatly, for I don't know how else to thank you.'

In view of the way he was dressed, she fully expected him to say no, as a man more knowing most certainly would. But Richard did not realize that he was supposed to decline. He wavered, considered, argued with himself. Jenny was not actually expecting him. It was not as if he were letting her down – and he was curious to see the inside of this very smart house.

Susanna, awaiting his refusal, was hard pressed to hide her surprise when he answered: 'All right, then. 'Tis good of you to ask me.'

There was nothing to do but carry it through. He was not suitably clothed, but she hoped her mama might overlook that when she learned who he was, for Papa had spoken well of Susanna's rescuer at the fair.

Mrs Tregear was already having tea when Susanna took him into the drawing room. Like her daughter, she was slight of build and perfectly groomed, but her features were thin and she looked her age, which was fifty-four. Her mouth popped open when she saw Richard, and she turned pointedly to Susanna for an explanation.

'Mama, this is Mr Rescorla – the young man who came to my aid at the fair. You remember, don't you? Papa told you all about it, didn't he?'

Understanding dawned on Mrs Tregear's face. 'Ah,' she murmured, surveying him with a tight little smile. 'Yes, yes indeed he did. We're obliged to you, sir.'

Richard, unsure what to do, murmured that it was nothing. Nervously, he stuffed his hands in his pockets, then quickly took them out again.

'And now he's been kind enough to carry my parcels home for me, so I think he deserves some tea.'

'Um – well, yes, I'm sure he does.' Still taken aback, but feeling unable to object, Mrs Tregear motioned him to take a seat.

Richard sat down, rolling down his sleeves and fastening his waistcoat, for the elegance around him made him uncomfortably conscious of his rough clothes.

Susanna went upstairs to change, while her mother ordered more tea. The shocking incident at the fair was raised once more and Richard was thanked all over again. The laws against public drunkenness were far too lenient, said Mrs Tregear, and both the quarrymen deserved a term in prison. Richard agreed that they were and they did, and called it a bad job that a respectable woman could not walk down a main street in safety.

When Susanna returned, she was wearing a crinoline of lemon silk, with many puffs, layers and gold bows. It was somewhat elaborate for afternoon tea, but Richard was enchanted and could barely drag his gaze away from her. Mrs Tregear was quick to notice this, and her look became very thoughtful.

'You must tell us more about yourself,' she said. 'We'd very much like to hear about your work.'

Encouraged with gentle questioning and murmurs of admiration, Richard was very forthcoming about his trade, his home and his parents. He spoke with enthusiasm of all three, and sometimes he exaggerated just a little. Mrs Tregear was sharp enough to recognize which was solid fact and which was garnish, but responded to both with the same rapt attention. By the time the mantel clock struck five, she had formed a fairly accurate impression of his circumstances.

Susanna, meanwhile, attended busily to his wants and his comfort. She did not say much and did not need to, since her ornamental presence was enough in itself. Ever smiling, she nibbled tiny sandwiches, crooked her little finger as she held her cup, and made a pretence of strain when she lifted the teapot to pour.

Mrs Tregear, with her watchful grey eyes, saw that the young man was captivated, and observed him with the greatest interest. Soon her formal manner disappeared and she began to use his Christian name.

'So you have no brothers, Richard?'

'No, I've two younger sisters, that's all.'

'And your enterprise is strictly a family concern?'

'Oh yes, Father likes it that way.'

Mrs Tregear seemed very satisfied with this reply. 'Quite right, too,' she said firmly.

When at last he was ready to leave, she kept him a moment longer, saying: 'Richard, I would like to offer you the loan of a book which I know will interest you. Do come into the study.'

The volume was a history of sailing vessels from earliest times up to the end of the Napoleonic wars. There were many beautiful illustrations and Richard was genuinely eager to read it. But he was also moved by the knowledge that it would have to be returned, and the hope that he might see Susanna when he brought it back.

As he went off down the front path with the book tucked under his arm, Mrs Tregear called out: 'We're always at home after four.'

When he reached the end of Morven Terrace, Richard stopped and debated for a moment, then decided it was too late to go and visit Jenny that day. Well, it hardly mattered, after all. They would see more than enough of each other in the coming years.

How badly mistaken Jenny had been in her assessment of Susanna, he thought, as he walked home. Few wealthy ladies would extend such a gracious welcome to a shabby young man. All the same, he did not intend to mention the visit to anyone – and that included his father. As soon as he arrived back at Boskenna, he took the book up to his room and hid it. He had no wish to be asked where it had come from.

41

5

One morning shortly afterwards, Mrs Tregear went to her daughter's room to have a private talk with her. Still in her drawers and chemise, Susanna was seated at the dressing table, having her hair brushed. Dismissing the maid, the older woman sat down in the armchair beside the window and regarded her daughter thoughtfully for a moment.

'What is it, Mama? I'm going out at ten and I'll need an hour to get ready.'

'Your social calls can wait, Susanna. I have something important to say to you and we must discuss it now, so that you may take time to think it over afterwards.' She folded her hands and a strange little smile appeared on her face. 'It's about that young man you brought home the other day.'

Susanna fidgeted uneasily. 'I'm sorry, Mama. Perhaps I did wrong to ask him in without your leave, and I know he wasn't suitably dressed . . .'

Mrs Tregear lifted a hand to interrupt her. 'No, no, child. I'm not here to rebuke you. But I have been thinking about him these past few days, and I have an idea for you to consider.' The smile became coy. 'I must say, he is quite handsome, isn't he? And pleasing in his manner, too. Soft-spoken, not at all clumsy.'

'Yes,' said Susanna, picking up her silver-backed hairbrush and stroking her locks. 'I noticed that.'

'So you found his company agreeable?'

The girl shrugged. 'Very pleasant, for a working man,'

she said absently, her attention centred more upon a tiny tangle than her mother's words.

'Within his own family's enterprise,' qualified Mama slyly.

Susanna made no response to this, so Mrs Tregear went on: 'I remember his mother, you know. We were not acquainted, but I knew her by sight. Rather a nice woman – quiet, dignified. Her people were clergy, I think.'

She peeped at her daughter in hopes of seeing some interest, but received only an indifferent nod. And so she said bluntly: 'On the whole, I think there is much to recommend him.'

At last she had Susanna's full – albeit suspicious – attention.

'For what?' The question came out low and wary.

'As a husband, my dear.'

Briefly, Susanna was too appalled to say anything. Then: 'You can't mean it!'

Her mother's expression had grown sober now. She leaned forward in her chair and said earnestly: 'I see possibilities in him, Susanna. You are in a difficult situation and he may provide a way out for you. It's not a perfect solution, I admit, but . . .'

'It's the most stupid, hateful suggestion I've ever heard!'

'Why, may I ask? We've just agreed that he's no clod. Young Richard is an only son, Susanna. Surely you realize what that will mean when his father dies? You would be the owner's wife.'

'I see no great honour in that! They build fishing boats, that's all. Mama, they're people of a different sort. They're not like us or any of our friends.'

Mrs Tregear was silent for a few seconds, then she said: 'That's true enough now, though you'd find no great differences if you could look back a generation or two. Of

43

course, you cannot remember the time when your father traded from a tiny shop in a sidestreet of Penzance. In those days we used two of the back rooms as living quarters and made just enough profit to keep body and soul together. You know nothing of that, because we were already rising in the world when you were born. But now let me tell you something. It was I who spurred your father on to expand his business, to buy a little house, then a second shop, and later still an even better house and third shop. You see, my dear, a wife can often guide a man and drive him on to gain advancement. Had it not been for me, your father would have stayed a poor haberdasher all his life. Oh yes, I know we're going to end up back where we started – but then, we've had uncommonly bad luck in the last few years. Thanks to my initiative, we came very close to considerable wealth, Susanna, and would have achieved it, had your papa's investments only turned out well. Think about it, child, for it may be that Richard could be moulded into something more than he is.'

'I don't care, I don't want him!' snapped the girl.

'Daughter, we must be realistic.'

Susanna suddenly remembered Jenny. 'Anyway, he's already engaged to be married,' she said triumphantly.

'Greater obstacles have been swept aside. The young man admires you very much. I noticed how he looked at you while we were having tea. A little encouragement is all he needs.'

'Well, I shan't give it!' The hairbrush hurtled across the room and cracked the glass of a watercolour picture before clattering to the floor. Mrs Tregear stiffened and a gleam appeared in her eyes.

'No? Let me list the alternatives for you. Will you be content to serve in your papa's shop? No, of course not. So – what else could you do? Well, the position of governess is said to be suitable for a gentlewoman in reduced circumstances – but you have no rapport with children, have you?'

Susanna darted her mother a sulky glance from under her brows, then stared moodily down at the rug, tracing its pattern with her toe.

'Or you could go and live with Aunt Hilda. She'll need someone to keep her company and take care of her in her old age. If you're dutiful and kind to her, she might even leave you her house when she dies. But Aunt Hilda can be very troublesome, can't she? How would you like to spend ten or fifteen years cooped up with a fractious old maid, knowing all the while that you'll probably end up as one yourself?'

The girl's expression had turned to one of helpless misery. 'Mama,' she whimpered, 'why are you being so cruel?'

Mrs Tregear reached out and stroked her daughter's hair. 'Because you must be made to face your situation. It's very hard for me to say these things to you, for I know that your father and I are largely to blame for your plight. All we can do for you now is to find the least unpleasant way of resolving it – which brings me to the final option. Marriage is still a possibility, my dear, but you'll have to lower your expectations.'

'No! No, there must be someone of my own kind.'

Her mother considered this. 'Yes,' she allowed reluctantly, 'I can think of one gentleman who might propose.'

Susanna's eyes widened with hope.

'Mr Pellow, the Town Clerk.'

Hope was replaced by revulsion.

'He has a very nice house and a good income,' continued her mother. 'Whenever I see him, he always asks after you. I think he regrets the fact that he never married.'

'He's nearly sixty! He's horribly fat and spits when he's talking!'

'Mr Pellow is fifty-three,' corrected Mama, 'but I quite agree that he is unattractive. I'm sure you can imagine . . .' She broke off, delicately moistening her lips. '. . . how unpleasant the marital duties would be.'

Susanna did not want to imagine it. Mrs Tregear saw that she had touched a nerve and so pursued the point a little further.

'When you were first engaged, I felt it kindest to warn you of the things a wife must bear, so that you would not receive a rude shock on your wedding night. Unlike most unmarried girls, you are not ignorant of the truth and I trust you are reconciled to it.'

'Yes, Mama,' muttered Susanna wretchedly.

'Since this contact must be endured, it is some consolation if the husband's body is wholesome. That's another point in favour of a young man like Richard. He's clearly healthy and well-made. I would shudder to think of you with such as Mr Pellow, but . . .'

'Yes, yes, I understand. But Mama, surely there's someone else?'

'I fear not. If we had wealthy friends or relations elsewhere in the country, I would send you away for a few months, in hopes that you might catch a husband. But we have no one to offer such help, Susanna. It's all we can do now to keep up appearances and we cannot afford to arrange travel or expensive social programmes for you. For the present, only our solicitors, our accountants and, of course, the bank, are aware of the true financial position, but our predicament will eventually be known to everyone. I advise you to seek a safe haven before it becomes obvious that you are in dire need.'

Her daughter fixed her with a sullen stare. 'You always

promised me I would have everything, and now you're telling me to make do.'

'Yes,' sighed Mrs Tregear, 'I'm afraid I am, and I hope you'll show the sense to make the best of a bad job. Think over what I've said, Susanna. When Richard returns the book I lent him, be as charming as you can. Cultivate his affection, and don't dally over it, for time is fast running out. At present you look no more than twenty-two, but don't be smug about that. Beautiful women are often inclined to fade quickly after a certain age. Richard may be your last chance, my girl, and believe me, you could do far worse. Despite all appearances, his people are more secure than we are. I've been asking a few discreet questions these past two or three days. Among others, I spoke to the Reverend Sobey's wife – she was a friend of Mrs Rescorla, you know. She tells me they have a decent little home, every bit as nice as the vicarage, and I understand they're never short of trade.'

'But he's too young,' whined Susanna, though she was beginning to weaken.

'And youth is impressionable, my dear. Youth is very vulnerable.'

6

By the time Richard returned the book, Susanna had come to terms with Mama's suggestion. Though hardly ideal, he was certainly not the worst of her options, and conscience had never been any obstacle for Miss Tregear. The Varcoe girl was young – pretty, in a way. She would find someone else. In any case, she was bred for work, which Susanna was not.

Richard brought the book at six on a Sunday evening, having spent the afternoon with Jenny. Noting his arrival by pony and trap, Susanna prevailed upon him for one more favour. Her aunt was ill, she explained, and she wished to pay her a call. Papa was using the family carriage – but perhaps Richard would be kind enough to drive her the three miles to her aunt's house and then bring her back again? The visit would not last for more than half an hour and it would be such a comfort to the old lady, who was a spinster and very lonely. Of course, if Richard was too busy, Susanna would quite understand. Yes, perhaps it was too great an imposition. She should not have asked . . .

Richard hastened to assure her that he did not mind at all.

The ride led to an invitation. Susanna was to sing and play the piano in a forthcoming musical evening at the church hall. The proceeds would go to the needy. The programme was to include recitations of prose and poetry, plus solos for flute and violin. Altogether a worthy and cultured event, she promised. Would Richard like to come? Oh, and Miss Varcoe too, of course – unless she would find it dull.

Richard decided he would go to the concert – it was, after all, in a good cause – but he did not take Jenny with him. He, of course, knew that it was all quite innocent, but Jenny would only upset herself again and imagine all sorts of silly things, so the kindest course was simply not to tell her. He assured himself he was not being underhanded, merely considerate.

When the concert evening arrived, he took a seat at the back of the hall, for he felt distinctly out of place. The audience consisted chiefly of females of the sort who possessed plenty of time and money to spend on charity work. The Teetotal Society had sent a squad of ladies, but none of the cottage community was present, except for Miss Drummond, who ran the Dame's School.

Richard could see Susanna sitting in the front row at the foot of the dais. She was with her mother, but did not look round to see who else was there.

Within a few minutes, the Reverend Sobey rose to introduce the first performer. Impatiently, Richard sat through half a dozen more or less passable efforts before Miss Tregear's turn arrived.

Dressed in a pure white muslin frock, with a simple silver locket at her throat, she sat down at the piano and began by playing a selection from Chopin. She was competent enough, and Richard, knowing little about music, marvelled at her talent. Finally, she stood up to sing the folk song 'Barbara Allen', and his gaze was riveted on this slender creature in her snowy gown. Susanna's singing voice was not strong, but it was pleasant. To the young man watching from the back row, she looked and sounded the very essence of sweetness.

Scanning the room as she sang, Susanna spotted him and was pleased to note that he was alone. When she finished, her performance was rewarded with genteel applause – and some rather more hearty clapping from the rear. Oh yes, he was impressed, all right. Returning to her seat, Susanna smiled with quiet satisfaction.

The concert ended at nine, and when she left the church hall she found Richard loitering outside. Mrs Tregear bid him a bright 'Good evening', then adroitly found someone else to talk to, in order that Susanna might have a few minutes alone with him.

'So you did decide to come,' beamed Miss Tregear. She had thrown a lacy shawl about her shoulders and she gathered it closer against the evening chill. 'I'm afraid it was all a bit stuffy. I hope you weren't too bored?'

'No, no. Some of the items were very good – especially yours. Anyway, 'twas a change.'

'You're very kind. We hold these little events every three months. Perhaps you'll come again?'

Richard agreed that he almost certainly would. They stood talking in the porch for several minutes, and when he asked after her father she confided that Mr Tregear's sixtieth birthday was only ten days away.

'I think it calls for a very special gift, but I've no idea what to buy for him,' she sighed. The blue eyes regarded Richard hopefully. 'I wonder if you could suggest something?'

He promised to give the problem careful thought. And then, remembering his monthly half-day, he went further and offered to accompany her to the shops in Penzance to help choose something suitable. Susanna made a show of protest – but only a feeble one.

And thus he stepped a little farther into the trap. Time he had once reserved for Jenny was no longer exclusively hers. There would be other rides now, and quiet walks and guarded meetings. As Mrs Tregear had said, he was easily beguiled.

* * *

The months went by and January came. On a Sunday afternoon, Richard stood at one of the windows of Varcoe's sail loft, gazing down into the street through the film of drizzle that coated the glass. It was a long, open-beamed room, where footsteps echoed on floorboards bare except for the chalked outline of a mizzen sail and the scuffed traces of other, similar diagrams. Here, in this loft, Richard and Jenny had played together when they were children.

She was sitting on her father's workbench that day, mending one of his shirts and talking about the future. Richard, his back turned, was not listening. His mind was on Susanna, and Jenny's plans did not interest him. They were all too familiar, too ordinary – and so, he felt with a stab of guilt, was Jenny. A terrible discontent had grown in him since Corpus Christi fair. Well, in truth, the seeds of it had been there far longer than that, and now they were sprouting like wild vines to choke an orderly little garden. That was half the trouble, of course. It was comfortable but dull to have his life mapped out. Everyone had always assumed he would marry Jenny, and he had fallen in with their expectations.

Perhaps they had assumed too much.

He loved her, of course, in a cosy, unexciting way, but surely there should be something more than that? Since meeting Susanna, he imagined there was.

Like a flood tide silently covering a sandbank, her influence had flowed swiftly round him until he was trapped and lost in it, as a man intent on the far horizon might suddenly look down to find the water risen to his waist and the shore a long way off. It was not just her appearance that lured and held him, but also the mystery of what might lie behind those ladylike ways which were both bait and barrier to him. She had given her age as twenty-two and had carefully made no mention of the

51

fugitive fiancés, so he thought her sheltered and fresh, like a flower grown under glass. He could look but he could not touch and was therefore filled with yearning.

Jenny, chatting about the children they would raise, had suddenly become aware that she did not have Richard's attention. She put down her sewing and watched him silently for a moment. She had felt for several weeks past that something was wrong, though he always denied it if she asked what was troubling him. But she was not blind, not stupid, and she knew him so well that his every change of mood, however slight, was clear for her to see. His visits, once regular, had become unpredictable. All the warm cuddling of the past was replaced now by a careless kiss when he arrived and another when he left. He used to stay for hours, but now he was restless in her company and often went early with little more than a weak excuse.

'Richard? Did you hear me?'

He turned from the window. 'What?'

'I said we should call our first son Robert John, after your father and mine.'

'Oh,' he murmured, uninterested, 'just as you like.'

'I've been thinking about girls' names, too. Which do you like best of these . . .?'

Suddenly, he snapped at her. 'Why must we spend so much time thinking up names for children who won't be born for years yet? Where's the sense in it? Why must we talk about children at all? Lord knows, we've discussed it all a dozen times before. We've planned every detail of our lives, from now till we're both dead and buried, and I don't want to go over it all again.'

Jenny stared at him and he returned the gaze with a mixture of pain and confusion. Her mouth had gone quite dry and for several seconds they both seemed paralysed by this outburst and what it revealed.

52

'I'm sorry if I bore you,' she said at last, the words scarcely audible.

He rubbed a hand helplessly across his forehead and muttered: 'No, 'tis for me to say I'm sorry. I'd no call to be sharp like that.'

'It's not the first time, Richard. 'Tis as if I'm a nuisance to you these days. What is it I've done?'

He sought an excuse and seized upon his work. 'I get tired, maid, that's all. Father's got three big vessels on order and we're working fourteen hours most days.'

'Yes . . .' Her smile was uncertain. '. . . I know that. Well, you'll be all right when they're done, I daresay.'

He nodded awkwardly and turned back to the window. Jenny quietly bent her head over her sewing. She had long since forgotten Susanna Tregear and could not understand the change in him. She only knew that he seemed to have grown away from her, and that he was not happy.

Nor was she, not any more, for the knowledge was already forming in her mind that her most treasured plans for the coming years were not so safely assured. All her fears were contained in a single question, and more than once she had been on the verge of posing it outright. But still it remained unspoken, except within her head. Richard, asked the inner voice, don't you want to marry me? But she dared not say it out loud.

No, he no longer wanted to marry her, but he was daunted at the prospect of facing her – and everyone else – with the truth, and so he allowed the charade to linger painfully on until the wedding was only ten weeks away. At that point, something occurred which drove him into the open.

It was March and he was walking with Susanna along the cliff path to the east of Porthgullow. They often met here, for the track was little used and it rambled through

53

belts of trees. Susanna called it her favourite spot. She chose it, she said, because it was pretty, but she knew quite well his desire for secrecy and had picked this place to make him feel at ease. How could she draw her net around a man who was constantly looking over his shoulder?

She did not fear to be alone with him. The days of chaperones were over for Susanna, and her situation convinced her there was little left to lose. Within her own circle she already had a reputation as a shrew, and that was stain enough to deter suitors. Richard, in any case, had shown himself to be respectful, never attempting any undue familiarity. She did not have to tell him that liberties were not to be allowed: he sensed and accepted it. After all, she was a lady.

Susanna paused at a break in the trees and stood for a few moments staring pensively out to sea. At length she gave a heavy sigh and he saw that her face was sad.

'Is something wrong?'

She shook her head and summoned a little smile that was brave and woeful all at once. 'No, not really . . . No, truly, it's nothing.'

'What's troubling you? Tell me.'

She seemed to wrestle with her conscience. 'I mustn't.'

'Why not? It can't be so terrible.'

'Not terrible, but better left unsaid. It won't help matters.'

'It might. Come on – please.'

Again the tragic smile. 'All right. I was just thinking that we won't be able to meet for much longer. It's quite close now, isn't it? Your wedding, I mean. I try not to dwell upon it, but the days are flying by.'

'May the sixteenth.' The reply was subdued. He did not want to think about it, either.

'Yes, well, I expect I'll go away for a little while when

54

the time comes. It's silly, I know, but I'll feel better if I'm not here.'

There was a brief, tense silence. Then: 'Will it upset you so very much?'

She bowed her head. 'I'll miss you dreadfully. Oh, I'll still walk here, of course, but it won't be the same.' She glanced at him to gauge the effect of her words and saw that he was filled with anguish. Lowering her eyes, she murmured: 'Forgive me, Richard, I shouldn't say such things. I've no right to embarrass you with my affections. I know you regard me as a friend and nothing more – quite properly so – and I mustn't make a nuisance or a fool of myself. If I'd known at the start that I would grow so fond of you, I would have kept my distance.'

There, she had made her 'confession'. It was all she needed to tip the scales. It all came out, then, all his desire for her, all his reluctance to marry Jenny and his dread of having to tell her so. Susanna shed a tear or two, she sympathized, she shared his distress and made a great show of her own. What a fearful dilemma, she said, what a painful plight for all three of them. Something would have to be done. Richard agreed, and she knew by the look on his face just what that something would be.

All was well. She had won. And as if to seal her success, fortune added another sticky thread to the web that day, for as they stood declaring mutual love, along the path came a woman of Jenny's acquaintance.

Her name was Alice Kittow. She was a fishwife who regularly walked the length and breadth of six parishes in the course of a day, bearing a basket on her back, from which she helped to sell her husband's catch. This was not Mrs Kittow's usual route home, and the crunch of her footsteps on the path made Richard and Susanna glance up with a start.

55

The woman looked at first surprised when she recognized Richard, but her face hardened as she drew nearer. Alice Kittow could smell mischief a mile off – and she had never seen a man look so guilty.

'All right, Richard?' The greeting was stiff, disapproving.

'Yes, Mrs Kittow. And you?'

'Ess, I'm well 'nough.'

That was all she said. It was all she needed to say. In a few seconds she was past them and walking on without a backward glance, but he knew the damage was done.

Concealing her satisfaction, Susanna asked anxiously: 'Will she tell anyone, Richard?'

He released a long sighing breath. 'I don't doubt it.'

'Oh, my dear . . .' She clasped his hands in her own. '. . . what trouble I've caused you.'

He considered briefly, then he said: 'No, perhaps 'tis just as well. Now everything's come to a head and 'tis time for me to do what's honest. I've put it off for long enough.'

7

Two days afterwards, in the late afternoon, fishermen setting out from Porthgullow noticed a young couple standing together at the end of the west quay. Everyone knew Jenny and Richard, and some of the men called out a greeting as the boats slid past and on towards the open sea.

There was no reply from the two figures on the jetty. The girl looked white and strained, her unbound hair whipping raggedly about her face. Richard, his head unhappily bowed, could hardly meet her gaze as he delivered his confession. Every so often he stole a nervous, sidelong glance at her and found her eyes fixed upon him in silent anguish as he stumbled through his welter of explanations and apologies.

'I won't plead with you,' she said, when his halting speech finally ended. 'I'd rather keep what's left of my pride. 'Tis enough that you've used and discarded me. I won't humble myself by begging you to change your mind.'

'Jenny, I'll never tell a soul that we were – indiscreet. You have my promise.'

'Your promise, Richard, is a thing of no great worth. Indiscreet, did you say? Well, well. It used to be a lovely bond between us. Now 'tis cause for shame. I see you've picked up some of Madam's attitudes and prissy talk.'

Richard winced, but repeated his pledge. 'No one will ever hear of it from me.'

'My, what a gentleman you are,' she said bitterly. 'I suppose I must thank you for leaving me that much dignity. I'll have enough to bear in facing this town, for I know of some who'll laugh at me and enjoy my misfortune.'

'A few, perhaps. A handful of mean, jealous girls. But they'll soon forget – and so will you.'

'You and I have been together all our lives! I can't set that aside as lightly as you do!' She turned her face from him, staring miserably towards the flotilla of fishing boats, outlined dark and angular against the sky as they fanned out across the horizon. 'I've never wanted anyone but you. I've never looked around and asked myself if I might do better with this one or with that one. You've been my whole life and all my hopes and plans were built around you. Because I trusted you, I let you share my bed. Because I wanted happiness for you, I thought you'd want the same for me. First I counted the months, then the weeks, and then the days till our wedding. Your cruelty's finely honed, Richard, to bring me this close and betray me this late. I always thought the world of you, but now I learn you're selfish and deceitful!'

Richard squirmed, but had no heart to defend himself. He could hardly deny the charges of deceit and betrayal, yet he firmly believed he was doing the right thing. Jenny, he thought, could not be expected to understand just yet. She was wounded, overwrought, and would need some time to recover. But surely it was better to suffer briefly now than to go ahead with a marriage that would cause them lifelong regret. They had made an error, that was all. They had been too hasty. Luckily, he had seen the mistake before it was too late – and Jenny would eventually recognize it too. How could he marry her when he no longer felt any desire for her? How could he keep up the pretence when his soul was filled with longing for Susanna?

'You'll find someone else,' he said awkwardly. 'Half

58

the young men in Porthgullow would be proud to take you for a wife.'

'Then why am I not good enough for you?'

'I didn't say there was any lack or failing in you. 'Tis just that I've had time to consider, to . . .'

'Compare?' The girl gave a wry smile. 'Well, I always knew you could have your choice of Porthgullow girls, but I never counted the likes of Susanna among them. My world is a small one, I suppose, and it's not often I look beyond these narrow streets and cottages, or people of my own kind. Do you have ambitions, Richard? Is that it? Do you want to better yourself and become a wealthy gentleman? You should have told me before. Or has it only come about since you met your fine lady? Perhaps she's filled you with ideas?'

'Susanna's position makes no odds to me – and it's not so very grand in any case. Her father's well-off, I admit, but he's no more than a shopkeeper, for all that. I've no thoughts of advancement, and Susanna's willing to accept a simpler way of life because she loves me.'

'My, you must feel flattered, Richard, to know she'll sacrifice so much for you.' Jenny regarded him thoughtfully for a moment, a flicker of grim humour playing upon her features, then she added softly: 'She's older than you, I think.'

'I'm nearly nineteen and Susanna's just twenty-two. 'Tis nothing to fuss about.'

'But virginity is, I suppose. I don't expect Miss Tregear allows you any liberties, does she?'

'You make too much of all that.'

'Oh? It wouldn't vex you, then, to find her without her maidenhead?' She searched his face and saw that, despite what he said, he did not care for the idea. 'No, you wouldn't wish to find her as you've left me. Tarnished? Is that the word? Don't worry, Richard, I don't think

Susanna would be silly enough to give away something for which she could ask a good price.'

'Don't be so insulting. She's not a schemer. Susanna and I can't help what's happened, and neither of us can go against it.'

Jenny's expression became a little pitying. 'Why, Richard, I always believed you a man of sound common sense and I never thought to hear such foolishness from you.'

Romance, that was what possessed him. It had scattered his wits and now held him fast with all its empty glamour. It was romance which had taken him from her, as much as the woman Susanna Tregear. His youth and his restlessness, his susceptible nature had done all this. Jenny had never before realized the value of mystery. No, she should never have parted with her virtue, or given Richard credit for better judgement than he truly had.

'I love Susanna,' Richard said. There was a note of pleading to the words. 'If only you could understand.'

But Jenny gave a derisive snort, shook her head and turned away without answering. There was no more to be said. His mind was made up and the anguish inside her was about to escape her control.

'I'll walk home with you,' he offered.

'I think you'd better not. I fear my father might break your neck.'

Sensing that his gaze followed her, she forced herself to keep a measured pace and upright bearing as she walked down the quay. It was not until she rounded the corner of Covenant Street that she broke into a run, fleeing homeward with the tears coursing down her cheeks.

The following morning, Richard faced his father with the news.

'If I had other sons,' John Rescorla growled, 'I would disown you. If you were not the only one to follow after me, to carry on my business and my name, I swear I'd turn you out!'

Richard's mouth had gone quite dry, for his father's normally genial face was suffused with a bloating rage. They stood facing one another across the table in the parlour, and Richard shifted awkwardly from foot to foot, trying to swallow the knot of tension in his throat.

The shipwright placed his hands flat upon the table and leaned forward, glaring at his son. 'I promise you, Richard, there's no joy to life unless you marry the right one. Choose badly and you may spend a lifetime paying for it. The consequences go on and on.'

'That's not your worry, Father.'

'No? I disagree!' Rescorla slammed his open palm upon the table. The epergne in the centre fell over and one of its trumpets snapped off. 'Did you spare any thought for the rest of us here in this house – how we might feel and how it might affect us? For a start, you've probably cost me the friendship of a man I've known and liked since before you were born.' He straightened up and drew a deep breath before proceeding. 'This is my home, Richard. I've the right to decide who I'll take under my roof. We'd all be proud and happy to have Jenny here – Judith, Esme, Hannah, all of us. But now you tell me it's not to be, that you mean to replace Jenny with a woman who's not suited to the type of life you'll offer her.'

'You haven't met Susanna,' objected Richard.

'I don't need to. 'Tis enough to know the lady lives in Morven Terrace. A woman of that sort could never fit in with our ways at Boskenna.'

'Mother did.'

'Your mother was brought up on Christian principles, among them humility. 'Tis rash to assume that this Susanna will gladly follow the same path.'

'She knows my situation's not as grand as her own, but

61

she wants me in spite of it. 'Tis a great compliment, Father. Susanna's very beautiful, she could have her pick of husbands.'

John Rescorla snorted and went to stand at the window, hands sunk in his pockets as he scowled out upon the little garden.

'Oh, yes, they all sigh for you, don't they, Richard? Even the fine and fancy ladies, it seems. Perhaps she's been reading poetry and silly novels. Perhaps she had dreams of giving up all for love,' he muttered scornfully. 'Believe me, boy, they'll soon turn sour, and so will she. 'Tis my guess you'll find her vain and spoilt. I fear she'll want more than you can give her.'

''Tis unfair to condemn her just because she was gently raised.'

'And to marry her on the strength of a few furtive meetings is so foolhardy that I almost doubt your sanity!' roared his father, turning from the window. 'To injure and abandon a girl who's loved you since you were a child is nothing short of wickedness! Since you're still a minor, poor Jenny's not even entitled to bring suit against you.' A thought occurred to him and he added a threat. 'By the same token, of course, I am able to forbid this marriage.'

'That won't force me to marry Jenny. 'Tis my resolve to make Susanna my wife and I won't be turned away from it. You can threaten whatever you like. Annear's are always glad of extra men. If you want to turn me out, then so be it.'

Richard knew, even as he spoke, that John would never do that.

The shipwright stared long and hard at his son. Richard returned the gaze with steady defiance. At length, John gave a short, mirthless chuckle. 'All right, Richard,' he said quietly. 'I know the mulish ways of young men. I shan't try to prevent it, since it's plain to me that you're caught like a fly in a treacle jar. Have your own way, then. Marry her. You're old enough to pay the penalty for your own folly. If she makes a good wife and thereby proves me a bad judge, I'll be man enough to apologize. But if, as I believe, she makes you wretched, then justice will be equally well served.'

'We'll see, then,' said Richard tightly.

He moved to leave the room, but was halted by a sharp command from his father.

'One moment, boy! I'm not quite finished. You've thrown aside Bob Varcoe's daughter and you shan't have my protection from his anger. You'll face him and 'tis best you show the courage to seek him out of your own accord, before he comes to find you. I shan't blame him if he takes his fists to you. As far as I'm concerned, he can deal with you as he sees fit, though I trust he'll stop short of murder. Best get it over quickly, eh? You'll go this morning.'

In Varcoe's sail lofts, the men went about their tasks that day in a manner more subdued than usual. There was little talk and no laughter. Keeping to their own section, the two riggers exchanged the odd gloomy shake of the head, sliding cautious looks towards the man who sat alone in the far corner. They could feel his rage, for it seemed to fill the room from end to end.

He was seated, as usual, upon a long, low bench. Across his knees and trailing over a large area of floor lay the tanned canvas sheets on which he was working. With his mouth compressed and forehead knitted in brooding anger, he performed the movements of his craft with a skill that was automatic and required no thought. But the violence with which he stabbed the bone spike through the canvas, or jerked the tarred twine with every flash of the needle, gave eloquent proof of his feelings.

As the door creaked open, the riggers glanced up and then stared awkwardly at Richard, wondering whether to offer any greeting. Deciding against it, they both stood up and left.

Richard ventured a few paces forward and the door clattered shut behind him. Varcoe's gaze lifted and fixed upon him with a mixture of loathing and disbelief.

'I'll grant you've plenty of nerve,' he said at last. 'Is it shame that's brought you here, or do you think to justify the way you've treated my girl?'

'Both.'

'Well, none of your shame will help her and none of your excuses will soften me, so I won't waste time listening to them,' snapped Varcoe.

'All I can do, then, is tell you I'm truly sorry that I've hurt Jenny and let her down after all this time. I know you must hate me, and you've every right, but I've come to apologize and to say I hope you won't hold Father in any way to blame. I'm sorely out of favour with him over this, and 'twas he who sent me here to see you.'

Varcoe's eyes glittered. 'Out of favour, is it? Yes, but that'll pass. You'll marry your fine lady and go on with your life without a backward glance and count it a small thing that you've ruined my child.'

Richard blanched and his eyes seemed to grow larger and darker in the whiteness of his face. It was a look so full of guilt that the sailmaker gave a grim nod of satisfaction.

'Yes,' he confirmed softly, 'that's right. She told me.'

Richard nervously moistened his lips.

''Twas long before I met Susanna,' he began. 'We weren't to know that everything would change. I'd no thought then of ever leaving Jenny.'

'No, but I'll wager the notion came to you soon after,' growled the sailmaker. 'I can't find it in me to chastise the girl, because I know how much she loved you and she's suffering enough as it is. But I expected better conduct from John Rescorla's son and I thought of you so highly that I never even troubled to caution her. Well, that was my mistake. I took you for a better specimen than you really are.'

He pushed the sail from his knees and stood up. He was taller by a head than Richard and, as he came forward, the younger man needed an effort of will to stop himself backing away. Since the content of their argument was such that he would not want it heard outside, Bob Varcoe refrained from shouting. Instead, his voice emerged with low-pitched, spitting intensity.

'I can picture the way you wheedled and coaxed her till she gave herself to you. But when you'd had your use of her you still weren't content. No doubt you told yourself there might be better elsewhere. Well, you'll find naught different under silks and satins, my lad. The airs and graces that look so fine in the parlour will bring you no comfort or fresh delights in the bedchamber.' He raised a meaty fist and shook it in Richard's face. 'How dare you dishonour my daughter and then decide she's not fit to marry! Who in the name of God do you think you are?'

'I had no need to wheedle Jenny or to coax her. She was freely willing . . .'

He was given no chance to finish. A bellow of fury burst from Varcoe's throat. The fist swung back and then was driven at Richard's face, with the whole weight of the sailmaker's great shoulders concentrated in the blow. Although Richard tried to dodge, Varcoe's hand struck the side of his head with a jarring thud and there came a hot, slicing pain. Richard staggered, lost his balance and landed on the floor in such a way that his right arm was bent under him. A terrible smarting of his scalp made him gasp and screw his eyes tight. As he rolled over to his left side to try and stand up, he saw four splashes of blood fall in rapid succession onto the floorboards.

Varcoe, still seething but once more in control of himself, stared first at Richard's gashed head, then down at his own fist. He was still wearing the palm, the leather strap that served to protect his hand as he forced needle and spike through canvas. The edge of the strap had opened Richard's scalp right down to the bone. The flesh was split along a diagonal of fully three inches and his hair was already sticky with blood.

The sailmaker stood back and allowed him to struggle to his feet.

'I forgot I was wearing the palm,' he said gruffly, but offered no other sign of regret.

Richard pulled off his neckerchief, wadded it and pressed it to the wound, returning Varcoe's angry stare.

'I never once tried to cajole Jenny against her will,' he repeated doggedly. 'And I don't believe she'd claim that I did. 'Tis you saying that, not her.'

Although his face did not betray it, the sailmaker felt a small tremor of guilt, for Jenny had never accused Richard of seduction. Bob recalled quite clearly the words she had used, between gasping sobs, to deplore her own eagerness.

'Get out,' he muttered, turning away. 'And don't ever set foot in my house again.' He sat down heavily on his bench and glowered at Richard. 'You're lucky to leave here with no more than a pat round the head. 'Tis only regard for your father that stops me from beating you senseless. I bear no ill-will towards John, nor do I hold him accountable, but I won't forget what's happened and I can't bring myself to carry on working with your people. This sail's the mizzen for the crabber you've just built. I took on the order, so I'll finish the job, but this'll be the last set I make for you. When they're done I'll deliver them and that'll be the end of it.' He jerked his head towards the door. 'Now get out of my sight. Your coming here has mended nothing and 'twould take very little to stir my temper again.'

Richard silently made for the door and a moment later he was gone, out into the streets where people turned curiously, whispering as he passed, for the blood had soaked right through the compress and was trickling down to the collar of his shirt.

He had, until now, harboured a certain short-sighted faith that all the hurts and differences would eventually heal and be forgotten. Time, he had thought, would put everything to rights. Now it dawned on him at last that the wounds were permanent, the damage irreparable.

8

Three days later, Varcoe paid his final visit to John Rescorla's yard, bringing with him the sails for the crab boat. He pulled up the horse and cart at the bottom of the lane and trudged across to the building sheds to find the shipwright. It was raining hard and Bob was wearing no waterproofs. His hair, his beard and his clothing were all saturated and his face was darker than the weather.

He went into the main workshop. There were two large boats in frame, and sounds of hammering came from the bay at the far end.

'John?' he barked.

The hammering abruptly ceased. Glancing about him, Varcoe saw Rufus Adams watching him silently from between the ribs of the new pilchard driver. Another man, blocking axe in hand, was eyeing him with uneasy curiosity. In the corner where the lathe bench was situated, Richard had stopped work and was obviously debating whether to step forward and speak. A bandage and a pad of lint covered the seven stitches the doctor had put in his scalp.

Varcoe ignored him. Seeing John Rescorla emerge from the bay at the back of the shed, he called out: 'I've brought the sails for the crabber. I'll want a man to unload them.'

'I'll come and do it myself.'

They went outside together into the rain. As he unfastened the tailboard of the cart, Varcoe said: 'There'll be no more after this. I told your son that. I take it he passed it on to you?'

68

'He did, but there's . . .'

The sailmaker cut him short. 'You needn't give my name to any owner from now on, and I shan't accept any order for sails for a vessel from your yard. I won't be coming here again.'

'Don't be such a fool, man, you'll lose money.'

'Better money than self-respect.' Varcoe hauled a bundle of folded canvas from the cart and dropped it with a wet thump on the ground.

'Bob, 'tis a bitter disappointment for me as much as you. Don't make it worse. Don't make a feud out of it.'

'Feud? I'm making no feud, John. That's the wrong word. I'm starting no war with you. I'm turning my back, that's all. I'll lose some orders, 'tis true, but not so many as you might think. See, I've turned down other work in the past because I was busy with yours. Well, I needn't do that any more, so don't concern yourself. I can get my trade elsewhere, just as Jenny can get a husband elsewhere.'

'Do I need to tell you how badly I feel about my son's conduct?'

'No, but it changes nothing.'

In this mood, he would listen to no one. The shipwright resignedly shook his head and then gestured up the lane.

'At least come up to the house and borrow some dry clothing and oilskins for the journey back.'

'Thank you, but I want no favours.' Varcoe went round to the front of the cart and climbed up on the box.

'There's no sense in this,' protested John, as he watched his old friend turn the vehicle round and start back up the lane. 'You're a hot-headed man, Bob, and . . .'

'And loyal to my own flesh and blood,' came the curt retort. 'Goodbye, John.'

*　*　*

Rescorla's mood was black when he went home that evening, and as if to try his patience further, he found a letter waiting for him. It was an invitation from Mrs Tregear.

Dear Mr Rescorla,

I write to tell you how pleased we are to learn of the affection between our daughter and your very fine son. Naturally, we are eager to meet Richard's family, just as you are no doubt anxious to meet Susanna and to know a little more about us.

We would therefore be delighted if you and your daughters would come to dinner at our home this Saturday evening at 8 o'clock.

Please inform whether time is convenient.
    Kindest regards,
        Yours,
            Edith Tregear

He read it, scoffed, screwed it up and stuffed it in his trouser pocket. After supper, he sat down to compose his reply. It was typically blunt.

Madam,

In answer to your note, I write to refuse your invitation, since I see no cause to celebrate. For the foolish reason that he's lovestruck over your daughter, my son has cast aside the girl he should rightfully marry. He's too stubborn to be talked out of it, and since it's plain to me that he puts his own desires above the feelings of everybody else, I'm resolved to let him go ahead and take the consequences. Richard and your daughter have injured a good many people, so I'm minded to let them live with their mistake. It's clear your Susanna has no qualms about taking someone else's young man. They're a callous pair and deserve each other, so I shan't stand in their way.

I see no good purpose in making your acquaintance, for we've nothing in common and we won't be socializing. I'm a working man; I don't go visiting and I'm either too tired or too busy to want people calling on me. As for your daughter, I daresay I'll see her soon enough. Richard can bring her here when he pleases, but we won't make an occasion of it.

Yours,
John Rescorla

Next morning, he sent Rufus into Porthgullow to deliver the letter by hand.

Mrs Tregear read it, muttered a few affronted words and promptly burned it, reflecting that the man should think himself honoured that his son was to marry 'upwards'. Even without money, Susanna was surely a cut above the Varcoe girl. The Tregears, after all, were 'drapers to the gentry', and it said so on their stationery, too. They had clothed any number of titled ladies, provided linen for their beds and their tables, curtains for their windows and coverings for their furniture. John Rescorla ought to be impressed.

But, of course, the locals were clannish and Richard had gone against his father's expectations, so perhaps a certain resentment was natural at first. At least John was not going to intervene, and she fondly imagined that his doubts would disappear as soon as he set eyes on Susanna and realized that his son had exchanged a mere daisy for a splendid orchid.

That evening, she said to her husband: 'Mr Rescorla sent his regrets that he cannot come to dinner with us. He's evidently overwhelmed with work and hasn't a moment to himself. I told you they were doing well, didn't I? But he said that Susanna may call at Boskenna whenever she pleases. Isn't that nice?' Brightly, she added: 'I think the engagement should be made official before the month is out. That will give us all the time we need to plan an October wedding.'

'And to scrape up the money for it,' grunted James Tregear.

This whole affair was more to Edith's liking than his own, but once again she had coaxed him into compliance. Hounded, now, by the bank and other creditors, he was disposed to take the line of least resistance, especially since his wife had quietly pointed out to him that Susanna, with her temper, would not be an asset in the shop. He had his misgivings, nevertheless. He grumbled a lot about the expense of a wedding, but in truth it was hard to say which troubled him more – the demand on his pocket or the murmurings of his conscience.

No amount of disapproval from those around him could dampen Richard's passion for Susanna. In fact, all the adversity served only to strengthen it and he saw his trials as hurdles on the road to bliss. To argue with him was simply to arouse that stubbornness inherited from his father. The more sharply Susanna was criticized, the louder he defended her. He assured everyone that she was deeply hurt by the suggestion that she had deliberately stolen him from Jenny. It was all the work of fate, he said. Susanna, he insisted, was a very sensitive girl.

Once engaged, she began paying twice weekly visits to Boskenna, where only the good-natured Judith attempted to make her feel welcome. John Rescorla, having assessed Miss Tregear as a 'mincing little madam', avoided her as much as possible and was distant with her on occasions when he could not escape her company.

Susanna had found Boskenna to be very much like the home of her Aunt Hilda – modest, but clean and comfortable. It was not to be compared with Morven Terrace, but she could no longer hope to remain there, whether she married or not. The days of grandeur were over. All she could do now was salvage as much dignity as possible. At least if she married she would not be called an old maid or obliged to take up some disagreeable occupation. Here at Boskenna she could spend her days in the parlour and take her meals in the dining room if she so wished. Except on Sundays, she would see very little of John, since he worked long hours and preferred to eat in the kitchen. There was only one unpleasant little person to be tolerated all day long, and that was Esme.

The child had always been fond of Jenny Varcoe and was fiercely hostile to the one who had taken her place, rudely outspoken despite all reproof from Judith and the odd cuff from her brother.

When, on the April afternoon of Judith's fifteenth birthday, Susanna called at Boskenna, she found Esme swinging back and forth on the front gate. The child stopped, holding it half open, and watched as Miss Tregear climbed down from her hired carriage and told the driver to wait. It was a day of light showers and Esme's lip curled with derision to see Susanna daintily picking her way between the puddles.

'Good afternoon, Esme. I've brought a birthday gift for your sister.'

Esme did not return the greeting. The brown eyes flicked contemptuously over Susanna's cream merino frock and took note of the package she carried.

'It's a silk shawl,' confided Susanna. 'I noticed that Judith hadn't any pretty shawls and every young lady should own at least one.'

'I expect you've got dozens,' observed Esme scornfully. 'You're always done up like a dog's dinner. All those bows and that big bonnet. Hannah says you're vain. She says . . .'

Susanna's indulgent smile vanished, to be replaced by a tight little frown.

'Hannah's opinions are of no interest to me. She is a servant and you're just an offensive, grubby little girl. I've tried to be nice to you, Esme, but if you carry on like this I won't ask you to be my bridesmaid.'

'I wouldn't be your bridesmaid for a thousand pounds!' declared Esme, quoting the largest sum she could imagine. Leaning forward, she hissed: 'I can't stand sight nor sound of you. You've got a voice like an east wind coming down a chimney. I hope you'll trip up in church and fall flat on your face. I don't want you to marry Richard and live at Boskenna. You don't belong here with us.'

'What you want is of no consequence,' said Susanna coldly. 'You're just a horrid child with too much to say for yourself.'

With that, she flounced through the gate. But as she passed, Esme quickly pushed it shut, trapping the hem of Susanna's skirt. The click of the latch was accompanied by a tearing sound, as a row of ruffles was ripped away.

Pulled up with a jolt, Susanna turned and gasped.

'You little brute! Wait till your brother hears about this!'

As if in disdain of any vengeance Richard might take, Esme promptly dropped from her perch on the second bar of the gate, landing with both feet in the puddle underneath it. A spurt of muddy water flew up and spattered Susanna's frock.

'I don't care what Richard says,' taunted the child, as she scooted off along the path and round the side of the house. 'Father won't let him spank me on account of you, so there.'

Shaking her dress, Susanna bustled up to the front door and rapped irritably at the knocker. Judith answered and was startled to find Miss Tregear on the step, fuming over the wet and tattered skirt.

'Look what your sister did to my frock! She hates me, you know. I've tried very hard to make friends with Esme, but she seems determined to upset me in every way she can!'

'Come in, Susanna, please. I expect we can mend it and sponge off the dirt. I'm so sorry – but it must have been an accident.'

'Believe me, Judith, it was quite deliberate. Esme's not like you, my dear. She's inclined to be spiteful.'

'Mischievous, perhaps,' corrected Judith, 'but not spiteful.'

Susanna was tempted to argue, but decided against it, for kindred were bound to stick together. She followed Judith into the parlour.

'I'm afraid I can't stay. I'll attend to the skirt myself when I go home. I've only called to bring you this.' She held out the parcel, which was wrapped in pink paper. 'Many happy returns of the day.'

Judith hardly knew what to say when she saw the shawl. It was white and lacy with a gold fringe – the prettiest item she had ever owned, and yet she knew she would not feel comfortable in anything so frivolous.

"Tis lovely, Susanna. Thank you very much.'

'I'm glad you like it.' The young woman delivered a peck to Judith's cheek. 'Fifteen years old! My, my! You'll be putting your hair up soon, won't you?'

'I wouldn't know how,' admitted Judith.

'Then I shall teach you. These things are so important, aren't they?'

Judith regarded her with a look of doubt and slight unease.

'We're not much concerned with fashion and social matters out here,' she said. 'Don't you think you'll be lonely? Richard says you're used to receiving friends at home and paying visits in return. People never call here unless they have business at the cove and – well, to be blunt, Father values his privacy.'

'Oh, of course, of course. Richard and I have discussed all that. Your brother is all that I need, Judith, and I'm sure I'll soon feel completely at home.'

I hope you mean that, thought Judith, as she saw Susanna out, for 'tis you who'll have to fit in with us, not the other way round.

10

Richard's wedding took place on October 20th, 1858. There were fewer guests than he might have hoped, for many of those who would gladly have come to see him marry Jenny Varcoe now made excuses or simply ignored the invitation. Most of the local people did not know Susanna, and those who had met her were apt to find her aloof or condescending.

The fishermen and their wives had always looked upon Jenny as one of their own. She was part of that cottage community and the life around the harbour where all were closely concerned with one another. The men, with faces furrowed by wind and salt spray, hands toughened by rope and tarred mesh, were sternly Methodist. Their perilous lives made them intolerant of those who were frivolous or unreliable. The womenfolk, as hardy as their sons and husbands, would vent their feelings in words loud and sharp when provoked. Much had been said about Richard Rescorla and his 'little madam' from Morven Terrace, and not many felt inclined to celebrate the wedding.

Susanna was not a bit concerned that so few of the Rescorlas' friends had turned up. A herd of her own relations and acquaintances made the event quite grand enough. They formed a considerable audience, before whom she could sweep triumphant to the altar in drifts of satin and Maltese lace.

A morose, disapproving presence in the second pew Rufus Adams attended the service out of loyalty to the family. Lined up beside him stood Rescorla's other employees, all just as glum. When the wedding march began, Rufus turned his head to watch the bride billowing up the aisle, and he sucked at his teeth, eyeing her with deep dislike.

Followed by four toddlers in blue muslin frocks and daisy headdresses, Susanna floated past him and stood demurely beside Richard. The congregation finished coughing and shuffling, while the parson leafed through his service book to find the right page. Richard smiled happily down at his bride. With her pale-gold curls, her ferns and flowers and dainty satin slippers, she looked enchanting.

He went through the ceremony like a sleepwalker, dazedly giving the responses. Susanna's replies, on the other hand, were prompt and precise, for she was overwhelmed neither by Richard nor the occasion. The experience was not a giddy one for her, merely the confirmation of success.

John Rescorla watched the proceedings with heavy resignation. Esme, who was always bored in church, slipped a mint humbug into her mouth and sucked it noisily while Susanna was making her vows. Judith made her spit it out into a handkerchief.

Half an hour later, Richard and Susanna stood in the autumn sunshine, a married couple, flushed and laughing amid a blizzard of rice and exultant pealing of bells. Surrounded by congratulations and wishes of good luck, neither of them spared a thought for Jenny Varcoe.

John remembered her, however, and guessed how she must be feeling. His gaze moved down across the rooftops of Porthgullow, away from all these people for whom he had so little liking and from whom he meant to escape without delay, now that the wretched business was over and done with.

He wished, in particular, to avoid James and Edith

Tregear, and when they encountered him after the service they found him abrupt as ever.

'A happy day for all of us, sir,' smiled Edith. 'I trust we may be good friends from now on? There's a fine wedding feast waiting at home for our guests and our new relations. Will you ride in our carriage with us?'

'No, I will not. I've no appetite for your food and drink, and none for your friendship, either. My daughters and I are going home now. Good day to you.'

With that, he pushed past them and went to find Esme and Judith.

Mrs Tregear was indignant. 'Dear heaven, what a boorish man he is! That was quite uncalled for.'

But her husband said, quietly: 'Was it? We've upset their lives, Edith. We've made cold, calculating use of his son and I'm not proud of it. Don't splutter about the man's rough tongue. He's honest, and that's more than we can say.'

'Jenny?' Bob Varcoe put his head round the door of his daughter's room and saw her sitting at the foot of the bed. She was staring through the window towards the church tower up on the hill. The insistent, mocking sound of bells came clearly across the mile between and her face was wet with tears.

'Jenny, are you all right?'

She nodded, wiping a hand hastily over her cheeks. Varcoe sat down beside her. Taking the briar pipe from his mouth, he slipped a brawny arm about her shoulders.

'Well, 'tis done,' he said. 'He's burnt his boats now, my love, boats of a kind he can't rebuild. Perhaps 'tis just as well, Jenny. If that's the way he is, 'tis better to have found it out sooner than later. When a man is callous and treacherous and sly, he can make no woman happy. There are other lads, maid, plenty of them.'

79

'None that I want.'

'Give it time, girl. You'll change your mind.'

She shook her head. 'I don't believe I'll ever trust anyone again. I'd known Richard all my life, and still I misjudged him.'

'You'll want children, Jenny. You'll need someone to look after you when I'm gone. Don't you let him spoil your life. Don't you grieve and shut yourself away. You were meant for husband and family.'

'I must settle for second best, then,' she muttered bitterly.

Bob frowned. 'Daughter, I've seen many a lad look at you with admiration. 'Tis unkind to speak of them as if they were stale bread or last week's milk. I know disappointment comes hard when you're young. You want your first choice in everything, that and nothing less. But don't turn your back on the other young men, there's many a good husband to be found in Porthgullow.'

Jenny was not listening. Her gaze had wandered to the trinket box on her bedside table and it lingered there as she recalled the day Richard had given her the gold and silver charm.

'I still have the little necklet he bought me,' she murmured. 'He said 'twas meant to remind me of our two lives, because the strands could not be separated. No matter how the pattern looped and turned, they'd still be bound to each other, even when they weren't touching, and would always mesh together in the end.'

Her father gave a small snort of irritation. 'You've no call to be sentimental about anything that came from Richard. 'Tis best to be rid of all reminders, Jenny. You must put that young fool right out of your mind.'

'I don't want to!' Her face crumpled as her voice rose and cracked. 'I want everything just as it was. Perhaps he'll grow to loathe her, perhaps he'll abandon her and come back to me.' She began to cry again and her body shuddered with sobs.

'Marriage is for life, my dear.' Varcoe took both her hands in one of his great fists and kissed the puckered forehead. 'And I won't have him sneaking round here thinking he can take up with you again behind his wife's back. I'd choke the life out of him before I'd allow that.'

'Perhaps she'll die,' wept the girl. 'I hope she does!'

'The misfits of this world are seldom so obliging,' sighed Bob. 'There now, maid, hush. You'll have a sore throat if you don't stop.'

'I hope she gets the smallpox!' raged Jenny. 'I wonder if he'd love her so well if she lost her prissy, whey-faced beauty. May she grow old and ugly long before her time! May he find her so repulsive that he can't bear to touch her!'

'I daresay she'll turn into a hideous hag in no time at all,' soothed Bob, stroking his daughter's hair.

'May they not see a day without strife,' hissed the girl, 'and may all her children hate her!'

'Now, Jenny, now, that's enough.'

'He made me a promise when he gave me that charm. His solemn promise, he said. But there was no parson to hear it and no congregation, so it counts for nothing. The Lord heard it, but He hasn't held him to it!'

'Enough, Jenny! You mustn't talk so.'

'How else should I feel? She's robbed me of the life I wanted. That's no small thing, is it?'

Bob offered a handkerchief and she blotted her eyes with it, then blew her nose.

''Tis less important than you think, my dear. There's no such person as the "one-and-only".'

'I wish I could believe that,' she said hoarsely.

'You will, and sooner than you think.'

The girl did not answer. After a moment she rose and

81

picked up a woollen shawl which hung on the back of a chair. Bob watched her sadly, noting that she had lost a great deal of weight over recent months.

'Where are you going?' he asked.

'Just for a walk – away from the sound of those bells. I shan't be more than an hour or two.'

'All right, maid. Best splash your face with water before you go. Don't let people see you've been crying. They say dignity's a cold comfort, but 'tis worth keeping, just the same.'

She walked out along the east headland towards the lighthouse, a distance of just over two miles. The day was bright and cold, with a lively breeze that carried the smell of the sea in over the heath. The footpath cut a narrow line through withered grass and bracken towards the outermost point, where the headland dwindled slowly down to a rocky shelf. Beyond it lay the little reef and Jenny sat for a while to watch the waves breaking against the base of the lighthouse. It occupied its platform of rock with barely a yard to spare on any side. Autumn sunlight winked on the slatted glass reflectors in the tower. Of the man who lived inside there was no sign.

Jenny's eyelids felt stretched and sore, and there was roughness in her throat. The ocean swell rumbled and surged round the rocks where she sat. They were dark as charcoal, but streaked with lines of lighter grey. Ten yards to her right, they were riven by a deep cleft, and here the sea boiled in with a booming and moaning, throwing up frosted showers as it reached the end of the gulley. The rift was six feet across and the water within it was milky-green with the foam of constant churning. At the brink the rocks were wet and slippery, their markings standing out glossy and clear where the water washed over them.

After a while she stood up and went towards the edge. The wind was in her face and needles of freezing spray flew up from the gulley to sting her cheeks. In her mind she could still hear church bells. They mingled now with the crash of water, and the pearly froth that clung to the sides of the channel was like delicate bridal lace.

'She's robbed me of the life I wanted. That's no small thing . . .'

''Tis less important than you think, my dear. There's no such person as the "one-and-only".'

Was it true? Jenny stood there for a long time, thinking it over. She had pined constantly for Richard these past months. She had fretted and fumed and suffered, thinking of nothing and no one else, contemplating this day, his wedding day, with dread. To the very last she had cherished a flicker of hope that he might repent and return to her.

Again there came an echo of Bob's words. 'Well, 'tis done. He's burnt his boats . . .'

Yes, it was over. That tormenting little hope was gone. But instead of despair, a strange feeling of relief was taking its place. It had been so painful to watch the worst approaching that she could almost be glad it had finally happened. Jenny had no fear that Richard's married life would be any cause for envy. The illusions would soon collapse now, and the long, long penalty would begin.

Father was right, she thought coldly. There were other young men to give her the children she wanted. And if they were poorer, less widely admired than Richard, perhaps they would value her the more. There was much to be said for a plain, contented man. Richard was not the only one she had known since childhood. What about Jack Behenna, who had given her his best marble when they were eight years old? Or Alan Norris, who would always bait her fishing hook for her? There was Luke Symons, who winked whenever he saw her, and Davey

83

Harte from the Male Voice Choir . . . Because of Richard, she had never given them a chance.

Suddenly aware that she was chilled to the bone, Jenny wrapped her shawl more tightly about her shoulders and retreated to a safe, dry footing.

To the devil with Richard, she thought. So he found her too ordinary. So he wanted the mystery and fancy manners of a woman like Susanna. Well, let him suffer for his stupid notions. It was just as well that he had gone ahead with his marriage. Self-respect was a very important thing, and Jenny could not have laid claim to much of that, had she been weak and humble enough to take him back. Richard, she promised herself, would be wanting her friendship before too long, and she would not give it, not ever. She would not spare him a word, a smile or any sign of forgiveness until her dying day.

11

'Mama has told me what to expect,' announced Susanna primly. 'I know my duty and will not shirk it. I only ask that you exercise as much restraint and consideration as your nature will permit.'

In their bedroom at Boskenna, Richard had just lit the oil lamp and a steady coronet of flame had sprung up. Susanna's words made him pause in surprise before slowly replacing the glass shade. He turned a wavering look on his wife and repeated uncertainly: 'My nature?'

'Your – baser needs.'

She was standing at the foot of the big brass bed, wearing an expression of fortitude and shame combined. Her eyes were downcast but her chin was lifted in a manner which clearly said that the spirit would remain detached and undemeaned, whatever the body had to bear.

'I understand and I'm prepared to submit, though I beg that you extinguish the light and keep silent whilst . . . That is to say, I don't wish to hear any – exclamations.' Seeing the puzzlement on his face, she wrestled for a moment with her sense of delicacy and then tried to clarify by adding: 'Sounds of relish, comments upon my person, things of that kind.'

A whirling gust of mirth rose up within him and he almost laughed out loud, but amusement quickly died away as he realized that Susanna's disgust was quite genuine, no matter how comically she expressed it. Although he had expected shyness, even fear, from his genteel wife, this cold consent to endure him was an unpleasant surprise. Susanna had never allowed him anything more than a chaste kiss, it was true, but that was merely the behaviour proper to such a lady during courtship. Once married, he had meant to guide and reassure her, introducing her to unknown joys. He had not bargained for an attitude of sufferance.

'I think your mama's been exaggerating. You know I'll treat you with care and respect. This part of marriage isn't supposed to spoil your happiness, Susanna, 'tis meant to complete it.'

'That is an attitude fit only for women of the commonest type and I can't believe that an act so coarse and so totally devoid of dignity could bring me anything but distress,' she said gravely. 'Naturally, I wish to bear you children, but you mustn't expect me to enjoy the necessary union. A lady never does.'

Richard emphatically shook his head. 'You're wrong, Susanna, I promise you. Whatever foolish tales you've heard . . .'

'I know precisely what is required of me, Richard. Please don't patronize me by trying to present an ugly bodily function as a pleasant experience. I'm a grown woman, well able to face reality.'

Doubting that any spoken argument would convince her, Richard made a move to encircle the tiny waist with comforting arms. By the glow of the lamp, she twinkled white and gold in her wedding dress and many a time he had pictured this moment as one of impending bliss. But she slid quickly from his grasp and went behind the dressing screen.

'I need no help to undress. Will you please put out the light.'

Her marital chore completed, Susanna slept quite well that night. Richard, however, lay awake all through the small hours and he watched the dawn break with mournful eyes.

She had lain there impassive, quite uninvolved, not answering his whispers of love and encouragement, unwilling to hold or touch him, completely refusing to acknowledge either his presence or what was happening. No persuasion, no insistence bestirred her. She gave nothing but a cold, detached compliance that wounded and insulted him beyond measure, for he knew he was being tolerated – as if she felt she was paying her dues, honouring a bargain. It was not modesty or fear with which he was confronted, but a complete absence of feeling.

'You mustn't expect me to enjoy the necessary union. A lady never does.'

Richard's thoughts turned to Jenny Varcoe and all those joyous romps he had taken so much for granted. He had found no reluctance and few difficulties there. It had never before crossed his mind that he had been uncommonly fortunate. Until this night, he had thought it reasonable to expect similar of any woman. But he wondered now if he might, perhaps, have been spoilt by Jenny's loving nature. He wondered, too, if those who married refinement always paid such a wintry price.

I'll have to be patient, he told himself at last. 'Tis her upbringing that's made her this way, but I'll overcome it in time. These are early days yet, early days.

But he had indeed been spoilt, for Jenny was a creature of singular warmth and affection. Faced now with a wife more chilly than most, it came to him forcibly that he had traded abundance for famine, and he had no way of telling how long he would have to remain hungry.

In the weeks that followed, Susanna found life at Boskenna to be tolerably comfortable and she did what she could to arrange things to suit herself. Because of her spinal weakness, she was able to perform very few household duties – a handicap for which she was now almost thankful. She did, however, consent to deal with all of the family's mending and sewing. The needlework, everyone admitted, was done extremely well, but apart from this her only pretence at work was to tinker with flower arrangements and do a little light dusting. In the evenings she would play the piano if asked, and even John agreed that this was very pleasant, but most of her accomplishments were of no benefit to anyone.

At first she was lost without her lady's maid, and she missed the convenience of having shops within easy reach. She was also injured to find that few of her old cronies seemed to think her worth the journey to the cove. Those who did come were so clearly uncomfortable at Boskenna that they seldom made a second excursion, and they did not invite her to visit them in return. She had, after all, slipped down the social scale. With Richard at work from dawn till dusk, she therefore lacked any agreeable company except that of Judith, who was little more than a child. Susanna had decided that she quite liked Judith, but the girl was too young to make much conversation and certainly too dowdy to share Susanna's interest in fashion.

For exercise, the new Mrs Rescorla sometimes went for walks along the cliffs, but very rarely did she venture down to the cove – because of the yard and the men who worked there. Once, she had gone inside the building sheds in search of Richard, and the experience had not been a pleasant one. There had been an atmosphere: she had sensed the men's dislike, their resentment of her presence in what was their domain. The yard was male territory; to go in there was to run the gauntlet of hostile or leering eyes, so Susanna stayed away.

Visits to Porthgullow were not frequent. She was unused to handling a pony and trap, and most of the time there was no one free or willing to drive her back and forth. So her days were mainly spent in the parlour – sewing, reading her poetry books and her *Lady's Companion* paper. It was, to her mind, a dull life but a safe one and for the time being she was simply glad to have escaped anything worse.

Flatly refusing to eat in the kitchen, Susanna took her meals in the little dining room, and during those first weeks of marriage Richard had his dinner with her every evening.

He was still being patient, considerate at night, though none of his pleas or his coaxing could elicit any warmth from her. She knew what was proper and what was not, and believed compliance to be quite enough. It was her part of the bargain to bear his carnal assaults, and she had done so without flinching. Not once had she refused him his unseemly relief. What more could a man expect?

With luck, she thought, he would eventually lose interest. Indeed, he already bothered her less often. From two or three onslaughts each night, his demands had decreased to two or three each week – just as Mama had predicted.

'All men become bored with a woman once she's conquered,' Edith had said. 'They're like children, they soon start craving novelty and seeking it elsewhere. No matter, though. Once the bond is sealed with a wedding ring, support and security are guaranteed.'

Richard and Susanna had never talked about this difficulty between them, for no lady could discuss such matters. So when she assumed his desire had cooled, she was not quite correct. Richard had not lost interest, but he was certainly losing heart.

12

Less than two months after the wedding, John Rescorla was obliged to pay a visit to the doctor in Porthgullow on account of a frozen shoulder. As he was leaving the surgery, he encountered a small, wiry-haired woman dressed in tartan skirts, a cape and an old poke bonnet. She was Mrs Esther Gammon, wife of the local solicitor.

'My dear Mr Rescorla, how nice to see you! I've been wanting to tell you how pleased I am that your son has married the little Tregear girl. Isn't it splendid! He's such a handsome young man and she's so very pretty. What beautiful children they'll have! Just think, you'll be a grandfather in no time at all.' Esther clapped her hands delightedly and rolled her eyes in glee. 'Please give them my congratulations.'

'Thank you, Mrs Gammon, I will.' He tried to brush past her, but she laid a detaining hand on his arm.

'Of course, the Tregears have had so much trouble and worry, haven't they? Poor things! It's quite uplifting to see them receive a stroke of good luck at long last. If only the financial problems would vanish in the same magical way – but I gravely fear that nothing can be done. Poor Mr Tregear. Prosperity is so hard to attain, so very easy to lose. A few unwise investments . . .'

'Mrs Gammon . . .'

'. . . a few bad debts . . .'

'Mrs Gammon, what are you talking about?'

The little woman ceased her twittering and stared at him with small round eyes that spotted every tiny nuance of expression.

'Oh!' she squeaked, peering intently into his face. 'But surely you know that the poor dears are in considerable difficulties? Their shop in Penzance has been sold off and they're shortly to lose the one here in Porthgullow as well. The bank will give them no longer, you see. Matters have grown steadily worse these past few years and they've now reached the point of . . . Well, perhaps it's too much to use the word "bankruptcy", but I'm quite sure they'll soon find it impossible to keep that house in Morven Terrace.' She paused, taking shrewd note of John's bewilderment, then pressed a hand daintily to her mouth. 'Oh dear, I believe I've been indiscreet. Forgive me, but I didn't dream you were unaware . . .'

'We've had little to do with Susanna's family,' said John gruffly, 'and we never thought to pry into their affairs. After all, 'tis the future husband who must give a good account of his prospects.'

There was an edge to his voice, a tone of rebuke that Esther could hardly miss. She merely ignored it and continued:

'But what does money matter anyway, when it's so clearly a love match? How wonderful that dear Susanna has finally found the right man after so many disappointments. Her mama was so worried – and she always confides in me, you know – because the child had been let down. And not just once, but twice, my dear sir! So sad. One of her fiancés simply decamped to the continent without a word of explanation, but the other made some very cruel remarks about Susanna's nature. Ill-tempered, he said – difficult and selfish. What slander! I was beginning to fear that Susanna was one of those unfortunate women who are helplessly drawn to men of harsh temperament, but I'm happy to see I was wrong. Richard is a perfect choice – and I don't think age is an issue of any importance, do you? She certainly doesn't look twenty-eight.'

Esther was almost jigging from foot to foot, made frolicsome by John's dismay.

'No,' he agreed stiffly, 'no one would ever guess.'

'Of course, she's had a very gentle upbringing – no hardship, no menial work of any kind. Small wonder she looks so much younger than she is. Susanna has always been accustomed to elegance and ease, but I suppose her poor papa could no longer maintain her in such comfort.' She peeped at John with a kind of sportive malice. 'What a mercy she's married! She might otherwise have been forced to take up some form of employment! An eleventh-hour reprieve – it's just like a novel!' Esther's mouth stretched back over yellowing teeth in a mocking little smile. 'I understand there's been some unpleasantness with the Varcoe girl, but that's only to be expected, isn't it? I think it's very courageous of Richard to face up to so much condemnation without wavering. I suppose he may have lost a few friends over that unfortunate business with Jenny, but just see what he has for compensation!'

With that, she swept off down the hill, leaving John to digest the full extent of the deception worked upon his son – and the knowledge that he himself had made a terrible mistake. Had he only been firm and forbidden the wedding, Susanna would probably have looked elsewhere for someone to support her. Had he only persuaded Richard to wait, her situation and her motive would soon have been revealed. In his anger, John had resolved to let the boy pay for his folly, but this was worse than Richard deserved.

Sick at heart, the shipwright went home to tell his son the truth.

* * *

92

Richard listened in white-faced silence as his father recounted the conversation with Esther Gammon. The last rosy veils of romance, already in tatters, finally fell away. Along with a terrible sense of loss, there came cold rage that Susanna had so thoroughly tricked and cheated him, and that he had made it easy for her.

That evening, Susanna dined alone for the first time, while her husband ate his meal in the kitchen along with his father and sisters. He had offered no explanation for this, but his mood was plainly dark and she could not fail to realize that she was the cause of it.

Nothing was said until they retired to bed at ten o'clock. Apprehensively she watched him undress, hoping his ill-humour meant he would not bother her that night. But a few moments later she knew she was not to be spared, and this time there was no hesitant, respectful approach. He climbed into bed without his nightshirt and rolled straight on top of her, bringing down his weight with a force that robbed her of breath.

'Come along, wife,' came the terse whisper, 'time to pay for your room and board.'

'Richard!'

'Well, that's the idea, isn't it?'

'I don't know what you mean. What on earth has come over you?'

She tried to wriggle away, but he pinned her down.

'Understanding, my sweet, thanks to an old acquaintance of yours.' He studied her intently and then grinned, for he could almost see her mind working, wondering who it was and what they had said. 'Father met Mrs Gammon today,' he explained softly. 'She had a lot to say about you.'

There was a long pause. He had half expected panic and protest, claims of innocence and assurances that

93

Mrs Gammon was full of false tittle-tattle. But Susanna's response, when it came, was flat and calm.

'I see. Well, now you know.'

Her face had grown hard, defiant. The truth could not be concealed for ever, there was no point now in denying it.

'You heartless bitch,' muttered Richard. 'By God, you've played me a sly game.'

'You wanted me and here I am.'

'Yes, but you didn't want me, did you? An easy life, a married name – you wanted them, all right. But not me, not the man who provides them. And I was conceited enough to think you loved me.'

'I'm – quite fond of you, Richard.'

'Are you now?' He raised mocking eyebrows. 'Quite fond, is it? I'm humbly grateful, dearest.'

'Don't be sarcastic.'

'No,' he said, jerking her nightgown up, 'it serves no purpose, I agree, so we won't waste any time on words.'

'Stop it! Leave me alone! I won't have you touch me while you're in such a foul temper!'

'Now, now, Susanna, we've a contract, you and I, and 'tis too late to go back on it. So, let's fulfil it as best we may. I'll give you food in your belly and a roof over your head, and in return you'll give me children. Fair enough? You're no friend and no lover to me, but I suppose you can breed, despite your age. At least, I hope you can, for there's nothing else to make you worth your keep.'

'What a vile thing to say!'

'Why so indignant, my love? Business is business and we have to agree the terms. I'll tell you what,' he added, pulling the nightdress up to her armpits, 'I'll even give you a little money for new clothing every month, because I know how important that is to you. Shall we say, five shillings? That's nearly three guineas a year.'

'Three guineas,' sniffed his wife. 'Papa gave me twenty.'

'Oh, you'll learn how to make the best of the money, Susanna. You're very skilful with your sewing machine, so you've only to buy the materials. Of course, if ever you refuse me, I'll feel entitled to make a deduction. On the other hand,' he went on, his voice silky, 'I'll give a little extra for every child you bear. How does that sound, eh? Are you ready to earn your finery?'

She glared up at him, checking the impulse to make a venomous reply. Caution told her to hold her tongue, for the man looking down at her was not the gentle, adoring Richard she had married. Because he was so much younger and so besotted with her, she had thought she could manage him, even when he found out the truth. Now, surveying his angry face, she realized he would not be so easy to handle after all.

As Richard brusquely took his rights, Susanna began to wonder if life with Aunt Hilda might have been better than life with a husband who was now promising to use her as a brood mare. She knew her mama and papa were about to sell their house and would soon be moving to Truro, and while Richard jolted and pounded out his fury, she even entertained the idea that she might pack her bags and go with them.

But when at last he subsided into exhausted sleep, she thought better of it. A few unpleasant minutes in bed were still preferable to whole days behind a shop counter.

13

On a Saturday morning in May of 1859, John made a trip into Porthgullow to see the shipsmith. He took his daughters with him, for Hannah wanted Judith to fetch some supplies and Esme would not be left behind. He pulled up the pony and trap in Covenant Street to let the girls out.

'You'll have to keep an eye on her,' he said to Judith, as the little girl jumped down. 'I know what a trial she is.'

'Don't worry, I'll see that she stays with me.'

John cast a warning glance at Esme. 'Don't you make a nuisance of yourself now, will you?'

She shook her head, grinning.

Placed squarely on top of Esme's head, and anchored under her chin with black ribbons, was a wide-brimmed straw hat. Beneath a gingham pinafore, her brown cotton dress was buttoned to the neck and the skirt reached halfway down her calves. From under this peeped the frilled bottoms of her drawers, leaving only an inch or two of white stocking visible above the black button-boots.

'Hmm, you'd better not.' John turned to Judith, who stood with a basket over her arm and Hannah's shopping list in her hand. 'Will two shillings be enough?'

'Oh, more than enough.'

He fished in his pocket and drew out a handful of change. 'There's an extra twopence for Esme to spend and . . .' He pressed another coin into Judith's hand. '. . . a shilling for you. Buy yourself something pretty.'

'Why, thank you, but . . .'

'Some little treat,' insisted John, stroking his daughter's hair. 'You're a good girl, Judith, and you never ask for anything. Be sure to spend this on yourself.'

With that, he drove on. Judith dropped the money into the pocket of her apron.

'Hannah says they're having a temperance play on the west quay at twelve o'clock,' she told her sister. ''Tis all about drinking and falling into debt, and how a man's family may suffer and starve on account of his vices. They've been rehearsing it these past three weeks in the church hall. We'll be able to see it. Isn't that lucky?'

Esme nodded dolefully. She had been to temperance plays before.

'Come on, then,' Judith said. 'We've time to buy a thing or two before it starts, and we'll finish the shopping after.'

Together they set off towards the greengrocer's shop.

By a quarter to twelve an audience had assembled for the performance. Some of the spectators carried silk banners, each embroidered with a teetotal motto. Judith and her sister, arriving just as the play began, found themselves at the back of the crowd and it was impossible to push through. Esme could see nothing but the tops of the players' heads, so Judith lifted her up onto the harbour wall for a better view.

The older girl was soon engrossed in the story, despite the loud heckling from some of the onlookers and the shouts of derision that rang out when the audience were invited to purchase tea and coffee whilst watching the play. Esme did not fully understand the plot, but perceived a censorious attitude and a tone of reprimand familiar from Sunday service, and she soon lost interest in the proceedings. When the story was only halfway through, she slid unnoticed from her perch and skipped off down the jetty.

At the far end, behind a stack of crab pots, she found five boys playing marbles. With cries of triumph or disappointment, they sat watching them bounce, bobble and click upon the worn stones. A jumble of bare feet, frayed trousers and untucked shirts, they bent their heads intently over their game. One of them, however, suddenly looked up and said:

'Who's that ole girl there?'

The others followed his gaze and met the solemn, slightly scornful regard of a freckled face under a flat straw hat.

'What're ee lookin' at, girl?'

'You,' said Esme, stout and unsmiling.

'Well, go 'way,' ordered the boy. 'We dawn't want no ole girls here.' He was the largest of them, and the darkest. He spoke in a rough dialect completely undiluted by education and his manner was vehement.

'I can look if I want.' She stuck out her chin and leaned with arms folded decisively atop one of the crab pots.

The boy sniffed, took disparaging note of her starched pinafore and clean frock, then retorted: 'Well, you needn' think we're goin' let ee play, 'cause we aren't.'

'I never said I wanted to play. Can't see much sense in it.'

'Thass 'cause you're a stupid ole girl.'

Esme's response was to reach down, grasp a tuft of his hair and pull hard. The other lads sniggered, but the big one rose angrily to his feet. It was only the intervention of a wavy-haired boy with an upturned nose that saved Esme from a cuff and a slap.

'Leave her be, she's only a li'l ole bit.'

His accent, too, was broad, but the tone of speech was more relaxed, almost lazy.

'You seen what she done. I aren't standin' fer that.'

'P'raps you asked fer it.'

'Why're ee stickin' up fer the cheeky li'l article?'

'Cause I d'like cheek, I spose.'

Hands on hips, the dark one glared a challenge at him. 'I dawn't want ee in me game, then.'

The smaller boy shrugged, stood up and glanced at the other with huge disdain. 'I was bored anyway,' he said lightly, and sauntered off.

Esme gave her antagonist a gratified smirk, then poked out her tongue at him in a most pugnacious fashion. Enraged, he made a grab for her, but she dodged him and bolted away down the jetty in the wake of her champion.

The lad had walked halfway along the quay. The tide was out and he descended a flight of stone steps to the beach, then set off across the sand with his hands in his pockets and his shoulders hunched. Esme went running after him.

'What's your name?' she asked, falling in step beside him.

'Tom Tregunna.' His answer was slightly curt and he did not seem entirely pleased to have Esme tagging along with him.

'I thought you were going to fight with that boy.'

He stopped and frowned at her. He looked to be no more than twelve years old and his hair was light brown, his eyes hazel. A few minutes' attention with soap, flannel and a comb would have rendered him a very attractive child. His clothing, however, was past redemption, the trousers shiny at the knees and seat, the shirt repeatedly patched.

'He's me friend. I wouldn' fight a friend awver no ole girl.'

He walked on, threading his way between the fishing boats left high and dry by the outgoing tide. Chastened, Esme followed him.

'Won't he like you any more?'

'Aw . . .' Tom shrugged. '. . . he'll come round. He'll forget it soon enough.'

'I'm called Esme.' She gestured proudly round her at the beached vessels with their black and white hulls, the tan-coloured sails rolled and tied. 'My father builds boats like these. Is yours a fisherman or something?'

'No, he's a tin miner – a tutworker. Knaw what that is?'

'Of course I do,' bluffed Esme.

The boy grinned. 'Liar. Wass your other name?'

'Rescorla.'

'Aw, ess, I've heared tell o' Rescorla the shipwright. So he's your faather, is uh?' Tom stopped and sat down, resting his back against the side of a boat. Esme dropped down beside him in the shadow of the hull. 'Do uh make a lot o' money, then? I 'spect he do.'

'We're not rich, if that's what you're thinking.'

'Better off'n my people, I'll be bound. Ever go hungry?'

'No,' admitted the girl.

'Do your roof leak?'

'No.'

'Do ee sleep in a proper bed?'

'Yes, but . . .'

'Then you aren't poor.'

'We don't have everything we want,' offered Esme lamely.

'Hmph, I dawn't get anythin' I want,' emphasized the boy. 'I spose you d'have a nice easy time of it 'n think you're somethin' important. Spose thass why you d'like to go round aggravatin' people.'

'I was only watching – and I'm not afraid of anybody.' She straightened her hat and lifted her head in defiance.

'No, I dawn't b'lieve you are.' He considered her for a moment. 'You'd be all right if you wadden an ole girl.'

Esme extracted the compliment from that and discarded the rest as irrelevant. They sat for a while in silence, Tom aimlessly scouring a pit in the damp sand with his heels, while Esme wrote her name on its surface. Suddenly, on impulse, she ventured an invitation.

'You can come to tea with us one day, if you like.'

Astonished, he stared at her, then quickly looked away. 'I'll think about it.'

'What for? Why don't you just say yes?'

'Well, I might.' He was both flattered and frightened by the idea of visiting this strange little girl and her supposedly rich relatives in their home, which he imagined to be something very grand.

'When?'

'Dunnaw. I'm busy, see. I d'go work most days.'

'Work?' Esme's eyes widened.

'In the buddle pit, up Wheal Merit. I dawn't go Saturdays nor Sundays, though.'

'What about school?'

'What about it? There's only the dame's school 'n Faather d'say she wen't teach a man nothin' worth learnin'. 'Tis twopence a week, too. I spose you d'go there every day?'

'Oh no, never,' Esme assured him. ''Twas Mother and Father taught us all to read and write. I go to the Sunday school, though – and I've seen you there once or twice.'

'Thass differnt. They d'give us free tay 'n heavy cake when 'tis awver.'

Esme pounced on that. 'You'll have a much better tea at our house. Will you come?'

Uncertain and therefore evasive, the boy muttered that he would still have to think about it. He was thankful when Esme, about to insist on an answer, was distracted by a familiar voice.

'Esme! Why did you run off like that?'

The child's face clouded with guilt and dismay as she

101

saw poor harassed, forgotten Judith hurrying towards her, filled with outrage and relief.

'How could you worry me so? I've been searching everywhere. You know you're not supposed to go about on your own. You always get into trouble.'

Esme looked sheepish and the boy started to laugh.

'This is Tom,' she said, glad of a diversion. 'He's my friend.'

Judith gave him a civil nod. 'How do you do, Tom? I thank you for taking care of my sister, but she has to go now.' She seized Esme by the hand and pulled her to her feet. 'Come on, hurry up, I still have groceries to buy for Hannah, and I've wasted nearly an hour looking for you.'

'I'll see you tomorrow,' promised Esme, as her sister hustled her away.

The lad wrinkled his nose. 'You might,' he said, 'if I aren't doin' nothin' else.'

'I don't want to go shopping,' declared Esme testily, trying to keep up with Judith's brisk steps. 'I wanted to stay with Tom.'

'Really? Well, that's a turnabout, I must say. What about your twopence from Father? Don't you want to spend it?'

Esme had forgotten that. A little more willing now, she trotted along to see what she could buy. Late with her round of errands, Judith had no time to think about spending her own shilling that day.

'She's nothing but trouble,' observed John, as he took them home in the trap. 'Always has been and always will be. What was she doing all that time?'

Judith explained about Esme's new acquaintance.

'I know of the man Tregunna,' John said. 'He's too fond of the beershop. They're a rough family, and that's putting it mildly.'

'Tom seemed quite a decent little boy,' ventured Judith.

'That's as may be, but his two elder brothers are drunkards already and I'm willing to wager he'll go the same way. Tregunna's brood are all known for thieving and they take a pride in their ignorance, as if learning were no fit exercise for men. In a few years' time that lad will be a foul-mouthed ruffian like the rest of them.' He paused to turn the pony and trap off the road and down the lane to Boskenna. 'I shan't forbid you to play with the child now and then,' he told Esme, 'but I won't have you mixing with that family of his. You're not to go near their place, is that understood? The last thing you need is a bad influence; you've enough tricks of your own without learning more.'

It was true that Esme had a liking for those who were wayward or otherwise unconventional. There were few things she admired more than daring, few she enjoyed more than devilment.

'I told Tom he could come to tea with us,' she said when they reached Boskenna.

'Did you indeed!' Her father, lifting her down from the trap, sounded indignant. 'Without so much as a by-your-leave!'

''Tis all right, isn't it?' wheedled Esme.

'Well, just once, perhaps. We won't make a habit of it.'

14

Tom Tregunna came from a family of eleven. His father and brothers were, as John had said, illiterate, uncouth and very much in love with drink. The boy's older sister was employed in dressing ore at Wheal Merit, but the other five children were as yet too young to contribute anything to the woefully poor income on which the family struggled to survive. Of the little money they had, far too much was spent at the beershop and the kiddleywink. They lived from day to day in a constant condition of debt and ignorance from which most of them showed neither the urge nor the ability to escape. William Tregunna had no great skill in his work and could teach his sons only what he knew himself. He was thirty-seven and his lungs were already seriously damaged by the conditions in which he laboured. There was no point in planning for the future, no hope of improving his lot, no care for that of his children.

In Tom, he saw only the means of acquiring a few extra pence for the beershop and had therefore sent the boy to work at the earliest possible age. He did not perceive the sharp intelligence in his son and would not have valued it anyway. In truth, the boy's better qualities were overlooked by most people, for he would steal and fight as readily as the rest of his kin when the fancy took him.

What Esme saw in him, however, was a promising partner in mischief. She had always looked upon the Sunday school as a thing to be grudgingly suffered, but it now offered a newfound interest. Whenever Tom made an appearance there, she would barge or manoeuvre her way into the seat next to him.

If, at first, the boy was vexed or embarrassed by the attention of this insistent 'ole girl', his annoyance was gradually replaced by a certain liking for her. Although he could neither read nor write, young Thomas possessed a talent for caricature and defaced the flyleaf of many a hymnbook with sketches to entertain Esme. Huddling together, always in the corner of the back row, they whispered, giggled and pulled faces, were frequently scolded and sometimes had their ears boxed.

There could be no doubt that Esme looked upon Tom as her best friend. Dolls and girls' games did not interest her and she would have sought the boy's company every day if given the chance. Tom's attitude was a little more nonchalant: he regarded Esme with a sort of fond amusement. She was, after all, just a girl, and could not be expected to understand or share in all the important projects and pursuits of a twelve-year-old male.

Whenever Judith went shopping in Porthgullow of a Saturday, Esme would go along too, in hopes of seeing her friend. He was not always there, even when he had promised faithfully to meet her, and his absence would fill her with gloom and disappointment for the rest of the day. Tom would not put himself out to see Esme if there was something else he would rather do, but no matter how much he teased her she would look for him every time she was taken into town.

Like many children of his kind, the boy was very well able to take care of himself. Despite the fact that there was just one year's difference in their ages, he thought himself far more grown up than his little friend from Boskenna. Indeed, there was only one point on which his jaunty confidence failed him: he was very reluctant to talk about his family or where he lived, becoming uneasy when questioned about these things.

One Saturday, after a morning spent on the beach, picking up driftwood, coloured pebbles and dead spider crabs, paddling and pelting each other with seaweed, the children were driven up onto the jetty by the incoming tide. They were sitting together on the quay, playing five-stones, when Esme asked: 'Why won't you show me where you live?'

'Aw, 'tis a long walk – too far fer a li'l ole bit like you.'

'I don't mind. I'd like to see. It can't be that far, Tom, or you wouldn't be in town so often. Is it out on the moor? That's only a mile or so.'

'I dawn't think 'twould please your father if I was to take ee home wi' me.'

Esme was silent for a while, considering some other means of approach. Still dusted with fine sand, their bare legs and feet dangled over the edge of the quay. The tide had come right up to the wall and a few small boats rode gently at their moorings, green weed hanging from the ropes like wet embroidery silk.

At last she asked: 'What's your father like?'

Tom shrugged. 'He d'work hard. Has a fine ole temper.'

Esme pushed back the tangled hair from her face and regarded him with eyes half shut against the sun.

'Does he hit you, then? Are you afraid of him?'

'No, he dawn't offen hit us, but he d'bawl 'n carry on like a mazed thing when he's drunk.'

'Are you going to be a tutworker too, when you're older?'

The boy pursed his mouth, so that the upturned nose gave a thoughtful twitch.

'No, I wen't be like he. I'll be mine cap'n, or maybe somethin' even better – somethin' venturesome, excitin'.'

The hazel eyes grew bright with conviction. 'I aren't goin' spend all me days in this place. I wen't live on scads 'n taties, neither, I can do better'n that. You'll think I'm talkin' foolish, I spose, but I want to be proper wealthy.'

He glanced at her to see the effect of his words. Esme did not laugh at him and so he added gravely: 'One day, p'raps, I'll take ee out to see our place, then you'll understand.'

'Why not now, Tom?'

'No,' he said hurriedly, immediately regretting his lapse. 'I ony said "p'raps" an I didn' mean soon. Tell ee what,' he added, after a moment, 'I'll show ee somewhere else instead. 'Tidn s'far to go, but you'd best put your boots back on.'

Unencumbered by footwear of his own, he waited while she hastily fastened hers.

'Ready? 'Tis this way.'

They walked eastwards along the waterfront for fifty yards, then down a little alleyway and through a number of streets with which Esme was unfamiliar. Finally, they emerged onto the long, sloping road known as Polglaze Hill. It began behind the main cluster of cottages and climbed steeply upwards, veering away from the Morven Terrace area and towards a wooded coomb. A row of bay-windowed houses extended halfway to the top. Here were found the doctor's surgery and the offices of Gammon the solicitor. When viewed from the bottom, the hill appeared to reach a dead end among a group of beech trees. From nearer the top, however, two pathways could be seen branching away from it, running to left and right.

'Where are we going?' puffed Esme, as they trotted up the road.

'You'll see. 'Tis me secret hideout, so you're lucky I'm

willin' to take you there. You wen't tell nobody 'bout it, will ee?'

'On my honour, no!'

'All right'n, come on.'

When they reached the top of the hill the lad stopped for a moment, glanced suspiciously around to see if anyone was looking, then raced off along the left-hand track, with Esme running behind him. This footpath, narrow and partly overgrown, continued for half a mile until it came to a broken-down gate set in a low hedge. Here the boy halted and waited for her to catch up.

'Look,' he said, as she arrived at his side. 'There 'tis.'

On the other side of the hedge lay what had once been an orchard. Some of the trees still bore fruit, but it was plain to see that no one had tended this place in many, many years, for it was overrun by weeds, nettles and long grass. Apple and pear trees stood with their trunks and lower branches smothered in ivy. The upper canopies, unclipped for so long, had grown together, interlocking and creating a heavy stillness beneath. And beyond this damp green tangle lay the house to which it belonged – a small derelict manor house, very old and crooked, deserted for more than half a century.

'Ooh,' breathed Esme. 'Can we go in?'

''Course,' he said proudly. 'Follow me.'

They climbed over the gate and made their way along a path formed by Tom's repeated visits, where the under-growth was thin and beaten down. The door of the house hung by just the upper hinge and few of the windows had whole panes of glass left in them. Convolvulus wound itself around the broken frames and great patches of lichen sprawled across the roof and walls.

The boy pushed hard at the door. It moved stiffly on its hinge and a gap opened at the bottom as it tilted. They both slid inside and Esme gazed curiously around her.

She had never seen so much dust. Mounds of it had collected in the corners, eddies of it swirled about her feet as she moved, and her pinafore was smeared with dirt in no time at all. The house was spartan, with rough plaster walls, slate floors and narrow stone steps. The height of the ceilings and doorways suggested that those who once lived there were either quite short or obliged to walk about with their heads lowered for much of the time.

'I'll show ee all round it,' said Tom. 'Mind now, there's places upstairs where you mustn' tread or you'll go right through, so stay by me till you knaw where they're to.'

''Tis a wonderful hideaway, Tom,' she said, as he guided her through the rooms, 'but what do you find to do here all by yourself?'

He paused and regarded her with amazement. They were standing in an upstairs chamber, one either side of a hole in the floor. 'I d'look fer secret passages,' he said, in a tone which implied that this should be obvious to anyone with an ounce of sense. 'I knaw they're here somewhere – an I b'lieve there's treasure, too. See, they was rich people that lived here. Must've bin. An I reckon they'd have hid a bit away. I've looked all awver, but I just can't make out where 'tis to. It'll come to me, though, sooner or later. 'Nother thing I do is to creep in here after dark to watch for ghosts.'

'Do you see any?' gasped Esme.

'Now'n again,' lied the boy, hooking his thumbs over the waistband of his tattered trousers. 'They dawn't worry me. Sometimes I d'stay here all night.' He dropped his gaze for a second, then tempered his falsehood with a sad confession. 'Truth is, I'm glad of a place to come to when th'ole man've had too much at the beershop. I d'just clear out of it 'n sleep here till mornin'.'

The girl nodded in sympathy, but said nothing.

'Anyway, you knaw all 'bout it now. Like to come here again?'

'Oh yes! I'll help you find the secret passages.'

'All right,' he said, 'nex' week, p'raps. We'd better go back now, though. I 'spect your sister's waitin'.'

She was filled with pleasure at the privilege Tom had bestowed upon her. He had shown her his secret hideout – and invited her back again. This was indeed an honour and a weighty gesture of trust. So delighted was she that she did not stop to consider how dreadful his home must be, if he preferred to take her to a ruin like the manor house.

Although he could not be persuaded to show Esme where he lived, the boy did at last agree to visit Boskenna one afternoon in late August.

She was waiting for him at the top of the lane and noticed immediately that he was somewhat neater and cleaner than usual. Fresh linen to wear and warm water in which to wash were things Esme had always taken for granted, and she did not dream that he had spent the previous evening scrubbing himself and his clothing in a cold moorland brook, spreading the old shirt and trousers on a bush to dry.

'Hannah's made rabbit pie and figgy pudding for us,' she told him, as they ambled down the track.

'Who's Hannah?'

'She's the woman who looks after us all.'

'Since your mother died?'

'Oh, longer than that. Hannah's been at Boskenna since Father was married.'

'An he d'pay her?'

'Of course,' laughed Esme.

Tom digested this in silence, for it seemed to him awesome that Esme's father could afford such a thing.

110

'Didn' knaw you had a servant,' he muttered.

'She isn't – not really. Hannah's more of a friend to us. 'Tis only Miss Hoity-Toity who calls her a servant.'

'Your brother's wife? Will she be there?'

'She's not having tea with us. Anyway, you needn't take any notice of her if you see her.'

''Course not,' agreed the boy airily, hoping Esme could not tell that his heart was in his throat.

His courage failed him for a moment when the house came in sight, and he hesitated, hanging back in a pretence of inspecting something in the hedge.

'Come on.' Esme tugged at his sleeve. ''Tis all right.'

'Are ee sure your faather wen't mind?'

'Certain. Anyway, he and Richard are both at work and they won't be home till half past six.'

So Tom squared his shoulders, swallowed his fear and followed her inside. The parlour and dining room doors were closed and Esme led him straight down the passage to the kitchen. There, he stopped on the threshold, face to face with Hannah. Brisk and plump and starched, she clasped her hands before her and surveyed him from head to foot.

'So this is Tom, is it? Dawn't knaw when I last seen a boy s'thin. Sit down, then. The pie's nearly ready.'

She motioned him towards the scrub-top table. He seated himself on one of the benches and Esme slid in beside him.

As Hannah served up the rabbit pie, the boy peered about him, round-eyed. The kitchen was warm and clean, simply furnished with a fireside settle, and a large dresser on which were displayed serving dishes, bowls and plates. A grandfather clock ticked peacefully in the corner. Bunches of herbs hung from the rafters, and the window sill was cluttered with tins and jars, salt and spice boxes.

Tom thought it a very fine room, and assumed the parlour to be splendid beyond words.

'Eat up,' ordered Hannah. 'You'm a wisht li'l mite, an no mistake.'

Esme had never seen him so quiet or so nervous, and she noticed how he savoured every mouthful of his pie. No, he seldom sat down to such a plate of food and even the simplest comforts were a treat to him. For a full half-hour he was cowed by it all – though not enough to blunt his appetite – but as the meal progressed the anxiety gradually left him. By the time Hannah produced the plum pudding, glistening with powdered sugar, he was almost his usual self again.

He had drunk a second cup of tea and was laughing and jostling with Esme when he suddenly heard the banging of the front door.

Hannah peered down the passage in surpise. ''Tis your faather, Esme. Wass uh doin' home s'early, I wonder?'

The girl said nothing, though she knew the answer well enough. Whatever other reason he might give, the fact was that he had come to inspect Tom Tregunna.

The boy turned apprehensively to Esme and received a reassuring wink. He glanced uneasily at his empty cup and pudding dish when John came in, as though he felt guilty to be found eating in Rescorla's house.

'Ah – you're Tom, I take it?' The shipwright's greeting was genial enough, but the black eyes assessed the boy shrewdly. 'We've heard all about you,' he added, grinning.

'Oh,' said Tom faintly, unsure of how to interpret that. He had expected someone more forbidding than this man in shirt-sleeves and open waistcoat, a face sharper and less humorous. All the same, he could tell he was being carefully scrutinized, and the knowledge set him very much on edge.

'Hannah's done well for you, I hope?'

'Ess – thank you – 'twas a fine feed.'

'What've ee come for?' enquired the woman, as John began to rummage through a drawer in the dresser.

'Iodine. Rufus caught his hand with a saw.'

'Aw, ess?' Her tone was knowing. 'Thought you kept some down there?'

''Tis all gone.' He found the bottle and slipped it into his trouser pocket. 'Might as well have a drink of tea while I'm here.'

'Aw!' Hannah's eyebrows lifted. 'What about poor Rufus?'

'He can wait five minutes more.' John sat down at the table. 'Well, boy,' he said, 'let's hear a bit about you, then. Esme tells me you've a surface job at Wheal Merit. Be going underground soon, though, eh? Can't say I know much about mining. Like it, do you?'

The replies, quiet and hesitant, were received with nods, murmurs of interest and more questions. Esme, watched her father hopefully for signs of approval and was partially rewarded with the impression that he did not, at least, dislike Tom.

'You childern go on outside 'n amuse yourselves now,' instructed Hannah after a few minutes. 'I've all this clearin' up to do 'n you'm gettin' in me way.' As Tom stood up, she passed him a piece of raisin cake. 'In case there's a corner left empty.'

'Well,' she said, when the two youngsters had gone, 'you've had a look at the cheeld. What do ee think?'

'Better than I expected,' conceded John, 'a lot better. He's not stupid, that's for sure, and he's able to mind his manners a bit. Still, he's not yet grown. See, 'tis all right while they're children, but just give him a few more years and I reckon he'll change. Wait till he's had his first taste of drink.'

'Ah, go on with ee. Dunnee think 'tis possible that family could turn out one good one? Seem to me he've got th'urge to do better fer hisself.'

'Oh yes, wants to be mine captain, wants to go travelling and all the rest of it. Well, I hope they're more than daydreams, Hannah, but I wouldn't stake money on it. Believe me, I'm sorry for the boy. He's sharp and he's very likely the best of a bad bunch, but 'tis my guess they'll start dragging him down before he's much older – and the moment I see signs of it, he'll be kept away from Esme.'

15

Almost exactly a year after his own wedding, Richard learned that Jenny Varcoe had found someone else and was newly engaged. He was standing on the west quay in Porthgullow one morning, talking with a fisherman, when he spotted her sitting on an upturned barrel outside one of the waterfront inns. With her was a burly man of medium height, wearing a navy canvas smock and thigh boots. She was smiling up at him, listening intently to what he was saying, and suddenly she let out a peal of laughter. Richard could just hear it through the rattle of cartwheels and the calls of the skippers and fish-merchants as they counted and bargained for the catch. The sound of it brought a score of good memories crowding into his mind – then an aching sense of loss.

The fisherman, aware that he had lost Richard's attention, stopped in mid-sentence and followed his gaze. Understanding came as soon as he saw Jenny. Everyone knew what had happened, and most had heard rumour that all was not well between Richard and his wife. A word from Hannah in the grocery shop had been enough to set tongues wagging all over the town.

'Knaw'n, do ee?'

'What? Oh – no. Well, only by sight. We've never done any business with him. Name's Symons, isn't it?'

'Ess, thass right. Luke, he's called.' The fisherman regarded Richard with a look that said: 'I'm sorry, boy, but 'tis your own doing.' Quietly he added: 'They're goin' to be marrid nex' March.'

Richard nodded and made an attempt at a smile.

'Good, I'm glad.' He meant it as sincerely as he could, but his gladness was not wholehearted. His guilt was eased and he hoped she would be happy, but she now seemed doubly lost to him. Stifling a momentary flash of jealousy, he tried to concentrate on what the fisherman was saying.

'Luke's a bit older'n you, I b'lieve – two or three year, p'raps. He've got his awn lugger that his faather left'n.' He indicated a vessel with the name *Sweet Eva* painted on the prow. 'An he d'live in one o' they li'l cottages awver there.'

The fisherman pointed to a row of four cottages facing out across the harbour, built no more than twenty feet back from the water. A strip of cobbles ran past the front door and beyond that lay the edge of the quay, where several rusty mooring rings were set in the granite.

'Luke's a good sort,' the man assured Richard. 'He'll give her the best life he can. Mind, 'twen't be same s'if she'd married you. 'Twen't be s'easy for her.'

A note of reproach was creeping in and Richard did not want to hear any more.

'No,' he said, 'well, I can't stand here talking. Too much to do. Good day to you.'

He walked off hurriedly, and as he reached the waterfront he saw Jenny take her leave of Symons, stretching up to kiss his face and touch his brown hair, before setting off towards home.

Richard felt a keen desire to follow her and talk with her. He paused, debating with himself. She would probably snub him – she had done so more than once before. Pride told him to save himself the effort. But perhaps she had softened a little, now that life had given her compensation? Perhaps he might at least reclaim her friendship? Indeed, mere civility would do for a start.

Mustering his resolve, he went after her. He would give

his congratulations, tell her he was pleased and wish her well. She could hardly ignore that, could she?

Jenny disappeared along an alleyway and he did not catch up with her until she was almost home. When she heard her name called she turned, half-smiling, to see who it was.

The smile dropped from her face in an instant when she saw Richard. She spun on her heel and quickened her pace.

'Jenny, please stop. I only want to say . . .'

She walked even faster, her heels clacking on the cobbles.

'. . . how glad I am about you and Luke Symons.'

He was beside her now, but she would not answer or turn her head, staring doggedly in front of her as she bustled along.

'For pity's sake, I'm trying to wish you well!'

They had almost reached her door and in desperation he caught hold of her arm and pulled her round. For just a few seconds they were face to face – and she looked straight through him. Richard's heart sank and his grip loosened. Quickly she wrenched her arm away, dived into her house and slammed the door.

He heard her shoot the bolt, and for a second or two he just stared numbly at the wooden panels. Then he glanced self-consciously around him. The street was deserted and he fervently hoped that no one had witnessed the incident from a window. Once he had told himself that she could not keep this up for ever, but now he was not so sure. Crushed, he slunk away.

Luke and Jenny's wedding was set for March 12th of 1860. With the ceremony just a few days away, the girl went one morning to the jeweller's shop at the foot of Polglaze Hill, there to sell and to buy. With the price obtained for her old engagement ring, plus an extra seventeen shillings carefully saved over the past year, she bought a silver pocket watch with a mother-of-pearl face – a marriage gift for Luke. The old jeweller offered to engrave the back for her.

Would it cost much, she asked?

No, not a penny, not to her.

Delighted, she thought for a moment, then told him what to put.

She could not wait to see if Luke would like it. That same afternoon, she went to his cottage and presented him with the little package wrapped in tissue paper. Her eyes followed the movements of his large, weathered hands as he opened it, and anxiously studied his expression when he took out the watch, examined it and read the inscription on the back.

> To Luke,
> With my Love,
> Jenny.
> 1860

He looked up, his sunburnt face beaming with pleasure.

'Why, 'tis a handsome watch, maid. Oh, yes 'tis a fine one, sure enough. I've a chain for it, too, somewhere. Bless you, Jenny . . .' He placed the watch on the kitchen table, kissed and hugged her with delight. '. . . I'm a lucky man.'

Yes, he knew that he was fortunate. He had always admired Jenny Varcoe and wished she could belong to him. Ruefully he had watched her with Richard Rescorla, accepting, like everyone else, that they were meant for one another. She had always been Richard's friend, Richard's sweetheart, and was bound to be Richard's wife. Luke still marvelled at the stroke of fate which had given him what he wanted. Providence had done him a good turn and, although he grieved to see Jenny suffer, he could feel no animosity towards Richard. Rescorla's loss was Symons' gain, that was how Luke saw it.

He had asked her very little about Richard and what had happened. The main facts were known to all and he did not have a jealous or inquisitive nature. It was enough that she was soon to be his wife, that she shunned Richard Rescorla and would not speak of him, except with bitterness. It was easy to guess how close they had been, but the severance was now so complete that this did not trouble him. She was his and that was all he cared about.

'I only wish I had better to give you,' he murmured. 'A better house, a softer life.'

Across her shoulder, his eyes, bright blue and deep set, worriedly surveyed the room. The kitchen made up the whole of the ground floor. Above it were two small bedrooms and outside was a shared privy. The ceilings were low, the windows small, the stone staircase narrow. And because he lived alone there was much male clutter but no touch of comfort. Against his chest, Jenny smiled.

'Keep faith with me, and that will be enough.'

'Oh, I'll do that, all right. By heaven, I will.' He chuckled, fondly rubbing her back. 'I'm a man who knows when he's well off.'

119

16

Jenny became Mrs Symons less than a week later. Richard knew the date and time, and was filled with despondency. On the day itself, wrapped in frowning gloom, he took himself off to a corner of the boatshed to work alone on a pilot gig, his mood varying between listlessness and agitated energy.

'Look at'n,' said Rufus to one of the other men, 'teasy as an adder, an 'tis no wonder. He've hopped awver a fine flower 'n landed on a piss-abed. I dawn't b'lieve he've had one happy day since he marrid that ole Susan.'

That was the truth, and when Richard climbed into bed that night, aware that his wife was feigning sleep, he did not trouble her to fulfil her duty, for he was too miserable to perform his part. He was sorely afflicted by the knowledge that Jenny – his Jenny – was now sharing Symons' bed and giving to him all the warmth of which Richard was deprived. Desolate, he turned out the lamp and huddled, sleepless, on his own side of the mattress, convinced that life could hold no consolation.

But on the following Sunday, Susanna surprised him with an announcement.

It was late afternoon and they were sitting in the parlour, she at her tapestry frame, and he at the table examining the half-model for a new boat. Warily, Susanna studied her husband, stealing furtive glances at him between stitches as she plied her needle. She knew the cause of his surly mood. Oh yes, she knew why he brooded and glowered. He was pining for that wretched girl, and what was worse, he seemed to hold Susanna entirely to blame for his loss – as if it were no fault of his own. If he thought his wife a scheming spider, he had certainly been a willing fly – yet he still considered himself cheated. Well, she had some tidings for him, some news with which to redeem herself.

'Richard,' she said, as she neatly finished off an end of wool and reached for another colour, 'I have something to tell you.'

'Oh?' He did not bother to look up.

'I've been to see the doctor. I'm expecting a child.'

At first he was more astonished than delighted. After nearly eighteen months of marriage he had begun to fear that she could not even do that for him. He put down the wooden model and his gaze flickered curiously over her figure. There was, as yet, no outward sign of pregnancy and he could not quite believe it. The red tartan frock she wore had a simple bell-shaped skirt, tight sleeves and a high-buttoned bodice. It set off her fairness in striking style and made a fine contrast to the white lace cap and its streamers. He imagined that she should look somehow different, softer, but there was nothing motherly about that slender, unwelcoming body.

Finally, he asked: 'When?'

'In September.' She threaded her needle and went on with her work.

'Well – that's wonderful news!'

For a moment he did not know quite what to do. He supposed he should kiss her or something like that. The occasion obviously called for a demonstration of joy – though Susanna did not seem at all excited.

'I'm glad you're pleased.'

'Pleased?' He stood up, went over and lifted her to her feet, then embraced her rather gingerly, for he fancied she must be more fragile than usual. 'I'll say I am.' He kissed the top of her head, adding hopefully: 'Perhaps things will go better with us now. 'Twill make a bond between us, wipe out all the bad feeling.'

'Will it?' enquired Susanna mildly.

'Oh, you'll see. 'Twill all be different when the baby's born.'

Susanna returned his smile but made no comment. Richard was apt to be carried away by enthusiasm, as she knew full well. Detaching herself, she went back to her tapestry.

'We've a cradle somewhere,' said her husband happily. 'I believe 'tis in the attic. I'll go and fetch it down.'

He lit a lamp and went up to the loft, there to search for the family crib. A child, he thought. A son, perhaps? Oh, it made no difference – a girl would be just as welcome.

Richard found the cradle, lifted it up and grinned broadly. It seemed that he might find some love and purpose in life after all.

Susanna did not find pregnancy easy to bear. She was sick and vapourish and complained incessantly. From the fourth month onward she suffered backache, swollen legs and constant indigestion, and she fretted a great deal over the state of her figure. Embarrassed by her condition, especially in front of men, she seldom ventured out of doors, but moped about the house all day, uncorseted and peevish. Huddled in her favourite armchair from morn till night, she stirred as little as possible, emerging only for meals or to lumber dolefully out to the privy. She found the latter such a hardship that a commode was finally installed in the bedroom for her. As the months passed, she spent more and more time letting out her clothes and grumbling that a pregnant woman could look nothing other than drab. By the eighth month, however, she was thankful, for comfort's sake, to borrow the plain garments Ellen had worn while carrying Esme.

As her pregnancy entered its final month, Susanna found it a great relief to go upstairs each day after lunch and lie down for a few hours. It was during such an afternoon that Esme found the bonnet.

The girl was now twelve years old, and the childlike urges for play were sometimes confusedly mixed with a dawning interest in pretty clothes. Much as she disliked her sister-in-law, Esme was often fascinated by Susanna's frills and trinkets.

The bonnet in question was made of shiny black straw, lined with cream satin and trimmed with artificial tiger lilies. It had cost Susanna ten shillings and she planned to wear it often when her figure returned to normal and she could once again be seen in public. Having decided that a few tiny gold bows under the brim would improve it, she had spent the whole morning twiddling bits of ribbon and stitching them into place. The work was not quite complete when Hannah brought her lunch, and Susanna left the bonnet in the parlour when she went upstairs for her afternoon doze.

Judith had gone out looking for blackberries, and Esme was wandering listlessly about the house in search of amusement. Boredom vanished the moment her gaze lighted upon the bonnet. Taking it from Susanna's sewing table, she turned it round in her hands, admiring it from every angle. The colours, she thought, were lovely. They would look very striking on auburn hair.

She lifted the bonnet over her head, then lowered it carefully into place. Tying the ribbons under her chin, she tweaked the bow till it stood out smartly, then standing on the hearthstool, surveyed her reflection in the mirror over the mantelpiece and was very pleased with the effect. There came a momentary wish that Tom could see how nice she looked. Her appearance had lately begun to seem very important and she was highly conscious of it whenever she met him.

After a moment, she hopped off the stool and hurried out to the wash-house to find Hannah.

In the nearest of the outhouses stood a brick-based boiling copper. A fire roared in the space beneath the pan, and the air was heavy with steam and the smell of harsh soap. A row of wooden washtubs contained items of clothing and household linen in various stages of soaking, rinsing or starching. At the end farthest from the door, Hannah laboured over a scrubbing board and the whole place was filled with a low murmur of bubbling and sploshing.

'Hannah, look,' said Esme, skipping across the wet floor. 'Do you think it suits me?'

The woman pushed back a strand of hair from her forehead and straightened up, wiping her hands on her apron. Hannah's face, already red with heat and exertion, registered sudden alarm when she saw the bonnet.

'Aw, my dear life! Take'n off, Esme. Take'n off 'n put'n back 'fore she miss'n.'

'I'm not doing any harm,' objected the girl. 'Anyway, she's asleep.'

''Tis nearly four 'n she'll be gettin' up soon. If she catch ee playin' 'bout with her hat, she'll have forty fits.'

'Well, just tell me what you think,' insisted Esme. She bridled, pouted, flounced back and forth between the washtubs, mimicking Susanna's querulous tones. 'It's my only good bonnet, you know. Richard doesn't care how I look. He never gives me enough money. I'm practically in rags.'

'You mustn' mock her like that,' warned Hannah, suppressing a snort of laughter.

'I'm sure I don't know what you mean,' persisted Esme, employing one of Susanna's favourite retorts.

124

Hannah hauled a sheet from one of the rinsing tubs and fed it between the rollers of the mangle. 'You knaw she can't stand t'have anybody poke fun at her – an you dawn't do much else,' she panted, forcing the handle round. 'She might have her awn back on ee one o' these days, an I dawn't mean just a trouncin'.'

'What, then?' demanded Esme, idly stirring her finger round in a basin of starch. 'I detest her and I don't care who knows it.'

'Ess, well she wen't forget.' Hannah raised cautioning eyebrows as the tail end of the sheet passed through the mangle. 'You go careful, maid. Go on in 'n put her ole bonnet back where he b'long.'

'Oh, all right.' The child shrugged. 'But I'm not afraid of her. She's just . . .'

It was too late. Susanna, having found the bonnet missing and searched all over the house, appeared at the wash-house door, demanding to know its whereabouts. To find it on the head of Richard's obnoxious sister was enough to kindle immediate rage.

'Give me that, you little beast! If you've spoilt it in any way . . .'

'I haven't harmed the stupid thing. I was only trying it on.'

Esme glared at her and quickly undid the bow.

'You had no right to take it without my permission. I don't like you touching any of my things. You're rough and clumsy and your hands are always dirty.'

''Tis only fit for an old witch anyway,' flared Esme, whipping off the bonnet.

Susanna held out her hand. 'Give it to me,' she repeated curtly.

Esme hid it behind her back and sidled away between the washtubs.

'Don't provoke me, child.'

125

'Do as you're told, Esme,' urged Hannah.

The girl took no notice, dodging further from Susanna's reach.

'She've done no damage, Mrs Rescorla,' Hannah said. 'Leave her be 'n I'll see 'tis brought back safe.'

'No damage?' queried Susanna. 'It wouldn't surprise me to find that she's caught headlice from that guttersnipe boy she brings here to tea. My bonnet is probably infested by now.'

Esme's fury was all on Tom's behalf. 'Well, I know just how to kill them off, then!' she exclaimed sharply.

And with that, she lifted the top of the boiling copper, hurled the bonnet inside and slammed the lid down again.

Susanna emitted a sound, half moan, half whimper. As Esme made a bid to dash past her, she seized her by the hair, jerked her head round and delivered a heavy smack to the child's face. She was about to inflict another, but Esme twisted round and sank her teeth into the fleshy pad below Susanna's thumb.

There was a shriek and the girl was released. She took her chance and fled, still rubbing her burning cheek.

'I told ee to leave her be,' sighed Hannah, returning to her work.

Susanna, sucking her wounded hand, look up and snapped: 'Let her be? Surely it's the other way round? Why won't she leave me alone? I want nothing to do with her. I'm in a delicate condition and yet I'm given no peace. She's impertinent at every opportunity. And as if Esme weren't enough by herself, we must have that foul Tregunna brat here to tea every week.'

''Tis ony now 'n again,' corrected Hannah. 'Three or four times he've bin here, thass all.'

'Far too often, anyway. They're always whispering and sniggering together about me. The boy pulls faces at me through the parlour window!'

'They're just childern, Mrs Rescorla. 'Fore long you'll have one o' your awn. P'raps then you'll learn to be more tolerant.'

'I hope her old thumb festers,' Esme said, when she told Tom about the incident.

The boy grinned. 'I knaw she's an ole misery, but you d'aggravate her somethin' crool.'

'Well, she has a nasty tongue.'

'Zackly what was it she said?'

'Never mind,' muttered the girl. She had carefully omitted to tell Tom of Susanna's remarks about head lice and of what she had called him.

The children were sitting together on the floor of an upstairs room in the old manor house. It had become a regular meeting place for them, and many hours had been spent there in games and exploration.

'Anyway, what shall we do now?' she asked.

He shrugged.

'We could play "house",' suggested Esme brightly. 'You could be my husband!'

'House?' Tom looked and sounded horrified. 'Thought you didn' like girls' games?'

Until now, she had thought so too.

'Great adventurers dawn't play "house",' he informed her indignantly.

'Oh. But they do have to eat, I suppose?' Esme's tone was tinged with pique. 'I've brought some food with me.' From the pocket of her pinafore, she produced a slightly squashed paper package and unwrapped two apple turnovers. 'Want one?'

Sheepishly, the boy accepted. It was when he reached out to take a turnover that Esme first noticed the state of his hands. The knuckles were bruised in some places and skinned raw in others.

'How did you do that?'

'Aw, didn' tell ee, did I? I'm workin' underground now – have bin since Monday 'fore last. Trammin, 'tis called. I d'wheel carts full of ore along the levels. In places where 'tis very narra, you're apt to scrape your fists.'

'What's it like down there, Tom?'

The boy munched thoughtfully for a moment. He was thirteen years old now, wiry and very strong for his age.

'Tunnels,' he said. 'Tunnels 'n more tunnels. Rubble 'n red dust everywhere. 'Tis hot 'n sticky, an the air idn fit to breathe. There's black pools, an slantin' walls o' rock shored up wi' big pine balks. Then there's great caverns wi' dark spaces awverhead that d'make echoes, an there's fearsome gulfs that go down 'n down, sometimes wi' just a plank slung aross 'em fer men to walk on. Thass how 'tis, Esme.'

'Don't you feel afraid?' she asked gravely.

'Ess,' he admitted, after a slight hesitation. 'I do, a bit. But 'tis no good to feel like that, 'cause I'll be spendin' most of me life underground. If 'tidn Wheal Merit, 'twill be some other pit.' His eyes flickered curiously over her anxious face and then he laughed. 'Wass matter, maid? Are ee worried about me?'

'Of course not,' sniffed Esme, hastily taking a bite of her turnover. 'You'll get used to it, I know. It sounds awful, that's all.'

But her face had turned red and for several minutes she could not look him in the eye. Esme had a very strong affection for Tom, but she knew he would only tease her if she confessed it.

17

Susanna's child was due in the fourth week of September. For the last fortnight before the birth, she hardly left her bedroom, since the kindly Judith had volunteered to bring all her meals on a tray.

'I think you're silly to run round after her the way you do,' said Esme one evening in the kitchen, as Judith prepared a light supper for her sister-in-law.

'She does deserve a bit of thought, Esme. Susanna's facing quite an ordeal – women sometimes die in childbirth, you know. And try to remember 'tis Richard's baby too.' She poured out a glass of milk to go with the cold pork and boiled potatoes. 'I expect her temper will improve when the baby's born. I've heard it said that women often change once they have children. They become less selfish.'

Esme maintained a sceptical silence and tried to push away the iniquitous thought that Richard would be much happier as a widower.

Susanna did not die in childbirth, though anyone who heard the screams that Friday morning might well have thought death was imminent. The pains began at just after four o'clock and soon became very severe. At a quarter to six, John set out to fetch the doctor, while Esme ran down to the cove to rouse Hannah. By the time the physician arrived, labour was well under way and Susanna was shrieking without restraint.

For a while Richard loitered on the landing, occasionally peering round the bedroom door with gauche enquiries as to Susanna's progress and whether he could help in any way. But he found himself brushed aside as a helpless nuisance, while Hannah bustled back and forth in response to the doctor's instructions. The moans and howls, and the panting, sweating figure of his wife presented a gruesome spectacle and Richard was not all sorry when the physician ordered him out.

For a time he sat in the kitchen, nervously drinking tea and occasionally jumping at the sound of a screech from overhead.

Esme kept him company, calmly shredding cabbage and chopping parsnips, quite unmoved by the wails echoing through the house. At around eleven o'clock an especially piercing shriek proved too much for Richard, so he quit the house and went down to the yard, there to potter about for a few hours.

In mid-afternoon, however, anxiety drove him back up to Boskenna to see if there was any news. As he came up the lane he was just in time to see the departing doctor's gig turning out onto the road at the top. Richard started to run and he practically vaulted the gate in his haste.

The house was silent when he stepped inside the front door. Quickly he went upstairs.

Susanna was sleeping. There were purple shadows round her eyes and her hair was lank with dried perspiration, but she seemed otherwise unharmed. Hannah, bundling up some soiled bed linen, turned and pressed a finger to her lips for quiet when she heard Richard come in. Then she smiled to him, nodding towards the cradle by the window.

Judith was bending over it, beaming with delight. She looked up and beckoned eagerly to her brother. Esme, equally fascinated by the child, assured him:

''Tis very red, and a bit creased, but 'tis all right.'

'A daughter, Richard,' whispered Judith, 'a lovely little girl.'

With eyes squeezed shut, the infant twitched and rolled her head, the puckered mouth working, the hands clasping and clenching at the air. A sparse growth of dark down upon her head promised that she would have her father's colouring.

They left Richard alone with the baby and he contemplated his first child with a mixture of pride and reverence. He and Susanna had not discussed the question of names, but it now came to him that he would like to call his daughter Katie.

His wife, who had opened her eyes and lain watching him for some moments, murmured: 'Are you disappointed, husband? I suppose you would have liked a son.'

Richard hastened to the bedside. He sat down and took her hand in a warm grasp. Filled with elation and captivated by the child she had given him, he was ready to forget all their differences.

'With such a beautiful daughter? How could I be anything but pleased? She's a fine, fine baby, Susanna.' He bent to kiss her forehead and found it cold, like the hand that rested limply in his own. 'How are you feeling? Is there any . . .?'

'I'm exhausted,' she said testily, 'as you might expect.'

'. . . anything you'd like?' finished Richard. 'Anything I can do for your comfort?'

'Hannah will see to it all, thank you.' She fixed her gaze upon the ceiling, as if willing him to go away.

Undeterred, he smiled and pressed her hand between both his own.

'Susanna, now that we have this lovely child, surely we can be happy together? Aren't you delighted with her? I know you don't enjoy my – attentions – but she's worth it all, isn't she? I only want your affection, Susanna. When you're well again and have the care of the baby, you'll be more content, I'm sure.'

131

Under their darkened lids, Susanna's eyes slid towards him in a hostile, sidelong stare and the lines of her mouth drew angrily down.

'You went out.'

'What . . .?'

'You went out,' she repeated tersely. 'You've been gone for hours. I asked for you when the child came, and Hannah told me.'

'I only went to work for a while.'

She snatched her hand away. 'Your concern for me was not so very great, was it? You didn't feel compelled to stay with me. Oh dear no, I was just left to get on with it.'

For a moment Richard was too astonished to answer, then he started to protest.

'There was nothing I could do to help. You know I wasn't wanted here. I can't believe you'd really like to have me in the room at such a time, and I'd only have been in the way.'

She ignored that. 'I might have died,' she continued. 'I've never known such anguish, and yet my husband, who so casually and selfishly consigned me to this suffering, hadn't the decency even to remain in the house while I endured it. A man likes to boast of his children, but he has no stomach for the unpleasant business of birth. He takes enjoyment from the making of a child and altogether too much credit for its existence, but he cannot take a share in the pain involved, nor does he care to witness it.'

Richard drew back and stood up, for the bitterness emanated from her like a vapour, poisonous and chill.

'I didn't mean to neglect you, Susanna. I just . . . That is, I thought the time would pass more quickly if I found something to occupy me.'

As soon as he had said it, he knew what her answer would be.

'More quickly for you, no doubt. There was no such mercy for me.'

Richard thought it wisest to let her have the last word in the matter and so, after a short hesitation, he changed the subject.

'I was wondering what to call her. I thought "Katie" would be nice. Katherine Ellen. Do you agree?'

Susanna turned her head away, but flipped a hand dismissively in the direction of the cradle.

'Call her what you like. It's of no interest to me.'

Her husband's eyes took on a stony look of withdrawal. 'All right,' he said stiffly. 'If she doesn't interest you, then she's all the more mine.'

Only a care not to startle the baby kept him from slamming the door as he left.

Judith's hopes that her sister-in-law might make a good mother were soon demolished. As Mrs Tregear had pointed out, Susanna had no rapport with children. An only child herself, she could not draw upon experience of baby brothers or sisters, and did not find infants at all endearing. She made half-hearted attempts at mothering, but proved so inept that Judith or Richard would usually step in and take over the task in hand. In the end, her role was limited to the necessary breast-feeds and the use of a dummy to stop Katie howling. She seemed incapable of bathing her daughter without soaking herself and terrifying the child. Soiled nappies filled her with revulsion and when, for the first time, Katie was sick on her shoulder, Susanna screamed aloud and all but dropped her.

So it was Judith who attended to most of the infant's needs, washing and changing her, crooning to her, rocking

133

the cradle. When Katie began to laugh and crawl and burble, reaching for everything in sight, it was Judith who sat in the garden with her on summer afternoons, or chased her round the parlour floor on hands and knees.

Susanna was more than content to let her sister-in-law amuse the child. If I had married in my own class, she told herself in justification, Katherine would certainly have had a nursemaid, and quite rightly so. Judith does almost as well and, what's more, she seems to enjoy it.

In the evenings it was Richard who tickled and bounced the little one, whispering the nursery rhymes and later the bedtime stories. It was he who took her paddling, built castles in the sand, pointed out flowers and shells and seagulls. Susanna's contribution to her upbringing was small indeed.

All the same, Richard was gratified to know that his wife could produce such healthy offspring, and eager to increase the size of his family. The baby was just twenty months old when Susanna conceived again.

18

1862 brought a long, hot summer and many outings for Esme and Tom. Both had passed the age of childish pranks and their meetings now took them for lengthy walks across the moors or cliffs, or else to some local festival such as Porthgullow regatta or the parish feast. On a footpath between the moors and the sea was a stile where Esme liked to wait for him, and there she would sit, surrounded by fern, foxglove and the drowsy hum of insects, until she saw him coming down the track.

She was now fourteen and the past two years had softened the inquisitive, foxy look of her childhood, bringing a certain poise along with rounded hips and bosom. Tom, too, had changed a good deal in that time. A dramatic spurt of growth had given him a height of nearly six feet. He was well past his fifteenth birthday and his voice had broken. The difference that most concerned Esme, though, was the change in his disposition.

He had grown less boisterous and was sometimes given to periods of brooding silence. There were moments when he seemed to feel uncomfortable with her. She thought she could guess why, but she sensed that he was troubled by something else as well, something more than the natural awkwardness of a youth in the company of a girl. He had long since progressed from the job of tramming ore to that of tutwork alongside his father, and here, it seemed, was the source of his unrest. He would still talk of his plans whenever they met, but he no longer appeared cocksure, as though a dose of harsh reality had brought him down from the clouds. There were, he once admitted, more obstacles before him than he had first thought.

One September afternoon, Hannah sent Esme over the moor with a dozen jars of blackberry and apple jam for the vicar of a neighbouring parish. The girl stayed to tea and was given a buttermilk cake to take home. It was nearly five o'clock by the time she started back to Boskenna.

Along the way, it occurred to Esme that a short detour from her homeward route would take her past Wheal Merit, with the possibility of meeting Tom as he left work. So she carried on for a few hundred yards, then turned southwards on a spur of the track.

She had walked another mile when a small group of men and boys from the mine, all of them weary and covered with dust, appeared over a rise, some distance ahead. Esme knew, long before they drew near, that Tom was not among them, for none was of more than medium height.

A trio of bal girls in white bonnets and soiled aprons next went by, followed by two young miners, and then an older man who seemed barely able to put one foot in front of the other. It was not until she came within sight of Wheal Merit that Esme spotted Tom. The track reached the brow of a low hill, and there, spread out below, was the wasteland round the stack and engine house, littered with stores, dressing sheds, dumps and surface machinery. Tom was among the last of those straggling up the road. Esme called out, but he did not hear and he turned east towards the wildest part of the moor.

She ran after him and had to shout his name several times before he finally paused and looked round.

'Why, Esme, what're ee doin' out here?'

Far from being pleased to see her, he looked and sounded distinctly uneasy.

'I had to take some preserves over to the vicar and I thought I might catch you on my way home.' She came to a halt, panting, and smiled up at him.

'Aw, I see.' Tom nodded, but glanced hesitantly down the track and then back at her. ''Tis late, though, maid. I dawn't think . . .'

'It can't be more than six. You're not in any hurry, are you?' She gestured towards a patch of high ground some half a mile distant. 'We could walk up on the hill and sit for a while.'

'Aw – all right'n!' He agreed to that with an eagerness born of relief. He had half feared she might wish to go home with him.

'Or else . . .'

Tom's heart sank.

'. . . you might show me where you live, since I'm this close. It can't be very far from here, and you've promised more than once.'

The lad shook his head. 'Esme, tidn the sort o' place I should take ee.'

'Why must you have this secret from me when we've known each other so long? I'm not such a tender flower, Tom, and it can't be as bad as you make out.'

'Can't it, now?' Annoyance furrowed his forehead. 'Am I a liar, then?'

She grinned. 'An awful liar. You take a pride in it.'

'Well I aren't lyin' 'bout this.'

'Please, Tom.'

With a snort of exasperation, he thrust his fists into the pockets of his trousers, then turned his back and ambled a few paces away, kicking up puffs of dust from the path. Finally, he spun on his heel, looked long and hard at her, then jerked his head towards the distant carn to the east.

137

'Come on, if you must. We'll settle this fer good 'n all, 'cause I'm certain once'll be enough.'

The words were very quiet, little more than a sigh.

The walk took half an hour, and in that time they passed a dozen lonely hovels that sat like growths upon bleak patches of moorland. Although less than two miles from Porthgullow, this was a desolate tract of country, where the land stretched away to a skyline raggedly sawn by the rocks projecting through the heath. Tom hardly spoke all the way and when at last he stopped outside a tiny cottage as mean as all the rest, he merely looked at Esme and nodded.

A farmer would hedge his fields with better walls. The stones were fitted together as well as their natural forms and a little crude shaping would allow. A filling of cob had been applied in places, but the whole was a pitiful defence against the wind and rain that raved across this treeless country in winter, and would offer no protection whatever against the cold. With sombre eyes, Esme saw that the furze her own family found fit only for burning was here employed as a roof.

'We've no privy,' Tom said harshly, 'just an open pit round the back. There's a ready supply o' water, though. The rain d'soak right through the thatch 'n trickle down the walls, so we're never short.'

Esme did not answer his bitter joke. She was still absorbing the sight of the meagre vegetable patch and the handful of sorry-looking fowls in a wire run at the side of the cottage. Just outside the door, two infant girls dressed only in grubby cotton shifts were staring blankly at her. Their bare feet, hands and faces were streaked with grime and she wondered if their hair had been cut or combed since the day they were born.

'Come on.' Tom took her hand in a rough grasp and

pulled her towards the door. 'You wanted to see, well here's your chance.'

The interior was so badly lit that Esme's eyes took some seconds to adjust, but the foulness of the air shocked her nostrils from the instant she set foot inside. Assaulted by the rank odour of unwashed bodies, peat smoke and boiling stew, the girl took a step back and a moment to compose herself.

"Tis all right,' jeered Tom softly. 'After all, you aren't such a tender flower.'

There were five people within the single room, in company with a pig. The animal, half-grown and snorting contentedly, was penned in one corner. A tall, bony man crouched over a table in another, avidly spooning stew into his mouth. Beneath the dirt, his hair was the same brown as Tom's and the facial likeness was very striking. This, Esme realized, was exactly how Tom might look after twenty more years of deprivation, twenty years of grinding labour. The man looked up, gaped at her and grunted through his food:

'Who's this'n?'

The question drew the attention of all to the figure hovering at the entrance. Mrs Tregunna, thin and lank-haired, with a baby clutched to her hip, was squatting to rake at the fire and she turned to stare nervously at the visitor. A boy of about thirteen regarded Esme with open mouth and dull eyes, while a girl of uncertain age grinned down at her from the rickety platform nailed beneath the thatch. A sagging bed, half-hidden by a greyish curtain, occupied a third corner, but it was clear that most of the family slept on piles of heather on the earthen floor.

The woman stood up and her gaze travelled over Esme's clothing with a kind of resentful stupidity, for though it was simple and plain, the girl's dress had neither a stain nor a tear.

139

'Her name's Esme,' Tom said. 'I've knawed her a long time.'

'Aw,' nodded the man, and he went back to his meal as if she were not there.

His wife seemed at a loss, as if no stranger had ever set foot in her home before, least of all a young woman wearing clean clothes and good shoes.

'We avn got nothin' spare,' she muttered at last. 'He've no business bringin' people here.'

Finding her voice, Esme hastened to reassure her. 'I only came to wish you good day and . . .'

'From the temp'rance, are ee?' enquired Tregunna roughly. 'One o' they women that d'knaw God personal 'n do all His talkin' for'n?'

Despite the horror of her surroundings, Esme began to laugh.

'No, I'm not from the temperance.'

'Thass all right'n.' He wiped a lump of bread around his plate and stuffed it, sopping, into his mouth. 'Betterfit they stayed home, 'stead o' traipsin' round wi' banners 'n warnin' 'bout hell like twadden here already.'

Esme looked at Tom and grinned, but all he could manage was a despondent ghost of a smile.

'You'd best go on home now,' urged his mother anxiously. 'We can't offer ee nothin', see.'

'Oh no,' protested Esme. 'I don't want . . . The truth is, I came to bring you this.' Flustered, she pulled the buttermilk cake from her basket and thrust it towards Mrs Tregunna. 'That's to say, the vicar's wife sent it.'

'There, I said 'twas temp'rance women at the back of it!' exclaimed Tregunna.

His wife, however, accepted the cake with an eager smile of thanks.

Suddenly sensing hostility, Esme glanced at Tom in

140

confusion. Humiliated, he glared at her with fierce resentment.

'We'll go now,' he said curtly, and motioned her to leave.

When she stepped outside, Esme was almost dazzled by the daylight and so collided with Tom's two elder brothers, on their way into the cottage. As shabby and dirty as all the rest, they ogled the girl and guffawed about her red hair. Esme pushed past them and hurried after Tom, who had stalked ahead without waiting for her.

He marched on, fully aware that she could barely keep up with him, until the ramshackle dwelling was well behind them and out of sight.

'Why are you so angry?' she panted. 'What have I done?'

He halted and turned unfriendly eyes upon her. His mouth was compressed and his whole demeanour howled of wounded pride.

'What've ee done?' he repeated. ''Tis bad 'nough that you need t'ask. Playin' Lady Bountiful, handin' out food to the beggars. I spose Mother should've dropped ee a curtsey? Had to knaw, didn' ee? Had to come 'n look. All these years, I've told ee 'twas rough 'n no place fit fer ee. I told ee there was more muck 'n stink than a barnyard – an you wanted to see it, like we was some freak show at a fair. Peerin' round ee, an wrinklin' up your nose – I daresay you'll want a bath when you get home?'

Esme listened to this outburst in amazement. The reality had, in truth, been more awful than she had imagined, but she thought it senseless that he should feel ashamed of misfortunes that were not his fault, and be offended by the gift of a buttermilk cake.

'All right, Tom, I'll admit 'twas worse than I expected. I can't deny that and I wish it weren't so, but you've no

141

call to say I'm haughty or accuse me of mean curiosity. You've always made a sore secret of your home and your family, and it caused a bit of awkwardness between us. I just thought I might put an end to all that. I'm truly sorry, Tom, that your lives are so hard and I wish I could help, though 'tis clear you'd resent me if I tried. No insult was meant when I offered your mother the cake. To be honest, I knew I'd done wrong in coming here. 'Twas the first excuse that entered my head.'

'Thass as may be,' he said sullenly, 'but I knaw pity when I see it, an you're the last one I want feelin' sorry fer me.'

'Huh! You're making more fuss than I am. 'Tis no great issue to me, Tom. I've liked you always, I like you still. You're no less my friend because of this.'

'I didn' want ee to see all that,' he said, shame-faced, 'specially after I'd bin to your house. I knaw I'm no angel – I've a hide tougher than most. Even so, I dawn't like to be made to feel small. Can ee look at me now without seein' that place behind me, an Faather with his food runnin' down his chin?'

'I see what's behind your plans and ambitions, that's all. You've not given them up, have you?'

'No, I have 'em still.'

'Well then, you'll rise above all this.'

The lad grunted and sat down on a boulder. 'I've lately come to see how difficult 'tis to make any money,' he said. ''Tis easy to talk big when you're too young to knaw better. In minin', a boy d'learn from his faather, see. 'Tis always the way. 'Nother year or so 'n there wen't be no more the'ole man can teach me, 'cause he dunnaw much hisself. Thass how we're trapped from one generation to the next.'

'But does it have to be mining? There are other things.

142

My father takes on apprentices from time to time and perhaps . . .'

'No, maid.' He shook his head. 'You'll think 'tis strange, I dawn't doubt, but there idn nothin' I want 'cept the name "Cap'n" an the white jacket that d'go with it. The bal's everythin', see. 'Tis the whole of life when you're born to it. Mother's a miner's daughter. Me older sister d'work in the sheds, dressin' ore, and so will all th'others in time. Every man in the family d'have his existence bound up wi' the pit. There's other things, thass true 'nough, but I've no taste for 'em. I wouldn' care to work on the land, thass certain. I spose I'd live longer if I was to go fishin', but I'd never be any the richer. Now, a man can do well in minin' if he've got wits enough, but I wen't have the teachin' I need if I stay wi' Faather. An thass why I wen't be stoppin' here much longer.'

'You're going away? But where?' Her consternation was immediate and obvious.

The boy plucked a stem of grass and stuck the end in his mouth. 'Redruth,' he said, chewing thoughtfully.

Esme gasped. 'Redruth? That's nearly forty miles!'

'Ess, 'tis best to put a good long way 'tween me 'n the 'ole man.'

'But how long will you be gone?'

'I shen't come back at all, not if there's chances fer me elsewhere.' His forehead creased slightly when he saw the dismay in her face. Discarding the grass, he rose to his feet and said seriously: 'Esme, I bin thinkin' lately 'bout you 'n me, an I b'lieve 'tis best fer us to stop meetin'. 'Twas all right when we was childern, but . . .'

'I don't see why it's any different now,' exclaimed Esme, her voice rising with panic.

'Oh, I b'lieve you do,' he said quietly. 'We've finished wi' chasin' round Porthgullow, an tormentin' your sister-in-law 'n suchlike. There's other kinds o' mischief fer us

143

now 'n 'tis you who'd lose by it, not me. I dawn't look at ee same way I used to, Esme. It've bin differnt fer me these past few months. Understand what I'm sayin'?'

Esme understood perfectly.

'Yes.' Her answer was firm and deliberate. 'I don't look at you in the same way, either.'

'I'll say it straight, then. I like ee too well to risk leavin' ee in any trouble, an I dawn't want to be tied. Think forty mile's a long way, do ee? Well, I plan to go a lot further'n that 'fore I'm finished, an I'll want me freedom to move round just as I please. I shen't want nobody else to worry 'bout. I aren't goin' stay here, Esme, an I wen't take ee with me, neether.'

'Oh,' she said faintly, 'I'd hoped one day we might . . .'

'Ess, I knaw, but 'tis no use, maid. I knaw the sort o' life you d'want, but I can't give it to ee – an it wouldn' suit me, even if I could.'

'Great adventurers don't play house,' she murmured forlornly.

'What was that?'

'Doesn't matter. I was just remembering something else you once said.'

'P'raps 'tis just as well you've seen how I d'live,' he went on. ''Twill be a long, long time 'fore I can offer a woman a decent life, an I wouldn' be willin' to put down roots in any case – not yet. 'Tis the way I am. You ought to knaw that by now.'

'Yes, I suppose I should. You always did have other interests than me.'

'I'm fond of ee,' he said. 'I wouldn' have cared what you thought o' me if twadden so, but thass all there is to it. Go on home, now, Esme. Think 'bout what you seen back there today 'n you'll understand 'tis the best way.'

'When do you mean to leave?' she asked wretchedly.

'Nex' spring, I spect.'

'Oh – well then, we needn't part quite yet.'

'We're partin' today, maid. I've gived ee the reasons already. 'Tis no good hopin' I'll change me mind in the meantime.'

There was a lengthy hesitation. 'Will you at least walk down to the coast road with me?' she asked finally.

Tom was about to say no, but she looked so woebegone that he relented.

'All right, Esme, just this once.'

The following evening, John found his younger daughter alone in the kitchen, while everyone else was in the parlour listening to Susanna playing the piano. Supper was over and Esme had just finished clearing up. It was unusual for her to insist on doing this chore by herself. She had even shooed Judith away, as if she were too bound up with her own thoughts to be bothered with anyone else.

'What's the matter, Esme?'

'Nothing, Father.'

'Yes there is, girl. You've been brooding on something since you came home yesterday. I thought your eyes looked swollen this morning, as though you'd been crying.'

'I didn't sleep well, that was all.'

She picked up a pair of serving platters and stood them on edge in the top of the kitchen dresser.

'Tell me what it is, Esme. You don't want your poor old father to wonder and worry, now do you?'

The girl wavered. She had always turned to John for comfort, even when her mother was alive.

'You'll be angry,' she warned.

He took down his pipe and tobacco from the mantel-shelf and tossed some turves of peat on the fire.

'Yes, I may well be, but let's hear it anyway.'

Esme went into the larder and returned with a chicken, killed that morning. She hitched a leg over one of the trestle benches by the table, sat down and took the carcase on her lap. 'I went to see Tom's home yesterday,' she said, pulling out a tuft of feathers.

'Ah.' Her father nodded and made himself comfortable on the settle.

'I know you forbade me to go – and he didn't want me there either – but I was curious and . . . Well, I had a shock, 'tis true, but 'twas something else that really upset me.'

'Go on.' John was filling his pipe and seemed quite calm, despite the knowledge that she had defied him.

'He says he doesn't want to see me any more,' blurted Esme. 'He says he'll be going away before long.'

'I'm glad to hear it.' John's tone was not harsh, but filled with a quiet satisfaction. 'Esme, 'tis just as well this has come to light. I've been meaning to speak with you about Tom for some time now. I've listened to you talking with your sister, and 'tis always "Tom this" or "Tom that". You're too fond of the boy and the time has come for it to stop. I think I know what's in your mind, girl. You'll be fifteen, come spring. A year or two more and you'll start to think about marriage. You speak of Tom as your friend, but I see the signs of something more and I don't want this attachment to grow any stronger.'

'Nor does he,' said Esme dismally.

'That's sensible of him. He couldn't provide for you, Esme, not in the way you need. 'Twould be a mean, miserable life such as you've never known. Poverty soon makes an old woman out of a young one. By the time you reached thirty, you'd look fifty.'

'It's not just that. He means to better himself and I believe he can do it, but he doesn't want to be – burdened – with me.'

146

She went on tugging and tossing away handfuls of down, and it floated to rest in gently stirring heaps on the flagstone floor.

'Is that so? Well, plain speaking is no bad thing. 'Tis hurtful sometimes, but the truth's the truth and you may as well know where you stand.' The shipwright puffed thoughtfully at his pipe. 'I confess I was afraid he might see you as a way of attaching himself to a more prosperous family. I'm pleased to find I was wrong. Now don't look so wounded, Esme. 'Tis my guess that the young man has a genuine care for your wellbeing and I thank him for it. I'm grateful, too, that he's saved me from having to intervene. If I'd been the one to stop you seeing him, you'd never have forgiven me, would you?'

Esme did not appear to be listening. 'I believe he thinks me a weak and coddled thing,' she muttered. 'I wouldn't be a nuisance to any man, no matter what the circumstances.'

'You're strong and determined, I know, but you weren't raised to endure such awful poverty. 'Tis good for a lad to have hopes and plans, maid, but they're not always fulfilled. You've seen what Tom could offer if all his ambitions came to nothing. Tell me truthfully – and think hard before you answer – could you live as the Tregunnas do?'

Esme ripped out another handful of down and cast it despondently into the air. She was silent for a moment as she sat among the flying feathers, and slowly her head sank with the acknowledgement that such a life would be unbearable.

John watched a feather drift gently down to settle in his daughter's hair, and he reached out to remove it. 'Now, the boy's done the right thing, Esme. I want your word of honour that you won't pursue him or argue the matter further. Your brother made a bad marriage – albeit in a different way – and I'll not see you do the same. I should have forbidden Richard to marry Susanna, but I didn't stop him and we all know the result. I shan't make the same mistake with you. Give me your promise, girl. You won't disobey me again, will you?'

She gave a helpless shrug. 'Oh, you have my promise. It makes little difference anyway. Tom meant what he said and that's an end to it.' With a soft laugh, she added: 'I was always more fond of him than he was of me. Perhaps he does have some concern for me, but 'tis freedom he cares for the most.'

19

It was setting and pay-day at Wheal Merit, an overcast December Saturday. Among the crowd assembled at the count house, Tom stood with his father and brothers, listening to the tributers bidding for a pitch.

This was easy ground, the captain said, with ore of middling quality. The men had already formed their own opinions, having inspected various sites within the mine and made judgements as to the likely reward for effort expended. They were knowledgeable, these tributers. They had to be, since they earned a percentage of the value of the ore they brought out. A man who could spot a promising pitch, work it fast and economically, might look forward to a healthy reward on pay-day. A mistake, on the other hand, could leave him with next to nothing for two months' sweated labour. Even the sharpest were caught out now and again, while others might do unexpectedly well from what had first appeared a meagre lode. It was something of a lottery, but one in which the odds favoured men of skill and intelligence.

There were several voices shouting offers, all undercutting each other till they reached the point where none would work for less. The captain took the lowest bid and the tributer signed the two-month agreement on behalf of himself and his five partners.

Tom liked the tributing system, seeing excitement in the element of chance and dignity in the way a man shared in the speculation. The tributer did not work for a fixed weekly wage. Like the owners, he gambled, and could win or lose according to his wits and his diligence. There was hardly a captain to be found anywhere who had not done his years as a tributer, and since it was Tom's ambition to rise to the rank of that man up there on the dais, he was far from content to continue as a tutman.

But tutwork was enough for William Tregunna. He had already taken a pitch that day; a simple contract, £7 per fathom to drive a tunnel through some barren ground. He did not care for the risks of tributing and had not the brains for it either. His money might be less this way, but at least he could be certain of it. Tom's elder brothers shared this view, often repeating that what did for Father would do for them as well. So the boy's work was chosen for him and he had no say in the matter.

Only once had he voiced his desire to make progress. He could clearly recall his mother's attempts to hush him up, and William's contorted features as they faced each other across the dirt floor of the cottage. His father's answer, angry and contemptuous, still echoed in his mind.

'Who ee think's goin' learn ee? I aren't no tributer. Faather to son, thass how 'tis taught. So waddee think you're goin' do? Long as you're livin' under my roof, you'll work 'longside o' me. We're your family. I didn' raise ee just to let ee go off 'n join up wi' some bugger else. An why should 'em want ee, any rate? Most men got sons o' their awn. Even if you was marrid 'n moved out of here, I'd 'spect ee to work wi' me, like I stayed wi' me awn faather 'n brothers till they was all dead. Thass what families do. Think you're goin' be better'n the rest of us? Well, you got 'nother think comin'!'

And with that final word had come a sickening swipe to the side of Tom's head. William was not habitually violent towards his family, and his health was not good either, but he could still deal the occasional dizzying blow to a son who enraged him, even though that son was six feet tall.

150

His fury, in truth, had little to do with family feeling. It was all about money, as Tom knew full well. The boy was a good strong back and a powerful set of muscles to swing a pick. He worked hard and fast and he seldom had need to sit down and recover his breath. Tom was an extra fathom or so of hewn rock, an extra few pounds on pay-day. He did more than his share of the labour – and received far less than his rightful portion of the money. That was why his father did not want to lose him.

It was William who bargained for the pitch and signed the contract, therefore it was William who collected the wages and doled them out. That was what they were waiting for now. As soon as all the bargains were concluded, everyone would be paid.

The rest of the day was a holiday and Tom's brothers were already debating the choice of beershop in which to spend their earnings. They were loudmouths, both of them, full of swagger and foolish opinions. While they bantered and grabbed at the bal-girls, the boy glumly watched his father join the queue at the office pay-window. A silent, reflective figure amid a throng of noisy talkers, Tom knew that he would be lucky to see a quarter of what was due to him. The rest would serve to keep William drunk till Wednesday. There were always many absent from work on the Monday following pay-day – 'mazed Monday', it was called – but only the worst, like William, would carry on the spree until mid-week.

Sure enough, his father handed him eleven shillings that day, though his proper share was nearly fifty.

'I made more'n that,' said the boy sullenly. 'Spose I needn' ask wass goin' happen to the rest of it.'

'You got lebm shullen fer yourself 'n thass 'nough. Waddee goin' do with it, anyway? Idn nothin' you need, is there? You avn got no wife nor cheeld to feed, an you

151

aren't courtin' neether. All I've done is took out some to give to your mother fer your keep.'

'Ess, an a bit fer the publican, too.'

'You can have a drop yourself, if you've a mind to. Might make ee more of a man 'n less of a moaner.'

'Aw, ess,' said Tom, 'you'd like that, wouldn' ee? But I aren't goin' end up like you. These two can please theirselves, but nobody's ever goin' find me lyin' in the street stinkin' o' three days' ale.'

'Ah, go to hell with ee, then. You d'sound like a Methodist, just bin saved 'n can't wait to spread the word. Come on,' he said to the older ones, 'let'n alone.'

The brothers nudged each other and chortled at Tom, then set off in William's wake. The boy scowled as he watched the three of them slouch off up the road. Saved? Yes, he meant to be saved all right, but only from William. Turning, he made his way over to the changing house to fetch his working clothes and his extra shirt.

In the small hours of Sunday morning, the cottage door burst open and William Tregunna stumbled inside, supported by his two sons. He was barely able to stand and they had half-carried him the last mile home. His eyelids drooped, his mouth hung slack and he could not hold his head up, but he kept up a ceaseless monologue of mumbling and cursing. The brothers were in somewhat better condition, but the smell of beer was heavy on their breath and clothing. Both wore witless grins and the larger of them was crooning to himself and spluttering with mirth.

The cottage was lit by a single candle fixed in an iron holder – a horizontal bar with a spike at the end which was driven into the cob wall. Mrs Tregunna always left it burning when her husband and sons had gone for their ale. Sometimes it helped them find their way back.

Startled from sleep, the rest of the family stirred, groaned, turned away or watched through slitted eyes, waiting for peace to settle again. Tonight the disturbance would not last long, for William and the lads were close to collapse, so there would be no ranting arguments, no clattering about or demands for food. Tom lifted his head to see his brothers haul William across the room and dump him clumsily down on the bed beside his wife. The muttering stopped and was quickly replaced by guttural snoring. Resignedly, Mrs Tregunna rolled over, clutching the baby against her and moving as far as she could from the great sodden bulk of her husband. He lay without a blanket, too drunk to feel the cold, and she did not trouble to cover him.

Tom laid his head down again and closed his eyes. For a few minutes there were thumps and scufflings while his brothers settled, then silence save for William's snoring. That was the end of sleep for Tom. He could not even doze now; he was wide awake and his mind was busy. Someone had snuffed the candle and he opened his eyes to total darkness. His thoughts roved back over the toil of the past two months, then returned to the mere eleven shillings he had gained for it. Fifty – he should have had at least fifty for his effort. But where had his money gone? Why, it was all around him – he could smell it in the air. It was vapour now, breathed out by his father and brothers, a cloying reek of beer.

He turned uneasily on his bed of furze, thinking now about Boskenna, about Esme's clean, sober family and their decent lives. Next spring, he had told her. Yes, he had meant to go in the spring when the weather was warmer. But he knew now that he could not wait that long, would not work another pitch with William or see himself robbed on another pay-day. Indeed, he intended to reclaim something from this one. There must, after all, be some money left. William was seldom spent out and begging credit before Tuesday.

Tom's heart began to thud at the prospect of going through his father's pockets, but he steeled himself with assurance that William could sleep through cannonfire and a marching brass band when stupefied by drink. Shivering, more with apprehension than cold, he huddled beneath his blanket, waiting for first light.

Hours later, when dawn relieved the darkness, he rose, pulled on his boots and buttoned his jacket, then crept over to where his parents lay. It took what seemed an age to cross those few feet of earthen floor, but when at last he knelt by the side of the bed he was rewarded by what he could only look upon as divine encouragement.

William lay on his back, his mouth wide open and his left arm trailing to the ground. His jacket had fallen open, exposing the inside breast pocket – from which there peeped the tip of a ten shilling note. Deftly, Tom extracted it, and then his gaze lit upon the rounded outlines of coins against the fabric of William's trouser pocket. Bolder now, the boy delved inside and withdrew a handful of half-crowns and florins. There were several shilling pieces too, some coppers and a threepenny bit.

For a second he hesitated, wondering whether to take it all. Then his resolve hardened, and his fist closed tightly on the money. It was only a fraction of what his father had taken from him over the years, and was destined for the beershop anyway. The family had always lived on 'tick' and this would make precious little difference.

Slowly he straightened up. He had no belongings to carry away from here. His other shirt and his working clothes were hidden at the manor house. He had only to go and collect them.

Still treading gingerly, he made for the door. But just as he lifted the latch he froze, transfixed by the grinning regard of his eldest brother. Head propped on one hand, the older lad surveyed him with amusement.

'Goin', are ee?' came the hoarse whisper. 'Clearin' out fer good?'

'Dunnee wake 'em, please,' entreated Tom.

'You wen't be able come back after this, boy. He'd as soon kill ee as look at ee.'

''Tis me awn money,' hissed Tom.

'Ess, but he wen't see it like that. He'd have mine too, if I wadde s'big 'n didn' buy'n a few mugs of ale.' The grin faded. 'Where ee goin' to?'

'Dunnaw,' muttered Tom untruthfully.

''Twen't be easy on your awn.'

For a moment Tom wavered, taking a last look round the cottage. Dreadful though it was, he had no other home. He wished he could say goodbye to his mother, but dared not take the risk. He would indeed be alone now, and it was strange that this brother – no friend to him, he had thought – should be the only person to see him go.

'No, I've thought 'bout that. Makes no difference, though. I can't stay.'

'Well, 'tis your life.' The other gave a careless sniff. But then he said: 'You're a dreamer, boy.' And with these words a wistful look came over his face, as if he remembered a time when he, too, had thought of a better life, as if, having lacked enough faith and courage himself, he envied Tom his dreams and his bid for escape. 'Still,' he added quietly, 'I wish ee the best o' luck. S'long, Tom.'

'Goodbye,' whispered Tom. Then he slipped out into the foggy morning.

Not until after Christmas did Esme learn of his leaving. Walking home from Porthgullow one bitter January

155

afternoon, she encountered his mother and could not refrain from asking after him.

'He've gone,' the woman said, wrapping her shawl more tightly round the infant she carried, as they stood in the freezing wind. 'Ran off after las' pay-day 'n we avn seen'n since. He wen't come back if he've got any sense. He took his faather's beer money, see. I dunnaw where he went or what he mean to do, but 'tis better for'n to go 'n I aren't sorry. He couldn' do no worse than stay here. Mind . . .' She smiled knowingly. '. . . I b'lieve you might have an idea where he's to?'

'No,' said Esme quickly. 'Why should I?'

Mrs Tregunna nodded, still with the sly smile. 'Thass all right, Miss. I wen't ask ee no more. I fancy we d'both want wass best for'n.' Her look became reflective. 'My Tom had quite a likin' for you, I b'lieve.'

'I don't know why he had to go away, then. I told him once that my father could probably give him an apprenticeship. Tom could have stayed with me if he'd really wanted to.'

'Ess, well, he was restless, 'tis true – always wanted to see the world. Tell ee this, though, 'twouldn' have bin s'easy for 'n to leave the bal 'n go work wi' your people even if he'd cared to. Might seem simple 'nough to you, but 'tidn so. See, his faather would never have gived he nor your family no peace, not while Tom was anywhere in reach, so dunnee go chafin' awver that. The boy done the best thing he could.'

And with that she went on her way. Esme gazed mournfully after her for a few minutes, then walked slowly on. A fine drizzle had begun to fall, shrouding the moors and the sea in grey.

Mid-winter, she thought. Dear Lord, what a time to leave home with next to no money and nowhere to go.

20

'Waddee goin' call her?' Alice Kittow gently pushed aside the blanket to inspect the ten-day-old baby in Jenny's arms. The child slept serenely on, undisturbed by the big red face of the fishwife beaming down at her.

'Eva,' said Jenny. 'We thought we should call our first daughter after the boat.'

'Ess, proper job,' enthused Alice. 'Nice t'have a girl this time. How old's the boy now?'

'He'll be two in April.'

Mrs Kittow seated herself on the hearthstool. Beside Jenny on the fireside settle, her son Michael was messily munching a slice of bread and treacle. It was February and a fire burned brightly in the grate. The mantel clock said ten to eleven and the women kept their voices low, for Luke was asleep upstairs, tired out by a night's fishing.

'I hear tell she out there's ready t'have her second,' said Alice, with a meaningful jerk of her head.

Jenny did not have to ask who was meant. Mrs Kittow loved to gossip and Susanna was one of her favourite topics. In this close-packed village, everyone knew everyone else's business and neighbours were constantly in and out of one another's houses, so Jenny never lacked for company or news.

''Tidn well with 'em, y'knaw. I d'offen see young Esme 'n she've tole me a thing or two. Sound to me like they d'live a cat 'n dog life. Serve 'em right 'n all. Do uh still try 'n speak to ee?'

'No, he gave up a long time ago.'

157

The infant began to whimper, but quickly went quiet when Jenny jigged her a little.

'Ess, I've seen ee go past'n s'if he wadden there.' Alice slapped her knees and chuckled. She had a streak of spite in her and a relish for feuding. Lacking a current conflict of her own, she could still find enjoyment in that of someone else.

Jenny said nothing and she wished Mrs Kittow would change the subject. She did not want to hear about the Rescorlas – any of them. They were nothing to do with her any more and she did not want to be reminded of them. In particular, she did not like to dwell upon the fact that Susanna's offspring had better food and clothes and toys than her own. It had been a hard winter and Jenny had to be grateful that her daughter was born strong and healthy – thankful just for life, without any trimmings.

'Did your husband catch anythin' much las' night?' asked Alice.

Jenny shook her head. 'He might as well have stayed home.'

'Ess, well, 'tis always poor this time o' year.'

And even at the best of times the rewards are small enough, Jenny thought. When the boat came in with a bumper catch there was sometimes money to spare for little treats, but more often the surplus was saved to see them through the lean periods, which were frequent. So many mornings when the nets were all but empty. And so many vigils kept through so many stormy nights, when Jenny could not sleep for fear of what might be happening to her husband out on the black, violent sea.

'Alice,' she sighed, 'does the time ever come when you stop feeling afraid when your man goes out? Do you ever stop thinking it might be the last time?'

'No, my dear,' said Mrs Kittow, grown solemn with understanding. 'Least, I never have.' Consolingly, she added: 'But there's this to be said fer it: you wen't have chance to get bored wid'n, nor he wi' you. You'll find more pleasure in your time together than they that d'live safe lives 'n get sick o' the sight of each other. Thass no small blessing, I tell ee straight.'

Richard's second child was born a week later. It was a boy and they named him Alan John. Although he was a quiet baby and seldom troublesome, Susanna showed no more enthusiasm for the care of her son than she had for the ebullient Katie, who was now two and a half years old. John Rescorla had expected no better from her, but what most disturbed him was not Susanna's apparent inability to mother the child, but Judith's eagerness.

She was twenty now and had never attracted a suitor. She was plain in face, almost matronly in her style of dress, and wore her hair in a neat, smooth roll that was far too severe for a young woman. Judith rarely caught a man's eye, and those who did attempt to speak to her were apt to find her unrewarding. She was too shy for banter, too innocent for wit, and her quiet 'yes' or 'no' answers made hard work of conversation.

In truth, Judith had never sought close acquaintances of any kind outside the family, for she had always been content with just her brother, sister and parents. And now, of course, there were Richard's children on whom to lavish affection. She could almost look upon them as her own – and who knew how many more there might be? Thanks to Susanna's shortcomings as a mother, Judith was allowed all the pleasure and satisfaction of caring for them, and assured of their love in return. It would be so much easier to remain at home, where she was safe and comfortable, than to enter the arena of pairing and courtship, where she felt she did not belong.

Sensing this, John feared that his elder daughter was

159

the kind of woman who might well become nothing more than a prop and a convenience for everyone else. Deprived of her own fulfilment, Judith would always be there, calm and reliable, to congratulate others on their successes, celebrate their good fortune or comfort them in their disasters. Such a life – a borrowed life or that of an onlooker – seemed less than she deserved, and he could not understand Judith's quiet acceptance of what appeared to him a most unsatisfactory state of affairs.

'Daughter,' he said one day, 'is there no young man who's taken your fancy? I know how you love children and you'll surely be wanting some of your own before long.'

She glanced at him, surprised and a little wary. 'There's no one, Father. I don't think I'm pleasing in that way. I know I'm plain and I've no clever conversation.'

'My dear girl, you're only as plain as you make yourself. Dress your hair in curls, Judith. Sew some pretty frocks – or ask Susanna to make them for you. She's a clever seamstress, I'll give her that, and I daresay she'll be flattered if you ask for her help.'

'I'm not a frilly sort, Father, as you well know, and my hair won't hold a curl, so I shan't waste time on it. Are you saying I should play the fraud and pretend to be something I'm not? That's how Susanna caught Richard, and you've called her false and devious for it.'

'So she is, so she is. Now don't you try to trip me up, miss. Let me tell you a sad truth, Judith: most young men are foolish creatures. However kind and faithful you may be, they won't take the trouble to find it out unless you first catch their notice and stir their curiosity.'

'It seems dishonest, all the same. Anyway, I never feel at ease in company and I don't long for outings or new friends. I'm quite all right as I am. Besides, I don't think Susanna can look after the children without my help.'

'While you're so willing to mother them, she'll never bother to try.'

'I don't mind. I enjoy caring for them.'

'They're not your own, Judith. Have you given no thought to your future? Perhaps you're happy now, girl, but in years to come, when I'm gone, you'll be a maiden aunt living with your brother and his wife, long after their children have grown and don't need you any more.'

Judith considered this for a moment.

'None of us can be sure that our young ones will stay with us,' she objected. 'It makes little difference whether we're aunts, uncles or parents to them. They grow up and we grow old. We can take no steps to ensure we're not left alone in the end. I know of more than one old widow whose children never visit her.'

Perceiving himself bested on this point, John spluttered a little. 'Well, yes, all right . . . Perhaps 'tis so – but I'll still think it a shame and a waste if you don't have a husband and a brood of your own. Be sensible, Judith. Find a good man to wed. 'Twould please me more than I can say.'

His daughter smiled weakly. 'I'll try to be more sociable,' she said reluctantly, 'if it will make you happy.'

But he knew by her tone and her wavering glance that she had no heart for it.

21

The next two years were to prove him right, for she grew, if anything, more spinsterish than ever, both in taste and habit. Prinking and flirtation had no place in her life. Her clothes filled less than half the space in her cupboard, so that the hangers made a hollow, clanking noise whenever the door was opened, and she still favoured dark blues, bottle-greens and browns, always with the minimum of trimming. Judith was seldom seen without an apron and, indeed, rarely engaged in any activity that did not require one. The children were all the amusement she wanted, and there was no need to dress up for them.

A new addition to her wardrobe was a very rare thing. One morning in June of 1865, however, John presented her with a length of pale yellow cotton and said:

"Tis the midsummer bonfire at Carn Clewse next week. You'll need a new frock, maid. I saw this in Porthgullow yesterday and I think you'll look well in it. Susanna says she'll make it up for you, so you'd best go into the parlour to be measured.'

Judith, who had just finished clearing up the breakfast dishes, gazed in astonishment at the fabric as he laid it on the kitchen table.

'But I'm not going to the bonfire.'

'What?' Her father's eyes widened with feigned surprise. 'Esme told me you were looking forward to it.'

'I said 'twas a nice custom, Father. I didn't say I wanted to go.'

'Oh – she mistook your meaning, I suppose.'

'I doubt it,' said Judith dryly.

John cleared his throat. 'Well, I've bought the material now. You won't let it go to waste, will you?'

'I'm sure 'twould look lovely on Esme,' suggested Judith.

''Tis for you,' said John firmly. 'Your sister has plenty of pretty things to wear. I went to Porthgullow purposely to fetch this. Don't you like it, Judith?'

'Yes, 'tis beautiful, but. . .'

'Then you'll wear it, won't you? I'd like you to go to the bonfire, maid. The outing will do you good. Anyway, I don't care to let Esme walk over the moors to Carn Clewse on her own at night. Either you both go together or I'll have to keep her home.'

Judith sighed. 'All right – I see I've been outfoxed.'

He reached out and stroked her cheek. ''Tis a thing to be enjoyed, Judith, not some terrible ordeal. Watch your sister, my love. Learn from her, and try to make one or two friends.'

She nodded wearily. Try to catch a husband – that was what he meant. As she picked up the soft yellow fabric and headed towards the parlour, Judith once more found herself wishing she was already forty and beyond these futile expeditions.

Susanna finished the dress on midsummer morning. She had made an excellent job of it. The skirt fell in three layers, with an edging of *broderie anglaise* to each one. The bodice was quite plain except for a small lace, but the sleeves were attractively puffed and bore a trimming of lace at the cuffs.

Alone in her room, Judith tried it on for a second time that afternoon. She had borrowed Susanna's cheval mirror and she studied her reflection with an anxious frown, thinking, as always, that the frock was too fussy for her.

For a while she stood smoothing the folds of the skirt. Then, hesitantly, she unpinned the tidily wound hair and tried twisting it up into a style more fashionable. The grey eyes travelled doubtfully over the image in the glass and finally she shook her head, releasing the thick ropes of hair. They merged once more into a shining curtain as they fell.

No, she would not cut a fringe, nor would she resort to curling tongs. The yellow frock made her feel quite clownish enough. Her father had paid more than seven shillings for the fabric and she would wear it just to please him, but she certainly would not submit to anything more. Bows and flounces and ringlets were for pretty women, just as the love of men was for pretty women – whether they deserved it or not.

Judith could not imagine herself as a wife. She had long believed herself destined to be an old maid, as if by divine decree. Marriage, so natural and inevitable for others, was a state not meant for her and the prospect of spinsterhood did not greatly distress her. If her father would only come to terms with it in the same way, she would be very thankful.

Carn Clewse was little more than a mile from Boskenna. The hill rose sharply from a rolling stretch of moorland and wore a crown of granite blocks, fractured and jointed by the weather. Midsummer celebrations were held throughout the county each year, and the Carn Clewse fire was always one of the biggest.

Dusk was falling by the time Judith and Esme arrived, and the luminous disk of a full moon was edging up from behind the dark boulders of the summit. It was well risen in a clear night sky when the torch was put to the bonfire. As the flames took hold, other pinpoints of light began to appear on hilltops or in hollows across the moor, all part of a chain of beacons extending from Land's End to the Tamar.

Most of those assembled round the fire were miners and farm workers. Many had brought small children with them, carrying the infants on their shoulders up the rugged path from the foot of the carn. To satisfy their stomachs there were sausages, several sacks of potatoes for baking, rough cider and many gallons of home-made ale, all donated by the local squire. For their entertainment, someone with a violin, together with drum and flute players, had come to provide the music appropriate to the circling dances demanded by long tradition.

Esme and Judith seated themselves among the rocks and watched the blaze climb to a towering height. Among the gathering they spotted a few familiar faces, but most were strangers or people known only by sight. Had she been alone, Esme would have found this no hindrance. At seventeen, she was very much at ease with young men and there were plenty here to claim her attention. If left to her own devices, she would quickly have fallen into conversation with a lad or two.

Her aim that evening, however, was to find someone for her older sister. Chattering brightly, she made several attempts to kindle a friendship between Judith and some passing male. Thinking herself very cunning, she would catch a man's eye, strike up a conversation with him, then try to hand it over to her sister. The ploy, however, was all too obvious and the men quickly made off.

At length, tired of these efforts to 'help' her, Judith finally put a stop to it.

'Esme, please, I'm sure you mean well, but I've had enough of this. I know that you and Father put your heads together in order to get me here, and 'tis perfectly clear what you're trying to do, but I don't like it.'

The younger one opened her mouth to protest, but perceived that her sister would take no more humbug.

'I'm sorry. We only thought you might meet someone nice.'

'Yes, yes, I know all about it. Just go and enjoy yourself,' instructed Judith. 'Join in the dancing and let me be.'

'I won't leave you sitting here by yourself.'

'I'll come to no harm, believe me.'

'Why don't you like to dance?'

'It makes me feel foolish, that's all.'

Esme relapsed into a glum silence and they sat for some time just watching the ring of people skipping clockwise round the fire. On the far side of it, where the wood was burned right through, two small boys could be seen hooking baked potatoes out of the embers with long sticks.

'Shall we have a mug of cider?' suggested Judith, feeling she had spoilt her sister's evening.

'Hmm,' shrugged Esme, 'I suppose we may as well.'

'I'll fetch it. I won't be long.'

While Judith was gone, the dancing stopped for a time and some of the young women began to throw garlands into the flames. Esme looked on despondently as she waited for her sister to return. These floral offerings were a regular feature of the annual ritual. One after another, she saw the girls step forward to fling circlets of flowers onto the fire – but she did not notice the big fair-haired man who approached a young lady at the edge of the crowd and offered her sixpence to sell her garland.

A few moments later, however, the little hoop of twisted creeper interlaced with betony, rue and wild flowers, was dangled before Esme's eyes. She looked up in surprise, to see a tall, well-built man grinning down at her.

'Most of the other girls brought one of these,' he said. 'You should have one, too.'

'Why thank you, sir.' Hesitantly, she took it. 'You're very kind.'

The man sat down beside her. Now that the firelight shone full upon his face, she recognized him.

'Ah – you're the gentleman I sometimes see in church.'

'Quite right, I'm Roger Carwarthen. You'll know the Halveor Inn, I expect?'

'Of course – I pass it whenever I go to Porthgullow.'

'Well, I'm the landlord since my father died last year. And you are John Rescorla's daughter – Esme.'

'How do you know my name?'

'Oh, a publican hears all about everyone,' said Roger lightly.

His manner was carefully casual. It certainly did not betray the fact that he had been watching Esme all evening. Indeed, he had admired her each Sunday for several months past, attending morning service purely in hopes of seeing her, and respectfully tipping his hat if given the chance to wish her good day.

It was Esme's hair which had first caught Roger's notice. Whenever he found himself sitting behind her in church, he would close his ears to the sermon and gaze fondly at the russet cascade that poured from beneath her hat and streamed in wavy tendrils down her back. He thought her freckles quite beguiling and his interest in this pert little female increased each time he set eyes on her. Until now, however, he had found no excuse to speak with her at any length.

'I've never met an innkeeper before. The men of my family rarely set foot inside a public house. Father enjoys his pipe of tobacco and a tot of brandy now and then, but he stays by his own hearth.'

'Oh, I've more to offer than just food and drink. The

167

Halveor Inn has the best skittle alley for miles around,' boasted Roger. 'There are five rooms to let, and I keep a fine hearse for hire, with two black horses to pull it. Some of my customers are men of means.'

'The live ones or the dead?'

'Both,' he said cheerfully. 'The Friendly Society dinners are always held at Halveor, you know, and the Reverend Sobey chairs the vestry meetings there too.'

Roger was anxious to impress her and he was not subtle about it. He had a plain but pleasant face, and a habit of tugging his earlobe or scratching his head at intervals while he spoke, as if everything in life was remarkable or something of a puzzle to him.

Esme regarded him with amusement. 'You're clearly a prosperous man, sir. I'd guess that most publicans are.'

'True, but mine's an establishment of the best sort. 'Tis no shoddy beershop or kiddleywink. I've a full licence to sell spirits, and the bill of fare is second to none.'

'My, my,' murmured Esme, smiling broadly. She glanced up as her sister appeared, bearing two cups of cider. 'This is Mr Carwarthen, Judith,' she said.

The man stood up and offered a civil greeting. Judith passed a mug to Esme, then shyly extended a hand to him. Roger clasped it warmly.

'You're Esme's only sister, aren't you?'

Tongue-tied, she simply nodded.

Roger relinquished the patch of dry grass where he had been sitting, so that Judith might have the more comfortable place. He seated himself between the two girls and continued listing the merits of the Halveor Inn. Although his interest clearly centred on the younger sister, about whom he wanted to know a great deal, he was careful to ask a few polite questions of Judith, so that she would not feel ignored. But his efforts to include her in the conversation brought little response. Shyness robbed her of words and coherent thought, and she could not conquer the reflex that made her lower her head, turning her face half away as she mumbled a reply. Esme, never intimidated by anyone, wondered sadly why Judith always shrank into this mouselike state when confronted by a strange man.

'Aren't you going to offer up your garland?' Roger asked. 'They'll be jumping the bonfire soon.'

'Seems a pity,' Esme said. 'I'd rather keep it.'

'Ah, but 'tis the custom and you must follow it.'

'Oh, all right.' She laughed, feeling slightly silly, then stood up and went to the fire and tossed the floral ring into the heart of it.

'Be sure to take home some ashes,' Roger said, as he came to stand beside her. 'They're proof against the evil eye.'

'Oh, I don't believe in such nonsense.'

Back in the shadows, Judith sat watching them. She saw her sister spread her hands in some expansive gesture, saw the big man throw back his head and laugh, then dodge away when Esme aimed a playful punch at him. They liked each other very much, Judith could plainly see that, and she felt she was a hindrance to their newborn friendship.

The last blackened spars of wood suddenly collapsed into a low heap, throwing up a fountain of sparks against the night sky. There came a billow of smoke and the spicy smell of it clung to the hair and clothing of those who stood close by. As it cleared, a young couple took a flying leap over the dying fire.

'You may not believe in witchcraft,' Roger said, 'but there are many here tonight who do. Will you jump the fire with me, just for good luck?'

Dubiously, Esme wrinkled her nose and was about to decline.

169

'You're not afraid, are you?'

The girl was indignant. 'We'll jump it six times over, if you like.'

Roger triumphantly grasped her by the hand and they paced back a few yards, then bounded forward and launched themselves over the bonfire.

'Now,' he said, as they landed on the other side, 'no one can wish harm upon us for a full year from this night. Not that anyone could desire misfortune for you,' he added softly.

'Oh, I know of one or two who don't love me.'

'Well, here's a man who admires you and wants to take you for a ride in his gig next Sunday.' Roger squeezed her hand and gazed hopefully down at her. 'Would you like that, Esme?'

A fleeting look of surprise crossed her face, but was soon followed by a smile of eager pleasure. 'Very much, Roger. Yes, I'd like that very much indeed.'

'You'll need to ask your father, I daresay?'

'I don't think he'll say no.'

An afterthought occurred to him and he glanced back to where Judith sat. 'I'll be pleased to take your sister along too, if she cares to come.'

It was a gesture kindly meant, but prompted by a feeling of obligation. He tried to sound hearty, but Esme could hear the reluctance in his voice.

'I'll tell her,' she said, though she knew quite well that Judith would not accept.

'And, of course, I'll escort you both back to your door tonight,' said Roger gallantly.

'Perhaps 'tis time to be leaving,' she agreed. ''Tis growing cold now the fire's gone down, and I think Judith will be glad to go home.'

It was past one o'clock when they set off across the moonlit moor, and almost a quarter to two when Roger left them at the gate of Boskenna. He bid them goodnight and went off up the lane, whistling merrily. Esme had promised to see him again, and so he was a happy man.

Despite the late hour, a light could be seen through the parlour window.

'Father's waiting up for us,' said Esme. 'I knew he would. He'll want to hear all about it, I suppose. Truth be told, I'd rather save it for the morning.'

'That's all right, you go to bed, for I know you're tired. After all, 'tis me he's really waiting for, isn't it?'

'Yes,' muttered Esme as they went up the path, 'and he's in for another disappointment.'

171

22

Judith's father never pressed her to attend another social gathering after that night, nor did he ever again bedevil her with talk of marriage. Glumly resigning himself to the fact that she was unlikely to attract a husband – and did not want one anyway – he finally left her in peace.

But the bonfire party had not been a failure, for Esme had found her future husband that evening. Always afraid that Tom Tregunna might return, John was delighted to see her develop a fondness for someone else – and especially a man like Carwarthen. Most people warmed to Roger within minutes of meeting him and were ready to call him a close friend within the hour, and Rescorla was no exception.

With John's hearty encouragement, the first Sunday gig ride was followed by regular visits and outings, which became ever more lengthy and frequent. The publican was humorous and tolerant, an entertaining guest and a generous host, successful in his trade and able to provide in ample measure for a wife and children. He would make a very agreeable son-in-law and an excellent match in every way for Esme. At twenty-six, Carwarthen was nine years her senior – which the shipwright deemed to be no bad thing. She had always been impulsive and peppery, so Roger's extra years and even temperament would make a healthy counterbalance. It was obvious that he adored her, and both men felt she was good material for an innkeeper's wife.

Esme had guessed almost from the start that Roger would ask her to marry him. He made it endearingly obvious by the way he gazed at her and hung upon her every word. It was a look that said, 'You're my choice, you're the one, there's nobody else like you.'

He's a good, kind man, she thought to herself. He makes me laugh and I feel at home with him, as if we'd known each other always. Esme Carwarthen. Yes, it sounds right, it already sounds like my name. 'Tis three years now since Tom went away. Such a long time and never any word of him, no news, good or ill. I don't suppose I'll ever see him again. Calf-love, Father called it, and perhaps it was. Anyway, Tom was right when he said I would want a settled life. So I do, and there's no one more steady than Roger. It won't be dull, though, not at Halveor. All in all, I don't think I could wish for more.

Carwarthen proposed to her on Christmas Eve that same year. She accepted him gladly, and John Rescorla readily gave his consent. Gathered round the Christmas tree at Boskenna, the family drank a toast to the young couple, celebrating their engagement with a bottle of fine old port Roger had brought specially for the occasion.

'Look at Father,' Richard whispered to Esme, while the glasses were being filled a second time. 'He's like a dog with two tails.'

John's face was glowing in the candlelight, as he chuckled and joked with his future son-in-law, relieved to know that one of his children, at least, was set for a happy life.

Esme winked at her brother, reflecting with amusement that Father was quite content to see her marry a man who sold ale, even though he had no time for those who drank too much of it.

The wedding date was set for June of 1866, just a month after Esme's eighteenth birthday. On the day before the ceremony, she took a mid-day meal down to her father and brother at the yard, and found John working alone, painting the waterline on a newly completed vessel. He put down his brush when he saw his daughter enter the workshop, then rubbed his hands on the seat of his trousers.

'What you have brought me, maid?'

'There's meat and potato pie, saffron cake, some cheese and half a barley loaf.'

She handed the package to her father as he seated himself on a bale of hemp. John glanced at her from under his brows as he unwrapped the napkin and picked up the chunk of cold pie.

'Sit down a while, Esme, there on the planks.'

The girl perched herself on a stack of timber. She had put her hair up and was wearing a topaz brooch – a birthday present from Roger – on the bodice of her fawn check dress.

'Well, the day's nearly here,' he said. 'Your new life won't be a soft one, but I think it'll suit you. It's not every woman who can fill the shoes of an innkeeper's wife, but you'll make a good landlady, girl, you're well fitted for it. My Esme wasn't made for a quiet existence, and 'tis certain you'll never be lonely or bored at Halveor.' He laid a hand on her cheek and regarded her intently. 'I'm very pleased about this marriage, maid. Roger's the sort of man I always wanted for you. Now, you've no regrets or doubts, have you?'

He had no need to mention Tom Tregunna's name. Father and daughter understood each other well enough on that score.

'I have no doubts about Roger, Father. I'll be content with him.'

'That's my girl. I'll miss you, Esme. I know the inn's not far, but the house won't seem the same without you.'

A sly grin spread across his face. 'Mind you, Susanna won't be sorry when you're gone. She's been counting the days.'

The following afternoon, Roger carried his red-haired wife over the threshold and into her new domain. Dressed all in white, she was now Mrs Carwarthen, landlady, and this would be her home for the rest of her life. The singing and cheering that surrounded the couple that day would carry on down the years, through countless luncheon parties and busy evenings. This house would always be full of people, and festivities like these, celebrations for others, would use up her time as she passed from youth into middle age and onwards.

The inn stood one and a quarter miles outside Porth-gullow, and just over two miles from Boskenna. Whenever John, Richard or Judith made an excursion into the town, they had to pass Halveor on the way and they seldom missed the opportunity to visit Esme. Although less than half an hour's walk from the inn, the town was hidden by the rolling of the landscape, so a guest who arrived at Halveor in the dark might wake next morning and think himself in the middle of nowhere. The coastal road made a broad curve at this point, and the inn stood at the centre of this arc with its back to the sea. Behind it, the land sloped gradually away for half a mile to the edge of a steep line of cliffs, and the Carwarthens' bedroom at the rear looked out upon a lonely sweep of rough green country, with the Atlantic beyond. No sign of cultivation, no other dwelling marked the land around Halveor. It sat looking lost and remote in its windy location between the ocean and the upland spine of the county.

The inn had the same stolid appearance as Boskenna, but was larger and built in an L-shape, with an archway at the junction of the two wings. The material was a dark, rough granite that came from the moors behind. Great blocks of it littered the hills, balanced in weathered stacks on their summits or lying half-hidden in fern on the lower slopes. Five generations had come and gone since the Carwarthens built Halveor, and no one of any other name had ever been landlord there. The sign above the front door was an oak board with the words 'Halveor Inn' burnt into the wood at the top, and a painted illustration of a moorland quoit below. A tariff, in Roger's own careful script, was displayed in a downstairs window. A large coach-house at the side gave space enough for the gig, the wagonette brake, and the hearse Roger kept for hire. With a brewhouse, stabling for seven horses, capacious cellars and a very large kitchen, it was a prosperous concern with a reputation for good food, strong home-brew and clean accommodation.

Esme felt immediately at home and she loved the smell of ale, spirits and aromatic pipesmoke that seemed to permeate the very wood. There was a small taproom at the back of the inn, with bench seating around the walls, and here the quieter patrons, mostly old men, would gather to drink their beer. The majority of Roger's customers, however, preferred what was known as the pewter room. His family had been collecting items of pewter for over a hundred years, and the best of it was displayed in the large rectangular room with the slate floor and low ceiling beams. Oak panelling and shelving had been specially fitted the length of one wall in order to set off the sheen of the pewter, all of which was lovingly polished every month. This task seldom took Esme less than a day to complete, for there were candlesticks, beakers and tankards, wine measures and flagons, chalices, porringers, basins and salt cellars in all shapes and sizes. Like every landlady before her, she thought the exercise well worthwhile, for the final effect was impressive. The pewter room offered only hard seating, yet there reigned an atmosphere of comfort and pleasure amid the twinkle of glass, the scent of cooking and the warm colours of rum, brandy and shrub.

The new Mrs Carwarthen was proud to be mistress of her own kitchen, especially as she now had charge of two young maids, Bridget and Dinah, who lived above the taproom. Roger also employed a hefty, sombre person named Ewan, who worked as ostler and cellarman and was sometimes called in to draw ale on busy nights. No one, however, could be said to have charge of Ewan. He always knew what had to be done, and he did it without being told.

Cherished by her husband, Esme soon found herself a favourite with the customers as well. She was pleased that the men admired her. She enjoyed their cheek and their compliments, often replying with some of her own. Sure of her affection and noting that trade had improved since Esme's arrival, Roger was rarely moved to object. He was a popular man himself, and more astute than his affable manner might at first suggest. Esme appreciated that, just as she admired his strength when he lifted heavy casks or ejected some ruffian from the premises by the seat of his trousers and the scruff of his neck.

Of those who frequented the inn, about a third were miners. Roger could have attracted more of them, had he been prepared to offer credit, as so many landlords did. In view of this insistence on immediate payment, and the fact that the beershops were cheaper, it was something of a tribute to Halveor that the tinners came at all. Esme, however, having seen Tom Tregunna's home, thought it less than surprising that some would pay a little extra to spend a few hours in pleasant surroundings.

In truth, it was just as well that the Carwarthens did

177

not rely too heavily on the mining population, for an exodus was taking place throughout the county at that time, a wave of emigration which had long been mounting and was now becoming a flood. Those who were venturesome enough, quick-witted and sufficiently provident to save a few pounds, could book passage for America, Chile or Australia, South Africa or British Columbia. Those who would not accept for themselves or their families the kind of life the Tregunnas led, those so poor they had nothing to lose, could choose from the four corners of the earth and strike out hopefully, taking little more than the clothes they wore, some bedding, a few pots and pans. Thousands had already gone and tens of thousands more would follow.

But as long as the travellers came to lodge, as long as the old men sat in the taproom with their ale, as long as pipes were smoked and stomachs patted after a good dinner, Halveor would continue to thrive. Even the nearby parish church was an asset to Roger's trade. He could always expect half the congregation, the bellringers and the vicar himself at the inn, before or after service.

Within a month or two, Esme came to know the ways and the characters of Roger's regulars and how best to deal with each one. There were those with whom she could safely banter and those of whom to beware. There were some to be turned away because they invariably caused trouble, and some who would always complain of short change or short measure, while others were so careless with their hard-earned money that it might as well have been a pocketful of seashells. They sang and they swore and they squabbled, they boasted or grumbled till late at night, holding forth with equal fervour on subjects of which they might know a great deal or nothing at all. As she bustled back and forth, filling plates and glasses, Esme often reflected that nowhere but a public house could a body hear so much nonsense so loudly and so earnestly voiced.

For resident guests or large parties, the inn possessed a sizeable dining room, which lay to the left of the front entrance. The Carwarthens, however, always ate in the kitchen, often at odd hours of the day or night, and their only private quarters were a small parlour and their bedroom.

Roger had never been more proud and joyful. Esme's appetite, whether for food or love, gossip or entertainment, was unashamedly large, and Carwarthen was ever thankful for his choice of wife. She had no need to simper and flutter for him, to rely upon wiles or lovely dresses. He thought her more alluring by far when up to her elbows in flour, when boning a joint or issuing orders to the scurrying kitchenmaids as thirty guests sat down to dinner. Whenever he found her in the brewhouse, bending over a steaming copper, he would slap the rounded haunches, cuddle her and tell himself that he was blessed. Whether arguing with Ewan among the barrels in the cellar, disputing with a gentleman over his bill or furtively buying game from a poacher at the back door, she was a constant enchantment to her husband.

Both looked forward with eagerness to the arrival of offspring, and it was always in the mornings, when Esme was mellow with sleep, that Roger wanted her most. There was no reluctance, no discord between the Carwarthens. Before long, they assured themselves, there would certainly be a child.

Esme could hardly be other than happy with the great congenial man she had married. She lacked neither love nor good living, and she knew he would be a perfect father when the time came. She was not unduly disturbed to see their first anniversary go by without any sign of a pregnancy, and she often dwelt fondly on the prospect of motherhood and all its rewards.

179

23

Susanna would not have agreed that there was any pleasure to be found in the raising of children. Apart from making their clothes and giving a few elementary lessons, she had very little to do with her own, and even this was a trial to her. She had found the girl, in particular, wilfully difficult.

'I don't want to wear it,' fumed Katie one morning. ''Tis a horrid colour, and 'tis too tight.'

'You most certainly shall wear it. I've spent three days making this frock for you.'

Susanna impatiently turned her daughter round, undid and then retied the sash in a larger bow. The ends were fringed with brown chenille, as were the hem and shawl collar. Katie looked down at the frock in disgust. It was tangerine and she felt swaddled by the close-fitting sleeves and bodice.

'There,' said Susanna. She spun the child round to face her again and nodded with satisfaction. 'What an improvement! For once you look quite presentable.'

She had brushed Katie's hair straight back off her face and fastened it with a large circular comb. The little girl stared reproachfully at her mother with eyes as dark and shiny as the new button-boots she wore. Richard's eyes. Oh yes, she was very much Richard's daughter. There was nothing of Susanna in her. The boy was the same; quieter, less defiant than Katie, but still another extension of the father. The girl was now nearly seven years old and Alan was four. There was no discernible mixture in either one, no evidence of Susanna's blood or temperament.

They were both Rescorlas, through and through, and therefore she knew they did not like her.

'You may go and play now – but stay indoors. You're not to soil that dress.'

'But what can I do?'

'You've three lovely dolls, haven't you? And a splendid dolls' house.'

'Yes, Mama.' The words were heavy with resignation.

'Very well. Off you go, then.'

Katie paused on her way upstairs, as the whirr and clack of her mother's sewing machine began once more. She scowled. Mama made clothes because it amused her to do so, because she loved colours and fabrics, braids and buttons. It was not for Katie's pleasure that Mama would spend a whole morning fiddling and stitching tiny tucks to ensure that a ribbon or a fold might hang just-so. Mama was quite well aware that Katie did not like fine clothes which allowed no jumping or climbing, no rough and tumble. Susanna did not know how to provide amusement for her, but she did not approve the forms of recreation the child chose for herself. She was always complaining that her daughter was 'not a little lady', that she was 'just like her Aunt Esme'.

Katie wished Judith were her mama.

The child stayed upstairs till past two o'clock. The dolls bored her, so she soon abandoned them and sat on her bed to flip listlessly through her picture books. Mama would call her down at three for the alphabet lesson, and after that she would spend an hour learning the piano or simple embroidery. The little girl gave a martyred sigh. Aunt Judith had taken Alan to Porthgullow for the day. She would have taken Katie too, but mama had kept her at home because of this beastly frock.

Tossing the books aside, she slid off her bed and went to the window. The day was golden with late August sunshine and she wanted very much to go out. Her gaze roved across the kitchen garden and came to rest on the apple tree.

It stood in the far corner, where the blackbery bush spilled its runners over the hedge. And there, on one of the middle branches, was a large, rusty-yellow apple. Katie's attention fixed eagerly upon it. There were many other apples among the branches – indeed, there were probably windfalls on the ground below, more fruit than she could eat in a week. But this, of course, was not the point. Katie was not even hungry, but the size and location of that apple offered something of a challenge. It was the biggest one on the tree and it hung at the end of a long, sturdy branch, just a little higher than she had ever climbed before.

The child hesitated for less than a minute, then she slipped out onto the landing and crept downstairs.

Hannah, scouring out a pie dish with a handful of growder, barely paused to notice when Katie scuttled past her and out through the back door. It was not until fifteen minutes later that a loud scream from the garden made her drop what she was doing and rush outside.

Up in the far corner, a bright orange bundle was struggling among the brambles. It whimpered and sobbed as Hannah hastened towards it. Several minutes were spent in gingerly freeing Katie from the tangle of thorns. She was a sorry spectacle, her hands and face badly scratched, her white stockings torn to shreds. The frock was a ruin, streaked with greenish stains from the bark, snagged in a thousand places. The fabric had ripped beneath each arm as the child hung for a few seconds from the branch before losing her grip and plunging into the brambles below. She had very nearly reached the apple, but those shiny boots with their slippery soles were never intended for climbing.

Richard arrived home that evening to find Susanna in a cold fury and his tearful daughter smeared with ointment. No bones were broken and the scratches were not deep, but they were certainly smarting. A slap and a severe scolding from Mama had completed the child's misery.

Richard picked up his daughter and cuddled her until she stopped crying. Later, he took her down to the beach to search for shells.

He sat on the sand for a while and watched her wandering back and forth along the tideline, stooping here and there to pick up a tiny ribbed cowrie, or a tellin with a lining of mauve, pink or gold. He smiled to see her inspecting them, discarding inferior specimens and hoarding good ones in the pocket of her pinafore. His Katie. Yes, he had two lovely children, and they were his consolation.

After a time, the girl stopped by the water's edge and stood for several minutes, looking out to sea. Richard rose to his feet and ambled down the beach to stand beside her. He picked up a flat stone and passed it to his daughter.

'Here, try and skim it. Let's see how many times you can make it bounce.'

She flicked the stone, low and level, over the water. It touched three times, then sank.

'Very good.' He found another. 'Watch, I'll teach you how to make it fly further.'

The child shook her head, then turned a grave face to him.

'Mama was very angry about the frock.'

'Yes, I know. She spent a long time making it.'

'But she didn't care that I hurt myself.'

Richard said nothing, but he silently ruffled the child's hair.

'It serves her right,' Susanna had snapped. 'She's a hoyden and she brought it on herself.'

Richard would not forget that.

Katie pulled the handful of shells from her pocket and looked at them moodily. She had lost interest already and so, one by one, she flipped them back into the sea.

She, too, would remember Mama's harshness.

Richard and Susanna's third child was born in March of 1868. He was the last of their offspring, for although his father was only twenty-nine years old, his mother was now almost thirty-eight. The difference in their ages, not readily apparent ten years before, was now becoming much more obvious, and no one thought it likely that Susanna would conceive again.

The baby was christened Peter and it was soon noticed – with astonishment – that his mother seemed fond of him. His eyes were blue, like hers. The downy baby hair was light brown at birth and darkened only slightly as he grew. To everyone's surprise, she paid him considerable attention, worrying over his little ailments, remarking each new achievement when he began to speak and stagger about, and showing unusual tolerance when he screamed or wet himself or spat out his food.

He was, without question, a beautiful child. His features were very similar to those of his mother, and Richard saw in this the only explanation for Susanna's attachment to the boy. Unlike the other two, he was recognizably part of her, and therefore a natural favourite. Because of this, Richard watched his younger son's development with deep suspicion, ready to intervene if Peter showed signs of becoming spoilt.

But, as time went on, he proved different from his brother and sister in only two respects – firstly, his appearance, and secondly, the fact that he seemed equally fond of both parents. It was, said Judith, a mercy that at least one of the children had not chosen sides – and nice to know that Susanna was capable of some maternal affection after all. Perhaps, she added hopefully, her sister-in-law would sweeten with age.

185

24

'Not too much sugar, an mind what you're doin' wi' they eggs!'

'How many do I put in?'

'Three's enough.'

Katie took a large brown egg and whacked it soundly against the rim of the mixing bowl. It was her tenth birthday and Hannah had said she could make her own cake. The egg smashed and its contents plopped into the mixture, taking a dozen fragments of shell at the same time.

'Aw, my dear life!' Hannah picked out the bits with a teaspoon. 'Look, maid – like this.' Expertly, she cracked the two remaining eggs into the bowl. 'Now, give'n a good stir 'n dunnee let'n curdle.'

The child took up her wooden spoon, grasping the handle halfway down, and began vigorously ploughing it round and round. Somehow, a streak of butter had found its way into her hair, and the floor round her feet was sprinkled with spilt sugar. Across the table, Alan sat watching and furtively snatching the odd handful of currants from the jar. When his sister began adding flour, he craned his neck to peer into the bowl, then wrinkled his nose in contempt.

'Look's like a pig's breakfast.'

'You needn't have any, then. You needn't come to my party at all.'

'Don't squabble,' warned Judith, who was making a batch of conference tarts for the birthday tea. 'And tie your hair back, Katie, or you'll have to have it washed

186

again. Your mama won't want you looking a fright this
afternoon.'

'Hmph, why does she have to be there anyway? She'll
spoil it.'

'That's no way to speak of your mother.'

'Well, she doesn't like me, does she? I'm always being
told off.'

'You don't understand each other, that's all,' said her
aunt awkwardly. 'Susanna doesn't think 'tis nice to romp
the way you do. I don't suppose she was ever allowed to
– or perhaps she wasn't able to after she hurt her back.'

'She doesn't like him, either,' persisted Katie, waving
her spoon towards Alan. "Tis because we take after
father and not her.'

'Nonsense,' Judith said, but her tone carried no
conviction.

'Childern dawn't miss much,' observed Hannah, mouth
pursed with satisfaction. "Tis only Peter she d'care 'bout;
she can't leave he 'lone fer s'much as a minnut.'

Judith experienced a tremor of sympathy for her sister-
in-law. 'It seems, then, that whatever she does is sure to
be the wrong thing.'

"Tidn right to coddle one'n neglect th'other two,' said
Hannah firmly. "Twoud've bin a bad job fer 'em if they
hadn' had you. It d'make me spit, 'specially when I think
'bout poor Esme, who've bin waitin' all these years for a
cheeld.' From the corner of her eye she spotted Alan's
hand edging once more towards the currants. She aimed
a slap at it and the hand retreated swiftly. 'Leave 'em be
or there wen't be none fer the cake. Come on, maid,' she
said to Katie, 'dunnee dawdle so. 'Tis lebm o'clock 'n
th'oven's ready.'

The tea party started at half past three. Katie had invited
a few children from Porthgullow and several more from

the cove. Esme came too, bringing a box of fudge and a book of puzzles for her niece. Large quantities of cake, biscuits and fruit pudding were consumed, and Judith then took them all into the garden to play blind man's buff, since there was no room indoors.

'Katie will be pretty when she grows up,' Esme remarked, starting to clear away the wreckage of the birthday spread. 'Her features are good and she has lovely teeth.'

Susanna was sitting in the window seat, where the two-year-old Peter stood with his nose pressed to the glass, watching the older children run about. Mama would not let him go outside with them. She said they were too rough.

'Pretty?' Susanna sounded amused. 'I hardly think so. She's not at all dainty – far too boisterous. I can't even keep her neat and clean. Her hair is always tangled and her nails are never free of dirt.'

'She's only a child yet. Just wait a few years and you'll see.'

'It's my opinion that ladylike behaviour should begin at an early age.'

'Oh? Well I don't believe in raising children prim and proper. 'Tisn't natural, is it?'

'Indeed? And what would you know about it? Since you've none of your own, you're in no position to instruct me.'

Esme's mouth went dry and a tremor of her hand threatened to tip the stack of plates and cups she held. 'Then take a lesson from Judith,' she said sharply. 'She's more of a mother than you'll ever be.'

Susanna was already tired of attacks upon her performance as a parent. Criticism from Esme, in particular, was more than she could tolerate. She took Peter onto her lap and arranged him as if posing for a photograph. The boy

188

wriggled, but she held him firmly, like a large doll on display.

'Esme,' she said gravely, 'I think I hear jealousy talking. It's not my fault that you've been disappointed, so don't vent your feelings on me. We're all very sorry for you, of course. Your father was saying just the other day how concerned he was that you still have no children after all this time.'

Esme swallowed hard. Was she jealous? Yes, in all honesty, she was. Only now did she realize how much.

'You don't deserve them,' she muttered angrily.

'Whereas you do. Yes, it must be very trying for you – and for your husband, too. How long has it been now? Four years? Well, I suppose it's too early to give up hope entirely, but I must say. . .'

Esme cut her short. 'I'm not worried, Susanna, so don't think it. When Katie was born you were all of thirty, and you've since borne two sons – which goes to prove that I've plenty of time yet.'

'Oh, you most certainly are worried, Esme. I think you're becoming very anxious indeed.' Susanna stroked Peter's hair and patted the dimpled knees, then hugged him a little closer. 'Tell me, my dear, does Roger feel that you've failed him? Of course, he's a very forgiving man, I know. Tactful too, I fancy. Even if he did feel you'd let him down, he'd never say so.'

'No, I don't suppose he would.' The reply was tart but slightly shaky. 'He's too kind and he loves me in spite of my "failure" as you call it. You know that your children are the only reason Richard tolerates you, so you ought to be more grateful for them. At least, you should care a little more for the other two.'

Susanna smiled indulgently. 'Now you sound just like Hannah.'

'That's all right. Hannah's no fool, which is more than

I can say for you. Susanna, you drive away those who might otherwise love you, and no one can afford to do that, especially when youth is well and truly past.'

Susanna's expression froze. The smirk remained, but it seemed to be fighting a downward drag of her facial muscles. Satisfied that her bolt had found its mark, Esme turned on her heel and left before her sister-in-law could fire back.

It was always a triumph to have the last word when dealing with Susanna, but the skirmish left Esme with no sense of elation. She did not return to the dining room to collect the rest of the dishes, for Susanna would see that she had been crying, and that would never do.

Next morning, Roger Carwarthen woke just after half past six and found the bed beside him empty. He and Esme were expecting a large funeral party later in the day, with a meal to be cooked for fifty mourners, and his first assumption was that she had risen early to make a start on this considerable task. He rose and dressed himself, opened the curtains and leaned for a while upon the window ledge, enjoying the sharp air of a brilliant green and gold morning. A milky haze hung across the skyline, with a pale diffusion of sunlight behind it and a radiance on the sea. Such days were inclined to turn out hot, and he thought it sensible of his wife to make all the preparation she could in these first cool hours.

When he went downstairs, however, Esme was not in any of the usual places. After a short search, he discovered her in the skittle alley, sitting on one of the benches that ran the length of each wall. In her hands she held one of the wooden pins, and she turned it absently round and round, tracing the circle of its iron collar with her thumb.

Roger stepped inside and she looked up with a jerk of

her head, startled by the echoing tread of his feet on the floorboards. She was still in her nightgown, with hair uncombed and her feet bare.

He sat down beside her, took the skittle away and rolled it gently along the floor to lie in a heap with the rest.

'What is it, Esme?'

She hesitated for a moment, still loath to speak of a subject over which they had both maintained an uneasy silence for the past year or more. But at last she said: 'I had a little – exchange – with Susanna yesterday.'

'Is that all? Nothing new, is it? Nothing to mope about? You're not going to tell me she got the better of you?'

'In a way, she did. Roger, she taunted me because we've no children.'

'Ah,' he said quietly. He slipped an arm about her shoulders and drew her close. 'Well, I'm not altogether surprised. She hates you and she knew just where to strike.'

'It wouldn't have hurt if there weren't so much truth in what she said. I don't understand it, Roger. It's been four years. Surely we should have a family by now? Richard and Susanna were never as close as we are,' she added bitterly. 'How is it that you and I haven't a single child, while Madam, who probably rations her favours, has managed to have three?'

'I wish I knew,' he sighed, stroking and squeezing her shoulder. 'Susanna didn't even want them, did she?'

Esme snorted. 'She'd as soon have done without. But she sat there with Peter on her lap and showed him off to me as if he were a prize possession.' She glanced at him miserably. 'She said I've failed you, and I suppose I have.'

'I want a family too, Esme, but I shan't think less of you if we can't have one. For all I know, the fault may be mine. Whatever the reason, I'm still a fortunate man.

191

Believe me, I don't envy your brother. I wouldn't have Susanna as my wife, not for a score of children.' He turned her face towards him and scanned her features with a worried frown. 'Does it matter so very much to you? Will your life be a great disappointment if there's only me? I try to make it happy for you in every other way.'

'I'm sorry, Roger.' She bent her head to kiss the side of his neck. 'No woman could wish for a better husband. I'm foolish, I know, to let that harpy upset me.'

Roger patted her softly on the thigh. 'Quite right. She's not worth a second thought. Imagine how she'd laugh to see you sitting here like this. Don't give her any victories, my love. Now then, come on, we'd better stir ourselves and make ready for the mourning party. You've a saddle of beef and a brace of fowl to cook by three o'clock. As we both know, there's nothing like a burial for sharpening appetites.'

Not everyone could afford to hire Roger's hearse and horses and some preferred, in any case, to spend funeral club funds on a splendid meal instead. The Halveor Inn was a favourite staging post for walking funerals, since it was little more than half a mile from the parish church. Many moorland cottages and mining communities lay to the west of Porthgullow, with the inn conveniently placed en route.

A large following had assembled that day to escort a forty-year-old tutworker to his last rest. He had fallen from the ladder at the end of his day's core, dropping more than thirty fathoms when his wind and his strength failed him, and he could no longer climb or even hold on. It was a manner of death by no means unusual, and likely to be shared eventually by some of the friends and relatives who carried his coffin or marched behind it that day.

They were all in fine voice, having called at the Halveor Inn beforehand to fortify themselves with a glass or two, and quite a few were unsteady on their feet. Hymns were sung with gusto in sombre Cornish bass. There were numerous heartfelt requests for mercy from 'The Loord', many scriptural quotations and much praise for the sterling qualities of the dead man. Loudly and earnestly, the mourners proclaimed his virtues as the procession swayed along the country road. When, at last, they arrived at the church, there was little left for the parson to say, since so many fulsome apologies and recommendations to the Almighty had already been tendered on the miner's behalf.

By the time the coffin was lowered into the ground, the singing had become a little raucous. Most were restless in their eagerness to have the business over and done with, so that they might return to Halveor for the sumptuous meal awaiting them. The moment the vicar concluded the service, there was an unseemly rush for the gate.

Drawn by their shouting, a small knot of women emerged from the adjoining church hall to complain about the noise, for a meeting of the Teetotal Society was in progress. They were just in time to see one hefty young man leapfrog a headstone. The clergyman, a patient soul, observed these antics with a shrug and a sigh, for he knew of old the habits and the disposition of these people. All but the 'saved' were improvident, uncouth and contentious, yet privately he felt a preference for these sinners: their rowdiness was almost light relief after a morning spent with the Teetotal Society.

The lady who led the local division was a most alarming person. Her name was Margaret Jory and she now stood at the head of her followers, frostily watching the last of the funeral party straggling away up the road. The Reverend Sobey caught her eye, smiled weakly and scurried back into the church by means of the side door, so that he would not have to pass her.

Miss Jory was not an attractive woman. She was thirty-four years old and five feet ten inches tall – a height discouraging to large sections of the male population. Her figure was lean and she always dressed in black or very dark blue. In her usual stance, with jutting backside, hands clasped in front of her and elbows poking out, she seemed always poised to argue or chastise. On a woman of better appetite, the face might well have been heart-shaped, but in Margaret it formed a narrow wedge. The pallid skin was drawn over bony cheeks and a nose that was flat at the bridge, snub at the tip. Set deep in this countenance were eyes with the glint of two faceted beads from a necklace of jet. On the rare occasions when she laughed, they would disappear completely, sinking back as the cheeks rose. But most of the time they were restive, minutely observant and utterly without humour. Straight black hair, brushed up and back from her face, was fastened in a bun at the nape of her neck. The only beauty to which Margaret might lay claim was a set of regular, marble-white teeth, but the grimly clamped mouth rarely allowed them to show.

Miss Jory was more than just a busybody. The crusading spirit was fierce in her. It inspired the other ladies and made her the prime mover in all their activities. She was energetic, dauntless, and so they took their cue from her. Lesser women might quail, but Margaret would fearlessly march into taverns filled with drunken ruffians, silence them all with a stony stare and denounce them in no uncertain terms. She never missed a chance to parade with her banner on fair or feast day, to chide the town bobby for laxity in his duty or the vicar for a feeble sermon. To Roger's relief, she seldom descended in wrath upon the Halveor Inn, if only because there were so many other establishments less heedful of the law. That day, however, the funeral party's conduct in the churchyard seemed to call for a visit, just as soon as the society meeting had finished its business.

Esme Carwarthen was out of temper. Some of the mourners had gone lurching home as soon as their stomachs were full, but many more, late in the afternoon, were still carousing in the pewter room, where twenty or so were roaring verses of 'Trelawney'. Ewan had already broken up a fight in the courtyard, and Roger had been forced to rescue little Bridget from a burly young trammer, who had followed her up to her room when she went to change a sweat-soiled blouse.

Esme's feet were throbbing and her hair had come loose from its pins. She too was hot and damp with perspiration. Her head ached and she sat sucking at a blistered finger, burnt as she took a tray of beef from the oven. Alone in the big dining room, she sourly surveyed the remains of the meal. There were scraps of food everywhere, spillages on the tables, on the benches, on the floor. Broken crockery and toppled tankards, all the usual debris of a successful party, littered every surface. It would take a full two hours to clear up. They had all enjoyed themselves, of course, and the profits would be handsome, but Esme was exhausted and the mess filled her with dismay. Wearily, she folded her arms upon the table and laid her head on them.

She sat like that for fifteen minutes and was just gathering her energy to begin the task, when the noise from the pewter room unaccountably died away. Esme's eyes flickered open and she cocked an ear in puzzlement.

After a brief pause the silence was split by a woman's voice, well-schooled, but strident and filled with outrage.

'Is death a cause for merriment, gentlemen? Is revelry a fitting way to mark the fact that your departed friend is cowering even now before the throne of God, to whom he must account for his deeds and shortcomings? Are you so confident of his virtue that you do not fear for him? You would surely do well to reflect on the awful prospect of your own eventual demise. Each man here must take thought for eternity and ponder the condition of his soul – not tomorrow, nor in an hour from now, but from this very moment. Do you not tremble at the knowledge that any one of you, at any instant, might join that man on his terrible voyage through darkness to the place of retribution? Let me assure you all that I see no one in this room with reason to expect clemency from on high. Today, you presented yourselves at the house of the Lord reeking so strongly of drink that the fumes of it must surely have reached His nostrils. To utter profanity and disport yourselves in the churchyard, among the graves to which you, too, must come! To behave without respect for your maker or those who have gone before! What hope can you have under such a burden of iniquity, what chance of escaping the pit? I doubt that any one of you could stand up straight before the Almighty, for the very weight of your offences would cause you to totter and stoop.'

Esme groaned, for she recognized the voice, then she sat up.

From the pewter room came low murmurings and shuffling noises, then a gruff 'Allelujah' and the sound of liquid being poured upon the floor. One of the listeners had evidently taken Margaret's message to heart.

'There!' exclaimed the voice triumphantly. 'At least there is one among you wise enough to know the truth when he hears it, and to follow advice that can only uplift him.'

Resignedly, Esme stood up, went out into the passage and across to the pewter room. In the centre stood the tall figure of Miss Jory. She wore a black serge dress, some eight or ten years out of date. On her head was a flattish felt hat, and in her hand a bundle of the usual tracts. Esme sidled quietly through the door and round behind the counter, where Ewan stood dourly listening.

'Take heed of a good example, my friends,' Miss Jory was saying. 'Do not finish those evil slops and harsh liquors that lie before you. As the hops and barley are steeped in the brewing of these foul concoctions, so the drunkard is steeped in wickedness. The shades of gold, amber and ruby that glow within these potions are nothing but snares to beguile and bring you to destruction. The seductive flavours, the pleasant sensations that come when your God-given minds are befuddled and your wits scattered – these are devices of Satan to rob you of dignity, make fools and brutes of you all!'

Her voice rose, impassioned, on these last words. The men sat spellbound, some with glasses half raised for a sip but frozen in motion by the gleam of her eye. Others were fidgeting, scratching, glancing uneasily at their neighbours and then back to Miss Jory. A few were already too drunk to absorb the tirade. When she stopped for breath, there came the clunk of a dark head hitting the table as somebody slumped unconscious. More were now drifting in from the taproom, and they crowded round the doorway, clutching their tankards and grinning.

'Wass matter wi' she?' whispered someone.

'Dunnaw, but she'm in some tear.'

'Temp'rance, is her?'

'Ess, 'tis that Jory woman.'

'Aw – 'nough said. Dawn't b'long come out here, though, do her?'

'I urge you now to forswear your weakness and your loutish ways,' continued Margaret. 'Do not allow depravity or the enticements of Bacchus to stain your souls!'

'Very impressive, isn't she?' Esme murmured to Ewan, as Miss Jory went on declaiming. 'Born for the stage or the pulpit.'

Ewan scowled. 'She's just a long streak o'misery, an' wherever she d'go, there's trouble. Where's your husband to?'

'In the brewhouse, I think.'

'Better go fetch'n.'

'There's no need for that. She'll just make her speech and go.'

Margaret concluded by handing out pamphlets, and only the bravest declined to take one.

'I am aware,' she said, 'that many of you are unable to read. Any man who wishes to learn will be welcome to attend my classes at the church hall each Tuesday and Thursday evening. I make no charge for my time and teaching. Tea, with bread and a large bowl of nourishing soup, may be purchased at the end of each lesson for one farthing. You would do well to avail yourselves of this chance for self-improvement. I beg you to come along, and to bring your families too. Most of you are poor. It is folly to spend night after night squandering your money in a public house. What little you have should be put to better use. Remember, Tuesdays and . . .'

Esme thought it time to call a halt. Miss Jory's concern for the poor was quite genuine and her efforts to help them were unstinting, but she was also a danger to Roger's livelihood.

'I think you've made your point, Miss Jory. I see no reason for you to remain here longer.'

Margaret turned and eyed her severely. 'Do you and your husband never feel a pang of guilt, Mrs Carwarthen? Can you deny that the men who frequent this house stagger home each night in a state of hopeless intoxication? That some return to their wives and inflict upon them bestial violence, unleashed by the influence of ale and spirits? Does it not concern you that poverty is made worse by fathers, husbands, sons who waste their earnings in places like this and even fall into debt to the publican who offers credit?'

'We don't extend credit.'

'But you do permit men to wager at cards, or over skittle matches.'

'Our customers aren't children to be coddled. You won't cure weakness by removing temptation. Forbid a thing and you only stoke up the craving for it – and swell the ranks of those who'll supply it in secret for a much higher price. This inn is run to good standards – better than most – and 'tis decent enough for the vicar to smoke a pipe and take dinner here three times a week. A publican has his living to make, like everyone else, and the work's not easy, either.'

'That's as may be, but let me warn you that I shall keep a closer eye on this establishment from now on. Good day to you.'

'She will, too,' said Ewan, when Margaret had gone. 'We'll have a lot more trouble from she in future. Even the parson's 'fraid of her, and thass a bad job for'n, 'cause she d'live right nex' to the church. 'Tis no wonder the woman's a killjoy 'n full o'talk about the hereafter. Her house d'overlook the boneyard 'n the first thing she d'see when she open her curtains is a row of headstones.'

199

25

In February 1872, a new gravestone appeared in the parish churchyard. It was that of Bob Varcoe, dead of a stroke at the age of sixty.

He had been buried a fortnight before the news reached Boskenna, and John Rescorla was badly shaken. It brought an unsettling reminder of his own advancing years, and a great sadness for the friendship that had never been mended. If the passing of time had diluted Varcoe's bitterness, he had never said so. In fourteen years, his only word for the shipwright had been a brief 'Good day, John,' whenever the two men met in the street.

Jenny had not afforded Richard even that much. Not a word or a smile or any sign of forgiveness till her dying day – that was what she had sworn to herself on that painful morning long years ago. And she had held very firmly to this resolution, even though the hurt had faded and life had given her much compensation. They were both past thirty now, and snubbing Richard had become more a habit than a token of ill-feeling. The cause was not forgotten, but the anger had spent itself and she felt almost nothing when she turned her head away and pretended she had not seen him. There were even occasions when she was almost tempted to forgive him, but having built the barrier, she was disinclined to pull it down too easily.

But on a day in March, soon after her father's death, she finally relented.

On his way home from Porthgullow, Richard was

walking by the parish church at about eleven o'clock that morning. A group of elm and horse chestnut trees grew just within the hedge bordering the graveyard. Their branches arched over the road outside, throwing shadows when the weather was bright, dripping gently when it was wet. The sky was overcast that day, with darker patches of cloud tearing and changing all the time against the white. Expecting showers before long, Richard was in a hurry and would have passed without stopping, had he not noticed a flicker of movement between the trees. From the corner of his eye, he caught sight of a dark-clad figure – that of a woman who had just risen to her feet, having knelt to arrange fresh flowers on a grave.

She was standing now, quite still and silent, gazing down at the mound of bare earth. All her clothing, including the shawl that covered her head, was black. Her face was turned away from him, but he recognized her form and stance and knew that it was Jenny.

Richard paused and stood watching her from the gloom beneath the trees. She was alone. There was not another soul to be seen in the churchyard, and the only sounds were the swish and rustle of leaves, the cawing of rooks. He could not recall the last time he had seen her in church, for her husband was a Methodist and she now attended chapel instead. But perhaps this was an opportunity, perhaps here he could talk to her at last – pour out his remorse, acknowledge his awful mistake, and . . .

And what? To what end? She might still refuse to speak to him, and nothing could come of it anyway, for they were both securely married. Richard had three children and Jenny now had seven. What could he gain, except come close for a moment to an old, lost happiness?

Suddenly, she turned from the graveside and stepped onto the gravel path leading up towards the church and the main gate. For a moment he thought she was leaving, and he hurriedly debated whether to approach her. But she did not go to the gate. Instead, she took the little pathway to the side door of the church and went inside.

Richard hastily made his decision and followed her. No, he could not hope to restore the old bond between them, but this time he would have his say, whether or not she wished to hear it.

Sitting alone in a front pew, Jenny heard the heavy door open and close, and then a quiet echo of footsteps as someone came slowly down the aisle. The footsteps ceased and she sensed a man standing there, almost level but still a little behind her.

'Hello, Jenny.'

Richard's voice sounded nervous to him, for the still and musty air accentuated every tiny change of note.

She twisted round, taken aback, and stared at him. Her first impulse was to stand up and leave without a word – but all of a sudden the gesture no longer seemed worthwhile.

'Hello, Richard,' came the quiet reply, and he thought how good it was to hear that warm voice again.

'I'm sorry about your father.'

'Yes, I miss him very much.'

He hovered briefly, then he said: 'Do you mind if I sit down?'

'This is God's house. You don't need my permission.'

So Richard sat, and edged along the pew to within a few feet of her.

'Are you well?' he asked, after a lengthy pause.

'I'm very well, thank you.'

'Good, good. And everything's all right? I mean. . .'

'You want to know if I'm happy with Luke?' she said bluntly.

He reddened a little. 'Well – are you?'

'Yes, Richard, he's a good man and I've seven healthy

202

children. Life's very hard sometimes because we've so little money, and I'm often afraid something will happen to my husband, but I still have much to smile about, and on the whole, I'm content.' Her tone changed slightly, acquiring a soft note of mockery. 'Don't let your conscience trouble you on my account. I haven't pined for you in many, many years.'

'You always did have plenty of sense,' he said, trying to ignore the sting in those last words. 'I wish I'd been the same.'

'Has it all been such a disappointment, then?'

He looked at her and found that she was studying him closely, and the brown eyes he remembered as merry were now gravely attentive. His own, so black that they rarely betrayed his feelings, returned the gaze with undisguised pain, because this was Jenny and he wanted her to see.

''Twas the greatest mistake I've ever made and I fear I'll never cease paying for it.'

There it was, confessed aloud. She had known, of course, just how it would be for him. The only unexpected thing was the lack of satisfaction she felt in hearing him admit his error and the trouble it had brought. Once Jenny would have counted this a victory but now, strange to say, she felt no desire to crow about it.

'Your children must be some consolation to you.'

A fond smile crossed his face. 'They are, that's true. I dearly love them all. And you've a fine brood of chicks yourself. There's one I often see playing on the quay outside your door – a little girl with curly hair. I don't think I've ever set eyes on a lovelier child.'

'You must mean Eva. 'Twas her ninth birthday last month.'

'Same age as my elder son, then.'

203

'I've seen your wife in town from time to time,' Jenny said. 'She's still very grand, very smart.'

There was an unspoken 'but' appended to these words, and Richard guessed what was in her mind. Susanna was fast losing her prettiness.

'She was a lot older than I first thought,' he said. 'I don't suppose that surprises you?'

Jenny smiled. 'No.'

'And the years are catching up with her,' murmured Richard, 'though I don't think she's realized it yet. Susanna and I don't talk much, and we certainly don't confide in each other. Most of our words are angry ones.'

'Well, Richard, I confess there was a time when I hoped she would make you miserable. Yet now that I find she's done so, it gives me no pleasure at all.'

'You had a right to wish me ill, I suppose.' Richard shrugged. 'Anyway, I've grown used to Susanna now. She's not what I first imagined her to be, and it does no good to a man's pride to know he's been made a dupe – but the worst of it has been the memory of what I gave up. If I hadn't enjoyed those years with you, I'd never have expected such a lot from her. I envy Luke Symons, I freely admit it.'

'He'd laugh to hear you say that. He leads a dangerous life for small reward. Luke and I are very close, 'tis true, but we've nothing else you need covet.'

'I suppose he has a poor opinion of me?'

'I don't know what he thinks. Luke never asked me very much about you. He didn't pry into feelings I chose to keep secret. 'Twas one of the things I loved about him from the start.'

As he listened, Richard studied the solemn profile and saw that she had changed very little in fourteen years. The hands clasped in her lap were roughened by hard work, but she gave an impression of strength and the healthy brown skin was as firm as ever.

After a slight hesitation, he asked: 'Where does he go for repairs and so forth?'

'Annear's yard.'

'I've heard they charge a lot. You know, Jenny, I'd be glad to do any work your husband might need, at a much lower cost. Father made me his partner about eighteen months ago, and 'tis up to me what price I set.'

'We're not in need of charity,' she said stiffly.

'I'm not offering any. 'Tis simply bad business to pay more than you have to. Tell him to come to me next time. Perhaps I can never atone to you for what I did when we were young, but I'd like to give the scars some help to fade.'

Jenny regarded him steadily and a faint smile crept across her face. He was no longer the callow youth who had deserted her, nor the treacherous Richard towards whom she had felt such rancour. She saw instead a mature and chastened man, clumsily trying to make amends as best he could.

'All right,' she said finally. 'I'll suggest it to my husband. You'd do a good job for him, I know. Everyone speaks well of your work.'

26

The Rescorlas' reputation was known for many miles around, and in late November of that same year it won them an order from a fishing company in Devon.

To begin with, the owners would require a single lugger, to be fifty feet long with oak planking. They had said they would want her ready in time for the start of the North Sea herring fishery the following May. Prompt delivery and satisfactory performance of the vessel would lead to orders for three or four more of the same type over the next two years. It was a profitable commission and the Rescorlas accepted without hesitation, despite the fact that their workshops were already occupied by four other craft at various stages of construction. Two of these were small, in any case, and one of them, the pilot gig, was near completion. The company's exact requirements were discussed, a half model produced and approved, and terms agreed.

The new boat would be built in the open and they set up the blocks on the left-hand side of the yard, in the sheltered hollow beneath the cliff. Several extra men and boys were hired to help with the work, and there followed twelve weeks of furious activity. Between dawn and dusk, the workshops were never silent. There was always the thud of an axe, the scrape of a saw, the sound of men whistling, laughing or cursing. With the promise of a bonus at the end of their labours, they chiselled and hammered, shaped with the adze and daubed with the pitching mop till all the work was well in hand and no customer could be dissatisfied with his delivery date. The pilot gig was finished and launched in mid-December, and the apprentices were able to complete the clinker-built punt with little supervision. Decks were laid to the mackerel driver in the main shed during the last week of January, and the crabber for Porthgwarra was ready for her sails just a few days later than promised.

By the end of February they were planking the big lugger and felt confident of finishing her on time.

'We've done well, John,' Rufus said, as they left work one Thursday evening. 'She's turnin' out nicely. Are ee proud of her?'

'I am, I truly am. She'll be the finest we ever built. Best materials and a generous price for the work. If we could add one such order to our trade every year, we'd all be a lot better off.'

As they went out through the gate he paused, turning his head to peer at the sky, and then at the sea. Both were deep grey, and tiny wavelets performed an agitated dance that stippled the surface of the water with foam.

'Wind's fresh tonight,' he said.

'Ess, south-east. We're nearly into March.'

John latched the gate, bade Rufus goodnight and started homeward.

At just after twelve that night, Judith awoke and heard Peter crying. She padded into the boys' room to pick him up, and found him sobbing with fright. As she lit the lamp and took him on her lap, Alan sat up in bed.

''Tis this wind, Auntie, it scares him. I couldn't sleep, either. Will there be thunder and lightning?'

'I don't know, my dear, but there's nothing for you to fear.' She cuddled the weeping Peter, enfolding him within the shawl she had thrown over her nightgown.

A strong east wind was bellowing around the house. The window-frames shook and the panes shivered as the billows struck them. There was no rain, but Judith heard the snap and thump of a falling tree branch, then later a metallic rattle as something toppled over in the back yard.

"Tis only a bit of a gale,' she assured them. 'I expect 'twill die down by morning, but you can both come into my room if you like.' She shushed the toddler, jigging him gently on her knee. 'Be quiet now, Peter. Your father and grandpa are very tired and you mustn't wake them.'

Richard, however, had woken once already, and he stirred twice more in the course of the night, going to the window between troubled bouts of sleep, listening and gazing into the darkness outside. He could see nothing, for dense cloud covered the moon, but the night was alive and filled with a ferment of baying, as the wind swung to north-north-east.

God help the men at sea, he thought. I hope for Jenny's sake that Luke's not out tonight.

But as dawn approached, another fear began to take shape in his mind. It was raining now, and first light came as the gale was reaching its height. Richard had dozed for twenty minutes this time, but his half-waking dreams revolved around crashing timbers and pounding seas. Never, in his lifetime, had any tide reached the boatyard. No storm had caused more than slight damage, and yet . . .

Dimly a memory came back to him, something he had heard from his grandfather when the latter was a man of sixty and Richard a boy of seven or eight.

'There was a gale one time, when I was young, a storm that broke down the gates. In all my years, I've seen no other to rival it. 'Twas like the devil was loose that night, and I thought the world would end.'

In the dim early light, Richard squinted at the clock. High tide in fifteen minutes.

There was a sudden cracking noise, then the sound of

something clattering down the roof, and finally a brittle crash as one of Boskenna's chimney pots hit the ground outside the parlour window.

High tide in fifteen minutes.

Richard sat up in bed, flung back the covers and reached for his clothes. His anxiety, as he dressed, chiefly concerned the fate of the new lugger if the courtyard were to flood. Logic told him there was little to be done, but instinct prompted him to be there anyway.

Susanna, who had never concerned herself with Richard's business, turned drowsily over and slurred: 'What's the matter? What's the time? Why don't you wedge those windows and stop them rattling?'

Richard ignored her and she promptly fell asleep again.

He ran downstairs and was pulling on boots and oilskins when his father came hurrying across the landing and thundered down after him.

'Richard! Father! What are you going to do?' Judith appeared at the head of the stairs, still clutching Peter.

'Whatever we can, which probably won't be much,' her brother said. 'Take the child back to bed.'

'Father, please, it might be dangerous.'

John came to the foot of the staircase. 'Now, Judith,' he said, grinning up at her with fond reproof, 'we're both big enough to look after ourselves. Just do as your brother says, maid.'

He winked at her, then followed Richard out into the frenzied morning.

Rivulets of rainwater had scoured channels down the track to the cove and the way was slippery with mud. When they finally reached the bottom, the sight before them was one of chaos and ruin.

The worst of the destruction had come within the last half hour, as the tide rose and swept in far beyond its normal reach. Those cottages built level with the sand had been battered by tremendous breakers, which had smashed in the windows and doors, sucking out furniture and debris, throwing tons of sand and shingle up over the little paths and gardens. A fishing boat wallowed at her moorings, three-parts flooded and likely to go under with the next wave. Part of another one grated and flopped against the rocks, as the sea worried it steadily to bits. Farther out at the mouth of the cove, wreckage of all kinds was bobbing and jumping in the swell.

The boatyard gates were gone and part of the wall had collapsed, so that the buildings on the right-hand side had taken a head-on pounding from the sea. The front and left sides of the smaller shed were down and its roof drooped at one corner. The lean-to canopy of the timber store had vanished altogether – and so had much of the wood. The large workshop had lost a door and the other hung, twisted, on one hinge. As they watched, another curling rampart of water roared in, exploding into spume as it struck the stone walls and poured through the gaps, then boiled around the buildings and drew swiftly back, making off with yet another lot of timber. But although the yard was awash, the big lugger still rested upright on the stocks, for she stood in that recess under the cliff where the wall was still intact and the jutting buttress of rock had broken the force of the waves. Water a foot deep was eddying round the poles that supported her, but had not yet dislodged them.

Soon, though, Richard said to himself. Any second now.

But John pointed through the veils of rain and bawled: 'More struts! We'll put more struts under her.'

'What? What!' His face screwed up against the rain, Richard shook his head in vigorous disagreement. 'You're mad. It won't work. She's bound to go over, and there's no use going down there.'

'It might save her. The wall's still standing on that side and she's sheltered by the spur of the cliff. Look, this yard's forty feet above normal high water. If we can just keep her upright till the tide turns, she may be all right.'

John started towards the yard, but his son caught him by the back of his jacket and pulled him round, grasping him by one arm and a lapel.

'Don't be such a fool, man. 'Tis lunacy even to think of it.'

'Take your hands off,' John snapped. 'I won't stand here and see the finest boat I ever built knocked to pieces by a cursed gale before she's even been launched.'

'For pity's sake, have sense,' yelled Richard. 'Before long she'll be smashed to bits – and so will you if you're anywhere near her.'

'Will you let me go, or must I take my fist to you? I can still do it, Richard.'

They glared at one another, hair sodden and clinging round their faces in the downpour. A grey haired man nearing sixty and his son of thirty-four, still much alike and stubborn when it pleased them, they silently defied each other for a moment more.

'I'm proud of that lugger,' shouted John, 'and I want the contract to build more like her. 'Twas us the owners chose, not Annear's with their five acres of premises, nor any other big concern. But if we lose her, we may not be given a second chance.'

'If you're killed you won't be given a second life, that's for sure. To hell with the contract. We've managed well enough without their business up to now. We'll just have to salvage what we can when the storm's over. Look, perhaps the damage won't be too bad. If that's the case, we can put her to rights.'

'And miss the delivery date.'

'That can't be helped.'

'Well, I say it can! Partner you may be, but I'm your father and I'll still do exactly as I see fit.'

With that, he wrenched free of Richard's grip and began to run towards the boatsheds. By the time his son caught up with him, John was wading through the water that swirled about the courtyard. It was up to his calves and carried a lot of drifting wood, which struck at his legs as the heaving sea propelled it this way and that. Dead-woods, knees and frames, shaped pieces representing hours of labour, were now just a hazard to be kicked aside while he searched for lengths of timber with which to support the beleaguered boat.

Richard knew the hopelessness of John's plan – and of trying to stop him. While the sea poured in through the gaps in the wall, sometimes over the top of it, he joined his father in the futile fight, wishing Rufus were there to reason with him.

Between them, they fixed three extra props beneath the hull on the side away from the cliff, but there was little on the ground to secure them against the constant drag of the tide. As John and Richard struggled to position a fourth brace at the stern, there came an inrush of water that jerked the struts out of place by several inches and left them at a perilous slant. The cradle of criss-crossed poles slid and folded a little. The lugger lurched, creaked, settled uneasily. She was no longer sitting quite straight, but leaning ominously over the two men.

'That's it!' yelled Richard. 'She'll go with the next big wave. In God's name, give up!'

He pulled desperately at his father's arm. But John, still working feverishly under the stern, flung him off and shouted something profane above the clamour of the storm.

'Do you want to die?' persisted Richard. 'If Mother could see you now, she'd call you all the fools in creation.'

Crouched under the hull, John faltered in what he was

doing. Yes, Ellen had always rebuked him for his obstinacy.

'Come away from there,' urged Richard. 'You know 'tis no use.'

For a moment the shipwright stared miserably round at the wreckage of his premises, then up at the lugger. Built for a deep water harbour, she reared high above him and her lines were elegant. He ran a caressing hand over the planking. So much wasted effort. He could not help but view this disaster as a personal affront, a jibe at his skill and his hard work.

'Let her go, man.'

John hesitated, sighed and swore again, then reluctantly made to stand up.

But he had left it a few seconds too late. Just as he moved away, another powerful wave rolled in, deluged the courtyard and surged around the lugger. Richard, only just clear himself, was knocked off his feet and swept back against the wall of the main workshop. His nose and mouth filled with salt water and he felt two painful blows, as chunks of loose timber hit him in the ribs and shoulder. Submerged for a few seconds in the freezing, grey-green murk, he did not see the flood hurl his father back beneath the hull and wash the supports right out from under it.

The cradle of poles fell apart and the lugger toppled with a groaning crash. As he saw it coming down on him, John opened his mouth in the despairing scream of a man who knew he was lost. But the sound was swallowed up in the shrieking of the wind and the cry ended abruptly, for the terrible weight took his life in an instant.

When the water retreated, all Richard saw were John's head and shoulders protruding from under the fallen boat. She had pinned and crushed him from his chest to his knees. Every incoming wave submerged the body for a few seconds, and Rescorla's head and arms rolled with the ebb and flow of the water.

'Father? Oh, dear God!'

A fearful pain tore at Richard's neck and shoulder as he struggled towards the body, and his left arm hung useless, sagging slightly inwards. He knelt, trying with his good arm to hold John's head up out of the water, though the wide, staring eyes and open mouth left no doubt that his father was dead. Richard began to sob with shock and grief – and with frustration too, for he could not drag the body clear. The hull weighed many tons and his broken collarbone rendered him all but helpless.

'For a boat,' he fumed, 'just for a damned boat! There was no need, no need. The owners would have understood. You and your pride and your stubbornness. Oh God, what a waste of a good man!'

Soaked and shivering, he remained for some time on his knees, holding the lifeless head in his lap and muttering snatches of prayer. But the storm went raving on and when another section of the outer wall collapsed, he knew he could stay no longer. Closing John's eyelids, he reluctantly allowed the corpse to slip beneath the water, then pulled himself to his feet and stumbled off in search of help.

Of the dozen or so cottages built at the cove, half had been devastated. Rufus Adams, however, was one of those fortunate enough to live higher up the coomb, and his home had suffered little damage. Since dawn he had taken in several unhappy souls who had fled their dwellings in fear, and when he heard the hammering on his door he expected to find a few more seeking refuge. But Richard's arrival and the news he brought were more than the old man had bargained for. He listened in sorrowful silence as the tidings were delivered.

'Poor John,' he murmured at last. 'Ess, 'twas his pride

and joy, see. He said so ony las' night. I'm some sorry, boy. Aw, 'tis a sad end for'n. We'll miss'n awful, wen't us? Good friend to me, he was – they dawn't come much better'n John.' He patted the younger man gently on the back. 'You d'need a doctor, Richard. I'll come home with ee 'n help break it to your sister. Then soon as this dies down, I'll send a man to Porthgullow to fetch the physician, an I'll find a few more to go'n free the body. Dunnee worry now, there'll be many willin' hands.'

Jenny Symons had never spent a worse night. Badly in need of a catch, Luke had set sail early the previous evening and she knew he must have been caught far out to sea when the weather turned black.

All through the dark hours she had stayed awake, soothing her children and reading from the Scriptures, then mending her husband's clothes with hands that shook and made the stitching ragged. And praying too, constantly praying, a silent mouthing over and over of all the familiar pleas for mercy and the safe return of men who put out to sea. *Sweet Eva* was such a little boat to stand between four souls and the power of demented elements. At times like this, the only hope seemed to lie in help from above.

Towards dawn she roused the children and prepared to leave the house, for the gale showed no signs of dying down and she knew what would happen when the tide came in. These cottages, built right on the quayside, always took a beating in stormy weather. Here, occasional flooding was an irksome fact of life, stoically accepted by the occupants. The sea was a dangerous neighbour and always prone to tantrums, so steps had been taken in self-defence. Unlike the cottagers at the cove, those who lived along the waterfront in Porthgullow were never taken by surprise. They had sturdy shutters fitted to all their windows and they kept sandbags in their back yards.

As waves began to smack against the quay wall, sending up great plumes of spray, Jenny ensured that every window was shuttered and barred. She piled sandbags at the foot of the front door, then pushed the kitchen table hard against it for good measure. The settle was dragged from its place by the fire and the high wooden back aligned across the window as an extra barrier. All the crockery and small furniture, every little movable possession, was carried upstairs and as much as possible was locked in the recessed cupboards in the bedrooms. She knew with certainty that the ground floor would flood, for water was bound to come down the chimney, but the roof was sound and the upstairs often remained dry.

Michael, her eldest was still only twelve, but he knew the procedure well. She left it to him to ferry the last few items up the stairs, while ten-year-old Eva helped her dress the younger children.

Ready at last, Jenny shepherded them out through the back door and up the road to the Methodist chapel. It was no more than fifty yards distant, yet all were drenched before they had even gone halfway. The chapel was already crowded with people when they arrived. Men, women and children, wet and shivering, worn out by a night without sleep. And some of the faces were stamped with fear, white and drawn, just like her own. Oh yes, she could tell at a glance whose husband, son or father was out that night, and which other women were sharing the torment of worry.

Present, as always in times of disaster, was Margaret Jory, doling out blankets, hot soup and bracing quotations from the Bible. Ineffectual by comparison, the preacher was making a tour round the pews, offering a few quiet words of comfort here and there.

They do what they can, Jenny thought, but there's nothing to ease this misery except the sight of your man coming home.

It was mid-morning before the wind abated. In the grey calm that followed, Jenny and a dozen other women gathered on the west quay to await the return of the boats – if any were to return. They stood together, seldom speaking, wrapped in their shawls and their private cocoons of hope and dread. The sea was like a millpond now, the silence unnatural. The whole town was still and the air had the strange, heady freshness that often follows a storm. An hour went by, two hours, and all the time the anxious eyes kept searching back and forth across the skyline.

At half-past two there finally appeared a speck, which soon became the tiny outline of a far-off sail. The women stirred, straining to see, tracing the approach of the boat with fixed and longing gaze. After a while they could plainly make out both the sails, and later still the shape of the black and white hull.

It could be him, Jenny thought. 'Tis a lugger about the right size.

But most of the others were thinking that very same thing, and when at last the keenest pair of eyes could read the number on the prow, the cry went up: "Tis Jack Behenna. Sarah, Sarah, 'tis your Jack.'

And Jenny had to be glad, for Sarah Behenna had a son on board as well as a husband. Wistfully, she watched the little woman run to embrace her menfolk when the boat at last tied up. Two other wives, their vigil over, went to welcome the remaining crewmen, and so the little group at the end of the quay dwindled to ten.

The hours dragged on. Another boat came in, and another woman walked off down the jetty, thanking God for the lives of her father, brother and two nephews.

He'll be here soon, Jenny told herself. If others came through it, then so will he.

A third boat arrived, but this one brought anguish as well as relief, for two of the five-man crew had been swept overboard. There was sobbing now among the women, for here were the first reports of death, and the time was nearing five o'clock.

That needn't mean anything, Jenny thought. He'd have made for the nearest port. He might be in St Ives or Newlyn, and if that's the case then he won't be home till tomorrow. It's only been a few hours, really. It just seems much longer, that's all.

But still she stood and waited. And finally, out of the gathering twilight, came the dark shape of one more lugger. The light was too poor to see any distance and no one dared guess at who it might be. The figures on board were mere shadows in the dusk and it was not until the vessel came within fifteen yards of the jetty that the number could be seen.

'PW 115'.

Jenny gasped and clutched at the hands of the three women whose menfolk sailed with Luke.

''Tis him! 'Tis my husband – and three men with him! They're all there, every one.'

And so they were, exhausted and shaken, but all unharmed. Yearning for hot food and a warm bed, they trudged up the steps to their waiting wives.

'Thank God,' whispered Jenny, hugging her husband. 'Oh, thank God you're back. Are you all right? No injuries?'

'We're all in one piece,' he said wearily, 'but half the nets are gone.' He bowed his head miserably onto her shoulder. 'There's no money for new ones, Jenny. Between the four of us on board, we've lost gear worth fifty pounds.'

218

'But you didn't lose your lives, and that's all that matters just now. Come on, my love, we're going home.'

She was too relieved to see him safe to worry about the nets. It was enough that she was not one of those two sad souls left waiting as the night closed in.

Whether by death or destruction of property, there was scarcely a fishing family in Porthgullow left untouched by that awful night, and the list of tragedies seemed endless. In the days that followed, reports of wrecks came in from many points along the north coast: a barque driven onto the stones at the mouth of St Ives bay, with the loss of eight lives; a little schooner capsized near Padstow, with no trace of her five-man crew; four fishing boats gone and every man drowned but one; a brigantine run aground and breaking up, the men saved but the cargo ruined – and so it went on and on. Had it not been a poor time of year for the fishing, many more would have been at sea and caught by the weather. But even vessels thought safe in harbour had sunk at their moorings, and John Rescorla's yard was not the only one destroyed that night. Throughout Saturday and well into Sunday, crippled ships and boats were arriving at the nearest port with ragged sails and splintered spars, part-flooded holds and tales of men washed overboard.

Eventually, a number of bodies were cast up on the rocks and beaches, but by no means all the dead were thus accounted for. On Sunday, the churches and chapels of Cornwall were filled with mourning. And on Monday afternoon, with a good congregation of friends in attendance, John Rescorla was laid next to Ellen, beside the south wall of the parish churchyard.

27

Susanna had long awaited the day when Richard would become sole owner of the family property, and was appalled to find his trade premises in ruins. She had ventured down to the cove on the Saturday morning, and clamped a hand to her mouth in horror when she saw the mounds of sand, shingle and splintered wood that buried the courtyard outside the tumbledown remains of the workshops. For days afterwards she kept bemoaning this calamity and agonizing about the future, until Richard's temper finally snapped.

'Stop whining,' he told her sharply. 'I've lost my father and all you can do is fret over money.'

'Surely you care about your livelihood?'

'Yes, yes, of course I do. 'Tis a grievous blow, I admit it, but we'll recover.'

'It will take months, years. What are we to live on?'

'Father told me some time ago there'd be a hundred pounds in ready money when he died. That'll tide us over, I daresay. We'll be almost on our feet again by autumn. I can build on the beach if I have to.'

'A hundred pounds. Think what we could have done with it if this hadn't happened,' grumbled Susanna.

'We'd have left it in the bank, my dear. None of it would have been given to you, so you needn't feel cheated.'

But that was just how she did feel. 'One day,' Mama had said, 'you'll be the owner's wife.' To see the yard demolished at the very moment she attained that position was, to say the least, disheartening. Sometimes Susanna felt that fate was poking fun at her. And still more disappointment lay in store, for when the will was read she learned that she could not even call herself sole mistress of her own home. Although he had left the business entirely to his son, John's wishes regarding the house were a little different. He was anxious to provide for his elder daughter, and so Boskenna became the joint property of Richard and Judith.

'What are you sulking about?' Richard asked, as he and his wife undressed for bed that night. 'I've told you we're not going to starve.' He pulled back the covers and climbed gingerly into bed. His shoulder was stiff and painful, his arm supported by a sling.

'We're not going to flourish, either. Not for a very long time – if ever. What has your father left you after all these years? Half a house and a pile of rubble. May God give me patience!'

She folded her arms and began tapping her foot. Richard knew what was coming next – a string of well-worn complaints, so familiar that he knew them by heart. Placidly, he allowed her to vent her frustration, boredom written all over his face.

'If only I'd married a man with prospects – a gentleman who'd buy me flowers and trinkets and pretty dresses, someone who could take me out and introduce me to people of consequence, people of culture and education. Dancing and dinner parties, visits to the continent, a residence to which I could proudly invite my friends – those were the things I should have had. Instead, I'm confined to this cheerless house, miles from anywhere, with neither amusement nor civilized company. I've only a paltry clothing allowance and no proper servants. There isn't even a decent carriage in which I may ride with dignity. It's no pleasure to be shaken about in an open dog-cart, Richard, and you know I can't easily manage that pony. I wasn't raised to travel in such a conveyance, let alone drive it. Mama and Papa had a brougham, let me remind you. Furthermore, I detest the accents and the manners of the men with whom you do business and I wish you wouldn't ask them into the house. The same applies to your employees: you invite them here every time a boat is launched, and you drink with them as if they were equals. My father only had dealings with gentlefolk and I was brought up in polite company. I've borne you three children, Richard. I've endured much insult and privation these past fifteen years. And now, at the very time when I thought my lot would be improved, I find myself no better off than before.'

All her grievances freshly aired, she turned irritably away and sat down before the mirror to brush her hair, using savage, dragging strokes. There came tiny sounds of tearing and tugging as she ripped at the tangles.

Richard was sitting up in bed with three pillows at his back. Bare-chested and still brown from the previous summer, he looked far more healthy than his pallid wife, despite all his bruises and bandages.

'You were never misled about the sort of life you'd have here,' he said mildly. 'As to my employees and my customers, I've more esteem for them than for you or any of your kind. You married a working man, Susanna – one with a small measure of prosperity and a little learning, but a man who works with his hands. You've known that all along, and if you feel you've married beneath you, remember 'twas desperation that made you do it, not love or any lies of mine.'

'Desperation?' She banged the hairbrush down on the dressing table and spun round on her seat. 'I was never without admirers! I've been courted by so many men that I'm scarcely able to remember them all.'

'Now you're sidestepping. You know what I'm talking about.'

Susanna ignored that and continued as if she had not heard it. 'There were gentlemen of breeding, wealth . . .'

'. . . and good judgement,' finished Richard. A twist of self-mockery tugged at the corner of his mouth. 'None was fool enough to marry you.'

He saw her nostrils quiver with fury. 'Hmph! It was usually I who refused them. Jeer if you like, but if you died tomorrow, I daresay I could find another husband without much trouble.'

She turned back to the mirror and dabbed a little lavender water round her ears and neck, frowning at the reflection of her husband in the bed behind her.

Richard's glance slithered over his wife with grim amusement. Her linen nightgown covered a body which had grown unquestionably scraggy. Tempted into a flash of cruelty, he said softly:

'I doubt that, Susanna. Believe me, you've faded over the years. You've nothing to offer a man any more. You're no longer young, your prettiness has disappeared and you've no love to give in its place.'

Susanna's mouth dropped slowly open as he spoke, and her hand crept up to clutch at the base of her throat. The blue eyes, stricken with anguish, flickered distractedly back and forth between Richard's reflection and that of her own face.

Every word he said was true. She was forty-three years old and time had not been kind to her. The blonde hair, once glossy, now possessed a slightly fluffy texture. It would crinkle but not curl, and for all her nightly brushing it never achieved a shine. Like a dry river bed, the skin was dull and etched with arid gullies between nose and mouth, scored by ripples across the brow and loose about the eyes, with a delicate cobweb of lines below them. The eyes themselves, still huge but not so brightly blue, took fearful note of the softening under her chin, and the way her bosom had lost its firm contours. For a few seconds, Richard thought she was going to cry.

After a moment, however, her features crumpled into a scowl. She stood up, walked round to the side of the bed and pushed her face close to his.

'If I am the worse for wear,' she spat, 'it's due to your lewd assaults and the bearing of your children. A lady should not be used too often, Richard. Her constitution is more delicate than that of a common woman.'

'All right,' he said, gently mocking. 'Let's see – it must be about a month since your last ordeal. If you like, I'll contain myself for six months more to see if the colour comes back to your cheeks. I shan't count it any hardship, my love. To do without you is to miss very little.'

Incensed, she lifted a hand to slap him, but he caught the slim wrist and forced it down on the bed, gripping so tightly that the bones ground beneath his fingers. Susanna emitted a small scream of pain, but glared back at him in defiance. Richard saw a working of her mouth, as if she were gathering saliva to spit in his face.

'Don't do it,' he warned quietly. 'Or I promise you'll be sorry.'

Almost imperceptibly, Susanna swallowed.

'That's better.' He released her and she hopped back out of his reach. 'I've never yet raised a hand to you, but don't provoke me too far.'

She eyed him sullenly. In the lamplight, her clamped mouth took on a wooden look. Richard decided that this would be an excellent time to lay down the law for the coming years.

'Now then, I want it understood that nothing is going to change in this house just because Father's gone. His ways are my ways too. You will not be the one to say who's welcome here and who isn't. And let me make a few things clear to you concerning money. . .'

He broke off for a second, turning to reach for the tot of brandy on the chair by his bed.

But Susanna did not intend to be lectured or put in her place. The instant he took his eyes off her, she lunged forward with clenched fist and delivered a sharp punch to his wounded shoulder.

Richard gave a bellow of agony and the glass clattered to the floor as he pressed his right hand to his collarbone and doubled over, rocking with pain. Susanna scurried round the end of the bed and bolted out through the door, her husband's curses ringing in her ears.

It took Richard several minutes to recover, but at last he struggled out of bed, shut the door with a crash and locked it behind her.

Susanna had fled downstairs and into the parlour, where she flung herself into an armchair before the fire. There she huddled and wept herself into exhausted sleep, sobbing with hatred for Richard and grief for her lost loveliness.

'Hannah! Will you come upstairs, please?'

Susanna woke with a start, then shivered when she realized where she was. It was past eight o'clock in the morning and she had spent the whole night in the chair.

'Hannah!' Richard bawled again. 'Where are you?'

Although the parlour door was closed, the sound of his voice came loud and clear. He was still angry – very angry. Susanna raised her head, listening intently.

'All right, all right, I'm comin'. My dear soul, whatever is it?'

She heard Hannah lumbering up the stairs and then a muffled conversation, as Richard issued terse instructions. There came a questioning murmur from the woman, followed by a few more curt words from Richard, then the slamming of a door.

Susanna shifted uncomfortably and slowly stood up. The fire had long gone out. She was stiff in every joint and very cold. From overhead came the thump of Hannah's heavy tread as she hurriedly set about some task, and also the sound of drawers and cupboards being roughly flung open and banged shut again.

Susanna opened the parlour door a crack, then slipped outside and padded along the passage to the foot of the staircase.

In the kitchen the children were all listening, wide-eyed. Judith, who had heard her brother swearing the previous night, closed the door and told them to get on with their breakfast.

Cautiously, Susanna went upstairs. The door to John's old room stood ajar and she saw Hannah in there, making up the bed with fresh linen. A moment later, Richard emerged from the couple's bedroom, bearing a bundle of Susanna's dresses. He barged past her without a word, threw open the door to his father's room and dropped the pile of bright silks on the floor.

Susanna gasped. 'What are you doing with my things? Those are my best frocks!'

Richard stalked by without answering and she scuttled after him as he returned to their room for another armful. She shrieked when he reached into her wardrobe and pulled three more gowns from their hangers, for she heard one of them rip.

'Here,' he snarled, hurling them at her. 'Move them yourself, but do it quickly. I want your belongings cleared from my room. You can take yourself and all your gewgaws out of my sight. I want no reminders of you left in here. Is that understood?'

His wife reached out to catch her ill-treated frocks. Her

flailing arms gathered in the mauve cotton and the yellow muslin, but her best cream taffeta fluttered to the floor. Richard trod on it as he crossed to the tallboy. He jerked the top drawer right out and up-ended it on the bed.

'Stop it! Stop it, you hateful brute! Leave my clothes alone!'

She snatched up the taffeta and hugged her frocks protectively as her husband pulled out a second drawer and emptied it in the same way. He had swept all her trinkets from the dressing table and torn off the cotton valance underneath. All her brushes and combs, her pins and aigrettes, her ribbons, her jewellery, her perfume bottles, lay strewn upon the rug.

She scrabbled to pick up a few precious items, then fled across the landing into John's room.

'Hannah,' she panted, 'for the love of Heaven, stop him. He's gone quite mad and he's ruining all my lovely things.'

The woman did not reply until she had finished tucking in the blankets at the foot of the bed. Then she straightened up and said calmly: 'What did ee 'spect, Mrs Rescorla? 'Twas bound t'happen sooner or later. It d'say a lot fer his patience that he've stood it s'long as he have. How far do ee think a man can be provoked? I suppose there was trouble here las' night? Whatever 'twas, you must've gone too far at last, an thass why he's movin' ee out.'

'Moving me out?' exclaimed Susanna. 'Out of my bedroom?'

''Tis his bedroom. You're t'have this one from now on.'

Susanna stared around her and two patches of florid colour appeared on her cheeks. She had seldom found cause to set foot in this room when John was alive, and what she now saw did not please her. It was less sunny than the one she shared with Richard. The paintwork was cream and brown, the furniture too chunky for her taste. The room was altogether very plain and masculine and she knew she could never feel comfortable in it.

'No! No, I will not be shoved away in here! It's like a waiting room at a railway station!'

Hannah shrugged. 'Your father-in-law liked it well enough.' She bent again to her task, turning her back on Susanna.

'Well I don't! If Richard wants to be apart from me, let him sleep in here.'

Hannah said nothing, but flapped open a plain white counterpane and laid it over the bed. Susanna rushed back across the landing to confront her husband, and found him scooping all her shoes, parasols and reticules into the basket normally reserved for dirty linen. He thrust it outside the door, then dropped an armful of Susanna's poetry books in on top.

'I will not be ejected from my room,' she informed him hotly. 'I'll be more than happy to sleep alone – God knows there have been nights enough when I've prayed to be left in peace – but you should be the one to move.'

She had drawn herself up to her full height – which was not very great – and lifted her nose in a manner meant to be imperious. But her tangled hair and baggy nightdress, together with the bare feet, were quite at odds with this haughty stance and made her seem ridiculous.

'This is my house now,' Richard said. 'I'll choose where I sleep and I'll also decide where you must sleep. If you don't care to accept that room, Madam, you can leave Boskenna just as soon as you please. You want to be spared my attentions, don't you? So you shall be. I'll never touch you again. You'll have a whole bed to yourself, a roomful of cupboards for your things, and all the privacy your heart could desire. Some fresh paint, a rug or two, and then 'twill be all your own – just as your body will be all your own to the very end of your days.'

It was useless to argue and she knew it. How, indeed, could she protest when he was giving her just what she had always claimed to want?

'Oh', she sniffed, 'very well. As long as the room is made decent, I can think of nothing I should like better.'

'Good. We agree, then. I'm going down to have my breakfast now, and I suggest you collect up the rest of your rubbish before I come back.'

And with that he pushed past her and thundered down the stairs.

Susanna's first night in her new room was a restless one. She kept waking every hour or two, wondering for an instant where Richard had gone. It was disconcerting to find that she actually missed the warmth of him beside her and could not sleep as soundly without it. The bed seemed unpleasantly large and she floundered about in it, turning constantly in an effort to regain the feeling of enfoldment to which she had grown accustomed after so many years of marriage. She had often complained that her husband's weight caused a slant in the mattress which made her roll towards him. Now she missed the support of his back, the faint, toasted smell of his skin and the restful sound of quiet breathing.

This banishment had shaken Susanna more than she cared to admit. No, she was no longer beautiful. She was also past bearing children, and since Richard had no other reason to want her, he could plainly do very well without her. The knowledge left her unexpectedly wounded and bereft, but her pride would never allow her to offer any apologies; she could never plead to be forgiven and taken back into her husband's bed. To ask would be humiliating, and instinct told her it was pointless anyway. As Hannah had said, she had goaded him too far.

28

Rufus and the apprentices took six days to clear the
rubble and sand from the courtyard. Although the building sheds were half demolished, it was found that the
vessels inside could be repaired and the men set to work
immediately on the crab boat and the mackerel driver.

The big lugger, too, could have been restored, but no
one, least of all Richard, had the heart for it, and the
owners would not want her in any case. She had killed a
man and therefore she was jinxed. No seaman would care
to sail in her, and since she was the first of a line, all the
others that followed would also be looked upon as
unlucky. The contract was cancelled, but Richard did not
care. One evening soon after the gale, the battered hull
was dragged down to the tideline. There, he doused her
in oil and pitch and burnt her.

The storm brought a heavy demand for repairs and
brand new vessels. Richard accepted all the work his men
could manage, including orders for two new boats, setting
up one in the courtyard and one near the top of the
beach. Throughout the spring he passed most of his time
down at the cove, doing whatever chores he could. At
first these were chiefly confined to light tasks and supervision, for although his shoulder healed quickly he was
unable to carry out any strenuous work until the end of
May.

By the end of July, however, he was fully fit again and
one of the workshops had been rebuilt. That summer was
particularly hot and it did not rain for weeks on end. Both
Richard's sons spent their days on the beach and around

the yard, or in and out of the water, almost free of clothing and tanned from head to foot, with a frosting of sand and salt glittering against their brown skin. For the men at the yard, the hours passed quickly, swallowed up by work. For the children they were long and lazy, and time meant very little. Alan, now ten years old, liked nothing better than to watch his father exercise his skill. He was keen to follow in Richard's footsteps, and full of questions about the craft. The younger one, however, had other interests and ways to amuse himself, and his brother was usually assigned to keep an eye on him.

One particular morning found Peter investigating the rock pools just round the point from the beach. He knew each one as a tiny self-contained world with its own landscape and shifting population of limpets, winkles and rubbery red anemones. The outgoing tide always stranded something interesting here – if not a hermit crab or a sea urchin, then perhaps a small jellyfish. That day, in his favourite pool, it had left him a blenny to catch.

The sunlight cast a mottled golden pattern over the bottom and fine tresses of weed stirred gently in the water. The fish nestled in a crevice between two greenish-brown stones. It was no more than two inches long and almost the same colour as the rocks. Only the softly undulating fins and tail had betrayed its presence when first he spotted it. For twenty minutes now, the blenny had eluded him, darting from one rocky cleft to the next, and Peter sat pondering the best means to coax it out of its refuge and trap it. His blue eyes lingered solemnly upon the fish, willing it to venture forth, but the blenny stubbornly declined to do so.

Peter wore nothing but a pair of cotton trousers, rolled up to the knees. He was perched on a shelf of rock, hard beneath his haunches and sharp to his bare feet, but he was not aware of discomfort, only an all-consuming interest in the blenny. Around him the air shimmered with heat and the sun scorched down on his back, relieved now and then by a fluttering breeze that touched his skin for an instant and was quickly gone again.

The catching of fish held a deep fascination for Peter. Here among the shallow pools, he could see all that went on – which was very interesting indeed. More absorbing still was the mystery of deeper water, dark green water full of secrets. Sometimes Father took Peter and Alan out to the rocks at the tip of the next headland, and there they would fish with handlines. The little boy never failed to feel a tremor of excitement as he watched his hook and sinker plop into the water, and saw his line fading inch by inch into who knew what strange regions. Far below there were unseen creatures swimming round his baited hook, and whenever there came a tug on that line, communication from the depths, Peter was almost beside himself with glee. Alan did not seem to understand or share his enthusiasm. Fishing was all right, he said, but he would much rather help Father at work.

'What are you looking at?'

Peter glanced up as his brother came to stand beside him, then he pointed to the blenny.

'Oh,' said Alan, uninterested. Then he tapped Peter lightly on the head and added: 'Mother wants you up at the house later on, don't forget. You have to put proper clothes on before she takes you into town.'

The boy groaned. 'I don't want to go. 'Tisn't fair.'

Alan squatted down beside him. He was tall for his ten years, and facially similar to his father. 'Best do as you're told, else she'll come down and fetch you.'

Peter pulled a face, feeling very much put upon. He was fond of Susanna, but could not help wondering why he was always the one singled out for her attention.

'Why doesn't she take you instead? She's only going to the shops.'

Alan grinned. 'Because 'tis you she likes,' he said happily. 'I expect she'll buy you something. She always does.'

'I share all my things with you,' Peter reminded him defensively.

'Oh, I know that. I didn't mean I was jealous.' Alan gave the smaller boy a reassuring nudge. Then, as his gaze lit upon an approaching boat, he murmured: 'Who's that, I wonder?'

Peter looked up and spotted a lugger drawing towards the cove. She passed within thirty yards of the rocks where the boys sat, but they recognized none of the men on board.

'What's her name?' Peter asked.

Alan stood up, squinting against the shimmer of sunlight on the sea. *Sweet Eva*, he announced after a moment. 'Don't know that one, she's never been here before. Wonder what her trouble is.'

The boat disappeared round the point into the cove.

'Let's go and see,' urged Alan, and he began scrambling across the rocks. With a last regretful glance at the blenny, the little boy tagged along behind.

Richard, too, had caught sight of the strange vessel. He climbed from the deck where he was fixing a mast and walked down over the beach. The incoming boat ran gently into the slushy sand at the water's edge and a man clambered nimbly over the side, a man in canvas smock and high boots. Richard's steps faltered when he recognized him, but the other came forward, extending a burly paw.

'I'm Luke Symons,' he said. 'Can you do a repair for me today?'

Rescorla shook him by the hand. 'We'll do our best. I'm, uh. . .'

'Richard,' finished the man. 'I know.'

There was a brief silence, while each summed up the other. Symons seemed cordial enough, though he was clearly inspecting the shipwright with curiosity.

Richard glanced towards the lugger. 'What's the trouble?'

"Tis the rudder. There's a great split in the wood and I'm worried it'll go further and break in half. Had a knock from some other boat, I expect. Suppose I'll need a new one.'

'You might, but I'll see what I can do with it. I've another job to finish first, then I'll have a look.'

'Fair enough.' Symons gestured towards the building sheds. 'I heard what happened here during the gale. You've picked up again, I see.'

'It's been a struggle, but we're all right now.'

Luke wryly pursed his mouth. 'A lot of my nets were lost that night. I had to cut them away and make a run for it. If I hadn't, we'd all have died for sure.' He jerked a thumb towards one of his crewmen. 'So now I've joined up with old Nathan there. He had twelve nets to put aboard, see.' His gaze strayed once more in the direction of the yard. Through the open doors of the larger workshop he glimpsed the keel, stem and sternpost of a new boat set up on the blocks. 'Do you have much work in hand?'

'A few good orders. That one's for Mount's Bay. Come and have a look at her.'

They walked up the beach together, talking as they went. Expecting awkwardness when faced with Jenny's husband, Richard was pleased to find him so agreeable. He had imagined he would resent the man, but decided instead that he liked him. They spent half an hour at the yard, discussing the merits and drawbacks of various craft and agreeing that they did not care for the coming of steam. Two firm believers in 'tradition', they had more in common than love for the same woman.

At length, Luke left Richard to finish the job in hand and went back to clean up his own boat while he waited. When he got there, he found two boys on board, pestering the crew with questions.

'These are Rescorla's sons,' the man called Nathan informed him. 'This one says he likes fishing,' he added, grinning at Peter. 'He wants to know if we'll take him out with us one night.'

Amused, Luke squatted down to speak to the child. Peter stared soberly back at him, hoping for a positive answer.

'Out in the cold and dark?' queried the fisherman. 'Think you'd enjoy that?'

'Yes,' insisted Peter. 'I want to catch fish like you do – hundreds and thousands of them.'

'You couldn't catch a blenny this morning,' teased Alan.

'Who cares about a blenny? 'Tis big fish I want – turbot and conger and skate.'

Symons chuckled. 'Longlining, eh? Is that what you like?' He reached out and playfully pinched the boy's chin. 'Listen, son, my eldest boy's more than twice your age and I shan't be taking him out for a year or two yet, so 'tis certain I can't take you.'

Peter hung his head with disappointment.

'You just think it over for a few years before you decide to go fishing.'

'How many years?'

'Oh, nine or ten. I'm willing to wager you'll forget all about it before then. Don't you want to be a shipwright and build fine big boats?'

'Suppose so,' mumbled Peter.

Luke glanced up at the older boy. 'What about you?'

'I'm going to follow Father,' announced Alan proudly. 'I'll be made apprentice in four years' time. I'm ten,' he explained grandly. 'Peter's only five. He asks all the fishermen if they'll take him on a trip and they always say no.'

Symons' eyes were slightly more sympathetic now, as he met Peter's crestfallen gaze. 'Is that a fact? Never mind, boy.' He ruffled the child's hair. 'Time passes faster than you think, and perhaps when you're fourteen or fifteen you'll be able to go. Meanwhile, take it from me, you're far better off in your warm bed at night.'

Peter was not convinced, but he knew that no meant no. 'Is it all right if I stay on board and look round, then?'

'So long as you don't interfere with the gear. Old Nathan here will teach you to tie knots, if you ask him.'

This was at least a step in the right direction. Peter smiled gratefully up at Symons.

'Will you be coming here again?' he asked.

'Yes, boy,' came the prompt reply, 'I believe I will.'

29

Like his father, Richard had always been a home-loving man. Most of his spare time was spent with his children, or in dealing with bills or fashioning half models on the settle by the kitchen fire. Sometimes he would read or make items of plain furniture, and these quiet pastimes had hitherto been enough for him.

That autumn, however, bereft of John's company and finding his business restored to normal, he began to feel the desire for something more, so he took to spending an evening or two at the Halveor Inn each week. Sometimes he just went for a meal and a mug of ale, but he liked the skittle matches too and soon became a regular spectator at games between rival parishes.

One such contest occurred in late October. Porthgullow were playing the team from St Ives and Richard arrived at the inn well before eight. The pewter room was already crowded with customers, the air hazy with tobacco smoke and filled with loud talk and ribald laughter. His sister served him a tankard of ale and asked if he had had any dinner.

'No,' he said, 'I've come straight from work.'

'Go on over and make yourself comfortable, then, and I'll bring you something to eat. The match won't start till nine, so there's plenty of time.'

The dining room was deserted and Richard found himself with a dozen tables from which to choose. He settled himself at a small one in the corner.

A few minutes later the door opened and he looked up, expecting to see his sister carrying a tray. But instead it was Roger who entered, and with him was a very striking young woman.

'Good to see you, Richard,' the publican said. 'Esme tells me you've come for supper.'

'That and the skittle match.' Richard stretched out a hand and Carwarthen clasped it amiably. 'All right, are you?'

'Oh, I'm as well as ever.' Roger then turned to the woman. 'This is Mr Rescorla,' he said. 'My brother-in-law.'

Richard stood up and wished her good evening.

The lady's glance swept over him with warm approval. 'How do you do, sir?' She lifted glossy dark eyebrows and inclined her head with a smile.

'Mrs Drew has taken a room with us, just for tonight,' explained Roger.

'I'm spending a month in Cornwall,' she said. 'I've made it my plan to travel down the south coast and return along the north. Porthgullow is quite charming – and I've heard many good reports of this inn.'

'You won't be disappointed,' Richard said.

'No indeed. My room is very comfortable.' She quickly scanned the other tables, then asked of Roger: 'Am I the only houseguest, sir?'

'I regret that you are, Mrs Drew.'

She regarded Richard expectantly. 'Then I'm fortunate to have a little company.'

He had not anticipated that, dressed as he was in his working clothes. 'Oh – please . . .' He gestured towards the chair facing his own, and Roger held it for her as she sat down.

'Thank you. I never care to eat alone.'

Mrs Drew was small and very dark, a lively talker and clearly a woman who meant to enjoy life. She had been to India and the Far East, she informed him, and she spent several months of each year in the fashionable resorts of Europe. Her late husband had left her very wealthy, as her costly magenta silk frock, rings and necklet bore witness.

As the meal progressed, Richard learned that Mrs Drew had many friends and interests. She chattered about opera and horse-racing, French fashion and various expensive pursuits of which he knew next to nothing. She made brief enquiries as to his occupation, but the mention of boats only served to send her into raptures over the romance of sailing ships and the sea.

Despite her frivolity, Richard found Mrs Drew refreshing. She was merry, irreverent and highly entertaining, describing in vivid colours the sights and the people she had seen. She led the kind of life for which Susanna had always longed, but there was not the slightest similarity in temperament between the two women. Mrs Drew was not genteel. A lady dedicated to good living could not be hindered by propriety.

'You must call me Maudie,' she insisted at one point, 'and I shall call you Richard. I can't abide stuffiness.'

Maudie, he noticed, had a mighty appetite. While Richard was content with lamb, she ordered turbot, followed by ginger pudding with cream and brandy. By the time they had finished the cheese and fruit, she had drunk five glasses of wine and was quite tipsy. It was at this point that her conversation began to touch upon the subject of intrigue.

Mrs Drew was unashamedly fond of men and she hinted at a lengthy list of lovers. From the way she twinkled at him, patted his hand and kept referring to the 'cosy, secluded little room' Esme had given her, Richard was left in no doubt that he was hereby invited to join that happy company.

He had no qualms about accepting, for abstinence did not come easily to him. He guessed, quite correctly, that

239

Maudie did not discriminate on grounds of social standing. Duke or tradesman, a man was a man, and fair game if she liked the look of him. Richard had never encountered such a thing before, and was altogether tickled by it.

As she shuttled back and forth, replenishing plates and glasses, Esme soon became aware of the way things were developing. She was therefore not surprised when, shortly after half past nine, she saw them quietly slipping upstairs together. When he turned at the bend in the staircase, her brother chanced to look down and spot her standing there. Esme grinned at him, winked, then went about her business, and Richard followed Mrs Drew across the landing to her room. The door closed with a soft click behind them.

'I thought he came to see the skittle match,' whispered Roger, when his wife confided the news.

'So he did, but he's found something better to do. I'm glad you introduced him to Mrs Drew. I think she'll be a tonic for him.'

'But I didn't expect him to bed her!'

'Lord knows, the lady's eager, so why should he refuse?'

'I only hope it doesn't lead to trouble,' said Roger darkly.

'Oh, for heaven's sake! Mrs Drew's only staying one night.'

'Yes, but whether you like it or not, Richard has a wife and three children, and once a man starts dallying . . .'

'He has what passes for a wife – and a mean, loveless thing she is, too. If I were in his shoes, I'd take whatever happiness I could find. Morals, propriety, even the law, could go to the devil!'

It had been such a very long time since Richard shared a bed with a woman who really wanted him. All the years of grudging compliance from his wife had built a pressure of need that astonished even Maudie Drew by its intensity. She was far too worldly to take offence when she heard the name 'Jenny' breathed in one forgetful moment, and although casual affairs were a way of life to her, she was sensitive enough to realize that he was venting more than simple lust that night.

Richard had told her he had a wife and children. They were obviously no remedy for whatever troubled him. Maudie was not inclined to pry, but as she lay amid the tumbled bedclothes with his sleeping form stretched half across her, she guessed that an encounter like this had been long overdue. Perhaps his wife was delicate or ill, she thought. Why else would such a fine, enjoyable man be going to waste?

When she woke in the morning, Richard had gone. He had left her a farewell note and she chuckled when she read it, savouring the compliments paid to her. It would be given a place in her secret album, along with others of its kind. Maudie stretched and sighed and mused contentedly for a while before getting up to dress. She left Halveor after breakfast, wearing a smart travelling costume and a hat with a big green feather, gaily waving farewell to the Carwarthens as her carriage pulled away.

'I can hardly believe it of her,' Roger said for the sixth time. 'She seemed such a lady.'

'She is a lady,' reproved Esme. 'I wish she'd stayed a little longer. Richard was in great spirits when he left here this morning.'

It was just before eight o'clock when Richard arrived back at Boskenna. Susanna was having her breakfast when she heard him come in. She had risen earlier than usual, after a sleepless night spent listening for his return. He went down the passage to the kitchen, said a bright

'Good morning' to the wide-eyed Judith, then took a jug of hot water and bounded up the stairs with it.

Never before had he stayed out all night. Susanna had hoped he would come into the dining room to explain himself. When he did not do so, she flung aside her napkin, rose from the table and followed him up to his room. There, she found him standing before the wall mirror in shirtsleeves, lathering soap over a considerable growth of stubble.

'Where have you been?' Her voice was pitched just above a hiss.

'Good morning, dearest,' he said to her reflection.

Susanna's mouth was so severely pursed that tiny lines crinkled the skin around it. Her eyes were fixed balefully upon him, the pupils shrunk to pinpoints.

'Did you hear my question? Where have you been?'

'Since we don't spend our nights together, why should my whereabouts concern you?'

He picked up a razor and stropped it slowly on the leather.

'A wife has a right to know of her husband's mischief.'

Richard tilted his head and began rapidly scraping the bristles from under his chin.

'All right. I went to Halveor.'

'Drinking,' snorted Susanna. 'I thought as much. Were you so intoxicated that you couldn't find your way home?'

Her husband sheared the line of growth from his top lip and smiled as he rinsed the razor in his shaving mug.

'I had a glass of ale and a drop of wine, that's all.'

'A drop, you say? Sufficient to make you forget your responsibilities, it seems. You should have been at work two hours ago.'

'I'm my own master, Susanna, not a slave to bell or clock – and I needn't answer to you for my comings and

242

goings. Do you always lie awake listening to find out what time I come in?'

'Certainly not. It's just that I normally hear you. Last night I didn't and so I began to wonder if something had happened.'

'What's this? Concern?'

'Only for decent behaviour. You must have been in a shameful state if your sister had to put you up for the night.'

Richard finished shaving, flicked the last trace of soap from his cheek and ran a towel over his face. Then he poured the hot water into the basin on the washstand and began to peel off his shirt.

'Oh well, if it suits you to think so, I can't be bothered arguing. Just go away and let me wash in peace.'

But his wife had ceased listening. Her gaze was riveted on his back and her eyes started in shock at what they saw there.

'How did you get those?'

'What?' He turned and saw that she was pointing at him, her mouth slack with astonishment.

'Those, those marks! Where did they come from? There, on your back! Look in the mirror!'

He twisted round to see. Sure enough, there were half a dozen thin red streaks scored from his shoulders to his waist. Richard chuckled softly and fingered the scratches. They were rough and slightly raised.

'They're just like clawmarks!' exclaimed Susanna. 'What on earth . . .?'

She clamped her mouth shut in outrage when Richard's chuckle became a roar of mirth. Inhibited as she was, Susanna really did not understand how he could have acquired the scratches. She had never hugged or clutched at him in passion, and would think it bizarre that such wounds could signify a woman's enjoyment.

243

'I see nothing humorous, Richard. And how did you get that peculiar bruise?'

Another glance in the mirror showed him the large, plum-coloured contusion at the base of his throat. It was just at the tip of that collarbone broken during the gale, and a little circle of dainty teethmarks was clearly visible. Richard remembered the exact moment when Mrs Drew had given him that bite and he felt his spine weaken once more with the recollection.

'Have you been fighting?'

Richard bent his head and soaped his neck. 'Just a friendly tussle, my love.'

Susanna continued to stare at him with a puzzled frown. Then slowly the signs of comprehension began to appear on her face. Briefly – very briefly – Richard felt a little sorry for her.

'Oh! Oh, my God! You've . . .'

'Yes,' he said pleasantly, 'that's right.'

'You've been with some whore!' gasped Susanna.

'No,' said Richard, 'I wouldn't call her that.' He soaped his hands again and started washing his arms and chest.

'A trollop!' spat his wife. 'A loose woman! Some filthy, diseased creature from the streets! How much did you pay her?'

Splashing himself with water, Richard shook his head. 'Not a penny, Susanna. The lady has more money than I could earn in a lifetime. She's a lovely little widow with plenty of warmth and wit, and men are just one of her pastimes.' For devilment, he neglected to explain that Maudie was only passing through and would probably never come back again.

So, the woman was rich and pretty. Susanna swallowed hard. A prostitute would have been preferable. A common slut was a purchased commodity, not a rival to the lawful wife. She saw herself reflected in the mirror,

244

realized that fear and anger made her ugly, and tried to compose her features into an expression of indifference.

'Well, well. I wondered how long it would be before you took to philandering. I hope you were at least discreet about it?'

'Don't worry, Susanna, the secret's safe within the family.'

'Oh, yes indeed. I'm sure your sordid little escapade had Esme's full approval, and naturally you can count on her connivance in the future. How very convenient that your sister is a publican's wife. You'll always have somewhere to take your little harlots, won't you?'

'The inn may come in handy from time to time,' agreed Richard, opening the linen chest to rummage about for a clean shirt. He found one and shrugged it on, then turned and laughed softly as he fastened the buttons. 'You ought to be grateful to Esme, you know. If I had nowhere else to go, I might bring a woman home one night and have her in my own bed.'

Susanna would hear no more. She was already on her way out, head high and skirts swishing. Richard put on the rest of his working clothes and combed his tangled hair. As he pulled on the jacket, Esme's parting words came back to him:

'There will always be a room here for you, Richard.'

Susanna's assessment of Esme's attitude had been quick and wonderfully accurate, he thought. Of course, women always understood one another in a way that men could never fathom. It was just as well for him, he told himself cheerfully, that no love was lost between his wife and sister. Yes indeed, what he had done once, he could do again. It was doubtful whether he would be lucky enough to see any more of Maudie Drew, but he knew several local women who would need very little encouragement to share a bed with him from time to time.

30

After that, there were quite a few nights when Richard did not come home. And now there appeared upon Susanna's dressing table an assortment of little pots and glass jars. They contained creams and scented oils, powder, solutions of eyebright and lotions for the hair, together with various substances to be dissolved in the bathwater, sprinkled on it or inhaled with the steam. Susanna also possessed a pot of rouge, but she kept it hidden in a shoe at the bottom of her wardrobe.

During the early years of her marriage, she would have claimed unconcern, even relief, at the idea that her husband could satisfy his needs elsewhere. In the event, however, she found it humiliating. Far from losing his attraction, Richard was improved by the confidence and maturity of his thirty-five years and Susanna knew that many women would find her husband highly desirable. She suspected there had been several others since Maudie Drew, and she was right.

Alone and brooding, she tormented herself with imaginings, recalling all those buxom, bright-eyed Porthgullow girls who had ogled him in his youth and probably admired him still. Sometimes she anxiously pictured him together with a youthful mistress, and wondered if they talked about her. Perhaps they made jokes at her expense. Perhaps Richard drew insulting comparisons and amused the little slut with details of his wife's decline, describing every tiny sag and wrinkle.

In truth, he seldom even thought of her at such times.

246

Richard did not bother to taunt Susanna with his adventures, but nor did he make any effort to conceal them. He did not speak of the subject or mention any names, but whenever he went out wearing his best clothes and returned in jaunty good humour the following morning, she could have little doubt as to how he had spent the night.

For the sake of her pride, Susanna tried to pretend indifference. Yet every so often her resentment and curiosity seeped out in disdainful enquiries as to which strumpet, which leprous Jezebel had lately been chosen to satisfy his vile desires. And she spent every penny she could on preparations designed to improve her appearance. She knew there was little hope of reclaiming Richard's admiration, but now that he had other – probably younger – women, self-respect demanded that the contrast should not be too extreme, too cruel.

On the question of grooming, Susanna's main source of advice was the *Lady's Companion*. Katie, too, had been finding the paper interesting of late. As soon as her mother had finished with it, she picked up the September issue and took it off to her room, for it carried the last episode of the current serial and she was eager to know the ending. On the cover was a pastel portrait of an Honourable Mirabelle somebody, who was shortly to marry an Honourable Finlay somebody and live in Sussex with him. Susanna always cut these covers off and kept them, for she was endlessly fascinated by the matings of the gentry.

Upstairs, Katie flopped down on her bed, turned to the index and scanned the familiar headings: 'Everyday Etiquette', 'In Confidence (with Doctor Guthrie)', 'Dire Dilemmas and Good Advice', 'Faith and Fortitude', by

Canon Parfrey. Then there were pages on fashion, hair-dressing, the household budget and management of servants, plus the monthly 'Sisters, Arise' article, invariably a radical piece suggesting that women should do all sorts of unfeminine things. Convention was always restored by the serial, which was very romantic and could only ever end in death or marriage. Katie leafed through to page forty-three and spent a happy half-hour learning that the outcome in this case was tragedy.

She had first been drawn to the *Lady's Companion* by the medical items, morbidly intrigued by accounts of other people's rashes, swellings, itches and cramps. She was strong and unblemished herself, but sometimes found something of personal relevance in coy discussions of 'female troubles', even though these were confined to the vaguest of hints. The girl was now nearly fourteen and very much concerned with such things, but guidance had never been given by her mother who would not, or Judith who could not, speak of these delicate subjects. It was from blunt Aunt Esme that enlightenment had finally come, and once Katie had grown used to the idea, the arrival of womanhood had begun to seem quite exciting.

Having finished the story, she flipped over a few more pages in search of Doctor Guthrie – but halted instead at a picture of a girl dressed for an evening out. Katie caught her breath, then slowly released it in a soft 'Ooh' as she took in all the details. A cream silk ball gown, an ostrich feather fan, a sapphire necklace and, oh, such a head of hair, waved and curled and pinned up with glittering combs.

Katie wished she could look like that. She glanced towards the mirror on the wardrobe door and pulled a face at the scruffy reflection she saw there. This, she told herself, would no longer do. It was time to have nice frocks, time to control that messy hair and learn a little grace.

But – she bit her lip, then started to gnaw at a thumbnail – it would mean asking Mother for help. Aunt Judith, to whom she normally turned, had no skill at fancy sewing or hairdressing. Aunt Esme might be of some assistance, but Mother was undeniably the expert when it came to primping. And Mother could, with some justification, say that Katie had never wanted the pretty things made for her as a child and had left it too late to change her tune.

For a moment she dismissed the idea of approaching Susanna. But then she looked again at the picture and mustered her resolve. Perhaps she would ask her on Sunday. Yes, Sunday, the only day of the week when the whole family sat down to a meal together, for then she knew her father would be there to back her up.

'Mother, I'll be fourteen next week. May I put my hair up?'

Susanna laid down her knife and fork, staring at her daughter in surprise. 'Oh, I think you're still a little too young for that, Katherine. Perhaps in a year or two . . .'

'Go on,' interrupted Richard. 'How many times have I heard you complain that she's not ladylike? Aren't you glad to see she's growing up at last?'

His wife's brows lifted and her lids lowered primly over chilly eyes as she attended once more to her lunch. 'Naturally, I shall be delighted if this heralds an improvement in Katherine's deportment. A little decorum would certainly not come amiss.' She cut a tiny piece of roast beef and conveyed it daintily to her mouth.

'You'll show me how to do it, then?' pressed the girl.

'Yes, yes, all right.'

Katie's face flushed with excitement. 'This afternoon?'

'No, Katherine. Peter and I are going to study The Children's Picture Book of Bible Stories this afternoon – aren't we, little man?'

249

The boy slid pleading eyes towards Judith, in hopes of rescue, but she said nothing and so he mumbled: 'Yes, Mama.'

'We're going to learn about Jesus and the loaves and fishes,' Susanna informed them all brightly. 'And then we're going to use Peter's new water colours to shade in the picture of the five thousand eating their lovely feast, aren't we, dear? We always have a nice time together on Sundays, don't we?'

He made a weak attempt to smile. 'Yes, Mama.'

Susanna turned to her daughter. 'I will dress your hair on your birthday, Katherine, as a special treat.'

'There, girl,' said Richard. 'Your mother will turn you from a hoyden into a beauty – and high time too, I think. Shall I buy you a new frock? Something pretty?'

'Oh yes! With a bustle and a tiny waist!'

'Don't be silly, child,' reproved Susanna. 'A bustle would be quite unsuitable and you're certainly not ready for stays or tight lacing.'

Alan spluttered with mirth. 'Imagine grubby old Katie done up in a corset and tripping about in a big skirt.'

His father silenced him with a light cuff across the head.

'Your mother's right,' Richard told his daughter. 'That sort of foolishness can wait. I meant a nice simple frock.' Then he added: 'Take her into Porthgullow tomorrow morning, Susanna. Help her choose a pattern and fabric.'

'Oh, very well.' Susanna emitted a forceful sigh of annoyance and threw an irritable glance at the girl. She was reluctant to spend time or effort on her daughter, whom she considered a lost cause in more than one respect. Her gaze slithered impatiently over Katie's loose cotton frock and the straight black hair that hung untidily round her face. She would never make a 'beauty', as Richard so foolishly promised. Moreover, the girl had no love for her mother and Susanna thought it too late to earn her loyalty now.

'I'm sorry to be such a nuisance to you, Mother.'

There was an edge to Katie's voice that made Susanna glance sharply at her.

'It's not that I really begrudge you my time, Katherine. I merely fear that your father will spoil you.'

'That's my privilege,' Richard said, winking at the girl.

Never, through all the years of Katie's childhood, had Susanna imagined that she would one day be fiercely envious of her daughter. Indeed, it was not until the birthday arrived that Susanna realized she had cause for such feeling.

The new frock was made of tarlatan. It was cornflower blue, with pearl buttons on the bodice, a scallop-edged collar of white lace and a deep frill around the hem of the skirt. Katie stood excitedly before the mirror, almost too thrilled to stay still while Judith fastened up the back. Pink-cheeked with delight, her black hair pinned high in curls, the girl twisted and turned in front of the glass, spreading the skirts and patting the glossy, upswept tresses. The urchin with the dirty fingernails and torn petticoats had decidedly gone for ever. In her place stood a graceful young woman of striking complexion, with a trim but well-developed figure that owed nothing to corsetry.

'Well?' she asked breathlessly. 'What do you think of me?'

'You're lovely, Katie,' Judith said, 'truly lovely. Your father will be very pleased, I'm sure.'

The girl turned to her mother, expecting similar expressions of approval. After all, Susanna's taste and skill had achieved this miracle. She surely had cause to be proud of her handiwork.

'Mother?'

Critical, unsmiling, Susanna surveyed her for a moment, searching for flaws, for signs of awkwardness. A faint frown creased her forehead and she took a while to answer. Katie's smile wavered and faded with uncertainty. She looked again towards Judith for reassurance.

'Yes, quite nice,' allowed her mother coolly, 'though now that I see you wearing it, I think the frock is a little overwhelming.'

'On the contrary,' said Judith, 'it's not a bit fussy and she has the bearing for it.'

'Forgive me,' said Susanna sweetly, 'but I think my judgement is more reliable than yours. I believe we should slacken these darts at the bosom . . .'

'The fit is perfect,' objected Judith. 'To alter it now would make her seem shapeless.'

'I beg to differ.' She turned a wheedling smile on Katie. 'And perhaps a smooth little chignon, instead of these unruly curls? We do want to look dignified, don't we? Now stand up straight, dear, head high, and don't wring your fingers like that. Gaucheness is not attractive.'

Even Judith, for all her naïveté, could see envy at work here. Susanna had been assigned to transform her daughter – and had done it all too well. The result was more than she had bargained for, and now she wished to modify it. Judith's mouth tightened slightly, then she said:

'Well, since we can't agree, we must let the head of the household decide.' She put out a hand and gave Katie a gentle nudge. 'Go and show your father, my dear.'

'Oh, but surely Katherine should look her best before Richard's opinion is sought? Men know so little of these matters,' cut in Susanna swiftly. 'They're apt to approve the first thing they see.'

'Only if 'tis something they like.' Judith nodded encouragement to Katie, who was beginning to look quite anxious. 'Go along now, quickly.'

'I wish you wouldn't interfere, Judith,' said Susanna, when the girl had gone downstairs. 'You seem to forget sometimes that Katherine is my daughter, not yours.'

'Till now, my dear Susanna, you've been content to forget it for most of the time. Is it mother love she's finally roused in you, or simple jealousy?'

Such a riposte from Judith was a thing so unexpected that Susanna's mouth sagged open in astonishment.

'Don't be ridiculous,' she said stiffly.

But she felt her face go red, and she hurried from the room in case Judith should decide to state any more embarrassing truths.

She's fading while her daughter blossoms, Judith thought. And she can't bear it. Perhaps, after all, my plainness has its compensations.

Down in the parlour, Susanna found Katie revelling in Richard's praise and admiration. As she watched her daughter spin round to display the frock, Susanna felt older, more stale and drained than ever before. None of her cosmetics could repair the relentless attrition of the years. They could not even disguise it, and nothing could ever give back to her the fresh lustre Katherine now enjoyed.

The girl turned to face her and announced triumphantly: 'Father likes me just as I am. He says we're not to change a thing.'

Susanna gave a small shrug and a careless flip of her hand. 'Oh, as you wish, Richard. If you think it suits her, I shan't argue.'

Richard cast a slightly puzzled glance at his wife. 'You've done very well for her, Susanna. I see nothing to criticize.'

'I thought the frock a little gaudy, that was all, and the curls a bit flighty. I seldom make an error of judgement in such matters, but I'd confess to one in this case. I

253

would have preferred an effect more demure.' She turned to Katie with a tight little smile. 'However, I must make allowance for the fact that your father's taste has become somewhat – flamboyant – in recent months. He doesn't care for shyness in a woman. It's boldness he admires.'

The girl's face clouded as she recognized the insult. She knew of the nights Richard spent away from home. She had heard her mother speak of women whom she dismissed as 'cheap' and 'vulgar'. Well, even if they were, the fact remained that Father preferred their company to that of his wife. Katie sat down on the arm of his chair and gave his hand a squeeze. Richard said nothing, but smiled up at her once more to reaffirm his approval.

Without another word, Susanna went to her sewing table and picked up the piece of work that lay there. Her husband had not answered the call to combat, but she knew he was watching her as she threaded her machine. It was not anger she sensed from him, but something closer to pity. Richard knew she was jealous. She could feel that he knew, and her cheeks burned with humiliation. Katherine was the beauty of the family now. She had her father's love and her whole life to live. Susanna almost hated her.

31

With every year that passed, Esme and Roger noted the disappearance of a few more familiar faces from among the pewter room crowd. The emigrant ships were taking more and more of Cornwall's mining men to far-flung places, and it could not be denied that the teetotal crusade was gaining ground as well. A kind of creeping respectability encroached from every side, as hardened drinkers found salvation, signed pledges and developed a liking for tea.

'Where's Jimmy Jackets?' Roger might ask of his customers. 'Haven't seen him for weeks.'

'Jimmy? Aw, he went to Australia. Left las' month.'

Or, 'What's happened to Charlie Oakie?'

'South America. Gone to Chile.'

'How about Denzil Paul? He's surely too old to go abroad?'

'Ah,' they would say gravely, ''twas the Teetotal Society got he. Denzil started worryin', see. 'Fraid fer his soul, he was.'

And so it went on. Miss Jory made a point of calling at the Halveor Inn at least once a fortnight to exhort the customers and distribute pamphlets. She also made occasional reports to the constable on minor breaches of licensing law – a subject of which she knew a great deal – and had twice succeeded in having the magistrates impose a small fine on the Carwarthens.

Most recently, Roger had caught her tacking a notice to his front door. It read:

ALCOHOL IS AN ABOMINATION
The Teetotal Society
Will be serving tea and coffee
with a choice of pastries and cakes
at
THE CHURCH HALL, PORTHGULLOW
on
FRIDAY 9th OCTOBER, 1874
at seven in the evening
ALL ARE MOST WELCOME
COME, SAVE YOURSELVES!
(No charge)

Roger had quickly torn down the poster and seen her off, but not before she had loudly announced the free treat to all within earshot. Naturally, a few of them took up the invitation and some were persuaded into abstinence.

''Tis the same all over the county,' Roger said in the kitchen that morning, as Esme grumbled about Miss Jory's effrontery. 'Cornwall's changing fast and the teetotal societies are only part of the reason. 'Tis Methodism, education, new laws, inspectors of this and that sent down here from London, and more bobbies in the towns. Between them, they've reformed almost everything these past thirty years. I can't object to most of what's been done. In all conscience, I can't even argue against moderation in men's drinking habits, but I resent the way that woman denounces me as if I'm Satan's henchman. 'Tis said she has a private income, but I have my living to make.'

'I told her that, but it made no difference,' said Esme, who was washing off leeks to go in a stew.

Roger grunted. 'There's no greater pest on God's earth than a withered old maid with a moral purpose to take the place of her natural one.'

The instant the words were spoken, he faltered in

awkwardness and regret, for a shuttered look appeared on Esme's face and she turned her back on him, seizing a knife and chopping at the vegetables with an agitated, jerky motion.

Inwardly, Roger cursed himself. He hovered briefly in the doorway, groping for words of reassurance, then decided not to say anything lest he blunder again. The matter had become too painful for discussion. Eight years had gone by and they had ceased to hope for a child. To make things worse, Dinah the kitchenmaid, married only seven months, was heavily pregnant already.

The stew, a whole gallon of it, went at lunchtime. For the evening Esme made, among other things, one of her celebrated pigeon pies.

The first slice was sold at just after seven o'clock. The inn was already very busy and while foraging under the counter for more glasses, Esme heard the clink of a coin being placed on the top of it, and then a deep voice asking for a draught of her own homebrew. She straightened up, pushing back the unruly hair, and reached wearily for the money. Then her eyes rose to the face of her customer.

'Tom!' It came as a startled whisper.

'How ee doin', maid?' The hazel eyes travelled over her in smiling appraisal. 'Surprised? Well, it've bin ten year, I spose.'

'Nearer twelve!' Her tone was indignant, but a shining smile lit her face. 'All that time, never a word, and now you turn up like this!'

'I've only lately come back this way. Soon heard tell o' you 'n your cookin', though. 'Tis said to be the finest, so I'm come to try it.'

His body had broadened and grown muscular, and the brown hair was slightly longer, more wavy than Esme recalled. At twenty-seven, he still appeared perfectly healthy. The dust and the damp and the gunpowder fumes had not yet begun to affect his lungs, and he showed no

257

sign of ever having suffered serious injury. Esme had seen men and boys much younger than Tom who were crippled and mutilated by accidents below ground. She had often thought about him, and shivered to imagine him in similar condition. But there he stood, strong and well, grinning at her in the old familiar way, and his presence filled her with delight.

'Oh, 'tis good to see you,' she said warmly. 'I thought you'd gone for ever.'

'So did I, at the start. But I've changed me plans half dozen times in as many years, goin' from one pit to the next, an now I've drifted back here.'

'You've a lot to tell me, then?'

'Ess, if you want to hear it.'

'You know I do. First, though, what would you like to eat?'

'Got any pigeon pie, have ee?'

'That I have, fresh-made today,' she said, handing him his ale. 'Now, see the little round table in the corner by the fireplace? Make yourself at home there and I'll bring your food over.'

Roger, pouring brandies at the other end of the counter, had noticed the young man – a stranger to him, but evidently not to Esme, for she greeted him with rare excitement. When she emerged from the kitchen soon afterwards, bearing a plate piled high with steaming carrots, potatoes, and a huge slice of pie, Roger paused to watch as she delivered it to her friend, laid out his knife and fork for him, and then sat down at the table to talk. Their conversation was lost in the babble of voices and the rumble and clatter from the skittle alley, but it was clear to Carwarthen that they knew each other very well.

'What's brought you back, Tom?' she asked.

'I've took a pitch at Balgadden.' He tried the pie, then winked approval at her.

258

'Balgadden? Why, that's only a mile or two over the moor.'

He went on eating for a moment, then laid down his knife to reach for the tankard. 'Ess, 'tidn far. I've made a nice bargain, I b'lieve. There's good ore comin' out o' this lode, tribute's fourteen shullen in the pound 'n there's only four of us to share the money.'

'Tribute,' repeated Esme, beaming. 'So you've made some progress, Tom.'

He nodded, looking slightly rueful. 'Some, 'tis true, but not nearly enough. I used to think I ony had t'escape from Faather 'n 'twould all come right. By God, though, I had some awful hard time after I left here. Can't tell ee how many nights I slept rough. See, I wadden fitted fer none but the simplest work. Still, in th'end I had a stroke o'luck – fell in with a tributer who'd lost both his sons. Learned a good bit workin' with he. He've gone now, though. Died six year ago.'

'What became of your own people? I never see any of them.'

'Th'ole man've bin buried since summer 'fore last. I didn' even knaw till I went out there las' week. I'm livin' in lodgins, see, close to the mine. Mother d'look s'if she wen't go on fer long, neether. As fer the rest of 'em, the girls are all marrid wi' babies, or else workin' on the bal.'

'And your brothers?'

'Aw, still on tut-work, still keepin' the beershops busy. They'll go same way as Faather, I dawn't doubt.' Tom jerked his head towards Roger. 'Your husband's a decent sort, I'm told. Treat ee well, do uh?'

'Yes, I love him very much.'

'I'm glad o' that. Wouldn't like to think of ee wed to some ole misery. How many children have ee got?'

Just for a second he saw distress flit across her face, then she forced a smile.

259

'None – yet.' There was no conviction in that last word, and he realized he had touched a nerve.

'Well, no hurry, eh?' He smiled awkwardly.

'What about you? No wife or family yet?'

'I always said I wouldn' be tied. Dunnee remember that?'

'Yes, but if you want to rise to be captain, you'll need to settle somewhere.'

He pushed his empty plate to one side. 'Not in Cornwall, Esme. 'Tis no good here. I'd hoped to be further ahead be now, but there's too many pits closin'. The minin's dyin' an I dawn't b'lieve 'twill ever thrive again, 'cause tin d'come cheaper from foreign parts these days. I've bin thinkin' it awver 'n 'tis clear to me that a man must go abroad if he hope to make anythin' of hisself. The outlook's better overseas, so I'll be takin' ship sometime nex' year.'

'Oh – I see.' Esme felt a stab of dismay, though she recognized it as senseless. I ought to be surprised, she thought, that he hasn't gone already.

'Of course,' she said, reaching out to squeeze his hand. 'Any man of ability would do the same. Where exactly will you go?'

'Chile, p'raps, or British Columbia. I avn decided yet. I'd have left 'fore now, 'cept that I want to gain some learnin' fore I go. The travellin' school's comin' this way nex' spring, see.'

'The what?'

''Tis a professor – a man o' science. He d'go round the differnt towns 'n stay fer three months or so, holdin' classes of an evenin' fer men that want to better themselves. March to May nex' year, he'll be in Porthgullow. Now, you knaw I never had no real schoolin', and though there's many a Cornish cap'n can barely write his name, I've heard that some 'o they companies abroad d'set a lot

260

o'store be book learnin'. 'Tidn good 'nough no more fer a faather to teach his son be example 'n plain speech. I knaw me job 'n I'm good at it, but I want that schoolin' too.'

'But you can't read, can you?'

'Not much – not yet – but I've started goin' t'ole Maggie Jory's classes down the church hall twice a week, an I'm comin' on all right.'

Esme looked quite taken aback, and Tregunna's grin broadened knowingly. 'She d'say I'm her best pupil. Mind, I dawn't spose she's any friend o' yours?'

Esme cleared her throat. 'We have our differences, as you might expect.'

'I can well b'lieve that.' His eyes danced with amusement. 'She've got her good points, though.'

A non-committal 'Hmm' was her reply. 'Well, Tom, I'll be very sorry to see you go again. Still, it's not for a good while yet, and I daresay you'll spend some evenings here in the meantime?'

'You can count on it. Me landlady dawn't feed a man the way you do.'

'There's a nice fruit pudding on the stove, if you've room for some.'

'Ess, all right, I'll try'n.'

'More beer?'

'No, maid, this'll do.'

Clearing away his plate and cutlery, Esme stood up and made for the kitchen. Roger followed her, and he loitered by the table while she cut up the pudding.

'Who's, um . . .? Who's that?'

'His name's Tom Tregunna. We were friends as children.'

She fetched some cream from the pantry. It was topped with a pale yellow crust and rich with the flavour that came from scalding over a peat fire.

'Oh?' said Roger curiously.

'He was telling me about his work.' Esme dug a tablespoon of cream out of the pan and shook it onto the dish of fruit and suet pastry. 'He's done a great deal to better himself, you know.'

'Has he, now?' Her husband seemed slightly uneasy and he noted that she added a second dollop of cream for good measure.

'And as soon as he's studied enough, he means to emigrate.'

'Ah,' said Roger approvingly. 'I wish him well, then.'

32

Balgadden was one of the deepest mines in the county, and its owners among the least particular with regard to the safety of their men. Any pit was a dangerous place, but conditions at Balgadden were the most hazardous Tom had ever known. The ventilation was worse than poor, the ladders rickety and ill-secured, the timbering and staging shaky. Deaths were more frequent here than in any neighbouring mine, whether by fall or suffocation, crashing skip or run of loose ground. If the shareholders had ever possessed any will to improve these things, it had lately been extinguished by the slump in their fortunes. Balgadden was full of high-grade ore, yet they could not obtain a good price for it. The situation had been growing ever more serious for several years past, and 1874 had proved the most dismal of all.

Balgadden's owners had never been among the more benevolent, even in prosperous times. Recent adversity had hardened them still further, and the men were subjected to many ungenerous practices. Fines were imposed for the smallest offence, and the company was uncommonly slow in settling up. A man might wait three months to be paid for his last pitch and the money was often less than expected. Tom Tregunna's first pay-day was a big disappointment to him and caused a bitter argument with the agents over the value of the ore he had brought out, for he did not trust their reckoning of the weight. Few concerns would cheat over this, but check-weighers were surely needed at Balgadden.

Still, he thought to himself, it idn fer much longer. This

time nex' year I'll be overseas. Least there I wen't be riskin' me neck for a pittance.

Avaricious owners, falling demand for Cornish tin, it all added up to the same thing for the man underground – scant reward for toil and peril. Like every other minor, Tom had known many a moment of terror. He could recall a dozen narrow escapes, and his first at Balgadden occurred in January of 1875.

Although the outside air was freezing, the depths of the mine were oppressively hot. However, the sweat trickling down Tom's body that morning was partly the result of fright. The last charge had exploded nearly half an hour ago and smoke still hung in the air. Tom had always been nimble and fast on his feet, but this time he had almost been caught in the blast, having turned his ankle while fleeing for cover over the piles of loose rubble. He had fallen headlong, landing on his stomach with a thud that drove the breath out of him. It could not have been more than two or three seconds that he lay winded and panic-stricken, aware of the fuses burning away behind him, but it seemed a very long time indeed before he scrambled to his feet, ran on a few short yards and crammed himself behind a sheltering outcrop of rock. The recess was shallow, uncomfortably near to the face, and he threw both arms over his head, huddling in close to the wall as the crash and rumble sounded. Heavy chunks and jagged shards of stone hurtled past him, missing by inches, and he felt a rain of grit upon his bare back.

He had been lucky and he knew it. Two of the other men had gone in to flap away the worst of the smoke, each with a cloth pressed over his mouth, while Tregunna sat down to recover himself.

A man should earn more than a meagre living for work like this, Tom told himself for the hundredth time. Those who tolerated such conditions deserved to be rich. They should make a great deal of money and make it quickly, so that they might have many years left in which to enjoy it. Patience was of no use in an industry where men were old at forty. Most of his waking hours were spent in this clammy world of heat and feeble candlelight and dripping water. He never thought about the half mile of rock above his head, for a few large boulders could just as surely kill him. But he knew what this depth could eventually do to his lungs. Ten years at levels like these would make him a shrunken, stooping wreck, with barely breath enough to climb the ladder at the end of his shift. An evil alliance of drink, pleurisy and bronchitis had finally claimed his father, but Tom was determined not to let the same thing happen to him. He had more intelligence, more ambition – and foresight had warned him to keep his freedom. There were, in truth, moments when he longed for a wife and a proper home, but dependents were a trap, they would tie him to the treadmill of day-to-day survival. Each year another child to feed, a little less strength and hope, so that in the end he would never break free of poverty.

He bent forward and rubbed the twisted ankle, which had started to ache and swell. He would face a painful journey to the surface later on. Two thousand two hundred feet, almost a vertical ascent. It was just as well for him that the arms took most of the strain. He would go to the Halveor Inn that evening, he decided. There was little comfort or welcome at his lodgings and he would want a good supper. Besides, he had a present for Esme.

He took off his hat for a second and wiped an arm across his forehead, then rose stiffly to his feet. His upper body glistened with sweat and he badly needed a drink. His shirt and jacket, discarded hours ago, lay in a heap beside the water keg. Tom swallowed several mouthfuls, then picked up his jacket and rummaged through the pockets. He pulled out a chunk of rock and bent his head to examine it.

The stone was as big as the palm of his hand, a slab of translucent yellow encrusted along one edge with tiny crystals of clear quartz, and it sparkled, taking fiery glints from the tallow candle on the brim of his hat. He had come across this mineral before. Indeed, in the past he had often made a few extra shillings by selling specimens of one kind or another, but this was the best he had ever found and he thought Esme would like it.

Tregunna's existence was lonely and spartan, so he found a little pleasure in going to see her on two or three evenings each week. Warmth and laughter and a fine dinner were things to which he could look forward through the hours of killing work and the bleak periods spent at his lodgings. Esme, he thought, had turned into a lovely woman, a great temptation to any man, especially an old friend who loved her company in so many ways. Tom the grown man appreciated it far more than Tom the boy or the restless youth. Had his circumstances only been better, he now told himself wistfully, he would have done very well to marry her.

Through the haze of dust and smoke came rhythmic thuds and a brittle chipping sound, as the rest of the pare set to work on the lode. Tom slipped the crystal back into his pocket, reached for the poll pick laying at his feet and went to join his workmates at the face.

'My, that's pretty! What is it?' exclaimed Esme, when he laid the crystal in her hand that evening.

He shrugged. 'Can't remember what 'tis called. Found it this mornin'.'

'But 'tis lovely, Tom, thank you! I'll keep it on my dressing table.'

'Well, 'tidn worth much, but I thought it might please ee.'

Roger had been watching them out of the corner of his eye. His wife stood with her back turned, but he saw that Tom had given her something. Tregunna was smiling up at Esme with a fondness Carwarthen did not like; he slipped out from behind his counter and strolled across to the fireside table where the younger man sat.

'What have you got there, Esme?'

She held out the stone for him to see. 'Look what Tom's given me.'

'Very nice,' conceded Roger. But he only half smiled and his eyes were suspicious as they met those of the tributer. ''Twas a kind thought, Tom.' He moved a little closer to Esme, sliding an arm about her waist.

Tregunna's smile did not waver, but he understood the warning signalled by Roger's presence. The challenge was quiet but unmistakable, and he sought to deflect it by means of humour. He sat back in his chair and grinned at them both.

'Thought I might be given extra beef 'n taties if I was to softsoap her a bit.'

Roger's smile broadened, but he was not fooled and Tregunna knew it.

'Did you, now? Hear that, Esme? 'Tis bribery. The man's in love with your cooking.'

'Oh yes, cupboard love,' she agreed lightly.

'Better go and take up some dinner for him, then.' Roger began to steer her away. As he did so, he nodded to Tom. It was not a sociable gesture, but one that said: 'Have a care, my friend. She belongs to me.'

The younger man did not return the nod. His expression grew sober, for he was mindful of the fact that Roger could bar from the inn anyone to whom he took a dislike.

Tregunna saw Esme disappear into the kitchen to prepare his meal – but it was Bridget who eventually brought it to the table. Roger had managed to occupy his wife elsewhere and he contrived to keep her busy for the rest of the evening.

Carwarthen was not jealous by nature. Esme had always loved to banter and flirt with the customers, but he recognized that for the harmless game that it was. However, there was something different about this man, something Roger found disturbing. He had noticed the way Tom's gaze followed Esme while she went about her work. What he saw in it was not the impersonal male desire that could light upon any pretty woman and switch with ease to any other. The feelings he perceived in Tregunna were deeper and specifically for Esme. Theirs was an old relationship, an affection established long before Roger had come on the scene. Carwarthen did not care for the fact that Esme was always so glad to see Tom, or that she seemed disappointed on the nights when he stayed away.

33

'Thank you, gentlemen, that will do for now.'

Margaret Jory closed her book, then took down her blackboard and easel. With much coughing and scraping of chairs, a score of men rose to their feet, another reading lesson over. Some made straight for the door, but most went down to the other end of the church hall, where two worthy ladies were serving up tea and soup. Only one man remained in his seat, still puzzling over something on the page in front of him. Miss Jory smiled and sat down beside him.

'A problem, Thomas?'

He pointed out a word. 'What d'that say?'

'Laughter.'

'There's no "f",' he objected. 'An why put they other letters instead? None of 'em d'make the right sound.'

'English spelling,' said Margaret sympathetically, 'is not noted for its logic. Ours is a hybrid language, you see, and somewhat disorderly. It has its rules, but exceptions are many. Practice is the only real answer. Practice and more practice, until you know these odd ones off by heart and don't even have to think about them.'

'S'if 'twadden hard 'nough as 'tis,' groused Tom. He flipped the book shut and handed it back to her.

'Not too difficult for you, Thomas. Now then, will you have some soup?'

'Thank you, but no. I'll be makin' tracks fer Halveor in a minnut.'

'Oh?' Margaret's smile disappeared. 'I hope you don't spend too much time there?'

'Aw, dunnee worry. I d'ony go fer dinner 'n t'see Esme.'

'Mrs Carwarthen?'

'Ess, we was good friends as childern. Still are, come to that.'

'Indeed? Well, I don't really know her, of course. Now and again we lock horns over the question of drink, but I daresay she's a good woman in other ways.'

'You'd like her if you knawed her proper. Come to think of it, the two of ee aren't s'very differnt.'

'How so?'

'You're a hard case with a soft centre, an so's she. Pity you dawn't see eye t'eye over the drink 'n all. You might've bin friends if 'twadden fer that.'

'Hmm,' said Miss Jory, considering. 'If we shared a common purpose, she would certainly make a splendid ally. But sadly, it is not so. You were companions as children, you say?'

'Ess, near 'nough up to the time I ran off'n went Redruth. She knawed I was goin', mind.' He smiled to himself, remembering. 'Some upset, she was. Wanted to go 'long wi' me. Course, I wouldn't let her. Didn' want be bothered, see.' His voice acquired a rueful note, filled with affection and tinged with regret. 'She was turnin' out pretty, even then. Wise man, ole Roger. He've got a lovely wife.'

Margaret frowned slightly. Tom's feelings towards Mrs Carwarthen were obvious and somewhat disturbing. After a second, she asked: 'How often do you go to see her?'

'Two or three nights a week, I spose. Never more'n that.' His tone grew wary. Those sharp black eyes of hers missed nothing and he suddenly wished he had not mentioned Esme, for he sensed an awkward question coming. 'I d'spend more time here than I do up there, what wi' your lessons 'n the minin' lectures too.'

'Are you lonely, Thomas? I should imagine you are. It can't be easy to live as you do. Most men of your age have wives, families – and homes, however poor.'

'No point, is there?' He was defensive now. 'I'm goin' away 'fore long, you knaw that. If a man want to better hisself, he ought do that first 'n then think o' marryin' after. Most of 'em try 'n do it th'other way round 'n can't get nowhere. Course I d'want company 'n a bit o' comfort, an there idn no harm in goin' see Esme, is there? I told ee I d'only have dinner like all th'other customers 'n talk with her a bit.'

'No,' conceded Margaret, 'there's nothing wrong in that.' But he heard a veiled warning in the words, a warning made clearer by her next remark. 'And I know you wouldn't want to leave any discord behind you when you go away.'

Tom was now looking extremely uncomfortable, so she ended quietly: 'As a Christian I felt it my duty to say that. Having said it, I shall mention it no more.'

'No, well . . .' Tom stood up. 'I'd best be off, I think, or 'twen't be worth goin' at all. Goodnight, Miss Jory.'

'Goodnight, Thomas,' came the grave reply.

He hurried outside and into the road leading up towards the Halveor Inn. It was ten past nine this April evening and the air was fresh and damp. Tom was troubled as he walked that mile in the dark. Miss Jory had read him correctly and pinpointed the danger straight away. Oh yes, it would be very easy to start an affair with Esme – and the end result would be pain for all concerned. He wanted her, all right, and he sensed how much she wanted him. Discord, he thought, was a very mild word to describe the trouble it could bring.

Early in August, a new poster appeared on the wall outside the harbourmaster's office. It was plastered over the torn remnants of past sailing schedules and alongside notices of other vessels soon to leave for various parts of the world.

DIRECT SAILING FROM PORTHGULLOW
FOR QUEBEC
at a fare of £3.2s.0d
The Barque 'JANE ENDERBY'
will leave on August 27th, 1875
Intending passengers should apply to
the Emigration Agents at the Town Hall

Tom Tregunna spotted it one evening, read it through and swore softly to himself, wishing the notice had appeared a fortnight earlier. He had decided on Canada for his new life, but had recently signed for one last bargain at Balgadden in order to have just a little more money behind him when he went.

It had proved to be a bad mistake. Although the payment was sometimes suspect, all his other pitches had at least produced good ore, earning him enough to live on and a bit to spare as well. But this time he and his workmates were unlucky, for the lode was turning out to be almost exhausted. Seven feet wide at the start, it had dwindled rapidly within the first few days, as the vein tapered off into barren ground. The rock was extremely hard and progress slow, yet after only a week the seam of ore had narrowed to three feet. The men faced nearly two more months of back-breaking toil, in the almost certain knowledge that the money earned for it would be pitifully small.

Another week went by, and as the vein became more and more pinched, the pare began to grumble that the cost of the blasting powder might well exceed their wages. They were bound by this miserable contract until the end of

September, and likely to end up poorer than when they started. A man might release himself on payment of a twenty shilling fine, but this again would leave him out of pocket. Those with families to feed, and not a penny in reserve, were well and truly trapped.

One day there came a shift that ended in a minor accident for Tom. He and two other men, balanced on makeshift staging, were boring a shot-hole. While one held the drill rod, each of the others took it in turn to drive it into the rock with a blow from a sledgehammer. The planks on which they stood were slung between two ladders and supported by a few props underneath, and they shivered with every thud. The temperature was above eighty degrees and over an hour of relentless pounding had driven the rod less than ten inches into the face. Soaked in sweat and light-headed with exertion, Tom lost his footing and fell, landing on the heap of rubble seven feet below. His hands and arms were badly grazed, large patches of his bare back were skinned or cut, and he was fortunate to find all his bones intact.

He was aching from head to foot and the grazes were still smarting when he made his way towards the Halveor Inn that evening. It was Tuesday, when he usually went to Miss Jory's lesson, so Esme was more than a little surprised to see him. She was standing outside the front door, talking with the Reverend Sobey, when she spotted her friend coming down the road. Bidding a hasty farewell to the parson, she waited on the step for Tom. As he drew nearer she guessed that something was wrong, for he seemed despondent, more weary than usual, and there was no answering grin when she raised a hand in greeting.

'Couldn't you face Maggie Jory tonight?'

'No, maid, I'm in no mood fer learnin'.'

'What's happened?'

'Aw, I had a bit of a fall just 'fore th'end o' the shift.

273

There's no great damage done. 'Twouldn' bother me, 'cept I knaw 'tis all fer nothin'.'

'Is it a bad pitch, then?'

'Ess, gettin' worse every day.'

His shirt collar was open and Esme suddenly spotted a streak of raw flesh at the side of his neck. She reached out and pushed aside the fabric to see. The redness extended down and backwards over his shoulder.

'Is there much of this?'

'Fair bit. 'Tis ony surface, though.'

'There's dirt in it still. Come inside.'

She led him down the passage to the parlour, but he hesitated to go in.

'Your husband wen't like this, Esme. These are your private rooms – yours 'n his. I only came here fer a supper, same as I always do.'

'I can invite a friend into my parlour if I want. Anyway, Roger's busy in the pewter room.'

Doubtfully, he followed her inside, sat down and took off his jacket. He had washed off the worst of the grime at his lodgings and put on a clean shirt, but brownish patches of dried blood had appeared all over it. The linen was stuck to his back and upper arms in a dozen places, where the cuts were still weeping.

Esme gingerly peeled it off and tutted indignantly at what she saw. 'There's grit and dust in those cuts, they'll fester if they're left like that. Is there no doctor at that mine?'

'He's only there to saw off arms or legs, an announce whether a man's dead or not. Things like this are left to the wives 'n mothers.'

'Are they, indeed? Perhaps Balgadden don't pay him much, either. Well, as you say, most of it's not deep – but it still needs attention. I'll fetch some warm water and dressings.'

Esme took over half an hour to clean out the cuts. It was a delicate, nervous task, for the raw patches were large and stung fiercely at her lightest touch. Absorbed in a slow, careful washing of his back and arms, the removal of every speck of dirt embedded in sore flesh, she forgot the minutes ticking past. Neither spoke much as she worked, but there soon grew a guilty awareness in Esme that she was quite enjoying herself. Her hands moved over him with a touch too fond and lingering to be casual. Here was an unexpected treat, a short space of freedom and familiarity. She still thought of him as her own, and her fingertips betrayed the pleasure.

'There,' she said at last, pushing the pan to one side, 'some lint, a few bandages, and then I've finished.'

'You're kind, Esme, to go to such trouble for me.'

''Tisn't much to do for someone I hold dear,' she said quietly.

He turned to look at her and was met with an odd little smile that was guilty and helpless all at once.

'You know how it is with me, don't you, Tom? Even now, after so many years, and despite the fact I'm married.'

In that moment he came within a hair's breadth of voicing his own desire. But Margaret Jory's cautioning words, so often dwelt upon these past three months, echoed once more in his head and he checked himself just in time.

'I do,' he sighed, 'an I have me awn regrets. I'm sorry I treated ee s'lightly when we was young. I was careless of your feelins sometimes, an I remember sayin' you'd be a hindrance to me, or some such nonsense. They was clumsy words – but I still b'lieve I did right to go, an I'm glad you've a good husband, maid. 'Tis no use fer me to feel jealous, things bein' as they are. I could never have provided fer ee the way Roger have. You was always used to better things than I could give ee, an I wouldn' ask any woman to leave a decent home fer a poor one. If you was free now an I was a prosperous man, I'd make ee me choice without a second thought, but thass not how 'tis.'

Esme said nothing, but pressed his head forward a little in order to lay a dressing just below the nape of his neck. Her conscience stirred uneasily as she silently carried on with her task, for she loved Roger and knew he deserved complete loyalty. Yet the old affection for Tregunna remained as strong as ever, and would not be quelled by regard for what was right or advisable.

The mantel clock struck eight as she tied the last bandage. With a start, she realized she had spent nearly an hour with Tom. Her husband would surely be wondering where she was.

'You'd better go across to the pewter room now,' she said. 'I'll see that . . .'

But her words were cut short, for the parlour door suddenly opened. There stood Roger, and his face registered astonishment, followed swiftly by anger, at the sight of his wife helping Tom Tregunna on with his shirt.

'What's all this?' He noted the dressings, the bowl of water and jar of ointment, and his eyes met those of the other man with deep hostility.

'Roger, he was injured at work today. I just . . .'

'I had a mishap, a fall,' Tregunna said. He stood up, pulling on his shirt and fastening the buttons. 'Esme was good 'nough to patch me up a bit 'n I'm very grateful to her.'

Roger's glance darted sharply from one to the other. 'Is that so? She's been a long time over it. I'm surprised a man who's still on his feet should need so much attention.'

Esme scooped up the pan and the ointment, then hastily placed herself between the two men. They were both large and powerful, the one wary, the other belligerent.

276

'Twas a fiddlesome job, Roger. You know it took me half a day to pick the splinters out of you when you fell through the floor of the loft. I'll just give Tom his dinner and then he'll be on his way.'

'Oh yes, dinner and all,' muttered the publican wrathfully. 'Some appetite he's got, too. I've seen the helpings you feed him – twice as much as any other man.'

Tom reached for his jacket. 'No,' he said calmly, 'I dawn't b'lieve I'll stay. I aren't s'hungry after all.' The hazel eyes turned warmly upon Esme. 'Thank you fer your care, maid. It dawn't hurt much now.'

He nodded stiffly to Roger, then brushed past him and left.

Carwarthen shut the door heavily and opened his mouth to reprimand Esme, but she was the first to attack.

'That was nasty, Roger. He came to have dinner, that was all. I noticed that his neck was skinned and I offered to tend to him. He didn't ask me to do it. You've driven him off now, and he's still had nothing to eat.'

'My, how you concern yourself with his welfare,' growled her husband.

'He leads a miserable existence and he hasn't a wife to look after him.'

'No, but you seem eager enough to play the part. Tell me, Esme, would you like to be a wife to him in every way? I suppose I should be thankful you didn't take him upstairs and undress him completely, in case he had any other needs you could satisfy.'

Esme's mouth dropped open and her face turned stark white beneath her freckles. For a moment she spluttered, unable to summon any coherent answer. Then, in fury and confusion, she hurled the bowl of water to the floor and lifted her hand to slap him.

She only narrowly stopped herself. For a second or two her upraised palm quivered in the air – but then she slowly lowered it, for she knew he spoke the truth. Fearful of what her face might betray, she gathered her dignity and stalked from the room.

'He won't be allowed here again, I'll see to that,' shouted Roger at his wife's back, as she marched upstairs. 'Next time he tries to set foot on my premises, I'll throw him out, by God I will!'

Trudging wearily back to his lodgings, Tom was mulling over what had happened. After a mile or so he paused at a rise in the track and turned to look back towards the sea. The sun was sinking low, a perfect disc of red, and the water looked like a vast expanse of ruffled grey silk. A wind from the west brought the smell of brine to his nostrils.

That was the way he meant to travel – almost due west – and now he knew it was high time to go. Suddenly everything had come to a head: the barren pitch, his fall that day, and finally this nasty little episode at the inn.

'Tis best, he thought, that I never go back there again. I'd love to see her once more to say goodbye, but I've stirred up trouble enough already. Carwarthen made that well 'n truly clear tonight. Besides, I'll have to keep out the way if I'm givin' up me pitch. I aren't payin' no fine to Balgadden, an I aren't goin' end up in gaol, neether. To hell with 'em. They wen't have one more drop o' sweat nor ounce o' strength from me.

Tregunna had never before given up a contract, no matter how bad it proved to be, but this time he knew he had nothing to lose. He had already saved enough money to pay his fare to Canada and sustain him for a few months when he arrived there. There was neither point nor profit in completing his contract and his grievances against Balgadden were many. He did not feel disposed to play fair with those who had not dealt honestly with him.

The setting sun threw a broad shaft of pink across the water and it looked like a bright highway stretching into the distance. Events had made up Tom Tregunna's mind. He was not going to miss that ship.

Roger Carwarthen was gratified to see a week go by without a visit from Tregunna. Esme, for the same reason, was secretly distressed, but maintained a prudent silence in order to keep the peace. Both ascribed Tom's absence to the incident in the parlour, and while Roger felt he had 'seen the misfit off', Esme was torn between vexation at her husband, shame at herself and anxiety for Tom.

Another three days were to pass before the full reason for his disappearance became known to them. A group of men from Balgadden, drinking in the pewter room one night, made mention of Tom and a chorus of laughter broke out among them. Roger caught the name 'Tregunna' and then the word 'gaol', and was instantly on the alert.

'What was that, gentlemen?' He strolled across to the window where they sat.

'One o' the tributers gived up his pitch,' supplied a stooped old man. 'He'll serve three months hard labour at Bodmin if he get caught.'

'Tregunna, you said?'

'Ess, Tom Tregunna. 'Tis said he went back to his lodgins Tuesday night 'fore last, cleared out his belongins 'n was gone be nex' mornin'. Nobody's seen'n since, an th'owners've said they'll put'n behind bars fer it. 'Tis 'gainst the law, see, to break a contract.' The man gave a throaty chuckle. 'Only they'll have to findn first, an 'tis my guess he's long way from here be now. Good luck to'n, I say. There's many another'd do same thing, if'twadden fer wife 'n childern.'

279

There came a rumble of agreement from those seated round him.

'And 'tis your opinion that he's long gone?' Roger joined in the general merriment. 'I don't suppose he'd be wise to show his face at any other pit near here?'

'Thass a fact, so 'tis. A lot o'comp'nies dawn't bother takin' proceedins – gived that up twenty year ago – but Tregunna didn' pay no fine, see, an Balgadden's owners d'always prosseecute a man who just run off 'n leave his pitch like that, providin' they can lay hands on'n. I wish the lad Godspeed 'n thass the truth.'

'So do I,' said Roger, smiling. 'So do I!'

Esme made little comment when her husband delivered the news. He informed her, not with triumph but with quiet satisfaction, as they undressed for bed that night.

'I'm not exactly surprised.' She tried to sound offhand. 'He was treated badly at Balgadden. Wherever he's gone, I hope he'll find things better.'

'I don't care how well or how ill he fares,' replied Roger. 'I'm just glad he's gone.'

'Hmm, well, at least we'll have no more trouble,' muttered Esme, slipping into bed.

That was all she said on the subject, but she lay awake for many hours that night, thinking of Tom and the probability that she would never see him again. She had little doubt as to what he would do now – indeed, he might well have sailed already. She had known, of course, that the time was drawing near, that the parting would be painful, whatever form it took. All the same, she had wanted the chance to say goodbye to him and was grieved to be denied it. Once again she was stricken by his going, reliving at twenty-seven the same wretchedness she had felt at the age of fourteen.

34

August 26th was the day of Porthgullow regatta. For the people of the town and all the surrounding villages, it meant a holiday filled with gig races and swimming competitions, greasy pole contests and various other sports. For the Halveor Inn it could have meant a slack day's trade, but Roger was never a man to miss an opportunity. Despite the fact that Porthgullow was amply supplied with public houses, there were always innkeepers from outlying districts who set up booths on the quay for regatta day, and Roger was invariably one of them. Having left Ewan in charge at Halveor, he and Esme arrived in Porthgullow in the wagonette brake just before ten that morning, to establish their stalls in the best positions they could find.

The waterfront was already lined with stalls and teeming with hawkers, but Roger managed to claim the patch of flat ground beside the lifeboat shed. He was fully aware that his licence did not permit him to sell drink outside his own premises. But, like every other sharp-witted man of business, he was acquainted with many a ruse designed to circumvent the law. Alongside the casks, bottles and glasses displayed on his stand was a very large hamper. What it contained was a stock of saffron buns. If challenged, Roger could innocently say that he had come to sell buns and nothing but buns. The price he was asking for them might seem a little steep, but the glass of ale or spirit served with each one was, of course, free of charge – merely an incentive to buy a bun.

Esme had spent the whole of the previous day cooking

for the event, and had risen before dawn that morning to finish her baking. Roger had dropped her on the other side of the harbour, where she had spotted a space at the far end of the quay. There, she set up her trestle table and spread out an array of pies and pasties, cakes and loaves, cold meats and homemade pickles. It was an excellent position from which to sell food, for the day was already very hot and she had the benefit of the shade from the four-masted barque moored alongside. The first gig race was due to begin at a quarter past eleven, and crowds of spectators were assembling along the street that fronted the harbour. In calico dress and starched apron, Esme stationed herself behind her table to await customers. They were not long in coming, and the first few copper coins were soon jingling in her pocket.

By twelve the games and races were well under way. Spurred to mighty efforts by the promise of trophies, prizes of cash, kegs of ale or sides of beef, the crews bent their backs and hauled on the oars, sending the long, sharp-prowed craft scything through the water, while those on shore bellowed encouragement. Above the cheering sounded the thump and bray of a brass band, rendering popular hymns with many a fine flourish, almost drowning out the raucous singing and ripe language that issued from the three public houses ranged along the waterfront. All the beershops had been open since eight that morning, a shameful state of affairs which had brought the Teetotal Society and its sympathizers out in force. In front of the dim and shabby lair adjudged the worst establishment in town, there stood a short but doughty person in a black broadcloth suit and high-crowned bowler hat. With a voice as loud and eye as fierce as any drunken tinner, he had drawn an audience of no small proportions, for this was 'Last Trump' Trickett, the Methodist lay preacher, a man with breath enough to denounce, exhort and threaten from daybreak till nightfall, if only it would save a soul or two.

Esme's place on the quay afforded her a good view of the happenings on the water. There were contests for every size and class of working boat, and she was gratified to see two events won by vessels her father had built.

It was three o'clock when she sold the last cake. The greasy pole contest was almost over and the gig and punt chase was just beginning. All that now remained on her table were a few slices of lamb and pork, together with a wheaten loaf and some blackberry tart. It had been a very good day's trade, she thought, testing the weight of her purse.

As she tucked the money away in the pocket of her apron, she noticed a thin, dirty little boy, barefoot and dressed only in a knee-length shirt. He was sitting on the granite bollard that secured the mooring line of the barque, and he reminded her strongly of those children she had once seen squatting at the door of Tregunna's cottage.

Esme smiled at him, beckoned and held out the round of fruit tart. The boy hesitated only briefly, then slid down from his perch and sidled towards her. He could not have been more than six years old and he needed both hands to hold the pie. He bit and chewed and swallowed with astonishing speed, ecstatic with enjoyment and the easing of hunger. Only when the food was half gone did he pause to gaze solemnly up at her, his mouth encircled by a smear of red-purple sweetness and pastry crumbs.

'Feel better now?' enquired Esme.

The child replied with a nod and his eyes swivelled hopefully towards the bread and cold meat.

'Yes, you can have that, too.'

Excitedly, he gobbled down the rest of the pie, wiped his mouth and then carefully licked his fingers. Esme put the rest of the food on a plate for him. The boy finished up every crumb and thanked her with a grin full of gaps and milk teeth. Just as he was about to run off, she reached out and caught him by the slack of his shirt.

'Wait.' Delving into her purse, she produced a shilling piece. The child gasped when she offered it to him, then grabbed it with delight.

'Don't lose it now, will you?'

He shook his head, clutching the treasure to his heart, then darted off along the quay and disappeared into the crowd.

Esme sighed heavily. There must have been a time, she thought, when Tom Tregunna was just like that – ragged and famished. It was cruel that those who could not properly feed and clothe their offspring should have so very many, while she and Roger, with a good home to offer, were denied even one. Brooding on life's injustice, she began to stack up her serving dishes. She was just folding the tablecloth when a rough voice enquired:

'Esme, is it?'

She looked up and found herself face to face with a big, hard-featured man. He seemed vaguely familiar, though at first she did not realize where she had seen him before.

'That's my name, yes.'

He grinned. 'Me brother asked me to look out fer ee today, an to pass on a message – s'long as your husband was nowhere about.'

'Your brother?' Her eyes widened with recognition. 'Tom?'

The man's gaze travelled over her with interest. 'I remember you,' he said, 'you 'n your red hair. Tom's li'l friend from the Sunday school. Come to visit our place once, didn' ee? Couldn't get out quick enough – nearly knocked me awver on your way. Didn' think you'd want

284

much to do wid'n after that. Still, never knaw wi' women, I spose.'

'Tom sent you to find me? So he hasn't gone away?'

'Not yet. Knaw he's in a bit o'trouble, dunnee?'

'I heard he gave up his contract. I was afraid he'd gone overseas.'

'Ess, thass what he mean to do, all right. He'll be leavin' tomorra, but he'd like to meet with ee 'fore he go.'

'Well, where is he?' urged Esme impatiently.

The man's face grew sober. 'You'll take care, won't ee? I wouldn' like see me brother land in a cell at Bodmin on account of a woman's waggin' tongue.'

'You have my promise. Please . . .'

The grin returned to his face. 'That ole manor house up top the town. Knaw it, do ee?'

'Yes – oh yes, I know it.'

'Tom said you would. Better go quick, maid.' He jerked a thumb towards the barque. 'This is the ship 'n she'll sail on the mornin' tide.'

He sauntered off along the jetty and Esme turned to look up at the vessel towering above her, its four great masts rearing into the blue summer sky. *Jane Enderby*, ready to sail on the morning tide – a little after dawn. She could have just two or three last hours alone with Tom, but even a short time was better than none and Esme did not mean to waste a minute of it.

She left her table, dishes and cutlery, and hurried down the quay to the street facing the harbour, where she wove her way among the crowds until she came to a tiny ope. She slipped quickly through it and into the maze of cobbled alleys behind, taking shortcuts known from childhood. Because of the regatta, these back streets were all but deserted. Where noisy bands of children would normally play and women would stand to gossip, the steps and courtyards lay silent in the sunshine. At last she came to the foot of Polglaze Hill. Here she paused briefly to draw breath, then picked up her skirts and began to run.

When she reached the top, she turned to the left along the little footpath that ran for half a mile to the manor gate. It took her some minutes to find a way into the grounds, for the entrance was hopelessly overgrown. The old house, more ramshackle than ever, was half engulfed by weeds and creepers. The orchard huddled round it, dark and lush, though many of the trees were leaning now and some lay toppled, their roots torn free of the ground. The branches were encrusted with lichen and flaking bark, and a cool, damp smell of decaying wood reached her nostrils as she searched for a gap in the hedge. At last she discovered a way in, and trampled a path through the nettles until she came to the rotted old door that still hung by one hinge.

Esme squeezed through and peered around her. Nothing had changed. She could almost imagine that she and Tom had played here yesterday, eleven and twelve years old again, hunting for treasure and secret passages.

From overhead there came a small sound, a muffled thud and the creak of a floorboard.

'Tom?' Her eyes brightened and she moved to the foot of the stairs. 'Tom, it's Esme. Are you there?'

Without waiting for his answer, she hastened up the stone steps. They opened straight onto the main upstairs room – and there he sat in the far corner, upon a bed of rough blankets. He was dressed in shabby corduroy trousers and a linen shirt, garments that were relatively clean, but much mended and frayed. Beside him stood a stoneware pitcher of water, together with a small supply of food and a book of essays Miss Jory had given him.

'Oh, I'm so glad you're still here!' As he rose to his feet, she stretched out her arms and flung them joyfully

286

round him. 'It's been two weeks and I was fearful you might have booked passage and left from another port. Have you been here all this time? If only I'd known, I'd have brought you food and bedding. I could have come to see you every day. Oh, 'twas stupid of me not to think of this place. Where else hereabouts would you be safe . . .?'

'Or welcome,' finished Tom humorously. He cuddled her fondly, but his next words were cautious. ''Tis just as well you didn' think of it, Esme. I knaw you'd have come here every chance you had, but 'twouldn' have bin a wise thing to do.'

'I'd have been careful, Tom, truly. Your brother was afraid I might give you away, but I'm not such a fool as that.'

'I'm talkin' 'bout your husband, maid, an the trouble I've already made 'tween the two of ee.' He lightly kissed the top of her head. 'If you want the truth, 'twas in me mind to go without ever seein' ee again. When I left th'inn that las' time, I thought 'twould be fer the best. I went 'n talked to me brother nex' mornin', told'n what I was goin' do. He've bin good, one way 'n another – brought me food every day, even booked me passage on the ship – so I had no call t'ask ee fer help. 'Twas just one thing made me change me mind 'bout seein' ee – I thought you'd be in town fer regatta day. I thought to meself that 'twouldn' do no harm t'have just one short meetin', not if the ship was leavin' early nex' mornin'. Ought say good-bye, didn' us, maid?' He gestured towards the pile of blankets. ''Tis rough hospitality, but come 'n sit wi' me. This ole place d'leak like a sieve every time it rain, but at least there's one dry corner 'n 'tis better'n Bodmin gaol.'

They sat down together in the shaft of sunlight that shone through the filmy little window. Everything's

287

always been harsh for him, she thought, as she felt the bare floorboards through the coarse bedding.

'Some of the men were talking about you at the inn,' she said worriedly. 'Is it true you'd be given three months' hard labour if you were caught?'

Tom scoffed. 'Dawn't look s'anxious, girl. Any miner'll tell ee that what they d'call hard labour at Bodmin is easier'n a few months down a mine, 'specially fer a man who've still got his health 'n strength. I aren't 'fraid o' that – though I'll admit I wouldn' care to be locked up 'n I'd hate to give th'agents the satisfaction of it. Most of all, though, I mean to be on that ship.'

She reached up to lay a hand on his cheek. 'Yes, you're eager to be leaving, aren't you? The time's here and there's nothing to hold you.'

'You're all there is, Esme, an you dawn't b'long to me.'

For a while they talked of the things he hoped to do overseas, the reports that came back of vast metal deposits abroad, of men who earned so much in the space of just five years that they would never need to work again. Tom had no illusions that he would find an easy life at the end of the voyage, but he placed faith in the promise of proper reward for skill and toil, and he cleaved to his belief that the end was in sight for Cornish mining.

'I'll miss you so much,' she said sadly, 'just as I missed you before. You're always leaving me, Tom. And no matter how good the reasons, it grieves me when you go. I can't help it, nothing changes it, not even the years I've spent with Roger. He's the kindest of men and I love him dearly, but I wouldn't be Mrs Carwarthen today if you'd asked me first. Hardship or no, if you'd said to me when we were young, "Let's run away and marry", I'd have gone without a second thought. 'Twas bad enough to lose you once. It'll hurt no less this time.'

His eyes grew troubled as he listened. 'Poor Esme,' he

murmured, 'I should've left ee alone. When I come back this way'n heard you was marrid – happy too, by all accounts – I thought 'twould all be differnt. But I've stirred up old feelins, haven't I, girl? You was content enough 'fore I turned up, an I've spoilt that. I'm sorry, maid. Roger've got good cause to hate me.'

She gave a wry laugh and shook her head. 'The fault's more mine than yours, yet even as I say that, I know I'm not sorry. After you left Halveor that night, I raised my hand to slap him. He's my beloved husband and I was furious with him because he'd driven you away, and because he accused me . . .' Esme hesitated, nervously moistened her lips. 'Because he spoke the plain truth,' she amended. 'He said I wanted you. And so I do, even now. Even if it's only once.'

For what seemed a long time, his eyes lingered on her face with an intent, questioning look.

'I'd love to,' he said at last. 'By God, I would. 'Twasn't fer that reason I asked ee to come here, but I can't deny I've thought about it time 'n again these past few months. I'd dearly like to, Esme. I'd be proud 'n happy, an I'd never forget. But you – you might be sorry after I'm gone. I dawn't want ee rememberin' me wi' shame. 'Twould always be somethin' hid from Roger 'n it might lie heavy on your conscience in years to come. Would ee count it worthwhile fer an hour wi' me?'

She curled her fingers round his, felt the pits and ridges of scars on his palms.

'Yes, I truly would. I'd remember that we were given this one chance, that we had just a little time left and we spent it well.'

It was past six o'clock when Esme finally parted from Tom. He walked with her along the footpath to the top of Polglaze Hill, in order to steal a few more minutes of her company. It could do no harm, he said. They were unlikely to meet anyone. The band could still be heard playing down on the quay and the games would go on until dusk, when the firework display was due to begin. The people of Porthgullow were busy enjoying themselves and he felt little fear of prying eyes that day.

There was, however, one small person who had not enjoyed the regatta much at all. Peter had wanted to spend the day with his brother and sister, but Mama had not allowed him to leave her side. Worse still, she had dressed him up in a sailor suit for the occasion. The collar kept flapping in the wind and he suffered constant irritation from the string that secured his hat. Denied any freedom and stung by the laughter of other children, who sniggered and pointed at his outfit, Peter had soon become sullen and fractious. Susanna's response was to fill him with cockles and pickles, sweets and fruit cordials. When, at last, he was sick and complained of stomach pains, she rushed him off to the doctor's house on Polglaze Hill, fearful that he might have contracted food poisoning.

Regatta day always had its casualties and the waiting room was half full when she arrived. The other patients included a rower who had wrenched his back, an elderly deaf lady, and two young men injured in a fight. Of the latter pair, one seemed to think his nose was broken – and indeed it looked as if it was. The other had lost a tooth, but was chiefly concerned about his left thumb which, he told everyone, had been 'jammed in a door, deliberate'. Both of them smelt quite rancid.

More than an hour dragged by, and when the old woman was called she kept the physician for another forty minutes. Peter was growing ever more fretful and his mother's patience was strained to breaking point. There was no one else left now except the two young louts.

Their odour was becoming unbearable and it made her feel queasy. As if to drive away the smell, she made a little fanning movement with her hand.

'Hot, are ee, Missis?' It was he of the crushed thumb who spoke.

'It's very stuffy in here,' said Susanna distantly.

'Ess, 'tis a bit. Shall I open the winda fer ee? Dawn't want ee faintin', do us?'

'I would be greatly obliged.'

The man stood up and went to the bay window. He pulled down the top half of the centre frame and there came a rush of fresh air. He turned to open a side window too, but something there caught his attention and he paused, squinting up towards the top of the hill.

'Here a minnut.' He beckoned to his friend.

'What ee want?'

'Come here 'n look.'

Reluctantly, the other man shambled over to the window. His nose was plainly bothering him a great deal and he kept dabbing at it with a blood-stained rag.

'Who's that, do ee reckon?'

'Courtin' couple.'

'No, 'tidn. You knaw she, dunnee? 'Tis Carwarthen's wife.'

'Aw, ess. What about it?'

'Well, that idn her husband.'

The second man looked pained and slouched back to his seat.

'What I want knaw that fer?'

His friend sniggered. 'Bet 'twould interest ole Roger.'

'You goin' tell'n, are ee? Want your neck broke to go wi' your thumb?'

'Aw, I was jokin', thass all.'

He opened the side window, and went back to sit down.

'Better now, Missis? Ess, I b'lieve you are.'

Susanna did seem much more alert and her eyes were very bright.

'Much better, thank you. Perhaps I'll go and stand by the window for a while. Deep breathing is said to be very healthful.'

She moved across to the bay, where she took a few exaggerated breaths. But as she did so, her gaze slanted towards the top of the hill and it fastened upon the two people standing together in the shadow of a great beech tree.

The man, observed Susanna, was poorly dressed, but she could not make out his features. The couple were no more than thirty yards away and completely absorbed in one another. With a grimace of distaste, Susanna saw the young oaf embrace her sister-in-law. What a spectacle! A dolt and a publican's wife, fondling each other in the street. Such a show of urgency and vulgar emotion, so many ravenous kisses. Susanna wrinkled her nose as if at a bad smell, and gave a little shudder when she saw the man pat Esme playfully on the rump. She could not help but assume complete intimacy between them, so hungrily did they cuddle and cling. Esme's clothing was dishevelled and the loud red hair fluttered raggedly about her back and shoulders, a gaudy banner proclaiming her a slut. Just like Richard, thought Susanna. The same blood, the same inclinations.

After a time the couple drew apart and stood talking for a while. Whatever the words that passed between them, they were many and earnest. At last, after a very prolonged hug and kiss, Esme stepped out into the sunshine and the young man followed, still clasping her hand. That was when Susanna finally recognized him. A single clear glimpse of his profile brought immediate recall of Esme's childhood friend.

Well, well. Tom Tregunna. After all this time, the

attachment was still strong. Susanna wondered if Roger knew of his wife's old love.

'Havin' a peep, are ee, Missis?' came the rude enquiry. 'You'd see better if you was to stand on a chair.'

Susanna whirled round and glared at him, ready with a sharp denial. But then the door to the surgery suddenly opened and the old lady tottered out.

'Mrs Rescorla? Please come in.'

The doctor was waiting, holding the door open for her. Susanna snatched one more glance at Tom and Esme, who were still exchanging words of farewell, then seized the unfortunate Peter by the hand and hurried him into the doctor's office.

After fifteen minutes she emerged from the surgery in peevish mood, having been soundly rebuked for feeding her son such a hideous mixture. On leaving the house, she paused outside the front door and peered up the hill, but Tom and Esme had gone.

'Are we going home now, Mama?' Peter asked.

'Soon,' she murmured absently. 'We'll go quite soon, but Mama has a little errand to carry out first.'

Roger's stock of ale and spirits had run out by six o'clock. Behind him were stacked a dozen crates filled with empty bottles. Every bun had been sold and the hamper was now piled high with dirty tankards and glasses. He had spent all day in brisk trade and he wondered if Esme had fared as well. For the third time in half an hour, he squinted across the harbour towards the west quay. He could not see her table, for the barque was in the way, but there were still plenty of people milling around over there. It did not occur to Roger that his wife might have sold out of food and abandoned her stall nearly three hours before. Had she finished early, she would surely have brought him her takings for safekeeping.

It was, he decided, time to go home in any case. It would take him another half an hour to load up the brake. He could then collect Esme and drive back to the inn by seven. His head was aching and the prospect of a quiet evening at Halveor was a very pleasant one.

However, the sight that met his eyes when he arrived on the west quay caused him to exclaim in anger and bewilderment. Esme was nowhere to be seen, but her table had been overturned, probably by passing drunkards, and broken crockery lay all around.

Roger climbed down from the brake and retrieved what remained intact, then scanned the crowds once more in search of his wife.

What could have possessed her? he asked himself. To leave a stall unattended on a festival day was an invitation to theft or destruction, and Esme knew that very well. He glanced at his pocket watch. It said twenty minutes to seven. Where had she gone – and for how long?

His brow furrowed with worry and vexation, Roger folded up the table and was just stowing it away in the brake when a woman's voice enquired:

'Are you looking for your wife, sir?'

He was less than pleased to see Susanna. He liked her little enough when her mood was sour. She was now wearing a prim and censorious look that he liked even less.

'Oh, 'tis you, Susanna. I hope you've enjoyed the regatta?' He winked at Peter, who stood shyly beside his mother. 'Had a nice time, boy?'

'Yes,' said Peter, but without much conviction.

'Your wife, Mr Carwarthen – where is she? You don't know, do you?'

'I expect she's looking at the stalls.'

Susanna's eyebrows gently lifted. 'I fear not,' she said, her tone meaningful. 'If only it were so.'

Roger's irritation suddenly boiled over. 'If you've got something to say, just spit it out and have done with. Don't waste my time with your hints and your prissy looks.'

Unruffled, she replied: 'Very well. I feel I should tell you that Esme found a far from innocent way to amuse herself this afternoon. You and I have something in common, Mr Carwarthen. The urge for adultery seems to run strongly in the Rescorla family and we are both victims of it. I have just been to the doctor's house on Polglaze Hill. From the window of the waiting room I chanced to see Esme – it was little more than half an hour ago. She was in the company of a young man. Their behaviour was lewd and furtive. I daresay they flatter themselves that it went unobserved, but I saw them and I think you have a right to know. She allowed him liberties permissible only between a husband and wife. Her hair and clothing were in disarray – indeed, she had the appearance of a woman scarcely recovered from an intimate embrace. I suggest you take her in hand, sir, and quickly, before she grows more brazen and makes you a laughing stock.'

Roger's response was a blend of astonishment and indignation. He was only too well aware of the feud between Esme and her sister-in-law, and of the spite of which Susanna was capable. He was not sure that she would go so far as to make up such an accusation, but she was certainly liable to exaggerate.

'You're a narrow-minded woman, Susanna,' he said, 'with rigid ideas of what's decent and what isn't. Esme and I have many friends and acquaintances. You might have seen her walking and joking with someone. I'm used to the way she flirts with my customers, and I know she means no harm. It doesn't take much to shock a prude like you.'

'The man in question may be one of your customers,

Mr Carwarthen, but he's more than a casual friend to your wife. I know him, you see. His name is Tom Tregunna. He and Esme were very close as children. In fact, I think she would have married him, given the chance, and it seems that the old fires still smoulder.'

As she spoke, Roger's face began to register dismay, and this time he could find no words with which to challenge her or strike back.

She nodded and said quietly: 'Yes, it is humiliating, isn't it? Now you know how I feel when my husband spends the night at your inn with some – creature.'

Roger doubted there was any similarity between her feelings and his own, but had no will to argue the point just then.

'Come along, Peter.' She pulled at the boy's hand. 'Uncle Roger has a great deal to think about, so we must leave him to it.'

His head whirling with doubts and questions, Roger turned slowly to fasten up the tailboard of the brake. If Susanna had vaguely cited 'some man' or even 'several men', he would have given it no credence. But she had named Tom Tregunna, the only one of whom Carwarthen had ever been truly jealous. It was undeniably true that Esme was inclined to take the moral conventions lightly when it suited her. There was proof enough of that in the way she condoned her brother's affairs, and Roger clearly recalled her words on the night when Richard had met Maudie Drew:

'If I were in his shoes, I'd take whatever happiness I could find. Morals, propriety, even the law, could go to the devil!'

Roger squeezed his eyes shut for a moment and bent his head, pressing finger and thumb to the dull ache in his temples. He was very tired and could not think clearly. He did not want to believe Susanna, and he sought again to reassure himself that she would magnify the slightest familiarity, that she must have been mistaken in thinking she had seen Tom Tregunna. After all, no one else had spotted or heard of him for the past fortnight.

Yet, something had prompted Esme to run off and leave her table unattended, and she was not usually so careless.

He took out his watch again. It was ten to seven now. In a sudden blaze of anger, he slammed his palm against the side of the brake and kicked some shards of broken china over the edge of the quay.

And then he heard a guilty voice say:

'Oh, Roger, I'm so sorry.'

He spun round, glaring, and there she stood, gazing about her at the shattered dishes.

'I went to look at the stalls and . . .' Esme faltered, a red flush creeping across her face. She had taken the time to pin up her hair and now presented a very neat appearance. 'I'm sorry,' she repeated lamely. 'I didn't mean to be so long, but there was such a lot to see.'

'Was there, now?' He looked down and saw that she held a paper package. 'Is that all you've bought? What is it?'

'Oh – something for you,' she said quickly. She tore open the wrapping to reveal a length of dark red satin, together with a set of pearl buttons and a skein of embroidery silk. 'There's a stand selling fabrics outside the town hall, and I thought this would make a lovely waistcoat for you.' She dug into her pocket and pulled out her purse. 'I did very well today. There was hardly a crumb left over. I haven't counted the money, but there must be nearly three pounds and I thought I could afford to buy a present for you.'

She was smiling, but Roger could tell that his scrutiny

made her uneasy. That candid, mobile face could seldom conceal very much.

Esme's expression became apologetic once more, almost pleading. 'I know 'twas stupid of me to go off like that. Don't be angry, Roger, please. The plates weren't worth much, and I won't be so silly again, I promise. I only meant to take half an hour. I just don't know where the time went.'

''Tis easy to forget the passing hours when you're enjoying yourself,' agreed Roger, still eyeing her suspiciously.

Esme smiled weakly. Contrition was written all over her face, but whether for broken crockery or broken faith, Roger could not be sure.

'You do like the satin, don't you?' she pressed. ''Tis very smart and I thought 'twould look grand with your grey suit. You don't think it's a waste of money, do you?'

Carwarthen's doubtful gaze lingered a moment longer. Here was the wife he had always adored. He had no wish to accuse her without just cause, especially on the word of a woman like Susanna. But something had happened that afternoon. He could sense in Esme a powerful agitation, compounded of more than simple guilt.

Roger looked away. 'I like it well enough,' he muttered curtly. 'Come on, we're going home.'

She climbed up on the box beside him. As he turned the brake around, her glance swept sorrowfully over the ship moored at the quayside. It would sail in ten hours' time and she would never see Tom again. It had been agreed that they would not even write to one another. Roger's impression of her mood was quite correct, for her mind was a turmoil of grief, gladness and troubled conscience. The satin was a token of reparation, yet she could not regret what had happened.

Her husband was silent all the way back to the inn, and

he brooded for the rest of the evening. There were many questions he could have asked, but he feared to hear the answers. He did not want to watch Esme struggling to find convincing lies. The truth, on the other hand, might prove even less palatable.

Perhaps 'twas just a chance meeting, he told himself at last, and nothing like it will happen again. It could be that Tregunna ventured back to Porthgullow today, thinking 'twas safe with all the crowds. But he can't stay hereabouts for long, and I'll give her no chance to slip away alone again, not for a long time to come.

The hour before dawn was chilly. Most of Porthgullow slept soundly after the efforts and excesses of regatta day, but on the west quay there was life and bustle as the crew of the *Jane Enderby* made ready to sail. Along with her human consignment she would carry a quantity of cargo. These crates and bales were already stowed away and now she was taking on her final load – water, perishable food, and passengers.

By lantern light they filed aboard, clutching what possessions they could carry. They numbered fifty-three, of whom eighteen were women, and among the last to climb the gangplank was Tom Tregunna. Like all the rest, he was taking nothing but a small bundle of belongings and a head full of hopes. But unlike some, he knew all too well how hard and how long the voyage would be. Six weeks of cramped living, sickness, bad food and bouts of foul weather. There would be deaths – there always were – and the ship would reach Canada at the start of a winter more harsh than any Cornwall knew.

'Faith, courage and dire need,' Miss Jory had said of the emigrants, 'those are the things that spur them on.' For the most part she was right, though Tom would have included greed and recklessness when describing some.

Day was brightening when the ship began at last to move out from the quay. It seemed to Tom as if the town were floating away from him, instead of the other way around – his old life receding, growing smaller. He was overwhelmed now by a sense of finality and he knew the others felt it, too. Subdued, they stood looking back until the barque rounded the point and only the tower of the parish church could still be seen. A few minutes later, that too had disappeared from sight.

By this time, *Jane Enderby* was almost in full sail. She was already rolling heavily and many sought shelter down below, seized by the first queasy turns of the seasickness they were long to suffer. Tom was lucky in that respect. The motion of the vessel hardly troubled him, and he meant to remain outside for as long as the weather stayed dry. Most of his life had been spent in holes underground, so he would not seek to be cooped up below decks for longer than was needful. Besides, he wanted one last glimpse of the places he had known with Esme. His mind was still full of her, all that had happened and all that had been said the day before – his last and best memory of home.

She, too, had risen before daybreak – in truth, she had barely slept all night – and in the early light she went out to the henhouse to collect the eggs as usual. Her basket filled, she stepped outside and latched the door. That was when she saw the ship.

It was unmistakably the *Jane Enderby* a mile or so from shore and setting a course to the west. Esme half raised a hand to wave, then dropped it helplessly to her side. Even if Tom were looking, he would not be able to see her from such a distance.

For a long time she stood watching the ship rearing and plunging in the choppy sea, every sail stretching in the wind. Her gaze clung to it as it drew farther and farther

300

away, till at last there was nothing to see but a dwindling speck on the skyline.

'Goodbye,' she whispered finally. 'God give you everything you seek, and a little more besides.'

As she guessed, Tom had not been able to make out the little figure standing in the back yard, but his eyes had lingered on the inn until it vanished from sight. And when the barque passed the mouth of the cove, there had been a last clear view of Rescorla's workshops, and Boskenna up on the ridge.

The land soon dwindled after that, the coastline falling away until it disappeared altogether and there was nothing but ocean on every side.

So, he reflected, thass the end of it. An 'tis just as well when all's said 'n done. All I ever had to give her was a bit o' shiny stone, an she deserve better'n that.

35

In the weeks after regatta day, there grew in Esme's mind a suspicion, attended by dread and excitement, that she might be carrying a child. Tom had been gone almost two months when the doctor confirmed it.

Ever the realist, Esme wasted no effort in trying to convince herself that Roger was the father. They had tried for too long without success and she was no great believer in coincidence. She went home to the inn that day in a ferment of worry and delight. On the way she toyed with thoughts of confession, weighed honour against expediency, considered the happiness a child would bring to Roger if he believed it to be his own, and the humiliation he would suffer if he knew it was not. Again, she rocked between loyalty to one man or the other. She did not wish to risk confrontation with her husband, nor did she relish the idea of lying to him. Her conscience would have a burden to bear if she allowed Roger to raise another man's offspring under the proud illusion that he was showering gifts and affection on his own flesh and blood. At the same time, however, she found herself rejoicing that she carried Tom Tregunna's child, for now he would not be entirely lost to her.

She pondered the question for several days before reaching the decision that her husband should, if possible, remain in blissful ignorance. The only stumbling block, she thought, was the problem of family likeness. There was surely nothing else to betray her, and so she resolved to take the gamble and pray that the child would not resemble its father too closely. With a little luck, it would favour the Rescorla side and the truth would never be known.

This is Tom's gift, she told herself – a child for me to remember him by, a child for Roger to love. This is providence at work, contriving to fill our one great need.

And so, four days after the visit to the doctor, Esme broke the glad tidings to her husband.

Roger was in the coach-house, harnessing a horse to the gig, and had not heard his wife approach. A shaft of sunlight fell across his back and his fair hair glinted brightly against the dark belly of the mare as he bent for a few seconds to examine one of her front hooves.

'Roger, I didn't know you had to go out today.'

He glanced round. 'I have to go to court, Esme. I fear we're about to be fined again.'

'Oh – yes, I'd forgotten. Well, never mind that. I've something wonderful to tell you.'

'Have you, now? What is it?'

'I'm expecting a baby, Roger.' The words came in a trembling rush. 'At long last, we're going to have a child.'

There was silence.

Carwarthen straightened up slowly and darted a wavering look at his wife, as if reluctant to meet her eyes.

'When is it due?' There was no trace of a smile.

'At the end of May.'

Another silence. He turned his back to her, adjusting the horse's bridle, and made a swift calculation. The end of May – nine months from the time of the regatta.

Esme had expected wild delight, hugs and whoops and showers of kisses, not the flat, almost sullen comment: 'Well, well, imagine that.'

'Roger, we've waited nine years for this.'

Yes, he thought, nine years. Was it not a little strange that she should conceive after all this time? Such things were by no means unheard of – but certainly unusual.

Esme was not the only one to doubt the likelihood of a coincidence.

'So we have,' he agreed coolly.

An awful sense of foreboding began to steal over her. Was it possible that he knew? Why else should he respond in such a manner? But how could he know? She thought she had been cautious enough. She had seen not another soul in the time she had spent with Tom.

'You don't seem very pleased,' she ventured. 'Why is that?'

'We'll talk when I come back.' He pulled his jacket from the nail where it hung, and shrugged it on.

'No, Roger, you'll not leave me to wonder and worry. Whatever's wrong, you'd better tell me now. We've always shared everything, good or bad.'

'Have we, Esme?' His gaze flickered over her in an odd way. 'Is there not even one secret between us?'

She felt the colour draining from her face. 'What do you mean by that?'

Softly, he asked: 'Where did you go on regatta day? How did you spend those hours in the afternoon?'

He saw that she swallowed hard and he waited in silence for her answer. For nearly half a minute he stared steadily at his wife, reading the signs of guilt and dismay on her face. There was no sound but the restless stamping of the horse, for Esme could find nothing to say. She felt as if the ground were falling away beneath her.

'Susanna came to see me just before you returned that day,' explained Roger quietly. 'She'd been to the doctor's house on Polglaze Hill and it seems she did a little spying from the window of the waiting room.'

Esme closed her eyes, felt her heart turn over. The doctor's house. Oh Lord, she had not thought of that.

'She told me . . .' His voice was calm and very sad. 'Well, I'm sure you can guess the gist of it.'

She raised her eyes to meet his, and the look he saw there was as good as any confession.

'It's true, isn't it?' He sounded more weary than angry. 'You and Tregunna together. Because of what Susanna said, I've scarcely let you out of my sight these past two months. In eight weeks you haven't put a foot wrong or given me any reason to accuse you, and I was ready to call her a liar. But how many times did you meet him before regatta day? How often have you betrayed me over this past year? After he'd run from his bargain, when I believed he'd gone away, you must have known where he was. Did it make you laugh, Esme? Was it exciting to have a secret and to fool me? Did you go to him and say, "My husband thinks I'm visiting my sister at Boskenna", or, "I told Roger I was going to the shops."?'

'No, Roger, I swear to God! I'd never mock you, I'd never wilfully do anything to hurt you. It wasn't a sly adventure. It was . . .' She thought helplessly for the words to explain, spreading her hands in a pleading gesture. '. . . a farewell. And a farewell happens only once, Roger. I promise you that was all. Until regatta day, I had no more idea than you where he'd gone. But his brother came to see me at the stall that afternoon, and he brought a message for me. Do you remember the ship moored alongside the quay? She was due to sail in the morning and Tom had booked on board her. He was going to Canada and he wanted to say goodbye. I knew 'twas the last I'd ever see of him. On my life, Roger, he'd never touched me before. But on that last afternoon, when time was so short . . .'

'It all became too urgent, so you followed your instincts.'

'He was going away,' repeated Esme wretchedly. 'For that very reason, I thought no harm could come of it.'

Roger's stare had hardened while she spoke, and he

looked at her now as he might at a stranger. 'You would have let me believe the child was mine.' His tone was dull, oddly detached. 'You must have thought me a fine old dupe.'

Esme felt the prickling of tears and a painful constriction at her throat. 'I wanted you to have the happiness of thinking 'twas your own,' she said, her voice cracking slightly. 'I've never believed in truth at any price, not when a lie's more thoughtful or silence more kind. And I couldn't be certain, in any case, that the child wasn't yours – though I know 'tis most likely that Tom's the father,' she finished reluctantly.

For a few seconds his eyes remained fixed on her in the same remote, unyielding way. Then, without a word, he turned, took hold of the mare's bridle and led her from the coach-house, brushing past Esme as if she were not there.

'Where are you going?'

'To court, as I said.'

She hurried outside after him and stood anxiously twisting at the fabric of her apron while he climbed into the gig.

'When will you be back?'

'I don't know.' He looked down at her, his expression shifting between anger and reproach. 'I used to trust you, Esme,' he said. 'God knows, I never thought you'd disappoint me so.'

And with that he shook the reins and clattered out under the archway, disappearing down the road towards Penzance.

Glancing through the kitchen window a few minutes later, Dinah noticed Esme standing alone outside the coach-house. The maid's mouth dropped open in surprise to see Mrs Carwarthen with her face buried in her hands and her shoulders heaving with sobs. Filled with concern, Dinah came bustling out.

'What is it, me dear? Whatever's wrong?'

But Esme did not answer. She simply shook her head, hiding her face, and fled past Dinah, into the house and up the stairs. She shut herself in the bedroom and stayed there till mid-afternoon, leaving Ewan and the girls to cope as best they could.

It was after four o'clock when she finally emerged, having calmed herself enough to cope with her work. There was a ham to cook and a pudding to be steamed ready for that evening. Ignoring the curious, sidelong looks from the maids, she put on a clean apron, set a pot of water to boil and went grimly about her tasks, answering queries or issuing instructions in as few words as possible. Bridget and Dinah, accustomed to chatter and levity in the kitchen, crept around with voices hushed, as if the house were in mourning.

Roger did not return until late that night. Esme had gone to bed and fallen asleep, her eyelids still swollen and her throat still aching. Worn out with misery, she had drifted off without turning down the lamp, and she did not hear the gig roll into the courtyard below at just after one o'clock.

The sound that woke her was the lifting of the latch and the creak of the bedroom door. Her eyes fluttered open, the lids feeling cold, sticky and sore, and they rested with apprehension on the tall form of her husband. Roger hesitated, surprised to find the room lit, then he softly closed the door behind him.

Esme lay wondering what to expect. She had no fear of violence, for Roger was no bully, despite his size and strength. What she dreaded most was to find him still aloof, contemptuous and unforgiving.

Silently he took off his jacket and hung it behind the

door. Then he sat down on the edge of the bed, unfastening his collar and cuffs.

'What happened in court?' Her voice sounded hoarse.

'We were fined forty shillings.'

'Did you have to wait long?'

'No, 'twas over by noon.'

'Then where have you been all these hours?'

His answer was slow in coming, and vague because he truly could not remember exactly how he had spent the day.

'Here and there. I drove around, walked for a bit, sat for a while . . .' His words tapered off, the explanation sufficient.

Esme said awkwardly, 'We were very busy this evening. Trade was good.'

'Hmm.' Roger nodded, but made no more of it. Then he said quietly:

'Well, Esme, I've done a lot of careful thinking today. I was in a rare old state when I left here this morning and it took me a good many hours to get things straight in my mind, but 'tis all clear enough now.'

She moistened her lips uncomfortably and waited as he weighed his words.

'For a start, I can see that the reason we never had any children was that I couldn't give them to you.'

She sat up in bed and reached out to stroke his bowed head. 'Roger, we can't be sure of that.'

'Please hear me out.' She fell silent and he went on: 'What I learned this morning was painful to me. A man has his pride and a delicate thing it is, too. I can't describe what I felt in knowing you'd been disloyal. You may have lain with him just the once, but there were months of longing beforehand, weren't there, Esme? I don't doubt that you love me, maid, but it wasn't enough to stop you.'

308

'I'm so sorry,' murmured Esme miserably. 'The last thing I wanted was to hurt you.'

'I know, I know. 'Twas wrong to accuse you of laughing behind my back. Whatever the feelings between you and Tregunna, they weren't frivolous. I resent them and I always will, but I don't think you took pleasure in deceiving me.' He turned at last to look at her, and there was understanding in his tired face. 'Well now, as I was saying, we've always been denied a family and it looks as though the failing was mine.'

She pressed her fingers lightly against his mouth to halt this line of talk, but he took them away, clasping her hand in his own.

'No, let me finish. 'Tis hard that a healthy woman should have no chance of a child, simply because she's married a man who can't father one.'

'Roger, I can't pretend to you that I went with Tom just in hopes of a baby. The thought didn't cross my mind. Like you, I'd given up after all this time.'

'Yes,' he said ruefully, 'and 'twas just the once. In nine years I could make no children, but you only had to go to him once. That was salt for the wound, and no mistake.' He shook his head. 'It galls me, by God it does. Believe me, 'tis well for Tregunna that he's out of my reach. If he ever comes back to look for you, I'll give him cause to regret it, damn him. Because he came between us, because he did so easily what I could not, I'm jealous, Esme, and I'll always hate him.'

'And the child?'

The question seemed to hang in the air for a very long time, though it was, in truth, only a few seconds before he answered.

'I was coming to that. You know, at first I thought I should throw you out of my house. Why should I feed and clothe his child, I thought, and always be reminded

309

by the sight of it that my wife betrayed me? But I can't be without you, Esme, and how could I separate you from this baby? If you had to choose between us, I'm not so sure I'd win. I know the power of an infant, the hold it has on its mother, especially when it's been so long in coming and there won't be any more. You haven't left me much choice, have you maid?'

He saw her face lighten with relief and gratitude. 'Oh Roger – are you saying you'll call it your own?'

'I'll make it my own,' he said emphatically. 'I'll raise it to be a Carwarthen. There's nothing else I can take away from him, but at least I'll have the child for recompense. It'll never have his name, and he'll have no rights to it, should he ever come back this way. There's some consolation in that.' He reached out to touch his wife's repentant face, and then pulled her towards him, cuddling her and patting her back. 'I wish to God I'd fathered it, but I can't begrudge you this child, Esme. You've always longed for one and I couldn't oblige – but he could, so I have to accept what can't be changed. There's no other course for me, is there? I'm not going to lose you on account of Tregunna. What would I do without my wife? There's wisdom in compromise, I suppose. By these roundabout means, we shall have what we want.'

'You do forgive me, don't you?'

'I have to, maid. If I cherish a grudge, we'll all be miserable – and where's the satisfaction in that? 'Tis easier in the long run, and far less costly, to swallow a bit of pride and be content instead.'

Esme's daughter arrived on a windy night in May 1876. She weighed nearly eight pounds at birth and a wispy growth of auburn hair was already visible on the little head. Locked out on the landing by the midwife, Roger heard the first lusty squalling at two in the morning, but had to wait another half-hour before the stout little nurse would let him in.

He wondered, as he sat on the stairs, how easy it would be to overlook the origins of the child. He had made up his mind to accept it; whether he could love it was another matter. His thoughts returned to all the congratulations and back-slapping from his customers when Esme's pregnancy had begun to show. He had laughed and joked in response, but oh, how uncomfortable he had felt, what a sham it had seemed. He knew that, for his sake, Esme had kept a rein on her own excitement these past few months. She had just grown quietly, happily larger week by week, and between themselves they had seldom spoken of the coming child, finding it easier to talk of other things. Now that it was finally here, Roger prayed that he could hold to his resolve and treat it as his own.

At last the midwife called him in. Her job complete, she went downstairs to the kitchen to have some tea with Bridget and Ewan, for the whole household was wakeful and waiting for news.

Lying with the child in the crook of her arm, Esme regarded her husband with eyes that were drowsy but watchful as he bent down and stretched out a finger to push aside the blanket and see the infant.

''Tis a girl,' she said.

A wistful look crossed his face and told eloquently what was passing through his mind. 'Yes, and she's beautiful.'

'Our daughter, Roger. I want her to be yours as much as mine.'

He smiled faintly. 'Well, I expect in time she will be.' Thoughtfully, he added, 'I'm glad 'tis a girl. 'Twould have been harder for me if you'd had a son.'

'Yes, I know. That's why I've been praying for a daughter.'

Some while later, Esme drifted off to sleep, and Roger

311

took the child and put her in the cradle by the bed. He stood for a long time looking down at her. There was already a likeness to Tom Tregunna, and again he asked himself if he could live with it.

Not mine, he thought. Not my flesh and blood.

Then, suddenly, the baby yawned, smacked her lips and yawned again. There was something so comical about the rubbery little countenance and the tuft of red hair standing straight up on top of her head. A slow grin spread across Roger's face, and he said to himself:

She's part of Esme, though. That's the important thing. Anyway, if I can't father any of my own then I'm lucky in a way to have this one. When I'm gone, there won't be anything left of me but the moulding I give to this child, so I'd better make a good job of it. She's Carwarthen by name and I'll make her a Carwarthen by nature. That's something, at least, to leave behind me.

The baby was christened Mary Evelina, and she soon repaid Roger's graciousness in love and laughter. From the time she began to crawl, it was clear that she preferred her papa, as small girls often do. If there was scolding to be done, Esme had to do it, and she sometimes wryly remarked that Mary would unquestionably take Roger, if forced to choose between her parents. She was his 'little maid', always climbing on his lap, wrapping plump infant arms about his neck and giggling in his ear. She won him easily, completely, and he seldom returned from a trip into Porthgullow or Penzance without bringing home a toy of some kind. He might even have been able to convince himself that she really was his own, had it not been for Mary's increasing resemblance to Tom Tregunna. The facial similarity was such that her parentage could not be doubted, so Roger simply chose to ignore it. He enjoyed being 'Pa' and he took comfort in the

312

knowledge that Mary would neither know nor want her true father if she met him now.

For her second birthday, he made a rocking horse with a red leather saddle, and she was shown off in the pewter room that afternoon, wearing the new frock her mother had sewn for her. Esme sometimes wondered if any of her customers had noticed that distinctive, upturned nose or asked themselves where they had seen such eyes before, but no one ever made any comment or looked askance at the child as she toddled about the inn. Men, Esme supposed, were less observant in such matters, and certainly less interested, than most women. She had the feeling that Bridget and Dinah were suspicious, but both were too fond of the Carwarthens to gossip or pass judgement.

At Boskenna, of course, there was little doubt of the truth, for Susanna had reported Esme's 'loose conduct' on regatta day, and Richard had spotted Tom Tregunna at the inn on more than one occasion. The news of the pregnancy had caused him to exchange thoughtful glances and whispered questions with Judith. Like Susanna, both had done their arithmetic and drawn the obvious conclusion.

'You know, don't you?' said Esme to her brother one day. 'About Mary, I mean.'

He dismissed it lightly. ''Twas easily guessed.'

'There won't be any talk, will there? About regatta day, that is.'

'From Susanna? Not if she values her hide. I've made that very clear to her.'

'Thank you, Richard. 'Tisn't me I'm worried about, 'tis Mary and Roger.'

'I know that, maid. Still . . .' He fixed her with a warning look. '. . . the child's just like her father, don't forget. People have eyes and they're not stupid. Susanna told me there were two young roughs in the waiting room that day, and they saw you with Tregunna.'

'Yes . . .' She bit her lip. '. . . and I've often thought Tom's brother might put two and two together.'

'Might and might not,' shrugged Richard. 'All I'm saying is, people may know more than you think, so don't be too surprised if, sooner or later, something's said. Life doesn't let us get away with much.'

36

Life was treating Katie very well. It was delicious to be nineteen and pursued by numerous young men who brought her posies and told her how lovely she was.

Standing at her bedroom window, she looked out on a spring afternoon, absently dabbing lavender water round her ears as she thought about them, each in turn. Some were poor and others were quite well-to-do, but however much or little they had, all were eager to lay it at her feet and hardly a day went by without a visit from one suitor or another.

Richard liked to play the stern father whenever he encountered one of these admirers. They were quizzed about their intentions, warned to keep their hands to themselves when they took her out, and charged to bring her home by such and such a time and no later. To hear him, no one would have guessed how proud he was of his daughter's popularity. Susanna had less to say to the young men's faces, but was often disparaging after they had gone. One was 'arrogant', a second had 'bad blood' in his family, a third was 'a bore', while others were variously condemned as unintelligent, clumsy and so on.

On this particular afternoon, Katie was expecting someone who did not warrant any such criticism – someone special, in fact. Of course, it was very enjoyable to be worshipped and sighed over, and she had been granted more than her share of that, but this was the first young man who had stirred anything more than liking in return. This one occupied her thoughts much more than the rest, and now, as she compared them all, he emerged as the only one she would want to marry. His name was Arthur Lovell and he was due to call at four o'clock.

Katie was very excited and eager to see him. She had spent quite some time in pondering the choice of a frock to wear, and finally settled on a cream cotton print with a row of little bows down the back of the skirt. Arthur liked her in pale colours and it was he who had bought her the lavender water. Her hair was dressed in a style on which he had complimented her, so all in all she was groomed especially to please him.

Four o'clock arrived and so did Lovell. Katie smiled wryly to herself when she heard the rap of the door knocker. She had not troubled to mention Arthur to her mother, for Susanna had come to expect her daughter's callers almost every day, greeting their arrival with resignation and little apparent interest. This time, however, Katie expected to see some enthusiasm, for not only was Arthur a newly-qualified solicitor, but he owned a house on Morven Terrace too.

Susanna opened the front door to find a willowy, fresh-faced young gentleman on the step. He was wearing a very fine suit and clutching a bunch of lilac.

'And which one, pray, are you?' came the weary question.

He told her – and her boredom vanished in a flash. The name Lovell made an immediate impact. Was he related to the Lovells of Morven Terrace? she enquired sweetly. Thrilled to learn that he was, she ushered him into the parlour, installed him in the best chair, then rushed upstairs to fetch her daughter.

'My dear,' she twittered, cupping Katie's face between her hands, 'why didn't you tell me you knew Mr Lovell? Why didn't you let me know he was coming? I would have asked Hannah to bake some special dainties. Ah well, it can't be helped now. We must do the best we can.

Now then, let me see how you look. Yes, very nice indeed – although your frock needs something to finish it off. I know!' She snapped her fingers gleefully. 'My coral brooch! We'll pin it on the bodice just so. Wait a moment while I go and fetch it.'

Katie stood patiently while Susanna fluttered around her, fussing over every little detail and issuing instructions for correct behaviour.

'Come along, hurry,' she urged at last. 'Your young man is waiting.'

If Lovell had hoped to see Katie alone, he was sorely disappointed, for Susanna seized upon this chance to reminisce about her upbringing in Morven Terrace. In any case, it was important to observe propriety most rigorously when stalking a man of this calibre.

'I remember your parents so well,' she told him over tea. 'Your family and mine were the best of friends. Of course, you were only eight or nine years old when my mama and papa moved to Truro, so I don't suppose you recall much about us.'

A twinkle appeared in Arthur's eyes. 'Oh, I haven't forgotten you,' he assured her with a big, ingenuous smile. 'I don't think anyone in Morven Terrace ever will.'

'How nice,' cooed Susanna, flattered. 'I expect your sisters have married and moved away by now,' she added. 'Such pretty girls, all of them.'

'Yes,' confirmed Arthur, guessing exactly what she wanted to know, 'so I'm all alone since Mother and Father passed on. Sole owner and sole occupant – except for the servants, of course.'

'Of course,' came the purring reply.

'Arthur's with Gammon and Jose, Mother,' Katie informed her. 'He's hoping to be a partner in due course.'

'And I'm certain he will, in no time at all.' She beamed

317

from one to the other. 'Tell me, have you known each other long?'

'About three weeks.'

'And you didn't breathe a word – you minx!' Susanna dealt a playful pat to her daughter's knee, then turned to offer Lovell a sandwich. 'Please tell us about your work, Arthur. Yours is a most intriguing profession.'

'Intriguing? No, not really. I'd sooner call it dull but profitable. Most of our work at Gammon and Jose is concerned with probates, squabbles over boundaries, that sort of thing.'

'Nevertheless, it's a much-respected occupation.'

'And you passed your examinations at the highest grade,' Katie reminded him proudly. 'Mr Jose told me so.'

'When did you meet Mr Jose, Katherine?' enquired her mother.

'Last week. Arthur wanted me to see his office and meet his seniors.'

'The old boys love to see a pretty face,' said Lovell. 'They were both enchanted with Kate.'

Susanna was ecstatic. This, she thought, was looking very promising indeed.

'Well, though I say it myself, Katherine is very lovely. Richard and I are so proud of her. She has a sweet disposition and feels quite at ease in any company.'

She caught an incredulous glance from her daughter and turned slightly pink. Arthur, who never missed anything, exchanged a grin with Katie, as Susanna hastened to pour some more tea.

Mother had never before made any effort to flatter or amuse Katie's guests. In the past she had seldom lost an opportunity to criticize the girl's manners or appearance, to belittle her in company and tell everyone what a fractious child she had been. But suddenly she was

318

praising her to the skies, and the reason was quite obvious.

Susanna looked upon Lovell as one of her own sort. Arthur's house was even bigger and grander than the one in which she had grown up. Morven Terrace – she pictured the wide staircase and spacious drawing room of her old home, the elegant bedrooms and the bevy of properly uniformed maids. Oh, to return to all that, if only as a visitor. How splendid it would be to have access to that smart house with its lovely garden. Arthur would no doubt assemble a collection of prosperous friends and clients in the years to come. There would be social gatherings to attend. Oh, how she would enjoy that. Any means of entry to the old, privileged way of life would be very welcome, and Susanna was quite prepared to call a truce with her daughter in order to gain that end.

'Will you come to lunch with us next Sunday, Arthur?' she begged. 'We so rarely have interesting guests and I'm sure my husband would like to meet you.'

'Delighted,' said Lovell. 'Perhaps I could take Kate for a carriage ride in the afternoon?'

'Splendid!' Susanna clapped her hands. 'One o'clock, then.'

'He's the most engaging young man I've ever met,' she declared, when Arthur had gone. 'At last you have a suitor worthy of you. I know you think I've been unkind about the others, Katherine, but I didn't want you to make any mistakes, my dear. None of them was good enough. I admit there were one or two who were fairly well-off, but they weren't quite right for you in other ways. There was always something lacking – refinement, intelligence . . .'

'A house in Morven Terrace.'

Susanna opened her mouth to make an indignant denial. But suddenly her face changed and she said bluntly: 'Yes, my girl. That is a very great advantage, and don't dismiss it lightly. Katherine, you have an opportunity for which I would sell my soul. I would love to be young again, to be courted by a man like Arthur Lovell and have the chance, if all goes well, to live in a lovely house. I'm sure you know the circumstances under which I married your father. I left Morven Terrace because I had to, and I've always grieved for the loss of that life. However wrong . . .' She checked herself. 'However ill-considered my decision to marry Richard, believe me, I have not gone unpunished. I am out of my proper element, Katherine, and you cannot blame me if I long for it. I hope you will marry Arthur. If you do, and when you have spent a few years in his house, Boskenna will come to seem small and spartan to you. I doubt you'll want to return here, except for visits. You'll grow accustomed to a smarter, easier way of life, and then perhaps you'll understand my feelings somewhat better.'

'Father gave you all he could, and you were glad to take it at the time.'

'Yes – well, that's my very point. It was more necessity than choice.'

You could have chosen to leave him alone, thought Katie. You could have learned to live with your own bad luck, instead of spoiling his life as well.

But she did not say it aloud, lest an otherwise happy day should end in argument.

That evening, Susanna went through her daughter's wardrobe and proclaimed it quite inadequate. Katherine, she announced, would need a complete set of new clothes – and Susanna would make the supreme sacrifice in order to purchase them for her. She would give up her own dress allowance for the next twelve months, and spend it on finery for Katie.

A sprat to catch a mackerel, reflected the girl wryly.

Mother had suddenly seen her in a different light – as a passkey to the kind of life she coveted. Oh well, Katie would not refuse the new clothes, and she guessed that for once her parents would find themselves in agreement over something. Father, she thought, was sure to like Arthur, and so there was every reason to hope she might become Mrs Lovell.

The proposal came in the autumn and the wedding was planned for twelve months later. Katie's engagement ring was set with a sapphire and four diamonds and she never grew tired of admiring it.

'It feels strange to be wearing something so expensive,' she said one day. ''Tis the same when I think of myself living in that fine house of yours.'

'Ours,' corrected Arthur. 'When October comes, it'll be your home and you'll soon grow used to it.'

It was early New Year and it was snowing. They were walking arm in arm to the gate of Boskenna. She had thrown a coat over her shoulders just to see him off, and he was wrapped and muffled against the cold for his short drive home. A little mound of snow had already collected on top of his hat, and Katie's black hair was sprinkled with melting flakes.

'I always took it for granted that I'd have to cook and wash clothes and make beds.' She laughed softly. 'Imagine having servants to do everything. We only ever had Hannah to help out, and she isn't able to do as much these days.'

Arthur pursed his mouth dismissively. 'I've two maids and a cook, that's all. I'm certainly not as well off as your mother likes to think. Father left me a bit of money along with the house, but as yet I'm only a junior with the firm, so I haven't been extravagant. Later on, though, when I feel established, I'll hire a lady's maid for you.'

'Oh yes,' murmured Katie, 'Mother always said she had one of those.'

Lovell unlatched the gate and pulled it wide enough for his gig to pass through. 'And she'd dearly like to have one again. Will we be seeing much of her after we're married?' There was a delicate note to the question. 'I think she may be hoping . . .'

'No more than duty demands, Arthur. She'll want to be invited and I suppose I can't just cut her out altogether. Aunt Judith says Mother can't help being like she is, and I must admit I've never made much effort to get on with her.'

Lovell took hold of the horse's bridle and led him up to the gate, then paused to brush the snow from the seat of the gig.

'I don't mind her coming to call, as long as it's not too often – for your sake, not mine. You're the one who'll be at home all day, and you'll have Mrs Gammon to contend with as it is. The old misfit likes to visit on Sunday afternoons and I daresay she'll make it more frequent once you're living there. She thinks she can drop in whenever she pleases and she's not the most likeable woman. But she is the senior partner's wife, so we have to be hospitable.'

'Hmm, I've heard Father say a thing or two about her.'

'Think you can tolerate her?'

'For you, yes.'

'That's my girl.' Winking, he whispered: 'I'll find ways to make it up to you.'

'Oh, 'tis enough that you'll be my husband,' Katie said, kissing him goodbye. 'After all, everyone has something to put up with.'

The engagement passed and the great day arrived. Susanna spent more time fussing with her own hair and costume that morning than with those of her daughter. Peter was badgered into Sunday suit and shiny shoes, and repeatedly tormented with comb and brush, as she tried to coax his floppy brown hair to stay in place. He was twelve years old now, and regarded the event as a silly female festival to which men and boys were merely incidental. Richard and Alan were inclined to agree, and they kept out of the way as much as possible.

The calmest members of the household were Judith and the bride. At eleven o'clock, wearing a simple frock of white taffeta, Katie rode to the church in a brougham hired for the day, in company with Richard. Her veil was fastened by a semi-circlet of salmon-coloured silk roses, and she carried a little prayer book. Susanna and the rest of the family had gone on ahead in another carriage, and Katie was glad of these few quiet minutes with her father. Throughout the journey she sat placidly beside him and neither spoke much all the way. But now and then he smiled at her or squeezed her hand, told her she looked lovely and that he was confident of her future happiness.

After the ceremony, a reception was held at Arthur's home, since Boskenna was not large enough for a gathering of fifty, and Susanna had protested fiercely against the use of the Halveor Inn.

'As if I care,' Esme had said to Roger. ''Twill be good to have someone else do the cooking and the serving and the clearing up for a change. I don't mind being waited on.'

Lovell's house was at the very end of Morven Terrace and therefore had gardens on three sides. When she stepped inside and gazed round ecstatically at the fine furniture and carpets, Susanna felt she was back where she belonged. Looking her best in an emerald green velvet suit, she wallowed in all the reflected glory to which a bride's mama was entitled, and was thrilled to be introduced to Arthur's friends and relations, some of whom held high positions. To meet the Mayor of Porthgullow, two local magistrates and Mr Annear of the shipyard, was an honour so great that Susanna was almost beside herself, and she could not understand why Richard was not equally overcome.

During the course of the afternoon she slipped away from the gathering in order to poke around the house. She investigated the study and library, admired the sunny conservatory and the chandelier in the hall, then quietly went upstairs to look at the bedrooms.

The first door she opened proved instead to be a bathroom, with an adjacent water closet, and Susanna clasped her hands in rapture to see such modern luxuries. All the bedchambers were beautifully furnished and curtained, and the largest of them, obviously prepared for Arthur and Katherine, offered a sweeping outlook across the bay.

Susanna crept inside and closed the door. She went to the window and stood there for a long time, remembering. More than twenty years had gone by since she left Morven Terrace, but the memories were still vivid.

In a house like this her childhood had passed with no trial or misfortune, except the accident to her back. At a similar dressing table she had sat prinking, making ready to receive the first of her many suitors. And on such a bed she had thrashed and screamed in hysterical temper on learning that yet another fiancé had abandoned her.

Susanna's gaze strayed towards the mirror set on the front of the wardrobe, and her mind's eye placed there two images of herself. The first was a smiling girl of eighteen, almost untouched by life. The second was a woman of twenty-eight, dressed for her wedding, but wearing a look of bitter acceptance instead of joy. Making do, settling for so much less than she wanted. Susanna closed her eyes, then looked again, and there she stood in her green velvet suit with its jutting bustle and tight jacket. The mother of three children, and soon to be a grandmother, no doubt. Alan, at seventeen, was already halfway through his apprenticeship. In less than two years, Peter would also be taken into the business. Her time had run away like water and most of her hopes had come to nothing.

Richard, upon whom she had looked as 'better than no one', did not want her now. An occasional night with some willing woman was clearly of more satisfaction to him than the services of an ageing wife. Just for a moment, Susanna experienced a sick, frightened feeling, and saw the future as an endless prospect of emptiness, a straight road on a bare plain, narrowing to infirmity and extinction, with no landmark or oasis along the way.

Ah, but things were not truly as bad as that. She would always have Peter, her favourite son. And now that Katie had become Mrs Lovell, she would have the pleasure of visiting Morven Terrace every week. If she remained on good terms with her daughter, she might even look forward to a stay as houseguest for part of each year.

Comforted, she patted her hair and adjusted the frill at her throat, then hurried downstairs again to join the company.

37

'Who are those people in funny clothes, Ma?'

It was July. Esme and her daughter, shopping in Porthgullow, had paused on the quayside to observe a curious spectacle.

'They're visitors, Mary. They come from big cities, like London, and towns a long way up-country.'

'Why?'

'To see somewhere different, I suppose. I hear tell the cities are noisy and dirty and full of people who've never set eyes on the sea.'

'Will they come to live here?'

'No, they only stay a week or two. 'Tis their holiday, you see. There were some here last year too – don't you remember?'

The child shook her head. Just five, she stared, round-eyed, at the frolicking herd by the water's edge. They were all men, for this was the 'gentlemen's bathing hour'. Wearing plain or striped serge costumes, they gambolled in the shallows or struck out boldly with the jerky strokes of the inexperienced. A lone figure in a boater and black bathing suit was performing knee-bends and breathing exercises, and a game of cricket was going on farther up the beach. There, too, a group of about ten people had chosen a flat spot on which to lay out their picnic. They sat around a starched linen cloth, eating from plates with knives and forks, and drinking from glasses, as if at a dining table. Mary seldom saw adults 'playing' on the sands, for the local people generally had better things to do, and she did not think the picnic party looked entirely comfortable. She admired the men's gaudy blazers and the women's pretty cottons, but marvelled that they did not at least take off their boots and unfasten a few buttons at the neck.

'Can't the ladies swim?' she enquired. 'I expect so,' said Esme, 'but they have to wait their turn. They don't think 'tis nice to go into the water with the gentlemen.'

Mary frowned, wrinkled her nose in puzzlement, then lost interest in the strange people.

'Have we finished shopping now?'

'Nearly. There's a crabber just come in. We'll go and see if they've a nice one for us, and then we'll go home.'

It was just past mid-day as they walked across to the east quay, the child trotting quietly along beside her mother. She was more obedient than Esme had ever been, and far less temperamental. It was Roger's influence that made her so. His patience and gentleness were already echoed in Mary and she would never have the fiery nature of her mother.

The harbour was busy that day. Besides the crab boat, several luggers had come in late with big catches and their crews were still unmeshing. The jetty was littered with crab-pots, nets ready for the barking tank, and maunds of fish from which trickles of oily water ran and collected in puddles on the rough stonework. There were shouts of 'tally' as pilchards were counted, and much cackling and chatter from the women who had come to load up the baskets they would carry round the neighbouring villages. Esme bought a fine cock crab straight off the boat, then loitered for a while, exchanging a little cheek with the fishermen and gossip with their wives.

She was just turning to leave when she spotted her sister-in-law making her way along the quay. Almost hobbled by a finely pleated skirt that was bound back over an outsize bustle, Susanna came mincing between the puddles. On her head was a hat crowded with nodding feathers.

'Well, well – Esme! I haven't seen you for some time, have I?'

Susanna was not in the habit of venturing out onto the jetties, especially when fish were being landed, and Esme thought it strange that she should do so just to bid good day to her least cherished in-law.

'I suppose 'tis a month or so,' she agreed warily.

'I've been to visit Katherine this morning,' announced Susanna importantly. 'She and Arthur have just returned from a stay in Bath, you know. Of course, he's doing very well and I daresay they'll travel a lot in the years to come.'

Ah yes, here was the reason. She loved to brag about her daughter.

'I'm very pleased for them,' came the mild response.

'Yes, I must say I'm delighted that Katherine's made such an excellent match. She's risen so much in the world. Naturally, it was what I always wanted for her – to move in better circles and have the good things in life. She and Arthur have some very charming friends and often hold dinner parties for them,' Susanna went on grandly. 'Of course, Katherine needs my help and advice from time to time, but all in all she's met the challenge very well. She's quite the lady now.'

'And 'tis all your doing,' said Esme wryly.

After twenty years of squabbling with her daughter, here was Susanna, puffed up over Katie's success. And exaggerating, too, if the truth were told. For the present, it was all Arthur could do to keep a wife and maintain the fine house his father had left him. The 'dinner parties' involved just the occasional guest or two, though Susanna made them sound like lavish entertainments.

'I venture to say that I had a hand in it,' came the smug reply.

'My, how you love to crow.'

The remark was not exactly meant to hurt. It was one of those bald statements of fact so often to be heard from Esme. There was even a trace of amusement in it, for Susanna was looking so blissfully, stupidly pleased with herself.

A woman less haughty and blessed with a sense of humour would have simply laughed it off. But Susanna took herself and her dignity very seriously. She had meant to impress, but thought herself mocked instead. Yet again she was affronted by the old outspokenness which had punctured her pride so many times before. In a flash her mood turned sour and the simpering smile vanished from her face.

'At least I have something to boast about,' she said coldly. Her gaze turned pointedly to the child at Esme's side. 'And nothing to be ashamed of.'

Sensing trouble, Mary shrank behind her mother. Susanna saw her sister-in-law swallow nervously and dart a glance around her. Most of the people on the quay were engrossed in their own talk and tasks, but Alice Kittow and two of her cronies were well within earshot, should they care to listen.

'You don't need to ask what I mean, do you?' added Susanna.

'I don't care enough to ask,' came the stiff reply. 'I'm not interested in what you think and what does or doesn't meet with your approval.'

'Perhaps not,' said Susanna quietly, 'but I'm going to tell you anyway. You like to be blunt, don't you, Esme? You like to say precisely what's in your mind. Well, I can do the same. This child – we know quite well whose she is, don't we? Except for that hair, she's the very image of

329

her natural father. I'm sure I don't understand how your husband can forgive such betrayal – and then take the result of it into his affections and nurture it, just as a sparrow feeds a cuckoo chick. No self-respecting man would tolerate such indignity.'

'All right,' breathed Esme, 'you know all about it. Of course you do, and you think 'tis shameful. That's no surprise to me, so you needn't waste your breath telling me what a disgrace it all is. I daresay you've a dirty name or two for me – and that doesn't bother me either. But don't you sneer at my husband, Susanna. You mind your tongue when you mention him.'

The warning went unheeded.

'The reason I came to speak to you, Esme, was to tell you that Katherine is expecting a child – and at least Arthur can be confident that the baby is his own. I think it's outrageous that you should be forgiven your sordid little adventure, but it seems that Roger doesn't mind playing the dupe. Not very manly of him, in my view.'

'One more word and I swear to God you'll regret it.' Esme's voice was low and fierce. It would have been sensible to stop there and then, but Susanna had the bit between her teeth. For five years she had stored this up and she meant to have her say.

'Most husbands would cast off an adulterous wife,' she whispered tersely, 'and they certainly wouldn't undertake the raising of another man's bastard.'

The words were so clipped, the mouth so prim. Esme's face flooded wrathful red.

There was going to be an outburst, Susanna could see that. She knew the might of her sister-in-law's temper and the usual result of provoking it. But what she expected was the sharp edge of Esme's tongue – not the flat of her hand.

The blow landed on Susanna's cheek with the force of

330

a swinging paddle. She reeled and stumbled sideways into a pile of nets, where the heels of her smart boots caught in the mesh, tripped her and sent her sprawling backwards. She landed among the fish baskets, scattering pilchards in all directions. One of the maunds toppled into her lap, depositing its contents all over the new fawn suit of which she was so proud. Her hat fell off, and her feet, still tangled in the netting, were splayed out in front of her as widely as the skirts would allow.

Screams rang out – not her own, but those of the women on the quay, howls of raucous merriment accompanied by softer rumbles from the men.

Susanna, her mouth open in astonishment and eyes popping with shock, was too badly winded to make a sound. She flung back an arm to seek support and overturned another basket, so that a cascade of pilchards slithered down over her shoulders. Oily water pooled around her, soaking the back of her skirt and bodice. She gasped, whimpered, raised her eyes in bewilderment – just in time to see Esme descending upon her with the clear intention of further assault.

Susanna's voice returned to her and she uttered a screech of alarm, striving to regain her feet. But the pile of baskets creaked and tumbled when she tried to lean upon them, and she collapsed amid a fresh avalanche of fish as her sister-in-law swooped upon her with a second slap. Clumsily, Susanna flailed at Esme in a doomed attempt at self-defence. The few smacks she managed to inflict were landed by pure luck, and most of her energies were given to warding off punches and shrieking for assistance. At one point she succeeded in grasping a handful of Esme's hair and she pulled savagely, gratified to hear a squeal of rage and pain.

For nearly two minutes they squirmed, biting and scratching, among the fish baskets. No one made any

331

move to stop them, though a crowd was fast assembling. Mary had run to Mrs Kittow, whose dimpled arms cuddled her against a vast bosom. Even as she soothed the child, Alice's eyes were sparkling with excitement and she avidly counted every cuff and kick. Susanna's screams could be heard right across the waterfront and spectators came scurrying from all directions. The picnic party abandoned their meal. Bathers rushed from the water to jostle for a good view. It seemed to Susanna that the tussle went on and on, and she wondered why the constable did not come to rescue her.

Esme was conscious of nothing and no one but the woman struggling in her grip. By now, she had pinned Susanna on her back and was using clenched fists in an outpouring of hoarded fury. Her mind was filled with the things her sister-in-law had said and done over the past twenty-four years. Feverishly, she slapped and pummelled Susanna the usurper, who had taken Jenny Varcoe's rightful place; Susanna the unfeeling wife, who had made Richard miserable for so long; Susanna the snob, who had called Tom a guttersnipe. Because of this creature, her father had lost his oldest friend. By her presence, Boskenna had ceased to be a happy house. This was the woman who had neglected her own children, yet once jeered at Esme because she had none. Here was the spy who had reported to Roger the things she had seen on Polglaze Hill, who had insulted him and sneered at his generous spirit. And finally, Susanna had dared to vilify Mary. For a full minute of frenzy, unreasoning rage suggested that this vixen was responsible for all the troubles and disappointments Esme and her loved ones had ever known. Susanna was the spoiler and scourging was long overdue.

It was fortunate for both of them that Margaret Jory arrived when she did, alerted by the sight of a crowd and sounds of battle. Followed by three other ladies from the Teetotal Society, she pushed her way through the ring of onlookers and uttered a wrathful exclamation at what she saw.

'Mrs Carwarthen, stop this at once! Do you hear me, woman? For the love of God, control yourself!'

The command, loud and sharp, would have stopped many a brawling miner without further ado. Esme hardly even heard it.

'Help me!' wailed Susanna, whose lower lip was cut in two places. 'Please, for pity's sake, help me!'

Esme's face was set like that of a woman intently pounding dough, but she suddenly found her upraised fist seized in a strong grip. A second later, she was pulled to her feet and whirled around to face the outraged Miss Jory.

'What, in the name of Heaven, is the meaning of this?' demanded Margaret. 'I'm appalled to witness such behaviour from two grown women.'

Panting, Esme snatched her wrist free and snapped: ''Tis my business and I don't welcome your interference.'

'Really? Would you prefer the intervention of the town constable? You'd best calm yourself, Mrs Carwarthen, and quickly, unless you wish to appear before the magistrate.'

Esme snorted, pushing back the tangled hair from her face, but she realized that Margaret had given her sound advice.

Miss Jory turned to Susanna, who had heaved herself up to a sitting position and was sobbing angrily.

'Who, pray, are you?'

'I'm Mrs Rescorla, from Boskenna,' sniffed Susanna. 'That, that harridan is my sister-in-law. We were discussing a family matter and she suddenly attacked me for no good reason.'

333

'A family matter,' muttered Esme scornfully. 'No good reason,' she mimicked. 'You mean, miserable article, with your dainty ways and your nasty mouth. 'Twas only a portion of what you deserve.'

'Enough,' interrupted Margaret. 'Whatever your differences, this is not the place or the way to settle them.'

Wild-haired and dripping with fishy water, Susanna succeeded at last in standing up. A large bruise was darkening on her forehead and another on her left cheek.

'You must have offered some sort of provocation,' Miss Jory told her severely. 'I don't wish to know what it was, but I've heard that you're given to courting trouble. We have not met before, Mrs Rescorla,' she added quietly, 'but I know you by reputation.'

Susanna's glance slid bleakly towards the teetotal ladies. Two of them blushed and shuffled their feet. They were both friends of Esther Gammon.

'Reputation,' she repeated thoughtfully. 'Yes, that's an interesting subject and very much to the point, as it happens.' The light of malice leaped in her eyes and she jabbed a quivering finger at Esme. 'Let's talk about hers, shall we?'

Oh, dear God, Esme thought. I shouldn't have let her goad me. Now it'll all come out.

As if she sensed her mother's distress, Mary wriggled free of Alice Kittow's grasp, scuttled across to Esme's side and clutched her hand.

'I believe in airing the truth,' continued Susanna loudly. Now that she had a big audience, she meant to ensure they missed nothing. 'That's why I've just been set upon – because Esme didn't like to hear it.'

'If you know what's good for you, you'll keep your mouth shut,' Richard had told her. But that was forgotten now. All restraint and caution had slipped away. She was sore and bedraggled, she had been humiliated in front of

334

the local riff-raff. All that mattered now was that Esme should be made to pay, and pay dearly.

'That child clinging to Esme's skirts . . .' The brittle voice shook with excitement. '. . . she wasn't fathered by Roger Carwarthen, you know. Oh dear, no. She's the outcome of a squalid little intrigue between my sister-in-law and a young lout named Tregunna.'

She gazed expectantly round at the bystanders. The teetotal ladies exchanged urgent whispers and peeped curiously at Mrs Carwarthen. The fishwives and the men on the boats stood as though transfixed. All were gazing at the red-haired woman and child.

Esme closed her eyes for a second, then lifted her head and stared defiantly round at the circle of faces. People were murmuring to each other. There were knowing nods and raised eyebrows.

'That's right!' declared Susanna. 'The child is Tom Tregunna's bastard! Just look at her features! Carwarthen likes to pretend the brat belongs to him, but I happen to know otherwise.'

Margaret Jory was indeed studying Mary closely and the expression that crossed her face was one of enlightenment.

Esme had no intention of denying the accusation or her connection with Tom. The damage was done and further argument could only make the incident even more ugly. Mary was frightened and asking for Roger, so her mother picked her up, patting and stroking her, then mustered her dignity to walk through the staring crowd.

It was then that Susanna's triumph turned to dismay, for one of the teetotal ladies hurried to retrieve Esme's forgotten shopping basket and handed it to her with a smile. Some of the men tipped their hats to her as she passed, and almost everyone made way for her in friendly fashion. Although there were a few female faces stamped with disapproval, the great majority seemed unmoved by the awful revelation. In fact, there was very little sign of surprise, as if most already knew and the remainder did not care. It was stale news and had no power to shock.

Richard was right, thought Esme dazedly. It must be common knowledge – but no one's ever said a word.

This was not at all what Susanna had hoped to see. She was not a true native of Porthgullow and had no understanding of these people. Methodists they might be, with rigid ideas of right and wrong, but their code did not accord with hers. They knew danger, they knew hardship, and they were not petty.

Her gaze shifted uneasily to the men on the boats. A bearded fellow in a navy smock and battered felt hat pulled a handful of pilchards from the net and mouthed something under his breath as he flung them with a slap on top of the mass of fish in the hold. A younger man in oilskins surveyed her with contempt, and two others pointedly turned their backs.

Now she recognized her folly. Her mouth opened and closed as she struggled for words that might earn her a little support and sympathy, but there were none to help her. She had made a blunder she would never live down, for the local people did not forget such things. The Carwarthens were a popular couple, but Susanna was an outsider.

The crowd was breaking up now and starting to drift away, with many a backward glance at the woman left standing alone among the fish baskets. On some of the faces Susanna saw loathing. On others were looks of derision and, worst of all, pity.

Only Margaret bothered to speak.

'We are all sinners, Mrs Rescorla. Few of us are beyond redemption, but I truly fear for you.'

As she watched Miss Jory march off, Susanna began to

cry, and she realized with dawning horror that she would need a great deal of courage to show her face in the streets of Porthgullow again.

'Mrs Carwarthen, please wait!'

Rushing up the hill towards home as fast as her feet would carry her, Esme had given way to tears and did not hear the approaching dog-cart until it was close behind her.

'May I offer you a ride? My errand takes me past your inn.'

Esme halted in surprise when Miss Jory's vehicle pulled up beside her.

'Please get in,' urged Margaret. 'The child is heavy and so is your basket.'

Esme was astonished by this gesture from an old adversary, but she was also tired and miserable, grateful for any kindness.

'Thank you,' she said numbly, and climbed into the dog-cart.

Margaret drove on and said nothing for a moment or two, then she remarked: 'I know the Tregunna family very well. Misfits, most of them. The father died of drink. But Thomas is an intelligent young man. I taught him to read and write, you know. He's very quick, very clever. He once spoke to me of you. I understand you were old friends.'

'Yes,' said Esme quietly. 'He sometimes came to the inn for an evening meal and he told me he was following your lessons.'

'Left in some haste, didn't he? I gather he broke a bargain with Balgadden?'

'That's right.'

'And went to Canada, according to his brother.'

'Yes.'

Margaret chuckled. 'I can't say I'm surprised. He was never a man to be tied down, was he?' She cast a quizzical look at Esme and there was a glimmer of humour in it. 'Not the kind to be bound or held back by contracts of any sort. I liked him very much. In fact, I took a special interest in him. He'll do well for himself overseas, I daresay. I was hoping he would write and tell me of his progress, but he never has. Do you ever hear from him?'

She clicked her tongue to the pony as they came over the brow of the hill and saw the Halveor Inn down below.

'No,' muttered Esme. 'No, and I don't know where he is.'

'Hmm – just as well, I expect.' Margaret glanced back at Mary and smiled. 'Leave it to the Lord to arrange everything for the best, eh?'

38

Hannah and Judith were astonished to see the apparition that arrived back at Boskenna that afternoon. Susanna looked like a hayrick after a gale and smelt like a fish cellar. She had been to the doctor and pronounced free of serious damage, but the many bruises, coupled with a split and swollen lower lip, made her a sorry sight. She ordered Hannah to prepare a hot bath and to burn the ruined clothing. Then, over a glass of brandy, she related to Judith her own version of the day's events.

The tale was repeated for Richard when he came in at half past six. Suspiciously, he sat and listened while she described Esme's 'insane outburst' and the 'bestial assault'. Perhaps, admitted Susanna, she had been a trifle tactless with Esme, perhaps she had chosen her words badly, but nothing could excuse such a brutal attack.

Richard decided to reserve judgement until he had heard both sides of the story. So he went to the inn that evening, there to receive a more truthful account from his sister and Roger Carwarthen. He was home again before nine o'clock. Susanna would have no chance to slink off to bed before he had given her a piece of his mind.

'Lord knows, you asked for it,' he said tersely. 'Will you never learn to control that tongue of yours?'

'Whatever I said, she had no right to strike me,' retorted Susanna hotly.

'So you hit back by calling her child a bastard in front of half the town. As if you haven't caused trouble enough already.'

'Everything I said was the unembroidered truth!

Anyway,' she added sullenly, 'it didn't seem to make much impression.'

'I could have told you it wouldn't,' snorted Richard. 'By God, I'd thrash you if Esme hadn't made such a good job of it already. But if there's a next time, Madam, it will be my hand that serves out punishment and you'll find it far heavier than her little fist. What a fool you were, Susanna, to make such a spectacle of yourself. I warned you, didn't I? My sister and her husband are well-liked. This will cost Carwarthen no respect among those that matter. The local people will think no less of him for being a father to Mary. Come to that, you can't even prove that he isn't her father. Esme's a married woman and her husband calls the little girl his own. The law wouldn't argue with him, no matter how the child looks. All right, 'tis true that her features tell the tale, but 'twas Christian to accept her, and most will see it that way. Now, you've done your best to humiliate the man, and he'll smart for a while, I don't doubt. But I fancy you'll be the one to suffer longest. Few of the townspeople ever liked you anyway. Now you won't be able to walk down the street without meeting hard stares or hearing somebody shout after you.'

Susanna swallowed nervously, but gave a small shrug. 'It hardly matters. Most of my visits to Porthgullow only take me as far as Morven Terrace anyway.'

'Just as well. If I were in your shoes, I'd think twice before venturing any farther down the hill. Those fish-wives can be very nasty when they feel there's cause.'

'It will grieve me not at all to avoid the lower part of the town,' she sniffed. 'I much prefer the company of my own kind.'

'My husband is very concerned,' said Esther, setting down her teacup. 'He feels that it's bound to reflect on Gammon

340

and Jose, because of your kinship to that woman. The whole town is sniggering and especially this neighbourhood. I need hardly remind you that those of us who derive our income from legal practice should be beyond reproach in our personal conduct, and the same must apply to our close relations. We who are paid to deal with the scandals of others cannot afford any of our own, least of all a performance as vulgar as that one.'

Katie threw a simmering glance at her husband and received a dour one in return. Esther Gammon, who had always thrived on other people's trouble, was less enthusiastic when notoriety came too close to home. Now sixty-seven, she was grey and skinny and long in the face, like a very old ewe. Her voice was no longer strong, but could still convey severity when it suited her.

'Of course, Susanna was always prone to outbursts of temper, though it seems she found herself outmatched by your aunt in that respect,' continued Esther gravely. 'I cannot say that I sympathize with either one of them, but it's your mother, Katherine, upon whom discredit has fallen most heavily.' She paused to help herself to a small piece of cake, took a bite and chewed thoughtfully for a moment, remembering. 'It's a pity your father married her. I knew no good would come of it. I knew there would be strife. She simply wasn't . . .' Mrs Gammon waved her slice of cake vaguely as she searched for a word. '. . . adaptable.'

'From what I've heard, you were very excited about it at the time,' Katie reminded her frostily.

Esther had just taken another bite, but her jaws stopped working and a fleeting look of annoyance crossed her face.

'You're mistaken, my dear.'

'Oh, no I'm not.'

She was ready to quarrel and Arthur stopped her. 'Kate,' he said warningly, 'never mind that.'

Mrs Gammon swallowed the cake and brushed the sugar daintily from her fingertips. 'Anyway, as I was saying,' she went on, 'I fear Susanna is something of an embarrassment to us. Your mother has made herself a pariah, Katherine, and I have to say that Gammon and Jose cannot afford to be associated with someone so widely frowned upon. What are we to do?'

'Perhaps I should give up my position?' suggested Arthur wickedly, for he knew they would not want to lose him.

'Good heavens, no! My dear boy!' exclaimed Esther. 'No, no, no! You're a very great asset to us. Mr Gammon feels that you have a brilliant future and he's very anxious that you should stay. Had there been any question of your leaving, he would have spoken to you himself. What I meant to propose was that Katherine should visit Boskenna more frequently, instead of asking her mother here.' The tone became persuasive, sticky. 'It would be best, wouldn't it, if she were not seen calling here too often?'

'And preferably not at all, hmm?' ended Arthur drily.

'Well . . .' Esther spread her hands and smiled from one to the other, as if sad but helpless in the face of circumstances. '. . . the situation is awkward, isn't it?'

'Don't worry, Mrs Gammon,' said Katie, stony-faced, 'I'll deal with it.'

'Of course you will,' gushed Esther. 'You're such a sensible girl.'

'The old crone!' fumed Katie, after she had gone. 'She'll never let me forget it, you know. She'll harp on it for ever more.'

Arthur poured himself a tot of whisky and one for her as well. 'Here,' he said, 'something for the pain.'

'She made me feel like a child being smacked – for what Mother did! I don't know which of them I hate the most.' She swallowed the whisky in one gulp.

Her husband was silent for a moment, then he said: 'Yes, Esther's a dreadful old woman. Still, on one thing I have to agree with her, Kate. I don't want your mother here again. With or without Esther's interference, I'd have asked you to put an end to the visits. I know you don't enjoy them; you've stood them for duty's sake, but here's a good chance and a damned good reason to stop them. Roger Carwarthen's a client of mine. I like the man and I don't think I could find a civil word for Susanna after what she did. She's not welcome in my house any more, and it's nothing to do with what Esther or the partners want. Old Jose was a bit agitated about it all, and Gammon spluttered a lot, but there weren't any threats. I just don't care to open my door to a woman who publicly insults a good man and a five-year-old child.'

''Tis all right, Arthur,' came the grim reply, 'you don't have to persuade me.'

Friday was one of Susanna's regular days for tea at Morven Terrace. She did not call during the week that followed the scuffle, for the bruises took some time to disappear. Her lip had not healed completely when she finally ventured forth, but all in all she felt fit to be seen after nearly a fortnight had passed.

She arrived at her daughter's house at four, but when she was shown into the drawing room the customary spread of layer cakes and dainty sandwiches was nowhere to be seen. Katherine had already finished her tea. The maid took away a small tray, set for one person, and the young Mrs Lovell did not ask her to bring anything more. Nor did she invite her mother to sit down.

'I wish you hadn't come, Mother.' Katie stood up and

placed herself resolutely in front of the big marble fireplace.

Susanna frowned. 'Why Katherine? Are you unwell?'

'No, 'tis nothing like that. I may as well be blunt, because I'd like to have this quickly over and done with. I don't feel inclined to mince my words, since you're so reckless with your own.'

Her mother guessed, then, what was coming, and her heart sank.

'Arthur and I heard all about the uproar down on the quay. He wasn't pleased to learn that his mother-in-law had been involved in a public brawl – one that she started by slandering a child.'

'The truth doesn't constitute slander,' replied Susanna swiftly. 'Your husband, of all people, must know that.'

'We won't quibble about the law, Mother. The fact remains that you shamed us all. I can't forgive what you said to Aunt Esme. She's always been kind to me and I'm very glad she has that lovely little girl.'

'I didn't seek her out to cause trouble,' protested Susanna. 'I merely went to tell her that you are expecting your first child.'

'And to brag about my marriage. Oh, I know what was said, I've been to see Uncle Roger. You ought to have known better, Mother. You and Aunt Esme have always been the same – like fire and powder.'

'It was she who became offensive in the first place, not I.'

'Don't tell me you didn't mean to irritate her. I think she called it "crowing", didn't she? I daresay that's just what it was. And from there things went from bad to worse. I can picture what happened, all right.'

'Very well, yes, I'm proud that you made a good marriage and I wanted her to know it. What is wrong with

344

that? If she hadn't been rude to me, I wouldn't have mentioned . . .'

Katie cut her short. 'I won't have you using me or my husband's position as cudgels in your feud. Until I met Arthur, you disliked me almost as much as you loathe Aunt Esme. And after today I expect you'll fall to hating me just as before, because there's no longer anything to be gained from me. If I'd married a fisherman, or one of Father's apprentices, you wouldn't give me the time of day, let alone boast about me. We've never cared for each other and we never will. You don't really relish my company, Mother, you just like coming here. We called a truce and kept the peace for a while, but we still don't have much regard for one another. Now, you've made me very angry and I don't want to see you any more. Please stay away in future.'

'You selfish little madam! If it hadn't been for my guidance, you probably *would* have married a fisherman or some such type. I doubt you'd have captured a husband like Arthur if I hadn't supervised the courtship. It was I who taught you how to dress and behave, my girl. Have you forgotten whose money paid for your lovely clothes? You're a spoilt, ungrateful young woman, Katherine. Your advancement has made you conceited.'

'Yes, Mother, I know you see it as your triumph, not mine. But I venture to say that I could have "captured" him, as you put it, all by myself, because he didn't choose me just for my frills and table manners.'

'You wouldn't have been a fit wife for him without them!'

Katie ignored that. 'I don't think we've anything more to say to each other. Now please go.'

Susanna left in a brave parade of high dudgeon, the bustle of her skirt and the cluster of sausage curls at the back of her neck wiggling and bouncing as if with right-eous anger, and that was the end of her treasured entrée to Morven Terrace. The cost of her skirmish with Esme had proved very great indeed.

Barred from her daughter's house, and aware that she was fiercely disliked by the townspeople, Susanna was rarely seen in Porthgullow from then on. Whenever she wished to buy something, she went instead to Penzance. It was a lengthy trip and not one to be made frequently, so she found herself increasingly confined at home, both by reluctance to visit Porthgullow and by a worsening problem with her back.

The twinges, which once struck solely after lifting or other exertion, had now become a constant ache that relented only when she went to bed. Her doctor advised a special corset, to be worn throughout the day. It was quite uncomfortable, but nevertheless preferable to the gnawing pain in the lower half of her spine. Despite the physician's insistence that this affliction was caused mainly by the old childhood injury, and almost inevitable in later years, Susanna held Esme entirely to blame. 'That vicious beating', as she always called it, was surely responsible for this onset of chronic lumbago and she would not entertain the idea that her age had anything to do with it.

She was now fifty-one and decidedly wrinkled around the eyes and mouth. She had taken to wearing high collars to hide her ageing neck, and although her clothes and hair were always kept in fashionable style, no trace was left of the fairylike creature Richard had married. As if for good measure, by the end of that autumn Susanna found herself obliged to wear spectacles, for she could no longer read or sew without them.

39

Peter's fourteenth birthday fell the following year, and Richard duly took him into the trade. The boy was now taller than his mother and she found it strange to be looking up into his face, instead of down at the top of his head. When she spoke to him, the reply came in the variable tones of a youth whose voice was breaking. His features were changing too. He seemed set, after all, to be a very plain man. Susanna could not deny that Alan was the better-looking of the two, but Peter would always remain her favourite and she was deeply proud of all that he said and did.

Both her sons were now at work for twelve hours or more each day. There was no one except Judith to keep her company through the long afternoons and have tea with her at four. Judith was nearing forty, but seemed hardly any different for it. She had always been slightly quaint. Perhaps she was now a little more so, but on the whole she did not appear to have altered a great deal.

But age took its toll of others in that year of 1882. Rufus Adams died that spring, just a few weeks after the start of Peter's apprenticeship. Richard sorely missed the old man, for Rufus had always seemed to him a fixture, as permanent as the very rocks. But one April night, without any previous signs of decline, he died quietly in his sleep.

'Well, there's no better way to go,' Alan said, to console his father, 'and, after all, he had a good long life.'

Shortly afterwards, the Rescorlas were deprived of another old friend, for Hannah was now sixty-nine and too arthritic to cope with the work at Boskenna. Her father had left her his cottage and a little money to live on, and so she regretfully gave the family notice to find another woman to help in the house.

The girl Judith chose to replace her was unused to domestic employment. She was one of the many bal-maidens forced by the closing of the mines to seek other kinds of work. Her name was Patience. She was strong, willing and jolly, with black hair, pink cheeks and a dimple. She was also noisy and fond of coarse jokes, so the boys found her very entertaining. Under Judith's instruction she became a very good cook, and ably kept Boskenna clean and well-ordered. Had Patience been a little less brash, Susanna would have found no cause for complaint. As it was, she had to resign herself to the girl's loud voice and the howls of rollicking laughter that rang through the house a dozen times each day.

Having a roving eye and a taste for the company of men, Patience liked nothing better than to go down to the yard at midday to take them their food and loiter about for a while. In the summer heat they all worked with their shirts off, providing a feast of muscular brown bodies for the girl to admire. Her fancy lit, in particular, on Richard's elder son, and for Alan there was always a bigger slab of heavy cake, an apple more juicy or cold meat more lean.

'Here,' she said to him one day, 'you have that one. He've got more currants in'n than all th'others.'

It was a saffron bun. Alan put down his work at the lathe and took it with a grin. There was cheese for him, too, and a hunk of cold beef. Up in the rafters, a wheel was set to operate the lathe. It was Peter's arduous job to turn it and he gratefully clambered down when his brother stopped work. Patience hung around while they ate their meal, chaffing the younger brother and flirting with the

348

older one. As always, she kept them from their tasks until Richard intervened and sent her packing.

'Like her, do you?' Peter asked his brother, as they watched the broad backside swaying out of the door.

''Course I like her. Always have a bit of fun with her, don't we?'

'You know what I mean. She's got an eye for you.'

'Oh – well, no, I'm not interested like that.'

'Why not?' Peter rolled his eyes. 'She's a bit rowdy, but she's nice and – round. You've noticed that, I know you have.'

His brother, caught between mirth and embarrassment, stifled his own laughter. It was not easy to keep his eyes off the girl's ample bosom and if Peter had seen him looking, then Patience had, too.

'Get back up and turn your wheel, or I'll clip you one.'

'You're always watching the girls nowadays,' persisted Peter. 'I believe you're on the lookout for a wife.'

'Up aloft, go on!'

Still chuckling, Peter returned to his perch. Alan paused to inspect his handiwork, then applied it again to the lathe as the wheel began to spin. A joke it might seem to his brother, but women were very much on Alan's mind these days. He was ready to marry, all right, and had seen several girls who took his fancy. It only remained to make a choice.

40

Winter was mild that year. Even January, normally cruel, was not much worse than a damp November. The fishing boats went out more often than usual for the time of year, and though there was little to catch, it was still something extra to help them through till spring.

One Friday morning in February found Jenny Symons in the grocer's shop, debating the best means of stretching the money in her pocket. Tea or currants, sugar or gingerbreads? Something always had to take priority, something always had to be left. There was never enough for everything on her list. The shopkeeper waited while she compared prices and thought it all out. If she wanted credit he would give it, but Mrs Symons was one of the few who rarely asked for that.

A second customer came in, so he left her to ponder and went to serve the other woman. Jenny made up her mind in favour of tea and treacle but was now obliged to wait her turn, so she wandered round the shop, looking at all the things she could not afford. It was when she turned to the jars of sweets in the window that she noticed her daughter Eva standing in the street outside.

She was talking to someone, a young man, very dark and somehow familiar, for all that his back was turned. Jenny smiled to herself. Eva was the prettiest of her daughters. She bore a mixed resemblance to both her parents and the result was a winsome face that drew the interest of every lad who set eyes on her. Slight of build and curly-haired, she had found herself besieged by admirers from the time she was fifteen. Most of them had received precious little encouragement, but Jenny could see a different look on Eva's face as she chattered to this one. She seemed to like him very much.

Curiously, Jenny stood watching, hoping he would turn around. And at last he did.

The smile dropped from her face and a chill seemed to touch her soul. It was like seeing Richard there in the street, Richard at nineteen, laughing with an adoring girl he was soon to betray. Everything about Alan was an echo of his father: the way he held his head, the way he stood, with one hand in his pocket . . . And then there came a gesture – he reached out and pressed his palm to Eva's cheek, just for a second or two, as he said something that made her smile with shy pleasure. Oh yes, Jenny remembered that as well. She could summon again the warmth of Richard's palm on her own face and knew that Alan had paid her daughter a compliment of some kind. It was just the same, exactly the way his father did it.

'Mrs Symons?' The other customer was leaving the shop and the grocer turned his attention back to Jenny. 'Have you made up your mind what you want?'

She did not hear. The couple had linked arms now and were strolling off down the street. She was seized with an urge to run after them, push them apart and tell Alan to keep his hands off her daughter.

'Mrs Symons? What would you like?' The grocer sounded impatient. She remembered, then, where she was, and the impulse died away.

'I'm sorry, Mr Dyer,' she said absently. 'I'll take half a pound of tea and a tin of treacle.'

I'll have to put a stop to it, she thought, as she paid for the goods and made her way homeward. I'll speak to her tonight, when all the others have gone to bed. 'Tis one thing to forgive the boy's father for what he did to me, but that's not to say I'll trust a Rescorla with any daughter of mine.

'Eva, stay for a while. I want to talk to you.'

The girl paused at the foot of the staircase and a look of puzzlement crossed her face. It was late and she was in her nightdress. Her father and elder brother had gone out fishing and the other five children were all in bed. Eva, too, was ready for sleep, and wondered why her mother should call her back. She went and sat down on the stool by the grate, hoping her mother would not keep her long.

By the light of the fire and a single candle, they faced one another across the hearth. Jenny had laid her sewing down beside her on the settle and her hands were moving restlessly, clasping and stroking each other in the way they always did when something troubled her.

'What is it?'

'I've something I must say to you, my dear. I'm afraid you may not like it, but I'm only thinking about what's best for you.'

Eva plainly had no idea what was coming, and she waited in silence for her mother to continue.

'I saw you with Alan Rescorla today,' explained Jenny quietly. 'I was in the grocer's shop and I saw you talking to him. And then you went off together, arm in arm.'

'Yes . . .' The girl still seemed mystified. '. . . what's wrong with that?'

Her mother looked incredulous. 'What's wrong with it? Eva, how can you ask such a question? He's Richard's son. You know what happened when I was young, how his father let me down.'

Eva frowned. 'But that was twenty-five years ago. What does it have to do with me, or with Alan?'

'Everything, because he's just like Richard was.' Jenny turned her eyes to the fire, where the driftwood burned with a softly wavering flame. 'It all came back to me when I saw him touch your face like that. All the love – and all the misery that came after it.' Her gaze flicked sharply back to her daughter. 'You mustn't see him any more. Steer clear of him, Eva. If you keep on meeting, you're sure to grow fond of him.'

'Mother, I already am.'

'Oh? You've known him a good while, then?'

'I've been walking with him a few times.'

Jenny's mouth tightened with the beginnings of anger. 'He didn't ask if 'twas all right – and nor did you. Why didn't he show his face here to see how your parents felt about it all?'

'He will, if you like,' said Eva mildly. 'I'll bring him home next time I see him.'

'I'd much rather you simply didn't see him, Eva. That's what I'd prefer. I'd rather you took up with somebody else.'

The girl regarded her sadly for a moment, her hair throwing dark, swirly shadows on her face. 'I thought you'd forgiven Richard,' she said at last. 'Father's been taking his boat to Rescorla's yard for the last ten years. 'Tis only a dim memory to me that bitter words were ever said about him. I thought 'twas all forgotten, Mother. I never dreamed you'd be set against Alan, just because he's Richard's son.'

'Oh yes,' conceded Jenny, 'the grudge wore itself out a long time ago. But the lesson hasn't faded, Eva. I don't dislike the lad – how could I? I've never passed more than a nod and a word with him, and 'tis no fault of his that Richard jilted me. But knowing, as I do, that he's followed his father in every other way, how can I trust him with you?'

'He's another man, Mother. He's not Richard, for all that he looks the same. You're not being fair.'

'I'm being careful – for you,' said Jenny earnestly. 'I'm trying to keep you safe, that's all.'

But Eva did not want to hear any more.

'There's no need to worry, Mother,' she sighed, standing up. 'We'll talk again tomorrow if you want, but I'm tired now and I don't feel like arguing. I'm going to bed.'

'Please . . .' The word was filled with urgency. 'Please, Eva, will you do as I ask and keep away from him?'

'No,' said Eva firmly. She bent to kiss Jenny's anxious face. 'I've always taken your advice before, but this time I think you're wrong. 'Tis no good telling me to take up with somebody else, Mother, for there's no one in this town I'd rather have.'

'You're her father,' said Jenny to Luke, as they walked across the waterfront together late the following afternoon. 'Talk to her, make her listen. If she won't see sense, then forbid her to meet him. A word from you would be enough.'

'No, Jenny, I won't do that.'

'Well, speak to him, then. Tell him to leave her alone.'

'Nor that, either.'

'Why not? You know how his father treated me. What if the same thing happens to Eva?'

'It might, 'tis true, but the risk is there for any young woman with any young man. Just because the lad reminds you of his father, you're thinking he'll act the same way. You're afraid treachery might run in the family, I suppose?'

'Yes, perhaps it does,' said Jenny tartly. 'He's Susanna's son, too, don't forget.'

'He may be all the wiser for that. Look maid, it seems like Eva's decided she wants him. Now, if he leaves her she'll hate him, just as you hated his father. But if we interfere, 'twill be us she'll hate. Anyway, in a year from now they'll both be twenty-one and we'll have no more say in the matter. We can't stop her, Jenny, and we'll only create bad feeling if we try.'

They had reached the place where *Sweet Eva* was moored. Here, Jenny always came to see him off when he set out for his night's work. Luke paused briefly at the top of the quay steps for the usual hug and kiss from his wife.

'We must give the boy a chance, Jenny. He knows the price Richard paid for his mistake. Alan's had some of the backwash from it, I don't doubt. The lad's grown up with it, lived with it all his days. I believe he's sharp enough to have learned from it. Now go on home. Stop fretting and leave well alone.'

He turned and went down the steps to board his boat, and Jenny stood watching as it slowly moved out from the quay and headed for the open sea.

Stop fretting? Easier said than done where her favourite daughter was concerned. Why, oh why did it have to be Richard's son? Luke thought well of Alan, she could see that. Of course, he knew him better than Jenny did, since the boy had done a few repairs to the Symons' boat. Yet, it was still no more than a slight acquaintance, and what did that signify? Nothing at all. How well had she known Richard before he deserted her? Seventeen years had not been enough to teach her all about him.

'Eva Symons?' Alan and his father were walking home from work and the name made Richard pause in his stride. 'How long have you been seeing her?'

''Tis about a month now.'

'And you're fond of each other?'

'More than that.'

'Do her parents know?' The question carried a note of apprehension.

'Yes. Luke's all right, but her mother doesn't like me.'

'Hmm.' Richard did not sound surprised. 'Well, I don't think 'tis that, exactly. She's just wary, son, unless I miss my guess. I don't have to tell you the reason, do I?'

Alan scowled. 'But why should I be made to pay for that?' He shook his head, giving a small snort of anger and frustration. 'Dear God, she knows how to make me feel unwelcome – that sidelong way she looks at me and the tone of voice she uses, hard and suspicious. I come to court her daughter and I'm treated like a criminal. I hate going to the house, so most of the time I arrange to meet Eva somewhere in the town. It makes me wonder why you grieved so much for Jenny. I feel more at ease with Mother, and that's saying something.'

Richard chuckled and they walked slowly on up the lane. 'Yes, I know what 'tis like to be on the receiving end when Jenny turns cold, I've had more than a taste of that. I earned it, mind, but . . .' He patted Alan consolingly on the back '. . . 'tis rough on you when you've done no harm. Still, don't take it to heart, boy. She's just protecting her chick, or so she thinks.'

He halted again and his smile disappeared as he turned an intent, warning stare upon Alan. 'I'm taking it for granted you're not just dallying with the girl. I'm right, aren't I? You're not to trifle with her, Alan. If you want her for your wife, if you've no doubts and you're ready to carry it through, you'll have my support and blessing. But if you injure Jenny's daughter, I'll do what your grandpa could have done by me. I won't be as easy as he was, so you'd better be serious, my lad.'

'I've told you I am. How else could I stand the way her mother behaves towards me?'

Richard seemed satisfied with that. 'All right, then, when will you bring the girl out to see us?' he pressed, as they went on their way.

Alan hesitated. 'I don't know. That's another breeding

ground for trouble. Eva's not keen to come to Boskenna – because of Mother, see – and that's no small problem, is it? How could I ask her to live in the same house with Mother? She won't want it – neither of them will, circumstances being what they are.'

His father grunted and scratched his head. 'No, you've a point there. I hadn't thought that far. Still . . .' He paused and flipped up the latch of the gate. '. . . 'tis early days yet, and there's always a way round everything. Meanwhile, you can always call in on your Aunt Esme while you're doing your courting. She'll make you more than welcome. Just one thing, though . . .' He wagged a finger at his son. 'No nonsense. Understand?'

The look on Alan's face spoke volumes and Richard coughed with embarrassment.

'I don't want you following my example in everything,' he ended sheepishly. Then, grinning, he added: 'Well, boy, I've warned you about one thing and another, and we've agreed there are one or two bridges to cross. But now let me tell you how pleased I am.' He reached out and gleefully ruffled Alan's hair. ''Tis the best news I've had in many a year.'

Just like Jenny Symons, Susanna was greatly alarmed by the couple's courtship. She was hopeful that nothing would come of it, but it carried on without faltering and, much to her disquiet, September brought their formal engagement.

'Truly, Richard,' she said, shortly after the announcement was made, 'I see an appalling situation in the making. Heaven only knows what her mother has said to her about me. Since I cannot expect the girl to like me, I suppose I must resign myself to sharing my home with an enemy.'

She was sitting at her sewing machine beside the parlour

window, and the light reflected off her spectacles so that her eyes appeared as two large glassy circles.

'Hardly that, Susanna. It all happened before she was even born, and there's no spite in her, anyway.'

'Nevertheless, we are bound to be uncomfortable.'

But Richard, having pondered on this from the start, already had plans to forestall any trouble.

'There's no need to fear, Susanna. We all know how awkward it would be for everyone. I've been giving the matter some thought and I believe I've found the answer. They can have a cottage of their own. There's one standing empty down at the cove. No one's lived there since the gale and 'tis in a sorry state, but we can set it to rights. I know the man who owns it and he says he'll sell it for fifteen guineas.'

'Oh.' She had not considered such a thing. 'I see. But where, may I ask, will you find fifteen guineas? I understand we've done poorly these last twelve months.'

'I can scrape together the money, don't worry, and the boy will repay me in the fullness of time. 'Twill take a year or so to make the cottage ready, but as soon as 'tis fit to live in, they can name the day.'

Susanna picked up her work again, feeding a strip of fabric under the needle as she turned the handle of the machine.

'In that case I suppose I can make no protest,' she muttered grudgingly. 'Alan will soon be twenty-one. He's entitled to marry whom he likes, of course. But it galls me that of all the young women in Porthgullow, he should choose one of the Symons girls.'

'I can well believe it.' An interesting thought suddenly occurred to Richard and he could not resist the urge to torment her with it. 'Now I come to think of it, Luke and Jenny have several more nice daughters, so you'll doubtless be praying that Peter doesn't set his heart on a "Symons girl" when the time comes.'

The wheel of the sewing machine spun free for a second, as Susanna's hand flew to her mouth. Chortling merrily, Richard left her alone to think upon that. Too upset to carry on with her stitching, she sat motionless for a long time after he had gone.

His words had touched a nerve all right. Susanna did not like to contemplate the inevitable day when some scheming chit laid claim to her own dearest Peter. Any woman who married him would be stealing him away from her. It would all be so much worse if the thief should be one of Jenny's brood. This union between Alan and Eva, which Richard welcomed so eagerly, made Susanna feel even more firmly excluded. She had once likened Mary Carwarthen to a cuckoo, but in truth she had long felt like one herself. An interloper, surrounded by creatures of a different breed. And now, as if Jenny's shadow had fallen across her, she felt an inward shiver.

The cottage destined to be home for Alan and Eva was little more than a granite shell when Richard bought it. The walls were sound, but many of the floorboards and roof timbers were rotten and would have to be replaced. Countless slates were missing, not a window remained intact and there was no front door. All told, it was a dismal sight, but not too great a challenge for men skilled at work in wood, men who could build a fifty-foot boat in the space of a few months. Standing within a stone's throw of the yard, it was handy by whenever father or son had an hour to fill, and much of their spare time was spent there throughout that autumn and winter. Knowing he would have to find another six pounds to pay for repairs to the roof, Richard had beaten the owner down a little, and the bargain was finally sealed at twelve guineas.

The roof came first and after that the upstairs floor. There were flagstones to the lower one and the staircase, too, was stone, which saved them a great deal of effort, but it still remained to make and fit new doors and windows. Nevertheless, by January Alan felt sufficiently pleased with their progress to invite Jenny to see the home he was preparing for her daughter.

She came along with Eva one Friday afternoon, and found him shovelling rubble off the front path. Jenny returned his greeting gravely – indeed, he rarely saw her smile – and he welcomed Eva with just a respectful peck on the cheek. In front of Jenny, he dared not do more, however much he might cuddle the girl when they found themselves alone.

'We'll have a good-sized plot, Mrs Symons,' he said, waving his spade towards the weed patch round the cottage. 'I'll dig it over, come spring. We'll grow carrots and taties – flowers, too, if Eva wants them.'

'That would be nice,' allowed Jenny. 'She's never had a garden.'

Encouraged, he pointed up to the roof. 'And look, 'tis Delabole slate, sound as a bell now all the gaps are filled.'

''Tis a proper job, I can see that.'

Again a favourable comment. Alan glanced hopefully at Eva and received a wink in return. Cheered by these few words of praise, he took them inside to look at the rest of the work. For Eva there were no surprises; she had been here times enough before. This tour of inspection was all for Jenny, an attempt to win her over and calm her fears.

'I'll whitewash the inside,' he said, as they looked at the back bedroom. ''Twon't be dark like this when we come to move in. We'll have plenty of furniture, too. Father'll let me have a good bed and a couple of chairs from the house. The rest we can make ourselves – tables, cupboards and so forth.'

360

'Alan can turn his hand to almost anything,' said Eva proudly.

'Another way in which he's like his father.'

The tone and expression said more than the words, and there followed such a hush that she might just as well have slapped him. Eva moved close to him, loyally clasping his arm.

So much for the truce, he thought heavily. He had fancied that Jenny was warming towards him, but that flat remark still told of distrust and it suddenly moved him to anger.

'How long will you keep on like this?' he demanded sharply.

'Until the wedding ring is on her finger.'

'There's an engagement ring there already.'

'I had one of those, from your father,' came the stout reply.

'Oh yes, yes, I know all about that and I've put up with a lot from you in consequence, but I've had enough and I'm sick of it. What more can I do to prove good faith? Father went in debt to buy this place, and in my turn I'm in debt to him. We do a day's work and then we come here, one or both of us, and put in still more time. Is there no pleasing you? Seems to me we could break our backs and you still wouldn't be satisfied.'

'Mother,' added Eva coolly, ''tis unworthy of you to be so unkind after all they've done here. You can harp too long on things that are past. In the end you put yourself in the wrong.'

Taken aback, Jenny softened just a little. She dropped her gaze for a moment, considering, then she said mildly, 'If I was hurtful, Alan, I'm sorry. You've done a fine job of work here and I give you all due credit for it. 'Tis a nice little house and I'd be happy to see my daughter living here. She talks about it all the time.' This with a

361

fleeting smile for the girl. 'Her heart's set on it, and on you. I'm wary for her, that's all, and perhaps it makes me harsh. I promise you, on the day you marry her, you'll have my love and my trust – but not before.'

'She'll come round in her own good time,' Richard had told him. 'I had to wait fourteen years, so don't think you can hurry her.'

Jenny saw Alan sigh with weary resignation and a glimmer of a smile appeared on her face. 'I'll come again to see how you're getting on, shall I?'

'If you're interested,' he said distantly, still very much affronted.

'Perhaps in the spring, then.'

'Hmm.'

Turning to Eva, she asked: 'Are you coming home now, or staying for a while?'

'I'll be back later.'

'All right, just make sure you're in before dark.'

When her mother had gone, Eva said soothingly: 'At least she's impressed with the cottage.'

'If not with me,' he grunted.

'Believe me, my love, once we're married, she'll never stop making it up to you.'

On her way up the lane, Jenny passed the gate of Boskenna without even glancing at the house. It was Susanna's territory and she would not dream of calling there. At the top of the track, however, she suddenly came face to face with her old rival, who was just arriving home from Penzance in the pony and trap.

Susanna pulled up, and for several awkward seconds they simply stared at one another.

'Good day, Mrs Symons.' The greeting was crisp, slightly curt.

'Good day.' The reply was flat and unfriendly.

'You've been to see the cottage, I take it?'

'Yes. I daresay it'll do.'

'Hmm. The best arrangement under the circumstances, don't you agree?'

'I'm sure it is.'

There was a brief hesitation. Both felt acutely uncomfortable, and yet each was deeply curious about the other.

Here, thought Susanna, was the object of Richard's remorse and all his yearning – this chubby-faced, simply-dressed woman. His rightful wife, displaced but never vanquished.

Almost like a schoolmistress, reflected Jenny, as she studied the older woman. More of a teasel than a flower. Still elegant, of course, but somewhat less sure of herself. She fancied that Susanna seemed slightly nervous.

'Do you approve of this engagement, Mrs Symons? Are you pleased by the situation?'

'No, I'm ill at ease with it, I'll make no secret of that.'

'Ill at ease,' repeated Susanna. 'Yes, so am I, but there's little either of us can do. I presume you're afraid my son might jilt your daughter?'

'I don't deny it.' Jenny regarded her sharply for a moment. Susanna's hands were twisting uneasily at the pony's reins. 'And what are you afraid of, may I ask?'

'I don't think any good can come from the joining of our two families. Richard is all in favour, of course, but to me it does not seem a – healthy – alliance.'

'Well, I doubt we shall often see each other,' Jenny said brusquely, 'so you needn't concern yourself about that.'

'I'm sure you're right. I shall attend the wedding ceremony, of course, but as for the celebrations afterwards . . .' A look of distaste flitted across Susanna's face. 'I assume they'll take place at the Halveor Inn?'

'Esme and Roger want it so.'

'I thought they would. Rest easy, Mrs Symons, I shall definitely not be there. I bid you good afternoon.'

With that, Susanna drove on down the lane and Jenny could not suppress a grin as she watched her go. She had not witnessed Susanna's scuffle with Esme, but mention of it still raised laughter in Porthgullow.

41

April of that year brought a fortnight of blustery winds, heavy seas and recurring fogs. The weather changed from hour to hour, mists descending or receding, winds switching direction twice or three times in the course of a day. Far out on Gennys Point, the lighthouse kept its lamp burning for the benefit of passing ships and the lonely sound of the bell could be distantly heard at Halveor.

Set on higher ground that Porthgullow, the inn suffered greatly from the buffeting of the wind. Whenever the gusts subsided for an hour or two, down came the creeping white vapour to hide the hills and the sea, curling silently round the house and outbuildings, drifting lazily along the road outside. Then, just as quickly, it would lift and disappear again. Only the ceaseless pounding of the ocean remained constant, as it carried on a heaving assault upon the coastline. Here and there, in places where the cliffs were already fractured by past storms, great slabs and pillars of rock fell away, collapsing into the swell below.

Sulky weather, reflected Esme. If a storm was brewing, she wished it would break and have done. From the kitchen window, she looked out on a damp afternoon and shivered slightly. Trade was slow and no one had taken a room for almost two weeks. She supposed that was why she felt so melancholy. This lull in business was unusual and the dreary, indecisive weather made her feel oddly unsettled.

She went into the parlour, where her husband sat before the fire with Mary on his lap. The girl was now seven years old and she was showing him how to make a cat's cradle, gurgling with merriment to see his fingers tangling in the string.

Dearest Roger, Esme thought, as she watched him cuddle the little girl, joking and chuckling with her, patiently enduring all the teasing, fidgeting and hair-pulling. There were few men who would love another man's child so wholeheartedly.

She bent to place another log on the fire, then seated herself on the stool beside the grate, resting her back against the surround.

'The fog's down again,' she said. 'Do you still mean to go to Penzance tomorrow?'

'Only if it clears.'

'Why must you go, anyway? What is it that's so important?'

Roger's attention was divided between his wife and the giggling Mary, who was now tying one of his hands to the arm of his chair. He glanced up absently and replied: 'Oh, a business errand.'

'What are you keeping from me, Roger? You've been teasing me for days with your hints.'

He eyed her playfully and grinned. 'Haven't you been wanting one of those new-fangled kitchen ranges? Well, I'm going to order one from the foundry tomorrow.'

'Oh!' It was a gasp of delight and her face lit up with excitement. 'Oh Roger, thank you!' The beaming smile wavered for a second. 'But won't it cost a great deal?'

'I think we can afford it.'

'Will it have a brass pot rack?'

'It will, sure enough.'

'Oh, bless you!' she exclaimed happily.

'Don't forget, though, it'll have to be black-leaded once a week and that's no pleasant task. Still, all in all, I believe you'll find your cooking made a lot easier. 'Tis a

366

workaday present, but I know 'tis what you want, so we'll have it put in forthwith. The fireplace will have to be widened and part of the chimney breast taken out, so there's bound to be a mess and I want to see the job finished before summer.'

'Did you hear that, Mary?' Esme slid from her seat and knelt down beside her husband's chair, there to hug both of them. She smiled up at Roger, then drew his face down to hers for a kiss of thanks. 'How lucky we are, we three,' she said softly.

'Yes, maid,' he agreed, 'life's been good to us all.'

In celebration, Esme went to fetch tea and hot muffins. Roger settled himself more comfortably in his seat, contentedly patting Mary's back as he watched the flames licking up around the underside of the log and throwing off showers of popping sparks.

When morning came, it was clear and blue, chilly despite the bright sunlight, but a cheering change from the dankness of the past weeks. Roger dressed in his best grey broadcloth suit and his red satin waistcoat, and tucked a wad of money inside the pocket of his jacket. Esme bade him goodbye with a hug, and it was just after ten o'clock when he climbed into the gig.

The road to Penzance crossed many miles of moorland before it came once more within sight of the sea. Roger drove briskly over the bleak uplands, where the track ran through scrubland or wound between stony crags and marshy hollows. The path across this wasteland was ill-defined at the best of times and it would have been a far slower, more hazardous journey if the fog had not lifted when it did. Sometimes the track would branch, making little detours towards some long-abandoned engine house or a moorland pool. On a clear day these deviations presented no problem, but in heavy mist they could be perilous indeed and the traveller making a small mistake in his course would soon find himself lost.

Roger paused at one point, peering against the sun towards the outline of a deserted mine stack that stood about half a mile off the road. Wheal Merit, like so many others, was now dead and forgotten. Those who had worked it were gone, not just to other pits, but often to other lands. Roger was not sorry to see the back of some of them, especially Tom Tregunna, but he knew that the steady decline in his trade was partly caused by this exodus, by the gradual failing of an ancient industry.

He clicked his tongue and the horse trotted on. After an hour, the path led down from the high ground to join the coastal track that ran for some miles along the clifftop to Penzance. It was on this stretch of road that Roger stopped again, this time to admire the sight of a jagged, sprawling headland which jutted into the sea from below the spot where he had halted. Away to his right was a staggered procession of rocky points. The nearest of these was low and ended not far out from shore. Beyond it lay a second spur of land, with sheer grey cliffs beneath its grassy cap, and farther out again, a third swept a long curve towards the skyline. Between them nestled a series of sandy coves, strewn with the debris of many a winter's rockfalls.

It was a fine view and Roger sat for a few minutes to enjoy it, while the horse quietly cropped grass beside the road. Every colour was brilliant, every outline sharp and clear. A sparkling horizon marked the division between the fragile blue of the sky and the deeper shade of a calm sea. Roger could not remember when he had seen a lovelier day and he felt profoundly happy with the peace of this place. He had not met a soul on his journey, and the only sounds were the sighing of wind and water.

But less than ten minutes had passed when he began to

notice a change. As if from nowhere, a fine mist appeared, obscuring the tip of the farmost headland, and the skyline suddenly became indistinct.

Within two minutes more it vanished altogether, lost in a subtle haze with only a gradual fading of dark blue into light to give any indication of where the horizon might lie. There was no longer any great sense of distance when he looked out to sea – almost as if the blueness were pressing in on him – and the two outer headlands were now completely veiled by incoming cloud.

Having lived at Halveor all his life, Roger had seen many a mantle of fog descend in silent stealth upon the moors. Here, the wisps and tendrils of white vapour came hurrying towards him like spectres racing in from the sea, twining swiftly over the grey-green arm of the headland below, darting past him, wrapping round him, cool and clammy. When he turned to look up at the hills behind him, those uplands from which he had only just come, he saw thick banks of mist rolling down on them.

Within the space of a quarter of an hour, bright sunshine had given way to a cloak of fog that was growing more dense by the minute.

With a few muttered words of lament for the spoiling of a fine day, Roger set off once more down the road. He had six miles yet to go and he could see no more than fifty feet in any direction. All the same, he was not unduly worried. The track was wide and easy to follow if taken slowly, and so he kept the horse to a walking pace.

By the time he had covered one more mile, however, the mist had closed more thickly about him. He could now see no further than twelve feet, and a slight unease started to grow in him when he heard the rumble and crash of waves breaking somewhere far below and to his left, hidden in the drifting whiteness. Roger knew this road very well and could not recall any spot where it passed close to the cliff edge. There had always been a margin of six or seven yards – and yet he felt apprehensive. After a while, he jumped down from the gig and walked, cautiously leading the horse over a patch where the road sloped abruptly down, then climbed just as steeply up again to a stretch of muddy ground that continued for nearly a mile. Having negotiated this unpleasant section of track, he got into the gig once more and went on a little more briskly.

When next he heard the muffled roar of breakers, still a good way off to his left, he assumed he was quite some distance clear of the cliffs. He made no move to check the mare when she trotted into a bank of mist which billowed with a strange, eddying motion, as if stirred by an updraught of air.

Roger knew his mistake the instant her hooves slipped and plunged into emptiness. She lurched forward with a shrill snort of terror, pitching him over her head as she plummeted, squealing, down into the gulf where there had once been solid ground. There was a grinding, splintering noise as the gig somersaulted and bounced over the steep scree below. Roger threw out his arms, clawing at the turf of the cliff edge. For a second or two it bore his weight while he groped frantically for a better handhold. But as his fingers closed on a spur of rock, the grass and soil tore loose. He did not feel the cutting pain, but his eyes clouded with despair when the sharp stone ripped through his palm and slid from his grasp. The drop was not sheer and his final fall was a long, helpless tumbling. It was Esme and Mary who filled his mind in the seconds before the last violent jolt that broke his neck.

Esme did not sleep that night. Anxiety had gripped her when the mist came down again in the early afternoon.

She tried to console herself with assurances that he had probably escaped it, since the weather on one side of the peninsula was often warm and clear while the other might be shrouded in rain or fog. But when evening fell, she found herself more and more frequently compelled to step outside the front door and gaze down the road into the deepening dusk, listening for the sound of approaching hooves.

'Isn't Pa home yet?' Mary asked, as Esme put her into her nightshirt and tucked her into bed.

'No, not yet.' Her mother tried to sound bright, unconcerned.

'Will he be here soon?' The child's question ended on a yawn.

'After you've gone to sleep, I expect. You mustn't try to stay awake waiting for him. Your pa had a great many important things to do. He might even have to stay in Penzance tonight. He'll go to an inn, you see.'

'Like the gentlemen who come to stay here?'

'That's right. Go to sleep now.'

Perhaps that was it, Esme thought as she went downstairs. Roger might well have decided to take a room for the night. It was surely foolish to worry just because he was a few hours overdue.

But the sense of foreboding would not go away. Time and again as the evening wore on, it urged her to peer through the windows or slip outside in the hopes that she would see her husband coming down the road. The night was clear by nine o'clock, lit by a moon almost at full. Esme stood for several minutes at a time in the stillness of the front courtyard, shutting out the muffled sounds of talk and laughter coming from the pewter room, straining to hear the tread of a horse.

But Roger did not come. The evening passed, the

customers went home and Ewan completed his tasks of locking up and dousing the lights.

'Dunnee worry, maid,' he said yet again. 'Go on up bed 'n get to sleep. He'll be back, come mornin'. He can look after hisself.'

Esme smiled half-heartedly, bade him goodnight and went upstairs with her lamp. In her bedroom she slowly undressed and lay down, but she did not close her eyes. There had, of course, been other occasions when Roger had come home late, but this time she could not shrug off the feeling that something was badly amiss. While the rest of the household slept, she shared the night with her fear and the ticking of the clock.

By noon next day she was distraught. At one o'clock she told Ewan to take the brake and go to look for him.

Although he would not admit it, even the cellarman was now becoming concerned. It was just before two when he set out to follow Carwarthen's route to Penzance. He crossed the moors with many a looping detour from the main track, but found no sign of Roger or the gig. And so, at last, he carried on down to the coast road. He was just four miles from Penzance when he came to the spot where Roger had fallen.

With a curse and a gasp of astonishment, he hurriedly pulled up the horse. He had almost come to grief himself, for the rolling contours of the track served to conceal the peril until he was nearly on top of it.

Part of the road was gone.

There before him, like a giant bite taken from the cliff, was a gap some twelve feet across. The track ran right into it, resuming on the other side and continuing for half a mile, then disappearing into yet another breach before proceeding unbroken the rest of the way.

Ewan glanced about him, appraising the road he had just been travelling and that which now lay in front. The coastline here had changed a great deal since the last time he had come this way. It had gone back many yards in some places, eaten away by the battering waves. Never, in the past, had the road run so close to the cliff edge. Even on a clear day, the drop formed a dreadful trap for the unwary. If a man were to pass here when the fog was down . . .

Fearful now, Ewan hopped down from the brake and moved gingerly forward to the brink of the rift. He knelt down where the grass and topsoil hung raggedly over, torn away by the tons of rock subsiding from beneath. The landslip had formed a steep incline composed of large craggy boulders, mounds of smaller rubble, earth and clay. Near the top, in a slab virtually unbroken, lay what he recognized as the piece of road the falling cliff had taken with it. At the bottom, piles of debris stretched out for some distance into the sea, and the water washed lazily in around them.

The scree descended for about a hundred and fifty feet. At first glance there was no sign of Carwarthen. Ewan was about to breathe a sigh of relief – but then, among the grey of the stones, perhaps two thirds of the way down, he spied a flash of bright colour. It was Roger's red satin waistcoat.

Carwarthen lay half in the shadow of the great rock which had, in the same instant, both killed him and stopped his fall. Of the horse there was no sign, for she had rolled right to the foot of the slope and the tide had taken her body some hours later. One wheel and a few splintered boards were all that remained of the gig.

'Aw, dear Lord, no. No, 'tis too cruel.'

Ewan bowed his head in sorrow for a man he had liked so well, and in pity for the widow and child left behind. The problem of retrieving Roger's body concerned him far less than the prospect of breaking this news to Esme.

He had rope, strength and a horse with which to achieve the first, but words did not come easily to him at the best of times, and he knew there could be none to soften these tidings.

42

Esme had always known that her husband was well-liked by virtually everyone, but the true extent of his popularity was made touchingly apparent by the numbers who turned out for the funeral. The parish church seldom saw such an assembly, since so many had turned to Methodism, but it was filled to capacity on the afternoon they buried the landlord of the Halveor Inn. Even ex-customers who had long since taken the pledge were present that day.

Despite all pleas from her brother, Esme refused to go home and spend a month or two at Boskenna. The inn was Roger's house, Roger's work, and she would not leave it. She preferred to live with the reminders: his chair in the parlour, the hollow made by his body on the right-hand side of the bed, his tankard and briar pipe, his clothes hanging next to hers in the bedroom cupboard. It would not help her, she said, to sit around in Richard's house, where she no longer felt she belonged. It was better to occupy hands and mind in her own kitchen and contend with her troublesome customers, than let herself be coddled and given too much time for thinking.

To her own anguish was added that of her daughter. Nothing Esme said or did could console Mary for the loss of her father. Only the placid Judith was able to calm the child or reconcile her to the idea that she would never see him again. It was therefore a huge relief to the widow when her sister offered to stay at Halveor after the funeral. Bringing only a small trunk, Judith moved into one of the guestrooms and promised to remain for as long as she was needed.

Throughout that spring and summer, Esme ensured that her days were packed with chores, and she went about them with a desperate energy. But in the small hours of the morning, with no merciful distractions, her head was filled with memories, regrets, and the bitter knowledge that they had all been robbed. For many months afterwards, Bridget heard Mrs Carwarthen crying each night behind the locked door of her bedroom. But Esme never wanted the tea or brandy the little maid brought for her, and would not share with anyone but Judith the grief and the anger she felt. The loss was much the greater because, for a few short years, her little family had been completely content. It was just as if fortune had been planning a cynical, malicious prank, waiting for the time when the blow would hurt the most.

The handling of her late husband's business was to prove both a burden and a blessing. Esme had always been a capable woman, but the running of the inn required certain skills and knowledge which were new to her. Roger had always dealt with all the book-work, but his widow was now obliged to take over this tedious and quite unfamiliar task. She spent many trying hours leafing through the ledgers and gazing at the columns of figures in an effort to understand the system. For a while it made no sense at all, but when insight finally came it was sudden and complete. The pattern stood out in simple clarity and the logic became obvious. When, in later years, she looked back upon this time, she was to say that the thrill of achievement obtained from this first small success was the start of a gradual healing – but only the start.

The brewing of ale, which had long been her responsibility, presented her with no problems. But she was now required to attend to the ordering of wines and spirits as well, to haggle for discounts from suppliers, pay the bills

376

on time and complain about poor quality, slow delivery and a host of other irritations.

By far the most formidable task was that of learning all aspects of the laws which governed her trade. Roger had known everything there was to know, but Esme's understanding of the subject was incomplete, to say the least. She realized with alarm that she would certainly find herself outmatched in this respect by the likes of Margaret Jory. And so she applied herself to the study of all the relevant rules and regulations, determined not to become easy prey for the teetotallers, who were always circling in readiness to swoop upon the careless publican with reports and summonses. Disputes of all kinds, brawls, or matters concerning the licence would demand her appearance in court from time to time and she meant to go well-prepared.

Had she found herself in softer circumstances, Esme might have pined a great deal longer, but the inn required her best efforts and all her attention. Roger had not left her with debts, but she could not afford to subside into mourning and forget all else. The grief, though it would linger on for a very long time, was tempered and deadened by the everyday concerns of work, and for that she was thankful.

Judith had expected to remain with her sister for several months, but in the event her stay was to last for more than a year. Esme was thoroughly grateful for the way Judith was able to comfort and entertain Mary, and glad of the extra help that allowed her more time to concentrate on her new duties. There was nothing to which Judith would not willingly turn her hand – nothing, that is, except serving the customers. She would happily cook and clean, fetch and carry from morn till night, but the idea of facing a roomful of brawny, ribald men was altogether too frightening for her. Much to the amusement of Bridget and Dinah, she never ventured into the pewter room or the taproom during the hours of business.

Christmas was not a happy time that year and Esme was glad to see the start of 1885, as if the change of date were another step towards healing.

As she grew more confident in the management of her premises, she began to think about making small changes. The notion first occurred to her one afternoon at the end of March, when a char-a-banc loaded with trippers pulled up outside. A member of the party was sent in to enquire whether the Halveor Inn could provide tea and cakes and sandwiches for twenty-four people. Always ready to take advantage of chance trade, Mrs Carwarthen assured them she could, and supplied a fine spread for the modest sum of one and threepence per person. These char-a-bancs, she had noticed, were becoming quite numerous now. From Easter to autumn, two or three of them might be seen passing the inn each day, bound for St Ives, St Michael's Mount, or some other spot deemed to be quaint or curious. It was a pity, Esme thought, to let all that custom go trotting by without making some attempt to lure it in. She therefore decided to have a signboard painted – a large, eyecatching notice to stand beside the road, announcing: 'Cream Teas at 1/6d'.

At the same time she began to think about the growing number of visitors who came to Porthgullow each summer. Esme had five rooms to let, but rarely rented out more than two of them on any particular night. Again, it was a waste. And so, after some thought, she determined to place a small advertisement in the *West Briton* newspaper, which was said to be read throughout the county.

'What do you think?' she asked, handing Judith a copy of the proposed notice. 'Does it sound all right?'

Her sister read the advertisement carefully. 'It seems excellent, Esme. I believe it'll bring good results.'

'I hope so. Anyway, I can but try. Local trade isn't what it used to be and 'tis no good fighting against the tide. There was a time when we could live on the takings from the pewter room alone, but those days have certainly gone.' She pulled a face and snorted. 'I suppose Maggie Jory will call it a victory when she sees I'm offering teas.'

'Don't worry, my dear. Your customers may be fewer these days, but they seem quite rowdy and thirsty enough to me. Now, let's hear again what you've said. Read it out to me.'

Esme cleared her throat.

THE HALVEOR INN
PORTHGULLOW

Comfortable Rooms to Let
Varied and Wholesome Bill of Fare

Bed	2/6d
Hot Breakfast	2/6d
Four-Course Dinner	3/3d
Afternoon Tea	1/6d
Attendance Charge	1/-
Special Weekly terms:	£3.10.0d

PROPRIETRESS: MRS ESME CARWARTHEN

Her voice faltered a little on the last line. Just under a year ago, it would have said: 'Mr and Mrs Roger Carwarthen'.

Judith laid a hand on her shoulder. 'I know your husband would be proud to see how well you've coped, my dear, and I'm sure he'd approve of your notice.'

'All right,' said Esme, smiling gratefully up at her, 'I'll have it printed in the newspaper twice a month and we'll see what comes of it.'

* * *

The anniversary of Roger's death plunged his widow into gloom and had it not been for Alan's wedding, she might have sunk deep in the mire of depression. May 10th, 1885, was the date fixed for the ceremony, and seventy hungry people were expected at the Halveor Inn after the service. Luke and Jenny had not the money to pay for such a feast, but Esme and Roger had gladly promised to provide one, accepting in return Symons' pledge of choice turbot and other gifts of fish in the years to come.

Esme began to make preparations a week beforehand, placing advance orders for meat and groceries, shining all the pewter and cutlery, and worrying over the seating of so many people. She moved all the tables around in the dining room, trying them this way and that, changing them back again and generally driving herself and everyone else to distraction. Chairs and benches were brought in from the pewter room, from the bedrooms, from the kitchen. Every napkin and tablecloth was laundered and starched. At the last moment she discovered that she did not have quite enough of either, and so had to rush out and buy more. Many extra gallons of beer were brewed, and much thought was given to the problem of organizing the cooking in such a way that Esme and Judith could attend the ceremony and then hurry back to the inn to put the finishing touches before the party arrived. In short, it was a great feat of labour and planning, guaranteed to take her mind off her woes.

The day came, the meal was cooked and served with barely a hitch, and the guests showed their appreciation with a round of applause for the landlady, with much whistling and stamping for good measure. Everyone was in great spirits and they did not seem to mind being crammed into a room that was never meant to seat seventy.

There was just one empty place and that was at the

bride's table. Susanna had gone straight back to Boskenna after the service, complaining of a headache. The Halveor Inn was not a place where she felt welcome and the company was not of the sort she enjoyed. Among such people she would never be anything but an outsider.

Richard was relieved when his wife elected to go home. He did not want Susanna seated stiffly beside him, picking primly at her food, poker-faced amid the jollity and pained by the noise. This was a very special celebration and he did not wish to see anyone dampen the merriment. When he looked at the radiant Eva, beautiful in white with spring flowers woven into her curly hair, and then at his flushed and self-conscious son, he saw a scene that should have taken place a quarter of a century before.

It was while Luke was standing to make a short speech that Richard glanced across the table at Jenny and caught her watching him with a similar look of remembrance. She smiled awkwardly and quickly turned her attention to her husband, who was full of gin and gladness and calling upon the Lord to bless the young couple in every possible way. Richard's eyes kept flickering over her face while she listened fondly to Luke. Jenny was forty-five now. Her features, like his own, had begun to soften a little – but only a little. The lines were there, but they were muted, gentle. Age would never make her ugly.

Later, when most of the party had drifted into the pewter room, he saw her slip outside alone. There was a wooden bench under the dining-room window and she settled herself on it. Richard hesitated for a second, then poured out two glasses of wine and followed her.

'Shall we drink their health again?'

Jenny had been lost in thought, gazing up at the ferny moorland slopes, and she turned with a start to see him holding out a glass to her. She reached up and took it

381

with a murmur of thanks, and Richard sat down beside her in the spring sunshine.

'To my new daughter and your new son, and to our grandchildren,' he said softly.

They clinked glasses.

'I owe Alan an apology,' she said, when she had taken a sip.

'There's no need. He's not a man to stand on his dignity.'

'I'll tell him, just the same. I've been hard on him.'

She was silent for a moment, thoughtfully savouring her wine. Then she said: 'Do you remember the necklet you gave me, the little charm with the gold and silver wires? You said our lives would always be bound together. And so they are, after all that's happened. From today, we're linked again.'

'Oh, I remember it, all right. How I remember it!' He shook his head, absently stroking a finger round the rim of his glass. 'The times I've thought about that promise. Once I'd married Susanna, I thought 'twas broken for good and always. But when Alan set his heart on your daughter I saw that, in a way, 'twould still be kept.' He smiled, though it was brief and wistful. 'This time there was no mistake.'

43

Alan and Eva spent their wedding night at the Halveor Inn and moved into their cottage the following day. That was when Judith began to think about returning to Boskenna.

I'll stay till the end of the month, she said to herself, and then I'll be on my way. It's been more than a year now. Esme doesn't need me any more and I'll be glad to go home.

But less than three weeks later, the fever came.

'Ma,' whimpered Mary one Wednesday afternoon, 'I feel poorly.'

Surprised to find the child huddled in an armchair on such a lovely day, Esme pressed a hand to her daughter's forehead and found it disturbingly hot.

'My throat hurts,' Mary said.

Her mother knelt down and turned the troubled little face towards her. 'Open your mouth, dear, let me see.'

Sure enough, the child's tongue was furred and the back of her throat was an angry red.

'Come on.' Esme lifted her from the chair. 'I think you'd better lie down for a while.'

Mary made no objection as she was carried upstairs and put to bed. She had seemed perfectly well that morning, and her mother was puzzled by the sudden appearance of this malaise. As soon as the child fell into a doze, Esme left her and hurried downstairs, meaning to send Ewan for the doctor. She had just reached the bottom of the staircase when her sister came through the front door.

Judith had spent the morning shopping in Porthgullow.

She seemed agitated and her voice contained a note of urgency when she said: 'Esme, there's something I must . . .' She faltered at the sight of her sister's anxious face. 'What's wrong?'

'Mary's ill, Judith. I don't know what it is, but she's running a temperature.'

'Oh, my dear.' Judith put down her basket and swiftly removed her coat. 'You must call the doctor straight away. I was just about to warn you, there's an outbreak of scarlet fever in the town. More than thirty cases already, I'm told.'

Esme's face registered shock and dismay. The Rescorla family were, for the most part, blessed with strong constitutions. This, together with their good fortune in living at the cove, had saved them from the fearsome epidemics that rampaged through the towns from time to time. Cholera, typhus, smallpox – her people had escaped them all. Confronted at last with a killing disease, she was almost bewildered, having grown to take good health for granted. Irrational though it was, the notion had long existed in her mind that fevers afflicted only the very poor, the dirty, the neglected.

Ewan was duly despatched to bring the doctor, who briefly examined Mary and confirmed her mother's fears. He peered sympathetically at Esme over the top of his spectacles and admitted that the attack seemed set to be a severe one.

'You must quarantine this floor, Mrs Carwarthen. None of the rooms must be let. In fact, you should close your establishment altogether for the next few weeks. Does anyone else live here?'

'Yes, the cellarman, one of the kitchen maids and my sister.'

'Move them out at once. Find some alternative, however makeshift.'

'I'll stay,' said Judith firmly.

'Have either of you suffered scarlet fever in the past? If not, you're both vulnerable, though admittedly less susceptible than a child.'

'No,' Esme said, 'no, we've never had anything like this.'

The doctor sighed. 'Well, we must hope for the best. I regret that I can offer you little outside help. The number of victims is fast rising in the town and local medical resources are not great at the best of times. It's all we can do to contain the spread of it in crowded areas, and I can't spare a nurse to attend one case at an isolated inn. I'll leave you detailed instructions for the care of your little girl, and I'll try to pay you a visit every second day.'

'All right, yes, I understand,' Esme said. But her gaze and her attention flickered distractedly back and forth between the physician and the fretful face of the child. Fear and confusion filled her mind, so she failed to absorb everything the doctor told her.

It was Judith, ever calm and efficient, who retained his advice, noting down the ingredients and proportions for various medications, the dosages and their frequency.

Mary was moved to a well-aired room at the back of the house. It contained a narrow bed and scanty furnishings, and would prove easier to keep clean than the child's own bedroom, with its rugs and toys and clutter. Esme lit the fire and then coaxed her daughter to drink a little milk and soda water, though Mary could not keep anything down for long. By mid-evening her temperature had risen to a hundred and four, and she cried with the pain of her headache. A heavy white coating had formed upon her tongue, and her palate was peppered with tiny, livid spots.

As the hours wore on and the fever grew worse, Esme immersed herself in a routine that served as much to allay

385

her own anxieties as to comfort and aid the child. The doctor's list of recommendations was considerable: every four hours a sponge bath with tepid water; every two hours a little swab to be made from wool dipped in equal parts of glycerine and water, for the purpose of mopping out the throat; cold compresses to soothe the swollen neck and, at four-hour intervals, the milk and soda water, with lemonade or barley water in between. Far into the night, Esme busied herself with the brewing of these beverages, the burning of soiled cloths and pads of wool, the emptying of slops. Till well past three o'clock, she managed to occupy her mind with the necessary round of scouring and disinfecting, the strict observance of all rules designed to keep separate every bowl, pan or cup, every item of linen used in the sickroom. It was a difficult, worrisome process, but one that succeeded in diverting her thoughts from the worst consequences of the illness.

But finally, in the hour before dawn, exhaustion caught up with her. Esme had neither changed her clothes nor eaten since the doctor left. She felt light-headed and her blouse was damp with sweat. Heavy-eyed, she sank down on a chair beside the bed and allowed the full tide of fear to flood in. Dreadful imaginings, hitherto held at bay, now began to work away at a spirit already depleted by loss. For thirty minutes she sat there alone in the lamp-light, her gaze fixed on the restless little figure in the bed, and dwelt in mute anguish on the possibility of losing all she had left. Tom had gone and would never return. Her husband had been taken from her. And now, perhaps, her child would die as well.

As the clock struck four, the door opened softly and Judith looked in, to find her sitting with her shoulders slumped and hair hanging lank about her face. A film of perspiration glistened on Esme's neck and brow. The hand resting in her lap held a sodden linen compress, and the wetness was soaking through her apron into her dress.

Judith set down her candle on the mule chest under the window.

'Go to bed, my dear,' she whispered. 'You must have a few hours' sleep. I'll take care of her now. I know what needs to be done.'

But Esme shook her head, rubbing eyes that were half closing.

'Don't be stubborn. I'm well rested and wide awake, so you must let me take my turn.'

'Judith, do you think she'll die?'

The question, breathed so quietly, carried a note of helplessness and a plea for reassurance. Poor Esme, always the fighter, was up against an adversary that could not be bested by a slap or a sharp tongue. Judith glanced at the child tossing and crying in the grip of the fever, and she framed her answer with care.

'Mary's strong and well-nourished. She has a better chance than most. We must expect several more days of this, but I think she can stand it. Now be sensible, Esme, go and rest.'

Her sister nodded wearily and dropped the compress into the washbowl.

'Will you call me if there's a change?'

'I'll wake you at once.'

It was not until she rose from her chair that Esme felt the ache which had set into every limb and was gnawing at the back of her neck so that she could barely hold her head up. As she dragged herself off to bed, her sister stoked up the fire and set about preparing yet another sponge bath.

By the time Esme woke, it was past eleven in the morning. She hurriedly dressed and combed her hair, vexed that she had slept so long. In the sickroom she found Judith still remarkably neat despite the night's labours.

'The rash is coming out,' Judith said, 'and her tongue has lost that awful coating, but she's still very hot.'

Sure enough, a crop of red dots had appeared about Mary's neck and upper chest, and was spreading steadily down her body.

By the afternoon the rash had covered her from head to foot. The ring of pallor round her mouth contrasted strangely with the deep flush over the rest of her face, and Esme found it unnerving. As evening approached once more and the high temperature persisted, she began to doubt that even the sturdiest of children could endure more than a day or two of such punishment.

The doctor called the following morning, as promised, and said that Mary seemed to be bearing up, but he could offer no assurances of ultimate recovery. There were, after all, so many complications attending scarlet fever.

Both Ewan and Dinah had already had the sickness and were therefore immune from a second attack. The cellar-man was a willing hand to fetch and carry supplies and fuel, but Dinah could offer no help at the inn, since one of her own children had also come down with the fever. Bridget, who had no immunity, had been sent back to her elderly parents, though not without protest. Richard had called on the Friday, but Judith would not let him in, lest he carry the sickness back to Boskenna. None but the doctor was admitted, for the front door was locked and a sign displayed upon it to explain why.

And so, cut off from almost everyone, Esme and Judith doggedly carried out the treatment by themselves. For almost a week the dismal programme of bathing and feeding went on, a vigil that turned day into night, always obliging one or the other of the sisters to sleep through the sunlit hours and then pass her waking time in the lamplight and shadows of Mary's room. By the Sunday a sense of depression had begun to affect even Judith, for she had privately asked the doctor about the situation in Porthgullow and learned that four children had already died, while a fifth had developed rheumatic fever.

It was on the sixth day that Esme suddenly became aware of an ache and a roughness in her throat. She had woken feeling listless that morning, and her clothing, though light, seemed much too hot. When she peered apprehensively into a mirror, she saw the beginnings of the telltale fur upon her tongue.

By tea-time she was weak, groggy and barely able to swallow, but these miseries were quite forgotten in the rush of relief that came when she noticed the change in her daughter.

Half dozing by the bed, she suddenly became aware of – stillness and silence. For the first time in days there was peace in the room, no tossing or turning, no crying. Mary's whimpering had ceased and she was sleeping quite soundly. She was cooler and the rash appeared less brightly red.

Excitedly, Esme called her sister in.

'I think she's past the worst,' Judith said. 'She looks much better, doesn't she? There, you see? Everything will be all right, though we'll have to keep a careful watch on her.'

But then she paused, inspecting Esme with a suspicious frown, and laid a hand on her sister's forehead.

'Oh Lord, you've got it too.'

'No, I'm just worn out, that's all.'

'Nonsense, you'd better go to bed. Mary's on the way to recovery and I can nurse her by myself. You may as well lie down now as later. You'll be forced to it in the end.'

As she predicted, Esme was thoroughly ill by midnight and thus began four exhausting days of single-handed

389

ministration for Judith. The child rapidly grew stronger, taking small meals of eggs, milk puddings, then fish and a little fruit. She was still fretful, however, irritated by the peeling of her skin, and Judith was ever alert for signs of any of the dangerous conditions that so often followed scarlet fever. With very little rest, she bustled from one patient to the other, smiling, soothing, anticipating every need, and no one realized how the strain was telling upon her – until, on the second Friday, the inevitable happened.

Esme was feeling a great deal better that day. She was certainly well enough to sit up and take notice when the doctor called, for he did not come alone.

Opening drowsy eyes in response to his knock and greeting, she was astonished to see Miss Jory standing beside him at the foot of the bed. Hauling herself up into a sitting position, Esme nodded warily to Margaret, then cast a questioning glance at the doctor.

'Miss Jory has come to assist you,' he explained. 'She's been of the greatest help in Porthgullow these past two weeks and has now volunteered to be of service here.'

Seized with alarm, Esme started to protest.

'I thank you, Miss Jory, but you mustn't risk the fever on my account.'

'I had scarlet fever as a child, Mrs Carwarthen, and am therefore unlikely to catch it again. As the good doctor has just explained, I've spent the last fortnight in close contact with its victims in Porthgullow. You can see that I'm perfectly well.'

'My sister's a very capable nurse and I'm sure you must be badly needed elsewhere.'

Margaret clicked her tongue with impatience. 'Your sister, I must inform you, is showing early symptoms of sickness herself.'

The doctor pursed his mouth in agreement. 'She's

running a temperature, Mrs Carwarthen. I saw she was ailing the moment she answered the door to us.'

Margaret removed the pin that anchored her hat. 'So,' she said decisively, 'you must tolerate my presence here, like it or not.'

Just as she spoke, Judith brought in a tray, on which was placed a dish of egg custard and puréed apple. When she set it down, Esme caught her by the hand and surveyed the tired face. The signs were unmistakable.

'Oh, Judith, I'm sorry. You're looking so ill. I should have noticed.'

''Twas almost bound to happen, Esme. Anyway, I doubt the attack will last any longer than yours did. I'll just take some broth in to Mary before . . .'

'To your bed at once, if you please,' ordered Margaret. 'I shall come along shortly to light the fire and see that you're comfortable.'

Like most people, Judith obeyed her without a murmur.

Esme, however, was filled with consternation. The thought of allowing her old adversary to take charge at Halveor was disturbing, to say the least. Fears of sabotage crowded into her mind, visions of Margaret seizing her opportunity to march down to the cellars, piercing and overturning every cask, opening every bottle on the premises and pouring away the contents. The prospect of finding herself beholden to Miss Jory for nursing care was not pleasing. To trust her with the freedom of the inn and access to its stock seemed unthinkable.

'I'm feeling much stronger today,' she informed the doctor earnestly. 'In fact, 'twas my intention to get up and help Judith with the cooking. I promise you, I can cope very well from now on.'

Margaret was watching Esme closely. An unexpected

lift at the corners of her mouth suddenly softened the severity of her face and the black eyes very nearly twinkled.

'Have no fear, Mrs Carwarthen,' she said wryly. 'It's true that we have our differences, but I'm not given to vandalism. I shan't waste my time lecturing you, either. Nor will I insist on prayers or Bible readings if you don't want them. I'm here because I'm a Christian woman and my faith demands that I give assistance where it's needed. I make no exceptions – and I do not take unfair advantage.'

Esme blushed, but stood her ground. 'I can manage,' she insisted.

'Don't be silly,' said the doctor testily. 'You're still weak and easily tired. You'll have to remain in bed for several days yet, unless you want to court meningitis or some other lethal complication. Think of your daughter, Mrs Carwarthen. She's already lost one parent.'

'Quite so,' said Margaret. 'Now then, where may I sleep? I'll require only a small room.'

Resigned but full of misgivings, Esme gave a shrug and a heavy sigh. 'We've four guestrooms empty. Use whichever one you like,' she muttered, sinking back against her pillows.

'Thank you. I shall first unpack my bag, then see how your daughter is faring. Don't look so wretched, Mrs Carwarthen. I assure you, I'm very efficient.'

'That's what worries me.'

'Believe me, you'll be glad of her,' the physician said, when Margaret had gone. 'She's a fire-breathing dragon,' he added, peering down Esme's throat and feeling the glands in her neck, 'but it's goodness that fuels the flames.'

Whatever Margaret's virtues, Esme was thankful to know she was over the worst of her illness and could at least retain the dignity of washing and feeding herself. And despite Miss Jory's assurance, she still felt the need for precautions. When the doctor picked up his bag and made for the door, she asked him to send Ewan upstairs to see her. Esme had certain instructions to give the cellarman – just to be on the safe side.

Somewhat to Mrs Carwarthen's shame, the doctor's faith in Miss Jory proved to be very well placed, for Margaret took care of them all with awesome competence and what her patients came to recognize as a brusque sort of kindness. Ewan, ordered to lock up and guard the stock, and generally keep Miss Jory under observation, did his best at first to defy her authority. But in the end he was bossed and reproached into grumbling compliance with most of her wishes, though he stoutly refused to let her use any of the keys entrusted to him by Mrs Carwarthen.

Judith's bout of fever developed into a very bad one. Already weakened when the disease struck, she had little resistance to offer. Margaret passed each night on watch beside her bed, dozing fitfully in an armchair but always waking more or less on time to administer the required treatments. However, none of them seemed to give the patient much relief and, as day after day went by without any hint of improvement, Miss Jory began to grow worried.

Early one morning, Esme padded into her sister's room, bare-foot and dressed only in her nightgown, to find out how Judith was progressing. What she saw was not very heartening.

Lines of angry red marked every crease in Judith's skin and she suddenly appeared much older. Having recovered from her own attack with relative ease, Esme had never imagined that the illness would present any great threat to her sister. The wasted and pitiable state in which she now found her was something of a shock.

'Dear Lord, she looks terrible!' Esme stood watching while Margaret applied a cold compress to Judith's neck. 'I didn't think she'd suffer so badly. She will be all right, won't she?'

Miss Jory's reply to the whispered question was hesitant.

'I don't know. She's extremely feeble. There's uncommonly heavy congestion of the nose, which seems out of keeping with the ailment. If she doesn't improve by this evening, I shall summon the doctor again.'

'But what more can he do?'

Margaret straightened up and regarded her gravely across the bed. 'There may not be anything he can do,' she said softly, 'but I'd like his opinion as to precisely what we're dealing with.'

'What do you mean by that?'

There was a brief silence. Between them, the woman in the bed lay like a fragile shadow of the old, healthy Judith. Reluctantly, Margaret explained.

'Well, I don't wish to worry you, Mrs Carwarthen, but I have a suspicion that there's something more than scarlet fever at work here.'

'What else could it be?'

'I'm not sure. I've done a certain amount of nursing, but I'm not a physician and it isn't my place to speculate. I may be quite wrong, of course. We shall have to wait and see. Please go back to bed now.'

'No. I want to stay here.'

'You'll be a hindrance if you do,' said Margaret severely. Then, more gently, she added: 'Don't distress yourself, I beg you. If you want to help, go and see to the needs of your little girl. I think you're well enough now to bath her and prepare the meals. That would be most useful, it would leave me free to give my full attention to your sister.'

'All right, but if anything happens you're to call me straight away.'

'Naturally, I shall.'

Late that afternoon, Esme was sitting on the edge of her daughter's bed, playing noughts and crosses with the child, when Margaret appeared at the door and beckoned her outside. Very disturbed, Miss Jory lowered her voice so that Mary should not hear.

'I know now what it is. Your sister has been taken with a fit of shivering. It's lasted for the past quarter of an hour and there's heavy perspiration on her face. I've seen this before, Mrs Carwarthen. I believe she's developed pneumonia.'

'Pneumonia?' Esme went white. 'Pray God you're mistaken!'

She started towards Judith's room, but Margaret caught her by the arm and tried to hold her back.

'It's best to keep away. You must think of your own health and that of your little girl.'

But Esme pulled free of Miss Jory's grasp and hurried down the passage. One glance at her sister assured her that Margaret was right, for Judith's body was shaken by violent chills. Her teeth chattered and great drops of sweat stood out on her forehead.

'We'll send immediately for the doctor,' Miss Jory said. 'In the meantime, please find me something to serve as a chest binder, for she'll surely need it later on.'

For seventy-two hours the relentless coughing continued, with its discharge of reddish-brown phlegm. While the scarlet fever rash faded, the breathing became more rapid and painful. Judith was given as much water and soft food as she could take, plus a tot of brandy every two or three hours, but at length her pulse began to fail.

At just after six o'clock on Thursday evening, the doctor took Esme aside and told her that her sister would not last another night.

'There's nothing I can do,' he said. 'Her strength is all but gone. She may fight for a few hours more, but she's dying all the time. That bluish colour is a very bad sign.'

For a second or two, Esme pressed shaking hands over her eyes, then lifted her head and gazed numbly towards the half-open bedroom door. Behind it, the rattling breaths went on and on.

'I must ask Ewan to fetch my brother,' she said quietly.

'There's a risk of infection.'

'Richard would never forgive me if I didn't send for him.'

'Very well, but it's best if he doesn't come too close.'

'I'll tell him, though I doubt he'll take much notice.'

Richard and both his sons arrived at twenty past seven. Ewan drove on into Porthgullow to inform Katie, but returned at eight o'clock with the news that Mr and Mrs Lovell were away in London. One of the maids had given him the address of their hotel.

'It'll break Katie's heart,' Esme said. 'She always loved Judith so much. I'll send a telegram in the morning, but 'tis bound to be too late.'

Miss Jory tactfully left the family alone in the sickroom, returning only now and then to see if anything could be done for the dying woman's comfort. Richard, Peter and Alan silently surveyed Judith's haggard face and knew she was near the end. Approaching death had already given its bony aspect to her features, and her eyes were sunk back in darkened sockets. They opened a little when her brother sat on the edge of the bed, stroking the damp skin of her cheeks and neck.

396

'Richard,' she murmured fondly. 'I'm glad you're here.'

'Alan's come to see you,' he said, 'and Peter too.' He moved back to make room for his elder son. On the opposite side of the bed, Peter clasped the small hand that lay limply on the counterpane and felt Judith's fingers curl weakly round his own. A faint smile crossed her face as she rolled her head on the pillow, gazing at each in turn.

'Two fine young men,' she whispered. 'I couldn't be more proud if you were truly mine.'

A fit of violent coughing seized her and allowed no breath for speech until several minutes had passed.

'We wanted to bring Katie, Aunt Judith,' Alan said, when the spasm had died down, 'but she's gone to London with her husband. We're sending her a telegram, so I daresay she'll be here to see you tomorrow night.'

The weary eyes regarded him with a trace of amusement. 'Don't try to fool your old auntie, my dear. We all know I can't stay that long. 'Tis all right. I'm content that she has a good life.'

For over three hours they sat round her bed, saying less and less as she grew more feeble. She allowed Esme to give her a few sips of brandy, but at last the time came when she would take no more. At half past ten, Miss Jory brushed the lank hair back from Judith's forehead, intently studying her face, then laid a sympathetic hand on Richard's shoulder and said softly: 'It's nearly over.'

The clock ticked away another ten minutes, then the wheezing grew fainter, the panting slowed, the heart stopped and the face became tranquil, assuming again the placid look it had worn through the forty-two years of her life.

44

Two years went by. Both Katie and Alan had given Susanna grandchildren, but she seldom saw any of them. The fact caused her little regret, for she was still awkward and ill at ease with infants and much preferred the company of adults. Of this, however, she was now almost totally deprived. At long last she was sole mistress of the house, though it brought her no satisfaction. She would gladly have exchanged this minor distinction for another twenty years of Judith's company. Loneliness had now become a familiar condition and was growing more intense with the passing years. Susanna had long ago lost contact with the friends of her single days, though every now and then she would read or hear that one of them had died. Her injured back added still further to her isolation, for it troubled her more and more as time went on and she found she had to retire to bed for two or three hours each afternoon, in order to gain relief from the rigid corset.

Richard was the last person to whom she could turn for friendship. Her pride would not allow it, and although he now went out less often, he still did not care to sit and talk with her of an evening. Even their squabbling had ceased, replaced by indifference. She no longer bothered to wonder whether he had been seeing the same woman all these years, or if there was a new one now and then. It hardly seemed to matter any more. Too late to worry, she thought. His affection was gone beyond recall and she was growing old.

So, alone with the ticking of the clock, Susanna sat

hour after hour at her embroidery. The first brown spots of age were appearing on the backs of her hands, a constant reminder that her sixtieth birthday was only three years away.

Richard was now forty-eight, with traces of grey in the hair at his temples, but he still seemed young to her. He was fit and vigorous, sunburnt from one summer to the next, and the crinkles at the corners of his eyes were quite becoming to him. He had his sons around him all day long, satisfaction from his work and, above all, the gladness that came from reconciliation with Jenny Symons. His time of discontent was over, but Susanna was still paying the penalty for the past.

There was just one beacon in her desolate life, one source of warmth and brightness on which she focused all the fondness she had: Peter was still her darling. He was now nineteen years old, tall and strong, unremarkable in his features, but possessed of a soft, pleasant voice to which she loved to listen. If he would have dinner with her each evening, if he would just sit for a couple of hours and talk about his day, Susanna found her existence worthwhile.

The boy was aware that she looked forward to the periods spent with him, and he seldom disappointed her. He felt a certain pity for his mother and was conscious of a strange sort of responsibility towards her. To have Susanna's affection was to be uniquely honoured, and he sensed an obligation to accept this rare tribute. Her life was a desert and he was the only well at which she might drink. Despite the knowledge that she had poisoned all the other waterholes herself, he could not deny her a little comfort, though he sometimes found her dependence very trying. It was a great burden to be a mother's favourite child, and not one that he relished. Peter was often exasperated by the stubborn pride that would not allow her to seek forgiveness from the rest of the family, yet he realized that she could not help it. To the bitter end, Mother would cling to her dignity, no matter what it cost her.

In January of 1887, Richard received a request for a small excursion steamer, a vessel to seat fifty people and carry them on trips up and down the coast. The project was a challenge for the Rescorlas, who had never before designed such a craft or built any boat to be fitted with engines. It was, however, the only substantial order that came their way that year, for their traditional customers brought them very little trade. The local seine fishery had suffered three very poor seasons, and the drifters, too, had complained of meagre catches for some years past. Fluctuations were natural, of course, but Richard heard it murmured more and more often that the fish were disappearing from Cornish waters. He could remember the days when Porthgullow harbour had bristled with the masts of her fishing fleet. There were fewer now, and the number dwindled year by year.

The steamer was finished and launched in early June and the men spent the next few months with little except repairs to occupy them. And so it came about that in September Peter once again asked to go fishing aboard *Sweet Eva*, since Richard could easily spare him for days, or even a week, at a time.

Luke Symons often put in at the cove to visit his daughter and grandson, and he never returned to his boat without calling at the yard to see his in-laws, exchange opinions and morsels of news, or lament the scarcity of fish. It was on such a day that he found Peter sitting on an upturned gig beside the launching ramp, whittling a doll out of a broken oar handle.

'Nothing to do, boy?' The fisherman morosely shook

400

his head. 'I've just been telling your father, 'tis one of the worst seasons I can recall.'

'We're having a lean time, all right,' agreed Peter mildly. He moved over for Symons to sit down beside him.

'My youngest son told me the other day that he's not going to spend his life fishing,' grumbled Luke. 'Says he'd rather sign on board a merchant ship and see some foreign places.'

'I wouldn't take much notice of that. In the end he'll stay with you, just like the others.'

The fisherman scratched his head and gave a dubious sniff. 'I'm not so sure. The middle boy's none too keen, either. 'Tis only Michael, my eldest, who's content to carry on after me. Truth is, I can't blame the younger ones for wanting something different.'

Peter laid down his knife and regarded him with interest. 'I'd like to make a trip now and again, Luke. Any time you're shorthanded and the yard is quiet, I'd be glad to go along.'

Symons looked surprised. 'Still fancy going fishing, eh? I thought by now you'd have given up the idea.'

'No, I still have an itch to try it.'

'Oh, yes,' Luke said knowingly, 'it might seem tempting by way of a change, I suppose. You'd find it less so if you had to rely on it for a living.'

'I daresay, but if you want an extra crewman I'll be willing to help out. We're family now, after all, and I don't like sitting idle.'

'All right.' The fisherman shrugged. 'The drift season starts in about a month. If I need an extra hand and you're still of the same mind, you'll be welcome to come.'

Richard made no objection to Peter's plans, but Susanna could not understand why he would wish to do such a thing, and she tried her best to dissuade him.

'Surely you can find some other way to fill your time?' she said one evening after dinner.

'What for, when fishing's what I like?' He was sitting in one of the armchairs, his long legs outstretched and feet crossed upon the fender. ''Twill only be now and again. 'Twont be a regular thing, so where's the harm in it? 'Tisn't as if I'm neglecting my own work, and if I'm to spend the rest of my days building boats for fishermen, 'tis as well that I learn what it's like to be one.'

'Your brother doesn't feel it necessary, does he? And after all, Mr Symons is Alan's father-in-law, not yours.'

Peter sighed heavily. 'You don't like to see me friendly with Jenny's people, do you? Luke never says anything against you, not to me, and nor does Eva. If that's what's playing on your mind, Mother, you needn't worry.'

'My . . .' Susanna's smile was one of gentle embarrassment and her hands stroked nervously at the arms of her chair. '. . . how easily you read me.'

'Oh, you make it very obvious.' Sympathy was mixed with slight impatience, as he added: ''Tis as if you think they're out to turn me against you. But 'tis all in your head, Mother, 'tis all about nothing. I know why you always ask me who I saw today and what was said, and what was meant by this or that. You torment yourself and me as well.'

'I'm sorry, Peter.' She dropped her gaze as she said it. He was the only one who ever heard her apologize. Only for him did she ever abandon her pride. No one else was allowed to see the lonely woman frightened by advancing age. The rest of the family might guess at her unhappiness, but never did she weaken enough to show it, neither by word nor tear. This was her one, perverse strength. Looking up again, the blue eyes vulnerable, she said: 'But you know you're all I have.'

'It needn't be so.' He felt for a moment as if he were

talking to someone younger than himself, to a child, almost. 'You could patch it up with Father. And Alan, it wouldn't take much to make a friend of him. Even Katie – she's not beyond your reach, though I know 'twould take some time and effort. As for Aunt Esme . . .' He caught his mother's incredulous glance and laughed. 'Well, all right, perhaps that's asking too much. But see what a family you could have. Look at the grandchildren. Why should I be everything?'

'I can't explain it, but you are and you always were. I simply never felt any bond with your brother and sister. With you it was different, though it's no use to ask me why. Don't most mothers have a favourite child? I think they do. I suspect that for Jenny Symons it's Eva. No one reproaches her for it.'

'But she still loves all the others, and her husband too.'

'To my knowledge, Mr Symons has never gone with other women. Your father has been humiliating me in that way since you were five years old. It's all very well to say that I should – what was your expression? – patch it up with him, but it's he who should ask forgiveness.'

'Mother, you drove him to it.'

'No, I did not.' She eyed him primly over the top of her spectacles. 'This is not a fit subject for discussion between mother and son, but I will say that I always fulfilled my duty.'

'Duty,' repeated Peter emphatically. 'That's what I mean – you drove him to it.'

She did not understand. 'He cast me off,' she insisted. 'As soon as your grandfather was gone and there was a spare room, Richard threw me aside and went out looking for easy women. Of course,' she muttered, her mouth twitching, 'I was no longer young or pretty. He told me so the selfsame night.' The words came tense and trembling. How it still rankled, that old affront to her vanity.

'If there'd been any love between you, I think he'd have overlooked that.'

She shook her head, musing. 'I'm nearly ten years older than Richard. We were always far apart in many ways and that was not the least of them.'

'Yes it was, the very least, and if you'd only make your peace with him now, you'd find out how little it matters.'

Susanna smiled indulgently. 'You're naïve, my dear – but that's the sign of a good heart.' She sighed, watching the firelight dancing on the brass fire-irons beside the grate. 'Judith was the same. I miss her, you know. I always liked Judith. Until you were born, she was the only friend I had in this house.'

Peter rubbed a hand wearily over his eyes and said nothing. He could have gone through the whole argument again, but he knew it would do no good. She thought herself more sinned against than sinning. Her memory was selective, accommodating, burying some things and colouring others to comfort her and suit her own version of the past.

'And now,' she went on, 'you're the only one. But you're enough. You're my dearest son and I can do without the rest of them.'

'You put too much on me.' Peter began to sound irritable. He fixed her with a steady stare, and in it was a challenge. 'Mother, what will you do when I marry?'

Her gaze flickered fearfully. 'Why – why do you ask? Have you someone in mind?'

'No one in particular.'

In truth, he had seen several he liked, but so far he had never brought any of them home. It was partly for fear of the way Susanna might treat them, and partly because he was not inclined to settle down yet. The situation might not arise for some years to come, but sooner or later it

404

would have to be faced and he was in the mood to sound her out.

'Then why do you ask?' she repeated.

'Because you'll have to love her and my children.'

She seemed briefly to struggle with herself. Then: 'And so I shall, if they make you happy.'

'No jealousy, Mother? No backbiting? I hope not, because I couldn't stand it. I'd have to do what Alan's done and live elsewhere.'

'Yes,' she said, almost timidly. 'All right, Peter, that's understood.' Then again the wavering question, 'But you're quite sure there's no one special at present?'

'I can think of a few that are nice, but . . .'

'None of them named Symons, I trust?'

Peter grinned. 'No one of that name. I take it that's another reason why you don't want to see me too friendly with Luke?'

A red flush swiftly covered her face. The tips of her ears burned with it.

'Yes,' he sighed, 'I guessed as much.'

Three weeks later, Luke unloaded the bait nets and long lines, and set about cleaning up his boat in readiness for the new season. Peter performed a few minor repairs for him and, together with Nathan Roskilly and Symons' eldest son, they spruced up the lugger and all her gear. The masts were scraped and smeared with pilchard oil. The bottom of the hull was scoured and repainted, the sails steeped in cutch water, the nets repaired. Against a fresh coat of tar, the number 'PW 115' and the name *Sweet Eva* stood out clear and sharp in white. Finally, they put on board the newly-barked mackerel nets.

The months leading up to Christmas were wet and windy that year, but Peter was hardy enough to weather the worst of nights at sea. He was also endowed with the stamina required to spend the long dark hours hauling in more than a mile of heavy net, sometimes on a pitching deck amid sheets of spray, unmeshing fish with his hands cut, chafed and frozen. As he worked he could not help but learn, absorbing from the others some knowledge of tides and currents, and the whereabouts of certain channels, rocks or sandbanks. They taught him the ways of finding shoals by the colour of the water, the behaviour of seabirds, the smell of oil or the sighting of a whale. And on a terrifying night of steep seas and lashing rain, he learned for himself that the boat was more than a mere object of wood, nails and tar. She was all that stood between him and eternity, and he would henceforth look upon his trade with more reverence.

Luke Symons seldom seemed greatly perturbed by rough weather, as long as none of his taboos had been broken. A deeply superstitious man, for whom conventional religion was never quite enough, he solemnly listed for Peter all the things that should not be mentioned or done whilst on board, for fear of frightful consequences. When life and livelihood stood at the whim and mercy of nature, it was wise to appease whatever forces there might be. Luke never left harbour without first reading to the crew from Psalm 107, and whether the catch was good or poor, he always called at the chapel on his return to offer thanks for their safety. Each homecoming was regarded as a personal favour from the Lord, and Symons made little of the part played by his own seamanship. No matter how well he handled his vessel, no matter how wise he might be in the ways of the weather, he did not believe these things would save him if he were foolish enough to antagonize any Christian or pagan power. He had reached the age of forty-nine and was convinced that these pious precautions had protected him through thirty-five years at sea.

A lifetime spent fishing was an awesome feat of endurance, as Peter soon came to realize. When Nathan slyly asked him if he would care to make it his chief occupation, he had to admit that he would not. As Luke had said, it was good to make a trip from time to time by way of a change. To face this toil nightly and depend upon its yield would be much less appealing.

When May came, Luke set out for the stretches of rocky seabed and the sites of wrecks where ling, conger, and sometimes cod, might be taken with the longline. This was the way of fishing that fascinated Peter most, but the summer that followed was a bad one, both for longliners and the men who relied solely on drifting. The fish were not plentiful and the merchants were paying a poor price for those that were landed. There was many a night when the crew of *Sweet Eva* could not even net enough pilchards to bait their hooks.

Midsummer was turbot season, Luke's favourite time, but all too short. Peter went along with him one night at the end of June, to join in the quest for this highly prized fish. The crew caught their bait around midnight, then worked through the small hours in cutting it up and attaching a morsel to each of the thousands of hooks. At dawn, Michael Symons began to shoot the line, paying out nearly three miles of neatly coiled twine.

The lugger rode quietly in two hundred feet of water and the day came up clear and sunny as they waited for the tide to turn. Far beneath them lay a sandy bottom that would yield skate, turbot and brill. Luke, in cap, smock and thigh boots, sat and read the Bible, while Nathan Roskilly stared at the skyline and sucked on the stem of his pipe. Nathan always wore his thick woollen jersey tucked into a large pair of trousers, suspended by wide braces, and his face was sombre beneath his black pompom tam.

After two hours, the men began to haul in the line. The arduous task of retrieving it and unhooking the fish was not even halfway finished by noon. They pulled in plenty of skate and a few stone of turbot, but there were many empty hooks – eight or nine stops at a time with nothing on the end. As Peter hoisted a big ray over the side, Symons deftly twisted it off the hook, then paused for a moment when he caught sight of a crowded vessel chugging down the coast towards Land's End. The sound of excited children's voices came clearly across the water and he could make out the parasols and bright clothing of the women. Nathan too, glanced up for a second, then went on dourly coiling the line back into the basket, methodically placing each hook in the cork rim.

'Pleasure ferry,' Luke grunted to Peter. 'Didn't your father build one last year?'

'He did – we were glad of the business, too.'

'I don't doubt it. Not so many working boats around these days. The fishing's going the same way as the tin. Everything's changing – started thirty years ago when they opened that railway bridge at Plymouth, though none of us thought much about it at the time. Now we've men coming down here from Lowestoft and such places, men with no religion, who don't mind fishing on a Sunday. What a Cornishman catches on Monday or Tuesday fetches next to nothing – if it finds a buyer at all – because the merchant's already had all he wants.'

''Tis hard on you, I know.'

'Hard? It'll put paid to us before long. And what will your family do if the fishing dies out?'

'We'll get by, I suppose. There's always a need for small boats of one sort or another.'

Peter carried on hauling the line, and a skate came up

408

from the green depths. Luke plucked it off the hook and held it up to the sun.

'Thin,' he snorted, tossing it into the fish berth with the rest. ''Tis the trawlers I blame, sweeping back and forth, mopping up the fry.'

'And cutting through local men's nets,' added Nathan. 'Not by accident either.'

'That's a fact,' agreed Symons vehemently. 'Trawlers and great ugly steamships, crowding us out of our own fishing grounds.'

Peter nodded soberly. He had witnessed one or two arguments between Luke and the East Coast men. Symons was a good-tempered soul, not easily provoked, but even he had been drawn into sharp exchanges with crews from up-country, who threatened his livelihood and offended against his religious principles into the bargain.

'They'll be sorry, mind you,' Luke assured him darkly. 'Sunday fishing is an outrage to the Almighty and they'll pay for it sooner or later. They'll be dealt with, one way or another.'

'You truly believe in fate and judgement, don't you?'

'I do, lad. Judgement because the Scriptures promise it, and fate because . . .' He hesitated, gazing thoughtfully towards the distant shoreline. '. . . because I see it at work all the time. Believe you me, there's order to life, to the way we're drawn together and what becomes of us all. Nothing comes about by chance, nothing. 'Tis all charted out, whatever's decreed for us, and we're carried along towards it, going with the current, like pebbles in the tide.'

Peter made not comment, but went on with his work. Thinking of Judith and Roger Carwarthen, he could not share Luke's faith in order and justice, and he did not care for fatalism.

'Turbot coming up,' he said, as a great rounded shape approached the surface.

'Ah, not a bad one, either,' observed Luke a little more cheerfully. 'Twenty pounds, if he's an ounce. I'll keep him for your Aunt Esme.'

45

Seven years. Esme paused in her dusting, picked up Roger's photograph from her bedside table and gazed wistfully at the face smiling out from the silver frame. She still missed him very much. It seemed to her that she had been without him for far, far longer, yet it was indeed a mere seven years.

She ran the duster over the picture and slowly set it down again. She could have taken another husband, of course. Several men had tried to court her since Roger's death. Not one, not even the best of them, had been a fit replacement for him. Opportunists, most of them, seeking a comfortable billet. Even those who honestly admired her, the industrious and the well-intentioned, were subjected to ruthless comparison and finally deemed unworthy. There was no one like Roger. It was better to remain alone than let some interloper take his place.

Esme turned briefly to the mirror. Still a handsome woman, everyone said. She peered critically at her reflection as she tucked a few tendrils of hair into place. Was she still attractive at the age of forty-three? It was said that one could never properly perceive the changes in oneself. Yet she saw that her features had softened, becoming just a little more full. It was, unexpectedly, a gentler face, and there were laughter lines around the eyes and mouth. Yes, laughter lines, in spite of everything. Her figure was slightly more rounded as well, but the strenuous nature of her daily routine did not allow her to grow fat. And of one thing she was deeply proud – she had not a single grey hair.

She surveyed herself curiously for a moment, then shook her thoughts back to the day's work. It was already half past eleven and she had five beds to change. Unlike the miners and fishermen, she had not fared badly from the changes stealing over the county. The Halveor Inn had certainly felt the effects, but Esme had found ways to turn them to advantage. Her advertisement had proved very successful and it was now usual to find all her rooms let on most nights throughout the summer months. She also found herself selling more food and less drink the whole year round, and this development was not unwelcome, since she was fast losing her tolerance of the rowdy. On this September day of 1891, her guestrooms were occupied by two elderly couples, a gentleman schoolteacher, and a quiet family of four from Berkshire. She could scarcely recall the last time she had cooked for a riotous funeral party. The skittle matches still went on, but the pewter room seldom saw a heated argument now and the sound of drunken singing was rarely heard, for the roaring, reckless, violent element had gone.

She went out to the linen cupboard on the landing, collected a stack of clean sheets and went to make a start on the teacher's room. But as she passed her daughter's bedroom, she chanced to look in and saw the girl standing before the mirror, staring intently at her own reflection.

Pushing back the half-open door, Esme went in.

'Mary, what are you doing? I asked you to help Dinah scrape the carrots.'

Mary turned around. She was fifteen years old now, as tall as her mother and very slender. Unlike Esme, she had no freckles, but the long wavy hair was an identical shade of red. It framed a pretty, rounded face, and whenever Esme met those eyes she could almost see Tom Tregunna looking back at her.

For a moment Mary seemed to consider, as if wondering whether to voice what was in her mind. Then she said steadily: 'I was looking at myself, because they say I'm very much like *him*.' That last word carried heavy emphasis. 'You know who I mean, don't you?'

Esme put down the pile of linen. Closing the door, she sat down on the edge of the bed. 'Who are "they" and what do they say?' she demanded tightly.

'Oh, this one and that one. Even the nicest people sometimes make – jokes. I don't think 'tis meant to hurt – not often, anyway. Most of them are just thoughtless. What was it Pa used to say? Where there's no sense there's no feeling. Take last Monday when you sent me to the ironmonger's for paraffin. I had to wait while he fetched it from the back store room. There were two women standing behind me and I heard them whispering about me. I asked what they were saying, and then one of them laughed and called me a "come-by-chance". She said, "You're the very image of your old man." It doesn't matter who they were, and I'm not upset about it. After all, it wasn't any shock to me. I've heard it times enough before.'

Esme looked down at the hands clasped in her lap and found the fingers painfully clenched. She released a long, shaky sigh. 'And I suppose you remember that day on the quay when I hit your Aunt Susanna.'

'Not clearly, but I know 'twas the first time I heard the name Tom Tregunna. I've known for a long time that it must be true. I look nothing like Pa, and except for my hair I'm not much like you, either. When I look at my face, I see somebody else there – some stranger. While Pa was alive I didn't care, and after he died I missed him so much that I couldn't think about anything else for a long, long time. But lately I've been wondering more and

413

more about Tom Tregunna and about what happened. Every day now, I go to the mirror and try to picture him.'

'Yes,' murmured Esme, 'of course you do. 'Tis only natural.'

The girl moved across to the window and perched on the little wooden seat. 'I know how you loved Pa, yet you must have hurt him a great deal. What kind of man was my father, that he could make you do that? Did he tell you lies and then run off? Did he have something against Pa? Did he know about me? Was he married? Have I any half-brothers and sisters? How should I feel about him, Mother? 'Tis time you told me.'

'Well, my dear, I suppose I've been waiting for you to ask. I knew you would, sooner or later.' Esme studied her daughter fondly. 'Oh yes 'tis true, all right. You're exactly like him. As the saying goes, he'll never be dead while you're alive. I haven't a photograph of Tom, but I don't need one. I can see him every time I look at you. And now you want to know all about him. Well, Tom and I were children together and that's where I must start.' She paused for a moment, considering. 'I think, perhaps, we'll go for a ride. We'll take the day to talk it over, plenty of time and no interruptions. Besides, there are things and places I want to show you, so you'll better understand. Would you like that? All right, make yourself tidy, then go and tell Ewan to harness the gig, while I change my clothes.'

They were ready in under half an hour. Esme had put on her cream linen suit. It was very fashionable, the skirt almost straight, the jacket double-breasted with leg o' mutton sleeves. A flat round hat, adorned at the front with a yellow satin bow, was skewered in place with a big gold pin. A fine woman, thought Ewan approvingly, as he watched her drive out under the arch with her daughter beside her. A strong, prosperous woman who had seen her share of trouble and come out of it well.

''Tis a lovely day,' Esme said, as the gig rolled off down the coast road. 'We'll make for St Just and then we'll travel home across the moors. I've told Dinah we're having an outing and won't be back till this evening.' She caught her daughter's expectant look and smiled. 'Now then, where was it I first met Tom? Oh yes, he was playing marbles on the quay . . .'

Mary had very little to say in that first hour or two. She simply listened while this shadowy, unknown part of her history was recounted in all the detail Esme's memory could supply. Despite the knowledge that her father was a miner, the Tregunnas and people like them, with their tumbledown shacks and toiling existence, had always seemed remote to Mary until now, not in time or distance, but inasmuch as they were set apart from the safe and comfortable life she knew. But as her mother talked, the hovels and the crippled men, the silent pits and the emigrant ships began to acquire a powerful and personal significance. Even the countryside through which they travelled offered glimpses into the circumstances and the changes which had helped to shape her parents' lives. A past more harsh than the present, yet somehow sad in its fading – she could see it all around her now, when Esme pointed out things that were 'never like that when Tom and I were young', things and places so familiar, Mary had scarcely noticed or given them a thought before.

Bumpy, narrow tracks had been levelled and made wider, and there were many more signposts along the route. But as well as these improvements there was much dereliction, and all of it had come about within her mother's lifetime. They passed several farms that had been prosperous and well-kept when Esme was a child, but now appeared run-down or abandoned, with gates rotting and broken, stone hedges collapsing and furze encroaching on the fields. The mining villages, above all, presented scenes of neglect and desertion. Cottage after cottage stood empty, the window panes cracked and opaque with dirt, the doors boarded over, roofs half stripped of their slates, and vegetable gardens turned to nettle patches. Never far away were the pits for which these little communities had once lived, but now the engine houses were mere stone shells, open to the sky and ringed around with brambles at the base.

'Look,' said Esme, when Wheal Merit came in sight, 'that was where he worked when I knew him first. Imagine, Mary, he'd been there since he was seven years old. Come on, we'll stretch our legs.'

They climbed out of the gig and walked up over the heath towards the mine. There was no longer any path to be seen, but Esme had not forgotten where it used to run. The engine house was coated in ivy and the acres around it were completely overgrown. Everything was gone – the count house, the dressing sheds, the stores, every last piece of machinery. Only the tumps and hollows still visible under the green remained to show where the waste-heaps and the buddle pits had been.

"Tis almost pretty now,' mused Esme, staring round her. 'Nature's covered the scars, and down below she's filled the shafts and levels with water. Water, deep and still, in place of dust and fumes and slogging men. I remember Tom describing what 'twas like underground, telling me about great chasms and caverns and the scores of miners, always digging and blasting, day and night, so 'tis strange now to think of all those miles of black, flooded tunnels running under these moors, for no one can ever set foot in them again. I think he'd be sad to see it if he came back today. But then, as I told you, he knew what was coming and that's why he went away.' She

416

smiled wistfully. 'He was right, you see. Wheal Merit's just one among many. 'Twill never be the same again.'

'Surely that's no bad thing? 'Twas an awful life, by all accounts.'

'Yes,' said Esme thoughtfully, ''twas gruelling, all right, but many had a taste for it and they were all hardened to it. Think of this, Mary. A man might walk five miles to work, spend six or seven hours swinging a pick or a sledgehammer in terrible heat and bad air, then climb nearly two thousand feet to the surface when his shift was over, and walk the five miles home. Every day but Sundays and holidays, and no one thought 'twas remarkable. Lord, they had such strength. 'Tis hard to know how flesh and blood could stand so much, and I don't think we'll ever see the like of them again. I'm afraid the best, like your father, are gone for good.' She linked an arm with her daughter and they started back towards the gig. 'Let's be on our way now. There's one more place you ought to see.'

Little remained of the cottage in which Tom had grown up. The walls had long since fallen down, the heath was growing over the rubble, and a clump of gorse bushes had sprung up on what was once the potato patch. Esme sat down on a granite boulder beside the track, while her daughter wandered round the ruin. After a time, Mary stopped and stood within the overgrown space that had once been home to her father, and also to a set of grandparents, aunts and uncles she would never know. Her back was turned to her mother and she did not move for quite some time.

She's trying to picture it, Esme thought. And she's wondering about them. 'Tis just as well they're dead and gone, or scattered to places where the mines are still working. 'Twould do her no good to know them. Tom wouldn't want her to, I'm sure of that.

417

At last the girl came to sit down beside her. Subdued, she said: 'I think I can see how it must have been.'

'Yes, 'twas wretched. He brought me here to see it when I was about your age. He didn't want to, but I kept on at him. Poor Tom, I can still remember how ashamed he was. You know, he always wanted far more than I did. Being so very poor, it made him want everything. Some people turn to religion and live on the promises the churchmen make, but Tom never found any consolation in that. He didn't want a brighter crown hereafter, he wanted the good things of this life.'

'I can't blame him for that.'

'I hope you don't blame him for anything, child. You see, I always did pursue him, even as a young girl. In those days he had grand ideas about adventure and what he was going to be. But life took some of the wind out of his sails and I think he was lonely when he came back here all those years later. Even so, what happened between us was mostly my doing, not his. You can't reproach a man for taking comfort when 'tis offered. I was always very fond of Tom and I believe he did care quite a lot for me, in his way, so 'twas nothing shabby like your Aunt Susanna said.'

'Do you still miss him, Mother?'

'No, my dear, 'tis your pa that I really miss. When Tom first went abroad, I used to look at maps and wonder where he was. But when I found I was expecting you, and I learned what a truly great heart I had married, I stopped thinking so much about him. He went his own way to chase the things he wanted and I wish him all good fortune. But Roger was the one I could rely on. Roger was the one who loved me best. He deserved no less in return. 'Tis strange, you know, Tom was always saying he had nothing to give me, yet he did for me the only thing your pa couldn't. He left me one great, important gift.'

She smiled and hugged her daughter. 'But if the Lord were to say to me now: "Esme, choose. I'll let you have one of them back", then I would ask for Roger, because he was the dearest soul and he's the one I long for, even now.'

It was less than a year afterwards that Esme received an unexpected visit from Miss Jory. She was seldom troubled by Margaret these days. The inn gave little offence to the Teetotal Society now and, indeed, the two women had found themselves on all but friendly terms since Judith's death. A little mellowing on both sides allowed a certain mutual regard to exist between them. So when Bridget came to tell Mrs Carwarthen that Miss Jory had arrived and was asking to see her in private, Esme felt more curious than concerned.

She found Margaret waiting in the passage. In her hand was an envelope – quite a large one.

'Good day, Miss Jory,' Esme said. 'Come into the parlour.'

Margaret hesitated. 'Can we speak alone there, Mrs Carwarthen? Your daughter, is she . . .?'

'Mary's out.'

'Ah, good.' Miss Jory followed her into the little sitting room.

'But what is it you don't want her to hear?' asked Esme uneasily, closing the door.

'May I sit down?'

'Of course.'

'I have some news, Mrs Carwarthen. You may wish to pass it on to her yourself, but that is for you to decide. I believe you should think carefully about what, if anything, you choose to say to her, just as I, in my turn, pondered deeply on whether to bring you these tidings.'

She looked so solemn that Esme did not know whether to laugh or feel frightened.

'Whatever is it?'

'Nothing bad – quite the reverse, in fact – but I hope I do right in showing this to you.'

From the envelope she pulled a letter and a large, slightly cracked photograph. 'Do you recall a local miner called Peter Jewell?'

The name meant nothing to Esme.

'No, well, he was never a customer of yours and he left these shores more than twenty years ago. But I still hear from him now and again, and last week I received this letter and photograph. I thought you would like to see them.' She handed over the letter first, pointing out a paragraph marked in red ink. 'This is the passage that will interest you.'

Esme frowned, scanning the spidery writing. She could not make much of it at first, but slowly the words were deciphered – and as she read her face began to lighten and lift, softening into a happy smile. Jewell had written:

See the man on the far right? That's Captain Tregunna. You'll remember him, I expect. He says he remembers you, says he's sorry he never wrote. Been captain here these last nine years, and a good one, too. All the men think well of him. That's his wife beside him, and their three children in front. Eldest boy's called Thomas. Can't recall the name of the other one. And then there's the little maid – Esme.

He went on to talk about other matters and other people. Esme laid down the letter and reached for the photograph.

It showed a group of forty or fifty people, assembled in front of what looked like a count house. Part of a signboard was visible above the door, showing the words 'Company' and 'Ontario'. Most of the men were miners in working clothes; some smoking pipes, several with picks slung casually over their shoulders, and others standing self-consciously to attention for the camera. Above the head of one was marked a cross, and this, Esme supposed, was Peter Jewell. At either end of the group stood two or three men in Sunday suits, most with families clustered round them. Esme peered closely at the one on the extreme right.

Yes, it was him. She stroked a finger over the picture, smiling to herself. His features had thickened a little with middle age, but it was Tom, all right. He looked like a man who was satisfied with life, satisfied at last. The woman at his side was dark, chubby. A kindly, comfortable sort, by Esme's guess, a provider of ample good cooking and cuddlesome flesh. The two boys were sturdy, grinning broadly at the camera, and between them stood a plain little girl, perhaps four years old. Esme. He had called her Esme.

'He didn't forget you,' Margaret said, as if she divined this last thought.

'No – no, 'tisn't a very common name,' came the pleased reply. ''Tis likely he was thinking of me.'

'I'm sure he was.' Margaret studied Esme's beaming face and then said gravely, 'As I've already told you, Mrs Carwarthen, I was in two minds about letting you see this and I still hope my decision was sound. It occurred to me that, since you are now a widow, this might serve to make you feel more lonely, and I certainly wouldn't wish that. This was a fear that caused me to hesitate for quite some time, but in the end I thought you would rather know what became of him than be left forever wondering.'

'You did right, I assure you. Oh, I'm delighted to hear he has the position he always wanted, and a home and a family too. When he was young, Tom never knew what it was to have comfort. Don't worry, Miss Jory, I don't feel any pangs. I'm simply glad to know he did well.'

'I thought you would be.' Margaret was silent for a few moments, allowing Esme to study the picture and read the paragraph again. She had another point to raise, one that worried her a good deal, so she saved it as long as she could. But at length she said tentatively:

'You realize, Mrs Carwarthen, that I've chosen to trust you by coming here today? I am conscious of certain risks and I shall feel sorely responsible if I've overestimated you.'

Esme looked up sharply, her smile fading. 'What does that mean?'

'Well,' said Margaret delicately, 'I hope you won't try to get in touch with him? Now that he has a wife and children . . .'

'Have no fear, Miss Jory.' Esme folded the letter and handed it back to her. 'I haven't looked at the address, and even if I had I wouldn't dream of making mischief. Tom never wanted to upset my life and I certainly wouldn't want to upset his.'

Reassured, Margaret tucked the letter in her pocket. 'So my faith was not misplaced. You please me greatly, Mrs Carwarthen. But tell me, what of your daughter? Is she to know?'

Esme thought for a moment, then handed back the photograph as well.

'I don't think so. I've told her all about Tom, but she still thinks of Roger as her father, and so he was, in every way but one. My own father always used to say, "Leave contentment alone". Mary's happy and I don't want to unsettle her.'

'Very wise,' said Margaret stoutly. 'I commend you for your good sense.' She paused for a moment, musing. 'I never thought I'd say such a thing about a publican, but you are an admirable woman, Mrs Carwarthen. You've survived a great deal, haven't you? I often hear it said that we're never sent any trial that's too much to bear, but it isn't always true. You are able to weather tragedy and remain standing firmly on your own two feet. Not everyone can do that.'

46

Late one afternoon in April 1893, Peter Rescorla walked
into Porthgullow and down to the quay to join Luke
Symons for a night's fishing. Ready and impatient to sail,
the rest of the crew were waiting on board when he
arrived. A steady procession of boats was leaving harbour
and less than four hours of daylight remained. *Sweet Eva*
had recently made good catches at a certain spot to the
south-west. Symons meant to head that way again and he
wanted to reach the fishing grounds before dusk.

Jenny, as usual, was there to see them off, one among
many women watching the departure of husbands, sons,
fathers. As Luke's vessel slipped out past the end of the
jetty, she raised her hand in a brief, parting wave, then
turned and went home.

Out between the headlands, leaving behind the broad
curve of Porthgullow bay and the tower of the light on
Gennys Point, *Sweet Eva* travelled within hailing distance
of several other craft for the first hour or more. The
evening was very clear and a lively breeze carried them
swiftly past Land's End, at which point the little fleet
began to disperse.

Symons was seeking an area to the north of Wolf Rock
and he set a solitary course in that direction. Water
surging away from the bow broke into a mottled pattern
of white upon darkest green, with a fuming of tiny bubbles
beneath, and Peter's face and hands were chilled by flying
spray as he leaned over the side to look for the film of oil
or the telltale colour that meant a shoal of fish. The wind
filled his ears, tugging at his hair and clothing, and he

could barely hear the voices of the other men as they talked and laughed together.

By half-past seven, however, the sun was beginning to sink and the crew no longer joked with one another, for their search had so far been in vain. All were now watching intently for signs of fish, and Symons was toying with the notion of trying elsewhere. The coming night promised to be a cold one and only two other vessels could now be seen in the distance, one fishing to the west, the other moving southwards. Perhaps his recent run of luck in these waters had ended, Luke thought glumly. He would give it another half-hour and that was all.

The light was failing fast and all were ready to turn back, when a shout from Nathan brought Luke and Peter running to the port side.

'Oily birds, Luke, see? And gannets, too.'

No more than half a mile away, a flock of stormy petrels stabbed at the water and fluttered above it, beating the surface with their feet. From high in the air a circling gannet suddenly dropped, folding its great wings to dive, causing only a neat spurt of white to mark where it entered the water. Another followed, and another. The first bobbed to the surface, its throat working to swallow its catch.

'I knew there'd be something here,' Luke said jubilantly. 'Let's go and have a look.'

The seabirds rose in a screeching mass as the boat drew near. They hovered overhead, flapping, swooping, perching on the spars, as the men peered down into the water.

'Mackerel,' Nathan said. 'No mistaking that green.'

Symons nodded. 'Let's get on with it. Twilight won't last long.'

It took them over an hour to shoot the nets. As the dusk deepened, the buoy that marked the first net drew farther and farther away until it was more than a mile distant from the boat. A line of cork floats, punctuated by an occasional white canvas buff, marched away towards it, and beneath this the nets hung six fathoms deep, a waiting curtain of tarred mesh.

The wind had dropped by the time they finished and the boat rocked very gently in the calm water. The others went below for something to eat, but Symons stayed on deck, content with a pipe to smoke. A single brass lamp burned on the masthead, but he sat in the darkness outside its circle of yellow light. Now and again the vessel gave a quiet groan, a faint creak – the usual sounds of complaint, so familiar that he scarcely noticed them. But somewhere out in the blackness of the sea, he heard the plop of a fish flipping over at the surface, followed by the flittering noise of many tiny splashes. Luke smiled to himself and puffed happily at his pipe. He expected a fine catch.

There was no moon that night, but the sky was speckled with stars and the sea reflected them back so clearly that it was difficult to tell where one ended and the other began. It was not only in times of storm or fog that he was most keenly aware of his mortality, but also on nights like this one, when he felt suspended in a great serene void, with untold depths below him and endless spaces all around.

At last he stood up, knocked out his pipe and went to see if the catch looked promising. He lit two more lamps, then dragged in several yards of line until he could lean down and grasp the headrope of the net. The very weight of it told the tale, and he could already see a shimmer of silver fading away into the depths. He clawed in a few feet of mesh and the rough twine dug deep into his fingers, hardened though they were. His muttered exclamation was a mixture of satisfaction and concern. These nets close to the boat were relatively new and therefore strong. The outer ones, however, were much older and less tough. If they were similarly loaded with fish, he feared they might rip or break away altogether.

Luke released the rope and hurried to summon the others. For the next three hours they laboured non-stop, heaving and gathering aboard the dark, soaking net and its gleaming burden, a riot of glistening white bellies and smokey-striped backs. Wriggling mackerel fell to the deck and slid about the men's feet, or were sent tumbling down into the fish berth. Boots and oilskins shed rivulets of water, and bundles of net were piled back in the sheet with quantities of fish still inside. Peter had found the mesh torn in several places by the sheer weight, but there was as yet no damage that could not be easily mended. Hauling in a pathetic lump of white feathers, Nathan untangled and tossed overboard a dead gannet whose last dive had trapped it in the net.

At two in the morning, Michael Symons paused, breathless. He glanced down into the fish berth and saw it was already overflowing. Turning to his father, he said:

'If it goes on like this, we won't be able to carry them all.'

Luke had plainly been thinking the same thing. He grunted and then scratched his head. 'I believe you're right, boy.'

'What's to do, then?' Nathan said. 'I've heard tell of catches that sank the boat.'

'I'm not fool enough to risk that,' retorted Symons.

'I'm only asking what you mean to do. We're low in the water as 'tis.'

'I know, I know.' Hands on hips, Luke made a grimace of irritation. 'I'm loath to spend the rest of the night hauling and unmeshing fish that I'll have to throw overboard, but it seems there's not much choice. We can't afford to cut the nets away, that's for sure.'

'You've one consolation,' Peter said. ''Tis early yet and the wind's risen again. We'll be able to finish hauling and reach Newlyn in time for the early market. 'Tis a fine big catch, Luke, and you'll get best price for it.'

Symons brightened a little. 'True enough. And maybe we'll throw out some ballast to make a bit more room. All right, we'll have twenty minutes' rest before we carry on.'

He and Peter took a lantern and went down to seek their bunks, while Nathan seated himself at the tiller with his hip flask and Michael Symons for company. For a quarter of an hour they talked, sharing the small bottle of warming spirits. A stiff breeze had sprung up and the lugger swayed restlessly. Behind the window of the brass lamp at Michael's feet, the flame shuddered and danced. There were, by Nathan's estimate, another eight nets to clear and he sat lamenting the waste of the fish that could not be taken on board or given to some skipper less fortunate. *Sweet Eva* was all alone that night, so the surplus could not be passed over to another boat.

It was when the conversation lapsed for a few seconds that a frown of puzzlement suddenly crossed Roskilly's face. Quickly, he turned his head, scanning the darkness and listening intently.

'What is it?' Michael asked.

'I don't know. I thought . . .' The words tailed off as the older main strained to recapture the sound he had first detected during a brief lull of the wind.

'There's nothing . . .' began Michael.

'Hush! I may be getting on in years, but my hearing's still sharper than most.'

Almost scowling with concentration, Nathan waited – and a few seconds later he caught the sound again. This time Michael heard it too.

A hiss and a whoosh, the rushing noise of a great prow cleaving the water.

In an instant they were both on their feet – and Michael screamed when he saw the towering shape bearing down upon them. A looming hull of steel, with tier upon tier of pale canvas above, the clipper reared up out of the darkness. Nathan could utter only the briefest plea to God for mercy. In the second before it struck, he saw its plates and rivets, even its rust, standing out stark and clear in the lamplight.

The fishing boat rolled, its keel lifted clear of the water, and both men on deck were hurled into the sea. As the ship rode over her, *Sweet Eva* cracked like a stick beneath a giant's foot, timbers splintering and snapping as she broke apart. Masts and sails collapsed on the water and were driven under by the hull of the clipper as she sliced the smaller vessel in half, brushing the wreckage aside in her passing.

When he came to the surface, Nathan heard shouting and the frantic ringing of the ship's bell. He floundered for a moment, amazed to find himself still alive. Then, shaking off panic and shock, he began to yell for his companions. The water was extremely cold and he had swallowed a great deal of it. His boots and the heavy woollen clothing under his oilskins would surely pull him down unless he quickly found debris to which he might cling. He called out several times before he heard the answering cry of Michael Symons, somewhere away to his left.

Numerous lights were appearing on board the clipper and he saw that she was slowly turning. God be thanked, she was coming back and would put out a boat to pick up any who might be saved. Nathan threw his arms around a piece of flotsam and bawled once more into the darkness.

'Luke! Are you there, man? Peter? For the love of God, answer me! Luke!'

But no reply came.

After what seemed an age, he saw lights approaching, low above the water. By the time the boat reached Nathan, Michael Symons had already been pulled from the sea and was shivering in shocked silence beneath a blanket.

'How many more to your crew?' asked a voice, as Roskilly was dragged aboard.

'Two,' he gasped. 'Both were below in the living quarters.'

The boat slowly moved forward. Dark figures with lanterns swept arcs of light over the water, revealing the wreckage strewn for twenty yards around. The bow section of *Sweet Eva* had upended and the stem now pointed at the sky. The stern, half-submerged, wallowed lazily amid a tangle of net and broken spars. A man wearing the cap and jacket of a ship's officer reached out and thumped upon the planking with an oar, and they listened for an answering tap.

It did not come.

They called out and knocked again, but still there was no response.

'We'll keep trying, we'll go on searching,' someone said, as a second longboat drew near, but his tone was not hopeful.

Around him, Nathan heard the whispers and mutterings of the ship's crewmen, but he was too badly shaken to absorb what they said. There were glimpses of strange faces, a confused bobbing and circling of many lights, and occasional shouts of discovery, followed by grunts of disappointment. A third boat had joined the search and cries rang across the water – suggestions, instructions and reports, always cheerless. No sign of life. Dazedly, he accepted a few swigs of something from the officer's flask, but did not even notice whether it was rum or brandy. A hundred yards away, the clipper lay waiting.

'We'd best take you back to the ship,' the officer said. 'The surgeon will tend to you both. Be assured we'll not give up while there's any chance of finding your companions.'

Nathan nodded silently and handed the flask to young Symons.

'They're gone,' said Michael numbly, as the longboat ferried them back to the clipper.

The older man, huddled under his blanket, did not answer.

It was daybreak before the bodies were at last retrieved, and early afternoon by the time the ship sailed into Porthgullow with her sad burden. A deputation went first to the home of the Symons family, bearing the corpse of Jenny's husband, while arrangements were made to hire a conveyance to carry Richard's son the three miles to Boskenna. A local fisherman, well acquainted with the shipwright, accompanied two men from the clipper to assist in breaking the news. Along the road where Peter had walked in good health and spirits the day before, they took him back, dead at the age of twenty-five.

Late in the afternoon, Susanna woke from her usual nap, dressed and went downstairs. At the bottom she paused in surprise, for the front door was open and Patience was standing on the step. Even though the girl's back was turned, Susanna could tell that one hand was pressed to her mouth and the other against her heart in what seemed an attitude of dismay. From the garden beyond came the sound of men's low voices.

Susanna went to the door, brushing past the startled maid, and halted at the sight of a horse-drawn brake pulled up just inside the gate. The tailboard was down and beside it stood Richard, in company with two strangers and a fisherman she vaguely knew by sight. All were looking at something that lay between the seats.

Seized by foreboding, Susanna took a hesitant step forward. One of the men glanced up and saw her, laid a hand on Richard's arm and whispered something to him.

Fear took firm hold on her when her husband turned round, for his face told of some terrible occurrence. Susanna rushed forward, pushing aside those who tried to restrain her, and then stopped short, staring down at the lifeless form outlined beneath a grey blanket. Trembling and sickly white, she reached out to lift the edge, emitting a tiny whimper of anguish as the smooth brown hair was revealed – and then the features.

Her cry changed to a desolate wail. She dropped the blanket and covered her eyes with her hands, shuddering from head to foot.

'Susanna . . .' Richard folded an arm about her shoulders and she spun around to clutch at him, weeping distractedly against his shirt. '. . . come with me.'

He began to steer her towards the house, but she tried to break away from him, stretching round and reaching for her son. The fisherman dropped his gaze in pity and the other two also turned away, for none had ever seen such a look of demented misery.

'No, Susanna, you don't want to stay here. Please, my dear, come along.'

She blinked up at her husband in confusion, her eyes darting back and forth between his face and the figure beneath the blanket. She opened her mouth as if to make a plea of some kind, but no words came.

''Tis all right, everything will be attended to,' Richard assured her gently. 'These men will take Peter up to his room.'

With that, he managed to coax her indoors. He took her into the parlour, while Patience showed the men upstairs to lay Peter's body on his bed. After they had gone, she tearfully fetched tea and brandy for the stricken parents.

'It happened in the early hours of this morning,' Richard explained shakily to his wife. 'From what they told me, I doubt he knew much about it. 'Twas a sudden accident, see, and quickly over.'

Susanna, hunched forward in her chair and rocking herself with grief, made no sign that she had heard.

Richard poured out brandy for himself and strong tea for Susanna, but she would not touch it. So he took another glass of spirit, knelt down and pressed it into her hand, carefully closing her fingers around it.

'Drink this,' he urged hoarsely. 'Please, you must take something.'

After a moment, she raised her head and hesitantly swallowed the brandy. Susanna, who had always eschewed spirits, did not wince or even cough as the liquid burned down her throat. She just sat staring into the black recess of the grate, as if she could see things in the soot and ashes. Her eyes moved, as though following people and happenings, and sometimes her lips moved too, but the shaping of the words was soundless and incomplete.

Richard watched her for a moment, then slumped into the other chair, head in hands. He had lost his younger son. Peter, blithe and good-natured, the last of his children, the one whose infancy and boyhood were still most fresh in Richard's mind. He had lost one out of three and the pain was indescribable. For Susanna, there had only ever been one. She had lost the single living soul she loved.

For a while there was silence and neither of them moved. Then, suddenly, Susanna sat up straight in her chair and a mirthless little smile appeared on her face. The dull gaze flickered, became strangely alert, as if some kind of insight had flashed upon her.

'Now I know for sure what it was I had to fear. It's her fault,' she croaked, in an odd, matter-of-fact way. 'She's taken revenge on me.'

Her husband was slow to grasp what she had said.

'What . . .?'

'I took you away from her, so now she has taken my son from me,' explained Susanna. 'It's quite simple. Old Testament justice, you see. She was once deprived of the one she loved most, and I must suffer the same.'

Richard's forehead puckered and he gave a soft snort of disbelief.

'Are you talking about Jenny?'

'Who else?' She nodded to herself with grim satisfaction. 'I felt afraid, you know, when Alan married that Symons girl. I sensed that a link between my family and hers could only bring misfortune, though I was never sure of the form it would take. You remember, don't you, Richard? Oh, I know you do. I recall that you taunted me with the idea that Peter might marry one of Jenny's daughters. Well, I confess I feared so, too. It would have been the perfect penalty if one of her girls had won him away from me, turned him against me. But that wasn't the plan after all, was it? There was something far, far worse in store. Fishing,' she whispered, 'oh yes, Peter always loved to go fishing, didn't he? And of all the boats along this coast, on which one did he sail? Of all the skippers in Porthgullow, with whom did he go? Of all the fishing families in this county, it had to be Jenny's people.'

Her husband could muster no anger at these ramblings, for she did not yet know the details or the full extent of the tragedy.

'Susanna,' he said quietly, 'Luke was killed as well.

434

Jenny was made a widow last night and Eva's lost her father. That's why Alan's not here with us now. He's taken his wife into Porthgullow to be with her family. There's no mysterious reckoning in this, no victory for anyone. As I told you, 'twas an accident. Luke's boat was run down by a big clipper ship. *Sweet Eva* was the Symons' living and there's nothing left of her but driftwood now. I don't know how it happened, or who'll be given the fault, but don't talk of malice and revenge, Susanna, for that's just foolishness.'

'Oh,' she breathed faintly. 'So Jenny is a widow, you say?' Nodding once more to herself, she gave a small sigh. 'Yes, I'm well and truly beaten.'

Her fingers loosened on the brandy glass as she fell again into musing. Richard reached out and took it from the limp grasp. He did not bother to ask what she meant. His own thoughts were in turmoil and he could not credit Susanna with any degree of sound reasoning at such a time of shock and sorrow.

'I think I should like to go back to bed,' she whispered, after a few more minutes.

Richard and Patience helped her upstairs, then gave her a dose of laudanum. Obediently she drank it, hardly aware of what it was or conscious of the fact that Peter's body lay in the room next door. Richard sat by her side until she fell asleep, then he went in to look at his son.

The house was completely silent. Rescorla felt old and broken as he stood at the foot of Peter's bed and allowed his grief to overflow.

A long time afterwards, he returned to the parlour and the brandy bottle.

47

Susanna declined rapidly in mind and body during the months following Peter's death. By the autumn she had wasted to a scrawny, bewildered creature who seldom left her bed and could hardly keep track of the days or the hours. Sometimes, for a short while, she would sit in the bedroom chair with a blanket about her, staring vacantly out of the window. But always she was thankful to lie down again, as if spine and muscles had suddenly grown too weak to support her.

Appalled at the state into which her mother had fallen, Katie came to offer reconciliation and took her to stay at Morven Terrace, in hopes of renewing her interest in life. But Susanna was back at Boskenna within a fortnight. She wanted, she said, to go home, where she could still feel Peter's presence. So home she went, and took to her bed once more.

When Christmas came she was persuaded to dress and go downstairs to have lunch with the rest of the family. But throughout the meal she simply sat in her place, detached and silent, scarcely aware of the assembled children and grandchildren and their efforts to make her talk or smile. She hardly touched her food, was not interested in her presents and made no attempt to follow the conversation, let alone join in. Her gaze wandered, the faltering hands kept dropping the cutlery, and as soon as the meal was over, she wanted to go upstairs again and sleep. There seemed to be no desire in her for recovery, nor even awareness of the need for it. The doctor said he had rarely seen such melancholy and he held out little hope that her condition would improve.

The boisterous Patience, though sympathetic and well-meaning, was little suited to the care of an invalid, so Richard hired a second maid, to live at Boskenna and tend to his wife.

The old Susanna, haughty, quarrelsome and spoilt, had ceased to exist and so she was not a difficult charge for her nurse, seldom requesting attention, greeting all services with docile acceptance. There was no vitality left in her, no concern for anything, and in place of selfishness and spite there was now pathetic confusion. No longer pettish or stubborn, she nibbled at whatever food was chosen for her, allowed herself to be washed, dressed or undressed, suffered her hair to be combed and her nails clipped, all without a murmur of protest. The maid, chattering brightly, received only quiet responses of 'yes' or 'no' or 'very well'. She knew that 'the poor lady' did not really listen or understand, and that her thoughts were always floating away to other days and places. Sometimes, the blank face was lit by a wavering, secretive smile, and Susanna's lifeless gaze would travel absently about the room as a pleasant memory conjured pictures in her fuddled mind. Whenever she saw this, the girl would sigh, shake her head in pity, and leave the old woman to enjoy her reverie in peace.

Richard's grief had turned his hair iron-grey and he no longer found so much satisfaction in his work. He was still only fifty-five and would never retire altogether, but his hours at the yard grew shorter as he allowed Alan a free hand in almost every aspect of the business. He had taught his son well and the younger man's enthusiasm for steam vessels and other new designs was greater than his own.

The Rescorlas had offered to build a new lugger for

Michael Symons, but he would not accept something for which he could not pay in full. The fishing community had made a collection for Luke's widow, raising a sum of thirty-four pounds. It enabled Michael to buy some nets and thus find a place aboard another boat. That, said Jenny, was enough, since all but one of her daughters were now married and her younger sons had long since carried out their threat to abandon fishing and sign aboard a merchant ship.

Richard's impulse at first had been to seek her company, to talk and talk and hug with her for solace. But though she shared his grief for Peter, her mourning for Luke was a private thing on which he could not intrude. Jenny had loved her husband and instinct told Richard to keep a respectful distance.

He was not free, in any case. His wife needed him as never before – indeed, they were close for the very first time. The only thing they had ever truly shared, he reflected bitterly, was this pain for the loss of their son. Susanna's pitiable state had moved him to forgive what had passed between them, and in the evenings he would often read to her for a while, or talk about the grandchildren and what they had said or done. He would never understand why she could not take comfort from the rest of the family, for all were willing to give it, but the fact remained that her love had always been reserved exclusively for Peter, and he thought that even Susanna could be punished too much.

Shocked by the change in her sister-in-law, Esme was forced to agree. She called one day, bringing a book of poems as a peace offering, and could hardly believe that the frail figure in the bed was the woman with whom she had done battle for so many years. Although in her middle sixties, Susanna looked closer to ninety, and she took the volume from Esme's hand with a mild 'thank you' and no sign that she recognized an old enemy standing before her. She was a sad sight.

Three years went by. One evening in May Richard was sitting reading to his wife from her favourite collection of verse. It was almost nine o'clock and the lamps were lit in Susanna's room. Richard had spent considerable time with her during the past month, for the doctor had warned him that she would not live much longer. He fancied that Susanna knew this too and he thought it a kindness that she should not be left alone too often. She seldom made much response to Richard's presence, yet he sensed that it pleased her and sometimes he stayed through the night.

That evening, as dusk fell, he was sitting on the bed with two pillows at his back. Susanna lay turned towards him on her side and Richard thought she might be sleeping, but he carried on quietly reading the poem, just in case she was listening.

Suddenly, a small movement made him pause. She had lifted her hand from under the covers and laid it on his arm.

'Richard . . . Richard, I'm so sorry.' Her voice was weak but the words were quite lucid. 'For all that happened, everything . . . Forgive me.'

He pressed the hand gently in his own. 'Of course I do,' he said sadly. ''Tis all past, Susanna. 'Tis all forgotten now.'

She said no more and he went on reading for a while. But just as he came to the last verse, something made him stop.

It was something about the hand clasped within his own, a subtle relaxation, almost imperceptible, yet . . .

He looked down at his wife. She had not moved or made a sound, but he knew she was gone.

Slowly, Richard closed the book. Beside him lay the

body of a haggard old woman with skin that hung loose upon a shrunken frame, the pinkness of her scalp showing clearly through the sparse white hair. She had aged far beyond her sixty-seven years and there seemed to be many decades between them instead of just one. How could it be that this poor thing was the girl with the parasol and pretty dress, she of the glossy curls and china blue eyes who had enchanted him at Corpus Christi fair? Forty years. Yes, it was almost exactly forty years ago.

He bowed his head and squeezed his eyes shut, pushing away all the memories of bitter strife. Their mistake, it seemed, had never been forgiven and the penalty had been slow, harsh, relentless, but at long last it was paid in full.

48

Summer stayed late that year. September came and the days were still hot and cloudless. The evenings were drawing in, but there was as yet no chill in the air to announce the coming of autumn.

More than three months had passed since Susanna's death and Richard had formed the habit of taking his Sunday meals with Alan and Eva down at the cove, after which he would usually go for a walk or return to Boskenna to read or snooze for a few hours. It was strange to have time alone after so many years surrounded by family. One by one they had gone, and at last the house was empty. He still employed the cheerful Patience, but she did not come to work on Sundays and he seldom bothered now to rise in time for morning service at the parish church.

Richard found the solitude quite pleasant, though there were still times when he woke from a nap and experienced a moment's alarm, wondering why the house was so silent. And just a little effort could summon echoes in his mind: the voices of his father, sisters and children, the rattle of Susanna's sewing machine or the swish of her skirts, all the laughter and fierce argument heard here through the years. Yes, it was strange to have Boskenna to himself.

On the last Sunday of the month, he decided to spend the afternoon walking on the moors. His route took him southwards as far as Carn Clewse and he climbed the path to the top of it, there to sit for a while and enjoy the view. Around him lay miles of moorland with barely a house in sight. Yet here, on top of the carn, there were many signs of human presence – a name scratched on a stone, the burnt patch left by the midsummer bonfire, a bunch of wild flowers someone had recently placed in a crevice between the rocks. Withered flowers, tied with red ribbon. Children, he thought, or a courting couple, perhaps. Yes, probably the latter. How many times had he come here with Jenny in the old days? Too many to recall.

But Richard still remembered how it was to be young. A magical, dangerous time, he thought, when folly was second nature and there was no suspicion of the price exacted for errors. Naïve, obstinate, thoughtless. Yes, in his youth he had been all those things. And a little vain, too? He feared so.

From the top of this hill he could see the moorland road. A mile distant, perhaps a little more, it wound its way towards Penzance. There was the road he had travelled with Jenny on the day of Corpus Christi fair. Then, as now, the heath was dried by summer heat, lying in burnished colours under the sun. Richard fixed his eyes on that strip of track and took himself away from the present, remembering the pink cotton frock she wore, the hat with the cherries round the brim, and the sweet, brown, laughing face beneath it. On that same road, a lifetime ago, they had ridden together by pony and trap, many and many a time.

After a while he went down the hill and made his way towards it. If he followed it for half an hour or so, the track would take him back to the coast. But he had not gone far along it when he heard a vehicle coming up behind him and a woman calling out his name.

He turned and saw that it was Esme in the gig. She was smartly dressed in an amber-coloured suit, her large hat firmly tied down with a silk scarf.

'Why, Richard, what are you doing out here?'

'Hello, maid. Just walking, that's all. I'm going back now.'

'I'll take you the rest of the way.' She moved over and he jumped up beside her.

'And where have you been?' he asked, as they drove on.

'To Penzance. I felt like an outing today.'

'Where's your daughter? Didn't she care to come?'

'Oh, Mary's courting,' said Esme brightly. 'She's found a very handsome young man and he's taken her to St Ives this afternoon. They're quite wrapped up in one another and I'm hoping they'll marry. 'Tis time, you know. She's twenty-one.'

'And you're impatient for grandchildren.'

'I don't deny it, Richard. You've eight of your own, so you know what a joy they are.' She cast a thoughtful glance at him. 'I've been meaning to ask you why Alan and Eva don't move back to Boskenna, now you're on your own. They can't have much room at the cottage, not with four children – and there may be more to come.'

'I made the offer,' Richard said, 'but Eva likes it down there and she wants to stay for the time being. Still, if, as you say, her family gets any bigger, she may be glad to change her mind. Meantime, I enjoy the peace and quiet.' He winked at his sister. 'I'm getting on a bit and I'm not as sociable as you are. You'll never have an empty house, will you, Esme?'

'Not if I can help it. Trade's been good this summer and I've three wealthy gentlemen staying at the moment.' She nudged him, suddenly gleeful. 'One of them gave me a bunch of roses yesterday.'

'Did he?' Richard chuckled. 'Still come courting you, don't they, maid?'

'Indeed they do, for all that I'm nearly fifty. I'll have none of them, mind you, but I do enjoy the bit of flattery.'

'You might still marry again, you know. There's nothing to stop you.'

'No, Richard,' she said, becoming serious. 'I had eighteen years with the finest husband a woman could want. I've known the best and nothing less would do for me now. Anyway, I'm used to looking after myself and I don't want to change.'

The moorland track had reached its end. She pulled up at the point where it joined the coast road. Left for Boskenna or right for Halveor?

'Will you come back to the inn, Richard? Stay for tea and supper. You needn't spend the evening by yourself.'

Evening. Something about the word distracted him, summoning again the memories which had come to him as he stood on Carn Clewse. Yes, he thought, that's my time of life, I suppose. The closing years, the close of day. Here I am at eventide, looking back, and how well I remember the morning, when Jenny and I were young and still together. 'Tis strange, but I seem to recall those days more clearly than the forty years that passed between.

'Richard? Did you hear me? You're not going home alone, are you?'

Well, he asked himself, am I? After all, it's not so very late. I'm still well and strong, and the evening is a lovely time if 'tis spent in the right company.

He was silent for a moment longer, then: 'Perhaps not, maid,' he said thoughtfully. 'Perhaps not this or any other evening, God willing. You can set me down at the inn, but I won't come in, thank you all the same. I've a mind to walk into Porthgullow for a while.'

She knew then, what he was going to do.

'You're going to see Jenny? And you've something special to say to her? To ask her?'

'Yes.'

'I'm glad, Richard, so glad. You've had to wait a long, long time.'

'The choice still lies with her,' he said, afraid to be complacent.

'Then the sooner 'tis made, the better,' declared Esme, and she clicked her tongue to set the pony off at a brisk trot.

She took him as far as the top of the hill above the Halveor Inn. From there he walked down to the harbour and across the waterfront to the little row of cottages facing the east quay. He stopped outside the last one and knocked at the door.

There was no reply, so he tapped again and waited.

'Are you looking for Jenny?'

Richard turned around and saw Nathan Roskilly seated on the bench by the harbour wall.

'Do you know where she is?'

'Try Gennys Point.' Nathan was whittling at a chunk of wood and he waved the knife in the general direction of the lighthouse.

'Over there? But why . . .?'

The fisherman shrugged. 'She likes to go walking by herself, that's all I know. Luke told me that was always her favourite path.'

Richard thanked him and went on his way. It was nearly six o'clock when he came in sight of the rocky point and the white tower beyond. On the grass by the side of the track, a solitary figure was sitting.

Jenny heard the crunch of footsteps and glanced round with a start. Her look of surprise was quickly replaced by an odd little smile. What would she not have given, all those years ago, to see him standing there like that?

'Nathan told me where to find you,' he said awkwardly, self-conscious now that he was face to face with her.

'Yes, I like it here.' She paused while he sat down beside her. Then: 'Why were you looking for me?'

'Oh, no particular . . .' Sheepishly, he cut short his pointless lie. There was no use in pretending. 'Well, I was out at Carn Clewse this afternoon and I was thinking about you. Remembering, you know, when we were together.'

He peeped furtively at her and the soft round face smiled back, still brown and lovely in its warmth.

'Such a long time ago,' she murmured.

'I was wondering . . .'

'Yes?'

His nerve failed him. He could not ask her outright, not yet. He would work up to it gradually. 'I was wondering how you are. Do you still grieve for Luke?'

'I'm all right now, Richard. It took me a long time to mend, but I'm all right now.'

'And you've everything you need?'

'More or less. I don't go short of anything important. The children see to that.'

Is that enough, then? he wondered. Do you want anything more – or have you become like Esme, satisfied to do without a man?

'Yes,' he said absently, 'they're good to you, I'm sure.'

For a while they sat there side by side, content, in the old, comfortable way, to remain silent. A ponderous green swell blossomed into foam around the rocks below, and waves plunged into the gully with a hollow roar, then sighed back again. The air was heady with the smell of the sea, and filled with the screams of wheeling gulls.

'I met my sister while I was out this afternoon,' Richard said at length. 'She asked me to the inn for tea and supper. I believe she thinks I'm lonely.'

'Is she right?'

He considered carefully. 'No, not really. I can see Katie and Alan and the grandchildren whenever I want, and there's plenty of company down at the yard. 'Tis just the house that's empty.' He laughed softly, shaking his head. 'Seems no time at all since my children were small and the place was full of life.'

'Richard,' she said quietly, 'I've told you this before, I know, but I'll never be free of regret for what happened to Peter. Fishing was Luke's livelihood, so he had no choice and I was always half prepared for disaster. But your son . . . Oh, 'twas needless waste.'

'It does no good to think that way. Peter liked to go fishing. Luck was against him, that's all.'

'And against Susanna, too.'

'Yes, 'twas more than she could bear. As you'll know, she rarely left her room in those last years.' He regarded Jenny intently. 'I'd hoped you might come to the house now and again, seeing Susanna had taken to her bed. You were always welcome, Jenny.'

'It was still her home and I had no place there.'

Here was his chance and he took it, though he felt as nervous as a youth of seventeen. 'You have one now, if you want it. You can spend the rest of your days at Boskenna, if you're so minded.' The black eyes held hers hopefully. 'I'd count it well worthwhile, Jenny. But what do you think? Is it too late? Have we lost too much time?'

Her answer came readily, because she, too, had pondered on this question, and had guessed that one day he would ask it.

'No, Richard,' she said gently, 'it's not what we've lost that matters now, but what we have left. And I say we should spend it together, be it one year or twenty.'

And so, at last, she was his again, and before them stretched their long and sunlit evening.